C000245724

Bruce Arnold was born in
Kingham Hill School in (
Ireland at Dublin Universi
and French. He is Literary Editor of *The Irish
Independent*, and has been a journalist working in
Ireland throughout his professional life. His books
include *Orpen: Mirror to an Age*, the life of the
painter, William Orpen, *Margaret Thatcher, A Study
in Power*, and a book on modern Irish politics, *What
Kind of Country*. His *Art Atlas of Britain and Ireland*,
and a life of the Irish Abstract Cubist painter, Mainie
Jellett, are to appear in 1991, as well as a book on
James Joyce and *Ulysses*. His *Coppinger Chronicle*,
a related group of four novels, will be followed by a
further sequence, on which he is currently at work.

Praise for *The Coppinger Chronicle:*

'These are marvellous stories. No one writes better of
the child's horror and humiliation at the careless hands
of the passionate, unpredictable, imperfect father who
doesn't measure up. What Arnold writes stays with
you; long after the detail is forgotten the base note of
anguish lingers to sound on in the reader's mind'
Grace Ingoldby

'The writing is confident, compelling, even beautiful.
What counts is the quality of his voice, the finished
style, the resonance of his language'
Financial Times

Other books in the *Coppinger Chronicle* published in Abacus:

A Singer at the Wedding
The Song of the Nightingale
Running to Paradise

The Coppinger Chronicle

The Muted Swan

Bruce Arnold

An Abacus Book

First published in Great Britain in 1981 by Hamish Hamilton Ltd
Published in Abacus by Sphere Books Limited 1991

ISBN 0 349 10207 4

Printed and bound in Great Britain by
The Guernsey Press Co. Ltd, Guernsey, Channel Islands.

Sphere Books Ltd
A Division of
Macdonald & Co (Publishers) Ltd
Orbit House
1 New Fetter Lane
London EC4A 1AR

A member of Maxwell Macmillan Pergamon Publishing Corporation

FOR GUY

'The silver Swan, who living had no Note,
When death approached unlocked her silent throat,
Leaning her breast against the reedy shore,
Thus sung her first and last, and sung no more,
Farewell all joys, O death come close mine eyes,
More geese than Swans now live, more fools than
     wise.'

Orlando Gibbons

'The imagination of a boy is healthy, and the
mature imagination of a man is healthy; but there is
a space of life between, in which the soul is in a
ferment, the character undecided, the way of life
uncertain, the ambition thick-sighted . . .'

John Keats, Preface to Endymion

'As for me. . . there is nothing which brings me closer
to you than to tell you everything and by my words
to make you a spectator of my life.'

Denis Diderot

Chapter One

I

Francis saw me first. He always did. Since our childhood together he had managed, somehow, to place me at a disadvantage. It was not only inevitable, inescapable. Somehow, it was right and proper as well. He would come upon me in whatever hiding place I chose. He would elude me whenever I sought him. He would make relations laugh when I was shy. He was always better at answering questions, quizzes, riddles. And if I should at any time hover on the brink of reversing this natural order, my elder brother would manage to turn that to his advantage as well. It was like a rule of the universe, as reliable as the sun coming up. And yet so much time had passed since we had been together that I had forgotten his inescapable supremacy. Indeed, too much time had passed altogether. And during the time away from him, the holidays we had spent apart, the period after he had gone from Coppinger leaving me on my own there, his superiority, which I had accepted automatically, almost thankfully, as one of the fixed rules in the science of affection, had faded, as had so much else.

Now he was resurrecting the old feelings again. Even before meeting, the arrangements made, in his authoritative fashion, had triggered off the beginnings of recollection. Now there came flooding back to me those myriad occasions which both mocked and quickened me in my fixed attitudes towards him.

His instructions had been simple and precise. And, accepting the old authority, I had obeyed them. Walking along the station platform, looking to left and right, I anticipated quite innocently that he would be there. It was familiar. And he would be familiar. He would come towards me, the inward-looking smile faintly playing on his lips, his eyes fixed on mine, his hands clasped behind his back. And the strange flood of feelings would surge up within me. I felt the warmth of expectation as I paced along the platform. Then I became unsure. He had told me the platform and the time. He had told me to keep the evening free. He had even told me to keep available the whole of the next day. To each detail I had nodded and voiced agreement over the telephone, not thinking, then, in my enthusiasm at seeing him again, of any capitulation to his superiority; not questioning for a moment his instructions; indeed, compelled to agreement and obedience by strong instincts of my own that I could bring about wider reconciliations, involving my brother and my father with each other once again, after several years of estrangement. For if I had a purpose in my heart at that time, in seeing Francis at all, then it was to bring about, in the midst of whatever else we did, whatever plans he had for us together, an extension of the two of us into a new friendship embracing Father as well. I had to amend the fact that Francis had elected to move away. Years before he had turned his back upon paternal authority, and had decided, with the help of odd relations and friends, to go his own way. He had viewed with I know not what feelings the strange childhood which I, in my turn, had chosen to pursue, trotting devotedly at the worn heels of this strange man who so doggedly performed frail deeds in his own blind world. And now I thought that perhaps the opportunity had come to bring them together again.

With so complex a set of desires and expectations stirring within me, it was absolutely vital that everything went well. Yet here I was, on Platform One of Paddington Station, in time, obedient to the summons, and where was my brother?

The minutes had already ticked beyond the appointed hour. Ridiculous, in the circumstances, but was I on the right platform? Had he actually said Platform One? Was it the Oxford train we were there to meet? Or had I got it all wrong? He had not told me who we were meeting, or why. His voice on the telephone had been tense and mysterious as though some precise, complicated drama weighed upon him. The words themselves had been frugal and filled with an authority that looked for unquestioning obedience.

I stared in both directions, and then moved further, pacing slowly back again, then once more turning in the direction from which the train would come. I was infected by the secrecy he had adopted, though I was handling it unskilfully, and I almost jumped when his voice sounded close behind me.

'So there you are. Late as usual.'

'Oh, Francis! But I was here!'

'I know,' he said. 'I've been watching you.' He was smiling slightly. He wore gloves and carried a walking stick, and on his head was a wide-brimmed hat. He stood a little away from me, as though engaging in an appraisal of my appearance. I looked at the clear, precise lines of his face, sharp, angular.

'We've time for a drink,' he said. 'You do drink?'

'Yes.'

'I wondered. I did truly. Aren't you going through some kind of religious phase? You were when last we met. I thought perhaps it might have made you teetotal. Given all the other circumstances.'

'You mean Father?' I said, with a laugh.

'You could say that he was a disincentive. Why aren't you staying with him?'

'He's on his own now. In a small room. He couldn't move to a bigger one, just for me.'

'Couldn't? Or wouldn't?'

I shrugged. 'It's easier being with Mr Porphyry.'

9

'You're lucky. But what about the religion?'

'I get by.'

'Do you still—' he paused and put his head on one side, the eyebrows quizzically raised—'pray?' He smiled: it was gently provocative, an expression of his own firm disbelief, an invitation to join him, a challenge to resume, once more, that perennial but uneven argument about God's existence and man's faith.

'From time to time,' I said.

'Oh? From time to time. I see.'

'What about you?' I said, not quite knowing what I meant, but feeling the need to equalise some shadowy disadvantage he had imposed upon me.

'I manage without prayer at present,' he said. His smile was watery. 'I make do with work. Jowett once told an idle student, "What does matter is the sense of power that comes from steady working". If you do it enough it takes on the force of prayer; at least, prayer as I understand it to operate. But I'm not an expert, like you.'

'Who's Jowett?'

'You've never heard of Jowett? He was an Oxford don. Classical scholar. Master of Balliol. Fund of intelligence. I suspect he prayed. Certainly he was in holy orders, though the two things don't necessarily follow.'

'Are you working very hard?'

We had walked down the station platform past the buffet entrance, and now turned back again.

'Frantically,' he said. 'My present regime does not really permit me to indulge in this—' he paused, and waved his hand vaguely in the direction from which the train would eventually appear—'this sort of thing,' and he dismissed it. He turned and I followed him into the buffet.

We ordered drinks at the broad marble counter, and carried them to a round table near the door. He paid.

'Have you seen Father?'

'Yes.'

'How is he?'

'Drinking a bit. Not too well.' I hesitated. 'He'd like to see you.'

Francis had his glass of beer half-way to his lips. He stopped and put it down on the table again. He looked at me for a while before speaking. Then, with a frown, he repeated what I had said as a question. 'He'd like to see me?'

'Yes.' It was my turn to pause. I gave some thought to how I should explain what to Francis was obviously a strange wish. 'He thinks you should meet again. Not continue this old business of not seeing him.'

'Is that the way he describes it? "Old business"?'

I recalled my father's face when he had said it, the look of faint appeal, half turning away as though years of separation could be dismissed with a nod of the head.

'Yes,' I said. 'That's how he describes it.'

'When did you see him?'

'The night before last.'

'When do you see him again?'

I shrugged my shoulders. 'Thursday, maybe. Or the next day. Nothing's arranged.' I paused. 'I kept tomorrow free, like you said. But after that I'll see him. I have to keep in touch with him. I'd like to be able to tell him.'

Francis raised his eyebrows. The expression in his eyes was eloquent, but non-committal. 'It will require some thought. My mind is preoccupied at the moment with other matters, which is why we're here. But I'll tell you before the end of the evening. Where is he, incidentally?'

'It's a place near Gloucester Road.'

'What's it like?'

'All right.'

'Is he with anyone?'

I shook my head. 'He's on his own. It's a small room.' I felt a stab of shame, as though apologising for him.

'No women, eh? He must be lonely.' Francis gave a short laugh.

'He is lonely.' I did not mean it as a reproach, yet it must

11

have had something of that in it, for Francis looked sharply back at me.

'Perhaps you have caused that,' he said.

'Maybe I have.' He made me feel that Father was my responsibility.

After a pause he said: 'What do you expect me to do?' He was quite serious, staring intently at me.

'See him? Would you?'

'Is that what you want?'

I nodded.

He shook his head. At first I thought he was refusing, there and then. His not speaking, his head just going from side to side, left me nonplussed. Then he said: 'I knew. I knew your game. I knew what you'd be up to.' His expression had changed, his features wrinkling up into a suddenly grotesque mask of cynicism and suspicion.

'Francis?' I felt a swift, cold stab of doubt about whether he was being serious.

'Yes, I know your type! You think you'll pull a fast one on me, don't you?'

I laughed, but a little nervously, as the muddled and indistinct recollections came back to me.

'Oh, Francis! Be serious! This is no time for joking.'

'Joking, eh? That's what you call it, you boys? You come here, conspiring against me. I know you. Don't think you can pull anything over me!'

The fixed, demonic expression of crippled outrage in his face stirred certain deep and uncomfortable layers of memory. I could not easily accommodate them, nor respond to him. I had none of his facility for imitation, at least of this particular ogre. I shared no equivalent range of recollection. I had not suffered the reality as he had.

After a pause I said, 'It's not a big thing, seeing him, is it? I mean, now, we just go, and meet. Isn't that it?'

He narrowed his eyes, resuming the caricature with an intense determination. 'I know you boys! I knew all along what you were up to! Conspiring against me, that's what it is!' He raised his finger, jabbing it towards me. I remembered, with a prickle of unease, that other, much bonier probe that barbed its way into one's ribs. 'A conspiracy!' Francis said. 'I know you!' But I could see now he was smiling.

'Be serious!'

He dropped his hand. His expression softened. There lingered on his face a smile that seemed to embrace a look of faint, private achievement. Then it all faded back into inscrutability.

I waited for him to answer. But he did not. Instead, he took another drink from his glass, and stared round the large, high-ceilinged buffet.

I knew then that he would not answer. He needed time. Though he had dismantled the protective barricades of his quite convincing imitation, what remained, that calm and neutral smile of faint satisfaction, was still a defence of sorts against me.

'He never used to drink when he saw us off, did he?'

'Maybe he did afterwards.'

'And when he met us?'

Francis shook his head slowly. 'He never obeyed any rules. None.' There was an indifference in his eyes, a vague dismissal. I smiled briefly. 'What are we here for? I mean, here at the station?'

'I can't say at this stage.'

'But are we meeting the Oxford train, like you said?'

'We are waiting for the Oxford train.' He looked at his watch then at his glass, which was about one-third full. He did not look back at me, and once again his face had become cold and expressionless, the eyes withdrawn. He turned them towards the door, but they sought nothing among the people coming and going. It was as if they did not even see.

We sat like that for a minute or two. I felt distinctly at a disadvantage. I had asked all the questions. He had evaded answering. I looked round at the other drinkers, remembered other occasions in that same place, waiting to go back

13

to Coppinger, or being met and treated to an unexpected drink in order that my father might demonstrate, by action rather than by words, the all too familiar reality that he was 'hitting the bottle' rather than being 'on the wagon'. Thoughts of him, muddled recollections, made me stare once again at Francis.

'Will you?' I said. 'Please?' It was a question and an appeal, both.

'See Father?' he said.

I nodded.

'I have news for you.' He paused and took a drink from his glass.

'News?'

'We meet our sister tomorrow for lunch.'

'Melanie? With us?'

He nodded gravely. 'Melanie indeed,' he said.

'Oh, Francis, how did you arrange it? How did you find her?' I could hardly control the excitement I felt. I had come to our meeting with what I had thought of as a strong enough hand, and here was my brother out-trumping me completely. I had brought the Jack of Clubs; but hearts were trumps, and he was playing the Queen. Melanie! Sister, brother, father, self: the whole family, reconstituted. Well, almost. I felt a shadow of hesitation: where might it lead?

'Tell me,' I said. 'How did you arrange it? Where do we meet? Is she in London? What's she doing?'

He finished his drink. 'All in good time, little brother. But you must be patient. I have arranged everything.'

'So had I,' I said, shrugging my shoulders. 'But you've done better.'

'I know.' He stared at me, then he gestured in an off-hand way with his gloved hand at the glasses on the table. 'We've time for one more.'

I got up and went to the bar to buy him another half-pint of beer, and myself the same. I was impatient to get back to him. At the same time, sitting down again at the marble-topped table, I felt the need to hold myself in check. I stared

14

across at him. And I remembered staring matches between us which Francis always won.

'Who do we have to meet?' I asked.

'I am unable to answer that question. We must wait for the train.' He paused. 'So you're with Porphyry now?'

I nodded.

'Did life with Father just become too much?'

'Oh, no,' I said. 'It wasn't like that.' I was desperately concerned that an adverse picture of the circumstances surrounding my own life might put Francis off from the project of seeing Father again. 'It was just the room, and Mr Porphyry having space in his flat, and there was part-time work for him as well. It just seemed easier.' My reasoning for the apparent dissolution of something which had governed my life since our childhood together, and from which he had turned away, sounded lame and faintly apologetic. 'I see him quite often. He does mention you. Asks questions. I can't answer many. I don't know, you see.'

'And how does it go with Mr Porphyry?'

'Well enough.'

'What does he think?'

'About Father?'

Francis paused, then he said 'Yes.'

I felt that if I had said 'About you?' he would also have answered in the affirmative.

'He thinks he's a bad lot.'

'Don't we all?'

I did not answer.

He lifted his drink and finished it. 'The train's due. We'd better wait on the platform.'

Even before I had finished he got up, and I had to hurry to make sure that we went out together. He led the way, without looking back. He stalked, rather than walked, ahead of me, tense, springy, making no concession. Without his hat, which he had taken off in the buffet and was carrying in his hand, I realised that I was now taller than him. The fact

15

was vaguely displeasing. I was so used to him being ahead of me. I did not want that to change.

His rather grim expression returned again as we reached the platform.

I attributed his general air of preoccupation, wrongly as it turned out, to what I had told him about Father's wish to see him again. I followed him out among the groups of people. 'Who are we meeting?' I asked.

He looked at me, as though debating whether he could tell me or not. And I had the urge to laugh at him since I would know the answer in a matter of minutes anyway. Whether or not this showed in some way on my face I cannot tell, but watching him it seemed that he gritted his teeth against some inner surge of expectation. I began to realise that the preoccupations which surrounded him related to matters other than Father. And when he then said, 'It rather depends on how things have gone,' I commanded my features as best I could, and put on a look of further intelligent inquiry.

He chose to ignore it. He did so in a faintly calculated way, his expressionless stare fixed upon me as though we were strangers. And that was what he made me feel, quite consciously. And in reality it was the truth. Growing and changing as we both were, even under normal circumstances as brothers returning regularly to the same home and to a stable parentage there would have been a strangeness, a divergence, and quite natural too. But we had not had that. It was now almost five years since Francis had left Coppinger; and in that time he had seen nothing of Father, had, by his own choice, cut himself off. It had divided us, and brotherly encounters had been irregular, uncertain, fleeting. They had even had about them a hint of guilt. Though it is an oversimplification to talk of 'two sides' to every family, there is, nonetheless, that primary divide; and it was with Francis and me, in our occasional encounters, that a brushing together, a touching, took place.

My dissatisfaction with this state of affairs was now

16

intensified by the realisation that, for him, it mattered less than the unknown encounter bearing down on us from Oxford. Perhaps even Melanie and the next day mattered less. He seemed to have put it quite firmly to the back of his mind, and was not prepared to talk further. He had not even divulged details of the next day's meeting. While I had come to him with an uncertainly planned family mission, which nevertheless filled most of my thoughts, he, with a considerably more precise arrangement and one that promised to be far more profound in its impact, was able to set it aside in favour of this other, and as yet unrevealed, preoccupation.

He had turned, with his hat back on his head, and pulled down over his eyes; and he was staring into the distance now, from where the train would come. He looked at his watch. 'Late,' he said. Then he stared round balefully. 'There are too many damned people here. The train from Oxford at this time is never full. What do they all want?' He stared angrily at the really quite modest numbers waiting, like ourselves, for the train; with a particularly vicious look he seemed to be singling out a couple in front of us who were talking loudly, and he fixed upon them a look of sharp disapproval. 'Why can't people be discreet?'

I shrugged. 'What are we doing, then?' I had meant the question to refer to the time after the train had come in, but in my own nervousness at my brother's tense behaviour I had fumbled the emphasis.

He reluctantly took his eyes off the couple in front of us and gave me a hard look, his brow contriving an unnecessary expression of inquiry.

'I mean, afterwards?' I said, hurriedly.

'We shall see,' he said. Then his expression softened. 'One thing is certain. Philpotts will be on the train. Who else, well that depends on the success he has had.'

It was another surprise, pleasurable, welcome, warming. My excitement at the prospect of seeing Philpotts again coincided with the appearance of the train and I said nothing more to Francis. At least I had an ally in the approaching

17

party, an ally I knew in some respects better than Francis. Whatever was going on, my own friendship with Philpotts might counterbalance my brother's strange and exacting mood of foreboding.

Philpotts was a friend. Three or four years older than me, he had been head of Forrest's house when I had been a junior in it. And his kindness had been of particular value during a strange set of episodes. Oddly, in the light of the pleasure I felt, we had met only once since his departure from Coppinger, and that meeting had been brief and not altogether satisfactory. Yet I knew the impending encounter would be all right. An unstrained and exact expectation of how he now might be filled me with a comfortable determination to fit in with whatever schemes Francis was hatching. And it was strange that I had not recognised the possibility that the two of them, both at Oxford, both from Coppinger, both more or less contemporaries, would be together.

The train stopped. Philpotts was among the first to alight. He stood, tall among other passengers following him on to the platform, and looked around. He was obviously alone. He noticed us almost immediately. I began to go forward towards him, but Francis stayed rooted to the spot he had chosen, his gloved hands resting on the pommel of his stick; and though he did not look at me, nor say anything, I stopped and held my position, a half-pace behind his shoulder, waiting with him for Philpotts to reach us.

Philpotts said nothing to me: just raised his eyebrows and nodded his head. But the gesture was more than sufficient. In its relaxed and familiar off-handedness it was welcoming of my obviously unexpected presence. I felt myself becoming more firmly part of whatever was going on. I did not grasp it any more clearly: Francis had seemed determined to keep me in the dark, the chosen sense of mystery and intrigue familiar from childhood days; and I had no reason to expect from Philpotts any sudden or complete clarification. But I sensed in his eyes that disposition of his to a normally frank outspokenness, which I had always so admired

18

in him, and I determined on patience as an answer to Francis's inscrutability. I adopted a not unfamiliar stance, though I had to rehearse myself back into it: that of my brother's favoured lieutenant, silent, obedient, a pace or two to his rear, observant as ever, ready for action, anticipating command in a sequence of events which had, in a way, taken on the faint colouring of a military operation.

Philpotts said to him: 'I failed to get Wedmore.' They stood facing each other. There was no real note of failure in his voice. He seemed quite relaxed about it; I almost thought he was pleased. Francis was not, however. At the corner where the sharp line of his jaw turned upward towards his ear the little grinding muscle jigged compulsively as he stared back at Philpotts. 'I can see that,' he said. 'Blast them, anyway.' He raised the stick and tapped it rather harshly on the ground in time with, and giving equal emphasis to, the three words 'Damn and Blast!' The expression seemed mild enough, but for the suppressed passion with which he spoke.

Philpotts said: 'There was nothing I could do. He's fairly totally enmeshed, you know.'

Francis nodded. 'It's a bad business,' he said.

'She was with him. Dorothy.' Philpotts said. 'And the mother.'

'I knew it.'

'Yes.'

There was a pause. I looked from one to the other, but they ignored me. I thought to myself that they were playing the sequence a bit like Cedric Hardwicke and Basil Rathbone playing Holmes and Watson, and I had the distinct though fortunately suppressed urge to laugh. Groups of people were moving past, insensible to our tense encounter. The many doors down the length of the train stood open, and occasional figures were still stepping down with luggage or pausing on the vantage point of the carriage threshold looking for friends or relations. The engine, not far from us, hissed steadily.

19

'Anybody else?' Francis asked.

'Scully was about. And Haverty. I didn't see them.'

'Vultures.' He clenched his teeth.

'Yes,' Philpotts said. But he spoke quite breezily, in marked contrast to the anger that seemed to have seized hold of my brother and was visible in the grim expression on his face. 'I might have known they would be there.'

My thoughts moved with the thickening drama from the superficiality of Conan Doyle to the more pervasive darkness of *Macbeth*: 'There would have been a time for such a word.' How could I anticipate, in their sombre presence, bringing to light things of my own which I had intended mentioning to Francis that evening, in addition to the matter already raised, though unresolved: whether or not he would agree to the meeting? I began to think we should move. Not knowing what it was all about, I felt that our particular position lacked conviction. And though I faintly suspected, from the rather different dispositions of the other two, that Francis was laying it on a bit, I had no means of judging the drama that was swirling in the air about us. It seemed to contain elements of movement, confrontation and rescue; there were these hideous 'vultures' called Scully and Haverty; and there was the prospect, in Philpotts's own appearance, empty-handed, of the adventure continuing.

Other dramas at Coppinger, which at that time weighed on my mind, and which I had half-intended to unravel to Francis that evening, seemed slow to the point of being entirely static when compared with the events which had brought Philpotts to London alone.

He now said, tentatively: 'Perhaps we should go to the flat. We're not doing any good—'

Francis interrupted him. 'Let me think a moment.' He paused. Throughout these exchanges he had entirely ignored me. Now he glanced over his shoulder. 'You did as I asked, didn't you? You are free all day tomorrow, aren't you?'

'Yes,' I said. 'You told me.'

'From early morning you could be available?'

20

I felt he was overstating my availability primarily for Philpotts's benefit. 'Of course,' I said.

'Good.' He turned back to Philpotts. 'Did you find out about Nicholas? Is he in London? Or out of the country?'

'Dorothy didn't know.'

Francis nodded. 'We'd better go to the flat.' He turned and set off, Philpotts and myself flanking him. When we got near the Metropolitan Line staircase he pointed at it with his stick and said to me: 'Three tickets to Notting Hill Gate. You have some money?'

I nodded and went ahead of them.

When we were on the train Philpotts spoke to me. 'Who were you with that time? In the theatre?'

He was recalling our earlier encounter, brief, memorable as always with him, when we had been at the theatre together, he with friends from College, I with Alice.

'Oh, that was Alice,' I said.

'And who's Alice?'

I could not possibly begin to answer the question to anyone's satisfaction who really wanted to know. 'Oh, she's a friend, Phillers.'

'Bit old, isn't she?'

'A friend of my father's,' I said.

He nodded. His recollection of our last meeting, brief though it had been, pleased me. I had clearly not dropped entirely from his general sphere of concern. And, more than in Francis's case, he could find time to express curiosity about my subsequent fate.

II

The flat was in Holland Park. It was really one large room, with two beds in an alcove at one end. Philpotts took his coat off and hung it up. Then he changed his shoes, putting the pair he had been wearing under one of the beds. It was only then that I realised he was staying with Francis. The fact added to my curious sense of exclusion. Not knowing this, not understanding what was going on, not drawn into the web of their action, I felt uncomfortably superfluous and awkward.

The room was dreadfully untidy. There were two tables, one on each side, both piled with books and papers; there were books and papers on the floor and on other pieces of furniture. Two armchairs were clear enough to sit on, and the end of a sofa. There were white painted wooden chairs at each of the tables. But I did not sit down. I waited near the door, inspecting the room, adjusting to their existence.

A third table, at the opposite end of the room from the alcove, had already been laid with cold supper. It appeared to be a rudimentary meal. There were two flagon bottles of beer, some cold meat and salad.

Francis asked me if I would like some beer. I said I would. He looked across at Philpotts, who had sat down in one of the armchairs, but Philpotts shook his head.

Philpotts said: 'Tell me about the dear old school, then. Merchant still trying to control things?'

'He *does* control things.'

'I wonder. All is not as it seems. Ever. You a prefect?'

'Yes.'

'You have a house?'

'Yes.'

'Forrest's?'

'Patterson's.'

'My God! He still survives? Does he run on a mixture of beer and spirits?'

I shrugged.

Francis gave me the glass of beer. He crossed towards the table at the end, his hands behind his back. Then he turned and stood there, looking at me. The exact position of his clenched hands resting at the base of his spine caused his shoulders to jut forward slightly, and this was further emphasised by the habit he had of lifting himself fractionally on the balls of his feet so that his heels were clear of the

22

ground. It was a physical manifestation of intent, the expression of intellectual resolve which was not necessarily related to the words he then uttered. They could, as I had experienced before, be devastating, and on those occasions the physical 'winding up' of the clockwork mechanism of his walk and the way he stood still, looking for all the world as though he might spring at one, seemed appropriate to the message that came from his lips. On other occasions the real mental tensions were entirely within himself. This time, the intended impact, as far as I could perceive, was moderate, and there was no way of detecting what ulterior force energised the strange tension surrounding him. He spoke to Philpotts; but he did not look at him, his eyes remaining fixed on me: 'He's staying with your friend Porphyry, you know.'

'I see,' said Philpotts. 'That's still going on then, is it?'

I shrugged again, and drank some of the beer. I felt uncomfortable, but not embarrassed. Francis continued staring at me.

'All that scholarship business is over though, isn't it?' Philpotts asked.

'Yes.'

'Petered out, did it?'

'Well, no, not—'

'Is he still a trustee? Still comes to Coppinger?'

'Yes, of course. Did you think it would stop?'

'I'm out of touch. Can't follow all these events. Coppinger politics.'

They were both looking at me, Philpotts less intently than my brother. There seemed to be, in their faces, a vague demand for further information. But Francis, across the room, knowing more, and having himself triggered Philpotts's questions, remained silently hunched and waiting. Equally silent, I resisted volunteering the slightly complicated explanation of how Mr Porphyry, when the period of the scholarship ended, went on to provide me with an ill-defined and unofficial guardianship to make good the growing deficiencies in my father. Even Francis knew only the vague outline.

23

'But he ended that religious nonsense?' Philpotts said.

'I'd forgotten you'd been a scholar,' I said.

'For my sins, you might say.'

There was a pause.

'No,' I said. 'It's not ended. It's only ended for me. He still awards the scholarship.'

'Queer your pitch?' Philpotts asked.

'Not really.'

'And who, might I ask—?' He paused, raising his eyebrows. 'No,' he shook his head. 'Don't tell me. Superfluous information. I wouldn't know him in any case.' He sighed. It was a dismissive expulsion of breath. 'I can't understand why I'm still curious about Coppinger. It exercises a certain hypnotic charm over the memory. I can't understand why.'

All this time Francis had been standing in the same position, quite still, hunched forward, following the slow twist of interrogation. Now, as Philpotts, in his mind, turned aside from the main issue, which concerned Mr Porphyry, Francis relaxed and looked down at the table, touching some item of crockery or food upon it. I had been conscious throughout of his curiosity; now I relaxed.

'Why do you never come back?' I asked.

'It might break the spell.'

'No. Seriously. Why don't you? You've never been back. Nor's Francis. You could come for Old Boys' Day.'

Philpotts laughed briefly. 'The idea's quite preposterous, going back.' Then his expression changed. 'Yet it does have a strange, novel attraction. What do you think, Francis? "I dreamt I went to Manderley again...." '

'I would be curious to meet Merchant. There are a few things I might usefully say to him. Is Parker still there, same as ever? And Forrest?'

'Yes. I'm not in his house any more.'

'So you said.'

'Who's head boy?' Philpotts asked.

'Danby.'

He frowned. Francis, who had left Coppinger even earlier than Philpotts, expressed no reaction at all.

'Wasn't he musical? In the choir when I was there?'

I nodded. 'Plays the french horn. You remember. He's head of Forrest's house, as well.'

'Any good?'

I looked at Philpotts, then at Francis. I was thinking about Danby and my last term at school which would shortly begin. 'He's all right,' I said.

'It's not the same as being good, is it?'

I laughed. 'It's an expression,' I said.

I suppose I was jealous of Danby. I had always thought of myself as better for the job, and I felt that in Philpotts's reaction there was a momentary agreement with this, and an unspoken question as to why it had not come about. It would have been too complicated to explain. It dated back to a certain brief period of instability related to one of my father's emotional lapses, when I had breached, though only in a mild way, school discipline in order to go to his aid. It had cost me, I believed afterwards, the position now occupied by Danby.

Sitting in the bow window at the front end of their large room, the golden light of the setting sun just catching, high up, in the motionless tracery of leaves in the mature plane trees that lined both sides of the road, we ate the quite frugal meal. Traffic was light and intermittent; occasional surges downward from Notting Hill Gate, the occasional tug of a bus coming up from the stop at Holland Park Underground.

I wanted to tell them more about Coppinger. Yet even on that subject, really the only one in which I felt I could be of interest to them, I was selective in what I wanted to tell. At the inner heart of what was happening at Coppinger was Wickham, and about him there was nothing I wanted to say, not even to Philpotts, whose own feelings for me, years before, had contained some of the depth of interest and of care I now felt myself for this younger boy. It was elusive and profound, what I felt. In the lemony gold stillness which

25

was now fading in the room to ochre and umber shades, I sat silently and recalled, with surprising exactness, his assured voice rising in measured notes through the register as he sang the line 'But as he which hath called you is holy, so be ye holy in all manner of conversation' from an anthem performed the previous term. By concentrating I could hear in my mind his powerful treble voice, full-bodied, swelling with attack. And from the imagined sound I could construct further: the glow of his dark eyes in his broad, angular features; the tangle of his hair, almost black, always too long, naturally curly; but above all his movement and gesture, agile, deliberate, as though he were putting on airs. And so he did—teasing even me, the head of his house, with a ripple of unquenchable impertinence. No, these things I could not divulge, not to Francis, not to Philpotts.

What I could say was important enough. What I wanted to tell them about was a certain stalemate reached between myself and my housemaster, Patterson, whose eccentricities had briefly interested Philpotts, though not Francis. Beyond the eccentricities darker forces were driving him to a state which had provoked the headmaster's interest, and at least part of Merchant's uncertain, exploratory curiosity about what was going on had been diverted in my direction. Yet my worries seemed trivial now, at a level quite different from that which mattered to them. They were curious, but only frivolously so. They wanted gossip; they wanted odd behaviour. Coppinger, to them, no longer represented real life. I could sense it in their mockery, their exaggerated reactions, in Francis's imitations of ogres out of a past which he and Philpotts knew, in a way they could not know the present which weighed upon me. I was more than ready to defer. Their cast of hidden 'characters'—Wedmore, Dorothy, Scully, Haverty—easily outshone any drama attaching to poor old Patterson, his wife, Bennett, Merchant, or, most secretly of all, young Wickham.

'Who is Wedmore?' I asked. We had finished eating and were drinking tea. We were still sitting round the table.

Purposely, I had looked at neither of them, addressing the question more or less to the debris of food in front of me. When no one answered, I looked up at Philpotts who himself had glanced across at my brother.

Francis said: 'He's a friend of ours at Oxford.' His statement had a finality about it. Yet it told me nothing I had not already guessed.

'Is there something wrong with him?'

'He has enemies.' Francis said it darkly, not looking at me or at Philpotts. He paused. Then he added: 'He's under enormous pressures. He could break at any time.' I sensed rather than actually saw, in the line of his jawbone, the clenching of teeth. Again he paused. I had the impression that Philpotts's anticipation of what might be said was almost as great as my own. 'Certain moves are being made against him,' Francis eventually said, 'certain moves which...'

I waited for him to go on. I relished the stillness of the room, the growing dusk, my own expectation most of all. Not to be part of their drama, and yet to witness it in this way, to be on the brink, as it were, to be even potentially a part, ready to be drawn in the next morning if it transpired that Francis needed me; all of this served as a stimulating and enormously heightened contrast to the ordinary stability of what I knew.

When Francis did not go on, I asked him: 'What moves?'

He looked across at Philpotts. 'What shall I tell him?'

Philpotts shrugged. 'It's up to you. It's your—' He stopped, unsure of quite what it was, and then left the phrase hanging incomplete.

'I'll give you an outline,' Francis said. He seemed once more to have become nervously tense about what he was describing. 'Wedmore has a certain amount of money. He's weak, and he's got into the hands of Scully and Haverty who we think mean mischief. Just don't know. There's this girl called Dorothy, who's a friend of theirs. And there's her mother. At the moment they're all together in a large house

27

in Charlbury Road. We thought we might get Wedmore to come down here. I'm afraid we failed.' He looked grimly at Philpotts, whose face betrayed no equivalent sense of foreboding.

'And who is Nicholas?' I asked.

'He's another friend of Wedmore's who just might have more influence than we have.'

'And are you going to see him? Is he here in London?'

'We don't know. We haven't made contact yet.'

I was intrigued by the mystery surrounding Wedmore. The thought of him 'breaking' at any time filled me with excited anticipation. I had no idea whatever of what was implied by 'breaking'. I assumed it meant some kind of nervous breakdown or physical collapse, but even these were hazy terms at that stage in my life, implying soft voices and darkened rooms, but otherwise being, once diagnosed, pleasurable and privileged experiences. I definitely wanted to be part of what was going on. At the same time I felt that perhaps I was asking too many questions and might prejudice my potential usefulness to them both in the days ahead.

'If I can help ...?' I said, and left the offer like that. Francis nodded gently. After a pause I said: 'What are you studying, Phillers? Do you have an exam?'

We had moved, and I was sitting beside one of the two work-tables. Though it was now quite dark, and there were no lights on, I had noticed that the general array of books referred to aspects of art. It had not been Philpotts's intention, when he left Coppinger, to study art, and I was puzzled about what he was now doing.

'I'm reading Auerbach at the moment. Coming to grips with the Tudor mind on art, and how its central purpose was portraiture. It's partly work for my finals, partly research for what comes after.'

'What do you mean? After?'

'I'm going on for a doctorate.'

I approached the table on which his books were scattered.

A slim volume lay open on top of several other books, and I looked at a smudged and grey illustration of a lady in Elizabethan dress. She seemed trussed up, and rigid. The quality of the plate was too poor to detect any expression in the face. I studied it, though. I wanted to understand Philpotts's mind.

'What do you think?' he said.

I hesitated. 'It's very stiff,' I said.

'It's very fine. Beautifully drawn. Look at the hand! The fingers! You should see the original.' He turned on a standard lamp.

I did not at first understand what he meant. To me the original was long since dust and ashes. 'What original?'

'The drawing, of course.'

'Where is it?'

'The V and A.'

'I'll go and see it,' I said.

He laughed. 'It's not altogether as easy as that,' he said. 'It's not presently on exhibition. But it can be arranged. I'll take you, if you like.'

I stared hard at the picture. The caption read: 'An Unknown Lady, Victoria and Albert Museum.' I turned over to a portrait sketch by Isaac Oliver; then another. They appealed to me more than the first, on that occasion. I did not directly answer Philpotts's offer. I was storing it up in my mind, savouring the prospect of once more becoming involved with him.

'What does it mean? A doctorate?'

'It's post-graduate work for which a—'

Francis interrupted from across the room, 'It's what the clever ones do, the cleverest of all.' I felt there was a hint of rivalry in the way he spoke.

'But you're clever,' I said, turning to him.

He nodded. 'I am,' he said, 'but I'm impatient. It takes a particular kind of mind.' He spoke with a level seriousness that made me feel a new surge of privilege being with them.

29

'And you haven't got it? The kind of mind?'

Francis was about to answer when Philpotts spoke, and I turned back towards him.

'It's not only that,' he said to Francis. 'You're ambitious. You want power.'

I looked back at my brother, and could see from the expression on his face that he had no inclination to deny what Philpotts was saying. He wanted me to accept that it was the truth just as Philpotts did. He wanted me to be engulfed by the tide of his endeavour. I, of course, was more than willing to drink in the romance of so clearly defined, so heroic an objective as power. It was preferable being his audience rather than trying to force him into being mine; his affairs had romance, mine seemed very gritty. What I now wanted was an alternative against which to measure it.

'And what about you?' I said, turning back towards Philpotts. 'If Francis is impatient, ambitious, and wants power, what do you want?'

He smiled; and behind the smile there was an evasiveness which reminded me of being in Forrest's house with him: he never told all that he wanted. It was not expediency, but principle. I thought that he would not answer. It was not in his nature, at least as I had known it since I was small, to say more than was necessary. And it was hardly necessary to divulge to me, younger than them, still at school, marginal to their passionately pursued purposes, so secret a thing as the mainspring of life's wanting. So I waited, as I thought, in vain, staring at him, occasionally glancing across at my brother.

Then his face became serious and thoughtful. He consciously cleared from it the smile that had been a form of concealment, and then he said, 'I want authority. This,' and he waved his hand across the crowded table of books and papers, 'will give it me. It is power in another form. I think it is the best.'

'How will you use it?'

'I think I've told you enough. That question belongs to another time.'

III

The flood of sound washed over me. It was the sea. It was the endless vigour of the waves. It was the determined pull of the tide. It had a pulsing, measured beat at the end, the notes reaching on, from bar to bar, calling and reaching forward, lovingly, soulfully, from love, through death, into eternity. There was an aching quality about it. In the room from which all light and most of the outside sound had been eliminated by putting over the heavy shutters, I lay on the carpet, and surrendered myself to the engulfing tide. It was a new experience. It was a new way of listening, too. It had been at Philpotts's insistence. 'Either we talk or we listen. Not both.' And he had put on the record and lain down, having first pulled across the shutters. He told me then to turn out the light. And having done so, I also lay down on the carpet. It seemed the right thing, an expression of faith in Philpotts by imitation. Francis stayed in his armchair. And thus we heard out the *Liebestod*.

Long after the final sustained note had died away we stayed where we were. And the silence began to loom in the darkness, and have sounds of its own in the mind, reinforced by the background hum of traffic. Then Philpotts said, 'Lights, ho!'

I obediently got up and turned on again the lamp which I had switched off when the record had started. Amid his books and papers Philpotts continued to lie full length on the floor. He now had his hands flat, one on top of the other, palms upward, across his eyes. Francis was looking at me, his gaze slightly bleary.

I had never listened to Wagner before. I had never listened to music like that. It had been not just music, but more. I felt myself to be in Philpotts's debt; he had contrived, perhaps unwittingly, an experience that had raised considerably the level of my response. He had made

31

sound palpable. He had insisted on a way of listening that really was listening. And I wanted to give expression to what was, in effect, gratitude.

'You know, Phillers, that—'

'No,' he interrupted. 'Don't speak. There's no useful comment you can make. None that any of us can.'

I realised this was true, and sat down again. I was across the room from Francis, but he was staring past me at the wall, in contemplation of some incorporeal wonder emerging from the mists of sound which, though they had died completely away, nevertheless seemed still to possess the room. His expression was stern. Dying for love was clearly a most serious undertaking.

We sat for a while like that. I did not mind any more the direction in which our conversation might move. It did not matter. It was to me more thrilling to be part of their world, drawn into it and absorbed among the intrigues and the ambitions, rather than attempting to explain my own. In anticipation, that was becoming steadily more difficult.

'I think that calls for a cup of tea,' Philpotts said. He got up and put on the kettle. He came and stood in the centre of the room. 'Are you brooding about Wedmore?' he asked.

Francis looked up at him. From the serious expression on his face it was clear he was brooding about something; but he raised his eyebrows in a look that disclaimed any deep concern at that moment for Wedmore. 'I was wondering what we should do next.'

A smile briefly flitted across Philpotts's face. 'I know what we must do. We must examine more closely this young brother of yours and find out exactly what is going on at Coppinger. I think he's concealing things from us. I have a definite wish to go down there for Old Boys' Day. I want to be put in the picture.' He went back across the room to make the tea.

I was excited by his interest, disturbed by the frivolity of his approach. Getting up and then sitting in the chair by his work-table I clenched my fists and wondered how I would

32

tell them about my feelings; even precisely what it was I had to tell them.

Francis was staring at me. '*Are* you worried?' he asked. 'I mean, about anything in particular?'

I nodded. I so desperately wanted him to take me seriously. And this urge induced a gravity of response which exceeded the tangible evidence I could offer to justify being worried. I felt inhibited. In my mind at that moment I was entirely of the view that his own problems over Wedmore contained the real drama of life, the stuff of human conflict and feeling, and that anything I had experienced was really quite trivial. Nevertheless, because they mattered to me, because I looked up to them both with admiration and affection, because they both had certain extended perspectives upon my life, very different, both in time scale and extent, but still there and inescapable, part of me definitely wanted to draw them in and make them an audience to my own endeavour, such as it was. I wanted to restore from the past bonds between us that had come undone, and it seemed to me then that the only focus for restoration could be either their principal concern, or my own.

We all sat drinking tea.

Philpotts said: 'What is it, then? Place breaking up? Probably about time.'

'No. It's not as bad as that.'

'Merchant cracking? I always thought there was something obsessive about him. Perhaps he's started to hit the bottle?'

'No. It's not Merchant. Not hitting the bottle, anyway. In a kind of fashion he's part of it, sort of. It's Patterson. He drinks. You see, his wife and Bennett...'

'Yes. You told me that. Now I remember. Quite outrageous allegations. Did he tell you?' Philpotts turned towards Francis.

'No. What was this?'

'Bennett is sleeping with Mrs Patterson.'

'On a regular basis?'

'I would suspect it happens irregularly.'

'Probably.'

'Yes.'

'I remember Patterson,' Francis said. 'Taught English, didn't he?'

'No. History,' I said.

'Married to a much younger wife. French, wasn't she?'

'No. Spanish.'

'That's right! Wasn't he in the Spanish Civil War? Rescued her there in some extraordinary encounter?'

'That's right,' I said. I had the urge to laugh, but suppressed it. Francis was recalling Patterson in the way my father used to recall Toynbee, a slow process by which memory is inefficiently dredged.

'Now it's coming back to me. He only taught me when I was a junior. Didn't he throw rather a lot of chalk around?'

'Yes. That's right,' I said.

'And he was accurate. I do remember that. It could sting. Keen on cricket? Wasn't that his big thing? Always obsessed with winning the house cup?' Francis paused. 'How has he survived all these years?' He ruminated on the phenomenon of Patterson. I watched him, then turned towards Philpotts.

'And Bennett's having an affair with Patterson's wife?' Philpotts said. 'Is that what's on your mind?'

'It's partly that,' I said. 'It's—'

'She can't be in the first flush of her youth, that's for sure,' Philpotts said. 'The Spanish Civil War wasn't today or yesterday.'

'But she was a child then, Phillers.' I paused. 'She's very beautiful. I think, anyway. Everyone does.' I turned towards Francis: 'Father thought she was—'

'He's met her?'

'He came down at half-term. When I first moved to the house. I suppose he wanted to see how things were.'

'Did he behave?'

I smiled at Francis, though I felt faintly annoyed with him. 'He's all right most of the time, you know. They got on, actually. She loves gardening. He told her all about his

34

last place, in Flood Street, the trellis he put up, and all the clematis.'

'And she didn't fall for him?'

I shook my head. 'He behaved.'

'He needs to be watched.'

I frowned at Francis, then looked away towards Philpotts: 'I think she was only six when he brought her back to England. Nobody knows for certain.'

'Tell me about Bennett,' Philpotts said. 'He's new, isn't he? Is he good?'

'He's super,' I said. 'He's a terrific teacher. He thinks I can get a scholarship. He gives me and Danby extra teaching. I like him a lot.'

'What does he teach?'

'English.'

'Your best?'

'Yes.'

'I suppose you're doing the Romantic movement and heavy dosages of William S. Is that the *mise en scène*? Hamlet? Lear? The crucifying tyranny of greatness before we are equipped to absorb it.'

'Not only,' I said. 'We do Eliot, Auden, MacNeice.'

'Aha! Do you hear that, Francis? They're investigating that decadent period. Communists and fellow-travellers on the one hand, high Church élitists on the other.'

'It seems to me that Bennett's a distinctly bad influence,' Francis said.

I shook my head. It was not Bennett's merits or defects that I wanted to expose. Nor was it the fact of his love for Mrs Patterson that I needed to establish, though I could if I wanted. It was not even Patterson's drinking. I was not totally sure that I knew what it was, but I felt in danger of their diverting me from my uncertain purpose.

'Eliot, of course, is a pernicious influence,' Philpotts said.

'Oh, no, Phillers! How can you say that?'

'Devious. Oppressive. Authoritarian. Exclusive. A masterly politician. The government of aesthetics.'

35

I looked at him in disbelief. Then I looked at Francis, who was nodding.

'Do you agree?' I asked.

'Absolutely. A fraud.'

I felt terribly crushed. I tried to remember the things that Bennett had said about him, but all I could recall was the occasion of his reading, one cold January evening in the school library, earlier that year, and how for days afterwards I was haunted particularly by the lines—

> I should find
> Some way incomparably light and deft,
> Some way we both should understand...

It suited the occasion now. And yet I felt, in contrast, quite unable to be other than clumsy and uncertain in my discussion with them both about Coppinger. It was not Eliot I wanted to deal with. It was not poetry or literature, though deep down I did want to ask Philpotts about Wagner, and about the art he was so voraciously studying. It was something else that was eluding me, it was power and conflict, and I could not put it into words. Power, conflict, and loyalty.

'And Patterson's your housemaster?' Philpotts said. 'Is that where the conflict lies?'

'He is,' I said, but did not answer the second part of the question.

'Do you get on with him?'

'Sort of. He's old-fashioned.'

It seemed from Philpotts's face that he was beginning to put together the shape and pattern of what I was trying to tell them both. I looked from one to the other.

Francis said: 'What do you mean? Old-fashioned?'

It was Philpotts, not me, who answered him: 'Well, you said it yourself. He flings chalk around at recalcitrant boys. He loves cricket. He wants his house to win. I expect he even manages to fit in occasional bouts of teaching. But he isn't really there.' He laughed. 'I remember thinking it at the time. It's coming back to me. Patterson doesn't really exist. He isn't there. He's unreal. Just the odd box of chalk, broken up and flying through the air. That's Patterson, more or less, a heavy deposit of carbonate of lime.'

Francis turned towards me. 'But is that what *you* mean by old-fashioned?' He was not sharing in Philpotts's sense of fun, at least, not at the same level.

I looked back at him, and smiled. 'Give or take the odd cricket ball, yes,' I said.

Philpotts stood up and began to pace up and down the centre of the room. He raised his hand and beat out in the air a silent rhythmn. Then, his voice solemn, he began to intone:

'He is younger than the boys among whom he sits;
Like Peter Pan,
He has been a child repeatedly,
And learned the secrets of perpetual youth;
He has bowled many balls,
And counted out the overs many times;
Boys have passed by him and have left
The trailing metaphor of their unfinished dreams;
He lives—'

Philpotts paused, and stood still, his eyes closed in concentration, his brow furrowed. Then he went on:

'He lives
Only within the compassion we extend
Towards his old-fashioned youthfulness:
Inexhaustible, endlessly renewed.'

He paused, standing in the middle of the room. 'How's that, then? Patterson? Near enough? What do you think?'

'That's very good,' I said. 'Did you just make it up?'

He nodded.

'But you must write it down. Can you remember it?'

Francis also nodded, but did not speak. He was sitting in an armchair, his hands joined in front of him, the forefingers extended and touching his lips.

'It's only pastiche,' Philpotts said. 'Pater did the real work. And even that wasn't too distinguished.'

I knew as I watched Philpotts and then Francis that I could not really tell them. I could not talk to them both together; it simply would not work. And while I considered the possibilities of saying more, it struck me that what I might say would have a superficial colouring; I would seek to meet Philpotts on his ground, ostensibly one of amused curiosity, or Francis on his ground, which was deeper, more solemn, more pertinent, but which manifestly could not be expressed side by side with the kind of observations which were being made by his friend.

Great issues were in the air. I was quickened by the prospect of meeting Melanie, yet could not talk about it. In its turn it had redoubled in intensity my desire that Francis would agree to meet Father; yet not only was I still waiting for an answer or a sign from him on this, it was quite obvious that I could not broach again in front of Philpotts so ridiculous a question. He would partially understand. He might even understand fully: after all, he had known us both for a number of years and had witnessed many of the intimate details of life which my father, in one way or another, was in the habit of letting slip. Even so, it was too like a baring of the soul. Idiotically, I was reminded of an illustration in a history book, long since left behind in the junior school, and based on the painting by Yeames: 'When did you last see your Father?' Only now the question had changed, and I was mentally substituting Philpotts and myself as interrogators, with a slightly modified question: 'When will you *next* see your father?' And Francis, dressed in pale blue silken suit, the trousers elegantly gathered at the knee, the stockings terminating in buckled shoes, was wearing the expression of concentrated doubt which even

38

now was on his face as he sat across the room from me, tense, preoccupied, expectant. Behind him, however, in the reconstructed genre work which was just then feeding my imagination to the point where I was on the brink of tense, embarrassed laughter, there emerged from the shadows a second figure, of a girl, Melanie, the younger sister, and to her also would be put an equally preposterous query: 'Are you prepared to see your father?' And while Philpotts and I, seated behind the great oak table in that large canvas, so often seen in reproduction, not seen in the flesh, so to speak, until years afterwards, Philpotts wearing a high puritannical kind of hat and leaning backwards, while, bareheaded, I leaned forward in eager expectation, endeavouring to pierce through the eyes to the mind, first of my brother and then of my sister. Both he and she were expected to make these momentous decisions by which they would alter the track and velocity of their lives upon this earth. It was too much. An explosive, an almost hysterical laugh, escaped me. Both of them looked up.

Philpotts said: 'You've a version of the same work for Merchant, I take it?'

For a moment or two I could not remember what he was talking about. Then I blushed. 'No,' I said. 'I was just thinking.' I looked weakly from one of them to the other. 'It was just about Patterson.'

'Do you want help with him?' Francis asked.

'It wouldn't work,' I said. 'It'll be all right.'

Philpotts said: 'He's giving trouble, isn't he?'

'It doesn't matter,' I said, though it did. 'It's nothing, really.' But it was everything.

IV

It was only later, when Francis went off to telephone Nicholas, or at least to try and locate him, that Philpotts said to me: 'Is there any difficulty? Bennett? Patterson? You know what I mean? Mrs Patterson?'

I looked at him without answering. The old concern was in his eyes, serious, questioning, emphasising the difference in outlook between us, the difference in age. I was glad for a moment that Francis was not there. 'I didn't explain it very well, did I?'

'I have the sense of it. It must be embarrassingly difficult being a witness. How are you so sure? About Bennett and Mrs Patterson?'

'I overheard them, once, talking. He said he loved her.'

'But is it just the awkwardness?' he asked.

I paused. 'No, it's more than that. It's Merchant. He asks me about them.'

Philpotts gave a short, dismissive laugh. 'And I hope you tell him to mind his own business.'

'But isn't it his business?'

'To involve you? No.'

'What about loyalty? That's what Merchant talks about. Loyalty to the school. Loyalty to him.'

Philpotts laughed. 'Merchant is clearly quite as dangerous a man as I always thought him. I think I shall have to come down to Coppinger for Old Boys' Day, just as you suggest. I'd like to have a few words with Merchant. I think he is quite a phenomenon.'

I felt a vague sinking feeling in my stomach. At the same time I could not help laughing. Looking at Philpotts's slightly plump face, his long, curly, untidy black hair, his open collar and rather crumpled suit, I could recapture in my mind, and revel in it, the feeling of confidence and strength he had always given me. The affection between us had changed. But the heart of it remained: I wanted him to understand about me, as I had tried, in the past, to listen to him and understand the things towards which he was striving.

'When Francis gets back we'll ask him.'

'Will you really come down?'

'Why not? We're near enough.'

'But what about exams?'

'They'll be over.'

After a pause I said, 'But what would you say to Merchant?'

He smiled. 'I'll have to rehearse that.'

'No, really, Phillers, tell me.'

'What does Merchant want?'

'I think he wants to get rid of Patterson. Patterson was there before he came. I mean, he was there before you, before Francis, probably before the war. Or nearly, anyway. He was certainly there for most of it.'

'But would it be such a bad thing?'

'What?'

'Getting rid of Patterson?'

'I don't suppose it would. But it's me that's involved.'

'Have nothing to do with it.'

'You don't know Merchant.'

'Well, I will. Come Old Boys' Day and I'll be in a better position to judge.'

'He's always on about loyalty.'

'Hm. We'll see.'

Francis had no luck with Nicholas. His face was tightly disapproving of the frustrations which were being put in his way, and he was even more put out, having told us of his failure to locate their friend, when Philpotts waved the whole issue aside.

'We have a question to ask you,' he said.

Francis looked from one of us to the other. The expression in his eyes was faintly suspicious, the line of his mouth slightly sardonic.

'Conspiring, eh? I know your kind.'

He made me wonder, quite forcefully at that very moment, what he thought of us; not what he thought of Philpotts, or of me; but how he saw the friendship between us. Philpotts was *his* friend, close to being his contemporary, at university with him. They were undoubtedly close. And

41

in as far as I knew either of them at all well, friendships were not numerous and did not come easily to either. That was the position now. Yet there had been a time, some years before, when Philpotts had been head of Forrest's house, and myself a junior, and when certain affinities between us, berthed in art or poetry or music, in addition to a natural enough affection, had brought us together. Because, as I thought, I had been Francis's younger brother, there had been a vague element of protection. Because of the general circumstances at one point, one winter wedding, in snow, near Coppinger, there had been a closeness between us. What did Francis think of that, if anything at all? How did he look upon it? I had never asked him. He had never volunteered any kind of view. All I could do was to *sense* how he felt, and what I sensed was a possessiveness; with assurance, Francis loved Wagner as Philpotts did, talked art, condemned Eliot, subscribed to the magnificence of *Lear*, the unquestioned superiority of *Hamlet*, and he behaved as though this gave a special bond to their friendship for each other. Perhaps it did. And perhaps because of this, or it may have been as a result of a conscious decision on his part not to consider the question, he simply did not realise how much Philpotts mattered to me.

His face remained screwed up with suspicion.

'Don't think you can pull a fast one on me, you boys. I've experience of you! As far as you're concerned I'm into next next week already, waiting for you to arrive! What's your trouble, then?'

'You cheeky monkey!' Philpotts said. He laughed. They both did. I joined in. 'Cut all this nonsense, Francis, and just listen for a moment.'

'You're plotting! Don't deny it.'

'To whom, or to what,' said Philpotts, 'should one be loyal?'

'I see. Trying to catch me out! A conspiracy! I knew it, all along. Can't go out of the room, but the pair of you—'

'It's serious , Francis,' I said.

42

He stopped now, and stared at us both. 'Tell me again,' he said. 'What's your question?'

Philpotts told him.

'The question arises,' Francis said, 'over Wedmore. No?'

I was about to answer, but Philpotts raised his hand. 'Okay,' he said, 'Wedmore. It does. But try and forget that. Just the thing itself. Loyalty.'

My greatest respect for Francis, then and later, lay in this activity: the objective analysis of ideas. Then, it resided in argument; endless, for its own sake, totally engrossing. Later, it was turned upon the things one did and how one did them.

'There is only one important loyalty: to principle. People do not really matter.'

'Wedmore?' Philpotts said.

'Is it Wedmore? Or is it friendship?'

'Is friendship a principle?'

'What do you mean? People do not matter?'

He looked at both of us and seemed to be considering our two questions equally. It also seemed that he looked upon them with relish. He did not quite rub his hands together, but there appeared on his lips the faint secretive smile I knew so well. He was anticipating an easy exchange with us both. He spoke primarily to Philpotts.

'We are concerned for Wedmore's independence, his freedom to choose. We want to liberate him from people he himself admits are a bad influence. He has told us he is weak. Remember when he broke down and cried in my room? Wedmore himself doesn't matter. He's quite tedious, isn't he?' Francis had raised his eyebrows, expecting some kind of challenge from Philpotts, but it did not materialise.

'He is quite tedious. Yes.'

'So why are we concerning ourselves in what is happening to him? We say it is because he is a friend. But I think we are compelled as much by feelings *against* those around him, for what they are doing to him, than we are by commitments to him as a person.'

43

'Does that answer our question?' Philpotts asked, looking across at me.

I shook my head. I had been put out by the use of Wedmore as a device by which loyalty should be examined. 'I still don't know what to think.' I looked from Philpotts across towards my brother. 'You see, Francis—'

'Wait a moment,' Philpotts said. 'Let's try again in the abstract. Francis says there's only one important loyalty: to principle. Principle is a fundamental truth on which we base our judgment of human action. Truth itself is a principle to which one can be loyal. That all men are equal, if one believes it and can define it, is another principle. So how do we add all these things into a pattern of loyalty?'

'We don't,' said Francis. 'That's the whole point. Loyalty doesn't matter. It is an unimportant factor. It is something used by people who seek power. They demand the loyalty of others to themselves and then use that loyalty as an endorsement of what they do. What they do can breach principles like truth and equality to the point where the whole fabric of a society can be undermined. I have little time for loyalty.'

I suddenly felt a warm flood of respect for him. It seemed that we had subjected him to a test which he had passed far more successfully than either of us had anticipated.

Philpotts said, 'I think we'll pass you on that. I think it merits an alpha. Do you agree?'

'Yes,' I said. I smiled at Francis. He had seemed isolated; now he was at the heart of things. I felt proud of him.

'Now, tell me,' he said. 'What's it all about?' He looked at Philpotts.

'Your brother will have to tell you,' Philpotts said. 'It's his story.'

I explained as best I could, going over what I had told Philpotts. Francis, of course, knew or remembered even less, and in explaining to him what it was that mattered and how it mattered; in going over the complicated conjunctions of the Pattersons, of Merchant, and Bennett, on which I could

44

be confused by question or misunderstood through indifference, it seemed that the fire of excitement generated by considerations of the sparkling permanence of truth, the integrated reward for doing what is right, were dampened down to the point of extinction when the detailed obligation of what one had to do was raised up for examination. I had really been answered, and was soon reduced to silence. I had come that evening to meet Francis with things I wanted to discuss. I had probably made more progress inside myself than I knew. Yet I felt curiously deflated, as if they and their world were racing onward, while I was heading back.

It was Easter time, and the shadow of my final term hung over me. I had holiday work to do, and revision, and on none of the detailed projects before me could I anticipate anything from them. They were solitary duties. I wanted to involve myself in what Philpotts was studying. I felt drawn towards the dusty littering of books and papers setting forth the iconography of the past; his interest gave it a vitality which was made more attractive, more mysterious, by the obscuring shroud of my own very limited grasp of what it was he was working towards. My own horizon seemed so much more limited: an abrupt sprint towards easily defined though not necessarily easily gained goals.

I left after that. Francis came with me to the door. It was a mild night, the air in front of the house scented with lilac from a large and untidy bush of it, the bracts of flowers miserably small, white in colour. I picked one to smell and to carry with me, but Francis took it out of my hand.

'I wouldn't,' he said. 'Not on the Underground.'

'But I like the smell.'

'So do we all.'

'Will you come and see Father?' I felt sure he would refuse. He was so richly immersed in what he was doing, and it did seem to me all-embracing. He twiddled the flower in front of his own face. His features were shadowy in the uncertain light of the street lamps. They looked drawn by overwork. Then his face softened into a smile.

45

'If you like,' he said.

'No,' I said. 'It's if *you* like.'

But his expression did not change. 'I'll come anyway,' he said. 'We'll talk about it tomorrow.'

'With Melanie?'

'I can't say about that,' he said. 'That's another story.'

I hesitated. 'Will you want me in the morning?'

'Not now. There's no point, without Nicholas. We'll meet for lunch. At the restaurant. About half-past twelve. I've booked a table. It's called Porter's. Quite easy to find. In Monmouth Street. Ask for a waiter called Albert.'

I stared at him. 'Should we meet before? Somewhere?'

He looked back at me. 'Why?'

I shrugged. 'I don't know. I just thought it might be better.'

'I won't make it before then. I have a meeting.'

'Okay,' I said.

He stood uncertainly on the step, looking down at the white flower in his hand. 'By the way,' he said, 'don't expect too much. It may not work out. It may not work with Melanie, the two of us meeting her, like this. Nor with Father.'

I stared back at him, waiting for him to look up at me. The doubt into which he had thrown me was momentary. 'It'll work,' I said. 'It'll work.'

I left him then, silhouetted in the doorway, standing with the bract of white flowers held in front of his chest. And when I turned at the gate it was already invisible. But the image was there, safely tucking itself away in my memory; so that setting off up the gently sloping pavement towards Notting Hill Gate, I was already busy at work, securing the future out of the uncertain past, the heart's transformation. He, at least, was clear before me; Francis was committed, part of the next day and the next, and everything was going to be all right.

Chapter Two

I

It was raining. Scuds of raindrops slanted across the window of my room in the flat, and I got back into bed, after I had drawn the curtains, and sat for a while watching the fresh green leaves on the trees in the small park opposite turn and twist in the wind. Though grey, the sky did not have that heavy, leaden look to it that presages a day-long downpour, and given the time of year it would probably clear up. Nevertheless, I was slightly disappointed; and my good intentions the night before, of getting up in time for breakfast with Mr Porphyry, faded a little now as I contemplated the light and tried to plan or orchestrate my determination that the day would go well. This priority, I must confess, had superseded any obligations I felt towards my unofficial guardian. Yet at the same time I was conscious of a measure of self-indulgence which adults, in the actions of adolescents, regard, perhaps unfairly, as selfishness. It is really the flow process of thinking things out. All of life, at eighteen, has to be thought out: repeatedly. And sitting up in bed, observing raindrops and the impact of wind, I was doing just that.

It may seem strange, the way I summon up and then dispose, as if for myself, my brother, my sister, my father even, in the service of a narrative that has reached a point requiring their presence. A bit *Bouvard et Pécuchet*, you

47

might say; the convenient bale of hay floating in the waters of the Seine. It was, in fact, the other way round. They, at that time, forced upon me considerations which were new and disturbing: the actual meaning, if I can put it like that, of 'brother', of 'sister', of 'family'. And once this was set in motion, the meaning of 'father' had to be subjected to a new and different interpretation in the wider context of the extended responsibilities we forced upon him. It was necessarily artificial. Some would say doomed because of that. Yet it was real as well. The decisions we had made, or were making; the things that came from them: all of that was real, just as all that we said, and all that we seemed to be doing, were intensely real, carrying forward, as it seemed, 'life' in its romantically conceived form. But it was the strange burden of questioning that seemed to establish the pattern of action, that Easter, and taught me a series of lessons. The lessons were far from satisfactory, as will be seen. And they derived from events which piled up, often, through my own engineering, at an inauspicious time, though I then thought quite otherwise. But it was their coming that set the pace, not the other way around.

Some of the events, of course, were there already; nothing I could do, no contribution I in fact made, changed the precise compulsion surrounding the strange involvement of Francis with Wedmore, Philpotts remaining oddly aloof in spite of being treated by my brother as an equal partner in the shadowy enterprise. But other happenings of far greater moment were contrived, I now see, to test out and discover answers in the thudding emotional world in which we moved at that time, not just me, but Francis as well, and, as I was to discover, Melanie; a world of definitions and inter-pretations of what we were and what we meant to each other.

I must confess to a certain sly evasion where Mr Porphyry was concerned. His mature judgment, I knew, would prick the bubbles of self-esteem which had blown up as a result of my lofty invitations to Francis, to meet Father again, and my own understandably enthusiastic but grown-up approach

48

to the impending encounter with Melanie. And this had kept me sitting up in bed when I should have been sharing breakfast with him.

I did not run away entirely, however. When I knew he would be on the point of departure I got up, dressed, and met with him in the hallway. I gave him a brief account of the previous evening and of the plans for that day. And in characteristic fashion he expressed his own views. They were a check upon me.

'I'm not sure it's altogether wise. No.' He was on the point of departure for the City. Already, his bowler hat was on his head, and he turned now, in the doorway, the familiar grey sadness in his eyes, making him look through me, into some unattainable middle distance of doubt and uncertainty and of careful, 'not-to-be-tested-too-much', spiritual hope. His craggy features were shadowy in the hallway of the flat.

'It will be all right,' I said. 'I just know it will.' I was standing in the doorway of the dining room, the light from the window behind me.

On what seemed a sudden impulse he came back past me into the room. And I expected from him the sudden, swift expression of his feelings about the imminent reunion on which his hesitations seemed uncertain enough to be easily countered by my own. But instead he said: 'So Philpotts is living with your brother?'

'Yes.'

'I expect they're working pretty hard, aren't they?'

'Yes. Very hard.'

'And he's interested in art?'

I hesitated. 'Yes,' I said. I could not understand why my own hurried, and somewhat guilty explanation, which had delayed his departure that morning, was being relayed back to me, delaying him still further.

'Has he met your sister?'

'No,' I said.

'But you'll be seeing something of him during the holiday? Art galleries? Museums? That sort of thing?'

I looked at him, puzzled by his questions.

'I don't think he'll have time,' I said. 'Anyway, there's Melanie. I'll be going out with her.'

He laughed briefly. 'She's a working girl. Her time'll be cut out. You can only hope you will. And another thing: you mayn't get on. Two determined—'

'We'll get on,' I said.

'She's grown up away from you.'

'I know.'

'She may be completely different.'

'Different?'

'From what you expect.'

'I just expect a sister.'

He smiled; it was an expression of resignation. He could not argue me out of my expectation. Rather lamely he said: 'Student nurses have a lot to do.'

'She'll have time off. I can fit in with her.' He spoke more slowly now. 'I do pray that it will work out,' he said. The blue eyes had focussed again on an indeterminate horizon beyond me, though looking straight at me, and the incipient doubt or reservation, which seemed to find expression now in the faraway gaze which he directed through me, and which mistakenly I associated with sadness, was heightened when he went on: 'I'm sure you have prayed about it as well, haven't you?'

I stared down at the carpet.

'Are you taking her out for the day? Or what's happening?'

'It's really Francis. He's arranged everything. I don't know what.'

'I see. And her people?'

I looked at him in some uncertainty. 'She's not at home,' I said. 'She's living in a nurses' hostel.'

The pale blue of his eyes had the quality of a penetrating fire. I found it difficult to look into them, and when I did I saw there the anger of love.

'There won't be any question of your father meeting her, will there?'

I shook my head. I tried to retain, in my eyes as I looked at him, that perspective of truth that I felt was slipping. 'It's just Francis and me and her,' I said.

'I mean, I know he's your father. He's lovable. But he's a rogue.' The craggy jaw, usually set in a somewhat grim expression, broke into a shy laugh. 'You may think I'm just being the over-cautious trustee. But it is casual and accidental decisions that often lie behind the difficulties which other people then come along and clear up.'

I waited after he stopped, not knowing what to say.

'I don't want to seem discouraging. I fully appreciate it's an important day for you.'

'I'm not discouraged,' I said. Perhaps there was just the faintest hint of defiance in my voice.

'But their permission?' he said. 'What about that? What has this brother of yours done about that? Matters of this kind should be arranged properly.'

'I'm sure he's done it right,' I said. But I looked down at where the reds and blues and browns of the patterned carpet glowed at our feet. And I thought to myself: it does not matter how he had done it, she is my sister. 'She is my sister,' I said.

'I know that,' he said, and smiled; it was a shy admission that he recognised that force within me, compelling me forward to the particular day's events. 'I'm only trying to hint at caution. I want you to be careful.' He paused, and once again seemed to gather himself for departure, gripping the handle of his umbrella, tracing the line of the edge of the carpet with it, once, slowly, then again. When he spoke it was gruffly: 'I just don't want anyone to get hurt,' he said. And abruptly, not waiting for an answer, he left.

Did I force the shadows to dispel? Were the shadows real? Nothing that Mr Porphyry had said could be described as anything more than the expression of caution. He was probing and questing for what was right, in his own eyes. Whereas I *knew*. And I was determined to, and did, surge past him.

51

I was a bit crestfallen, though. Alone in the flat, I wandered from room to room, reasserting within my mind the rightness of what we were about. Of course Francis had got permission, if it was necessary. But why did it arise? She was *our* sister. We had a *right* to meet.

The determination created its own excuse. The force of it soon neutralised within me the disturbing impact of Mr Porphyry's questions, and by the time I left the flat to go and meet Francis and Melanie, I had persuaded myself that Mr Porphyry was in favour of the meeting and was simply expressing a natural caution which I had to applaud. And it *was* natural. This was our first meeting since childhood. It was not as strange a phenomenon as I contrived in my own mind to make it, both then and for years to follow. Worse things have happened to others, more total dissolutions, more insoluble questions, mapping, over vast territory, the permanent rage and damage of the world's dismembered families. But to Mr Porphyry, and people like him, whose choice and discretion is exercised against ancient laws of charity and compassion which inevitably fail to match the agonised cries for help, my own situation, that of my brother, my sister, my father even, was real enough for him to take hold of it, and endeavour to understand it.

In Melanie's case the facts were prosaic: adopted in childhood after our mother's death rather than infancy she had grown up in the knowledge of what she was, one of the dispossessed, and of who she was, holding always in the back of her mind the expectation, one day, of meeting Francis and myself. We were fulfilling that for her; and she was a willing participant. What could be more natural?

II

We met in Porter's, though not quite as arranged. It turned out to be one of those comfortable establishments in which pub and eating place were tangled together in an untidy

52

succession of small, low-ceilinged rooms running off one another. The tables were mostly in cubicles of stained oak, the high-backed seats lined in dark red velvet. It was well chosen. I was impressed, all over again, at the way Francis *knew*. It was not just knowing London, and choosing where; it was planning ahead and being right, even down to the detail of the table, and the waiter, Albert, who looked at me in an openly appraising way and said, 'You have to be the brother, no mistake.' I nodded. He was thin and elderly, with a colourless complexion and black hair tightly brushed and showing, in places, the yellowish tone of his scalp. He had spoken without expression; now, rather bleakly, he smiled and said, 'Young lady waiting for you'; and set off to lead me to her. And though he said nothing about Francis, no message, no word, it did not seem strange to me because I was suddenly flooded with presentiments of what lay ahead, the tightening in my throat of excitement. 'He was particular about the table, sir,' Albert said, and headed through into another room and crossed it towards the line of windows, and the cubicled tables for four which lined that side of the room. And then he stopped. 'There you are,' he said. 'You settle yourself, nice and comfy, and I'll be back in a moment or two.'

And then I was looking at Melanie and she at me, and smiling, and wanting to laugh, and slipping sideways into the seat opposite her, beginning to sit down, and putting my hand out to shake hers, she laughing at me, and saying, 'Well, give me a kiss, then!' And I leaned across and kissed her on the cheek, and then held both of her hands in mine and looked into her eyes. And I said to her, 'Oh, Melanie! This is wonderful.' And all the time I was thinking furiously: Is she pretty? Is she beautiful? She's like Francis. She's like me. And where is Francis? Why isn't he here to help out? And what will I say to her, this first time? Her hands in mine were warm; but we did not look down at them, nor move them at all. We just looked into each other's faces, and hers was serious now, the blue eyes gazing in level curiosity into mine. I was disconcerted by their directness. She had light brown hair, curly and quite long. And she wore no ribbon or clip. There was a fine determination in her features, a strength of character that soon appeased me after the superficial disappointment of not finding her obviously pretty. Why I should have anticipated that is a puzzle, yet, for want of expecting other attributes, that is what I had foreseen.

'I'd have known you. Anywhere.' It was more or less true.

'I felt the same,' she said.

'How long is it since we...'

'Since we *met*?' She stressed the word and laughed, turning her hands in mine, wanting to disengage them. 'I was thinking, before you came, what word was right? And I couldn't decide.'

I held her hands for a moment or two longer, looking down at the way they were clasped across the table. I thought of Father, and realised that the self-assurance of holding on to her like that was imitated from him. Melanie was experiencing him, through me, without knowing it. I withdrew my hands to the edge of the table, looking down at them briefly.

'We were different people'

'No,' she said. 'We weren't people at all.'

'There's no point looking back.'

She shook her head vigorously. 'It's here that matters. And now.' She paused. 'You're going to university?'

'I'm trying to.'

'I wish I was. What will you study? What are you good at?'

'Mr Bennett—he teaches us English—he says it doesn't matter much. I'm doing English—and History. Geography, Art.' I hesitated, feeling the burden of the work I had not done during that holiday. It looked even more certain now that it would not get done, and the shadow cast by this thought was faintly oppressive.

54

Melanie said: 'I would have done English if I'd stayed on. I loved it.'

'Why didn't you?'

She made a small gesture with her shoulders and looked out of the window. I tried to understand the meaning, but all I could comprehend, behind the overwhelming realisation that she was my sister, with indissoluble links of blood that were recognisable in skin, hair, eye, gesture, was her strangeness as well. She was a stranger, sitting there. Brought together by circumstances still not fully explained; clearly, emphatically, close kin; yet there was not, with her, that tugging sense of the past which I had felt so strongly the previous day with Francis, investing with order, with authority—his over me—the way we behaved towards each other. I had been more than willing to accept it then; and with it, the flooding residue of remembered incident, trivial, irrational, yet important. This, now, was quite different.

Albert appeared at the table. His long, plain white apron reached almost to his black trouser turn-ups, which were short, and showed the lacing of his boots. He placed an old-fashioned, picture frame menu holder on the table and asked, 'Would you or the lady like a drink, sir?'

Unsuccessfully, I tried to smother the smile of vague, uncertain pride. A bit ponderously I said to Melanie, 'Would you like a glass of sherry? I'm going to have one.' I did not know what else to order, except beer. And I regarded that as ill-suited to the occasion.

'Thank you,' she said, nodding.

'So that will be two sherries? Dry?'

'Yes, please,' I said.

Albert went away.

'Why not?' I asked, pressing for an answer. 'Why not university?'

'Mum and Dad didn't think it was right. No one else in our street went. They thought it would put me above them.' She shrugged her shoulders. She was vaguely embarrassed.

'But these days,' I said. 'Surely everyone clever enough—?'

55

She shook her head. 'It was too posh. That's what they felt,' she said. She made a face.

I looked into her eyes with an expression of concern. I suppressed any astonishment I might also have felt. It seemed odd that Francis and Philpotts, and now myself and Danby, and then Archer and others at Coppinger, might be setting their under-privileged eyes on a place at Oxford, while my dear, new sister should have been turned away from such a goal by a strange form of inverted snobbery. It suddenly invested Coppinger with new value.

I wondered where Francis was, and looked round. It was early, and not many people had come into the restaurant, though there was a hum of conversation from the nearest bar, two rooms away.

'Did Francis ring you?' I asked. 'Say he'd be late?'

Melanie shook her head. 'It's better you should come one at a time.' The smile she gave was one of satisfaction, almost smugness. I was content with this at first; I dimly conceived it to be an assured self-centredness.

'How did Francis find out?'

'Aunt Julie told him. He's been asking her for years, off and on, and she did nothing. She refused to tell him where I was. It was considered not the right thing.' She emphasised 'not the right thing' in a hoity-toity voice, making the attitude old-fashioned; then she laughed.

'So what changed it?'

'I asked her.'

'Aunt Julie?'

'Yes.'

'So you remembered? You remembered us?'

She laughed at my urgency. 'Of course I did. I knew this would happen one day. All along, people said it, if I asked about you. I didn't expect to have to start things off.'

'Was it because of your...' I could not bring myself to say 'parents'. I thought for a moment of 'mother and father' or 'Mum and Dad', but neither came readily to my

56

unwilling lips. I stared at her, a slight flush of embarrassment coming to my cheeks.

'Mum and Dad?' she said.

I nodded. 'Did they stop it?'

'For a time. Until I left home, went into the nurses' hostel. Then they said it was all right.'

A shower was falling outside, the rain slanting along the street, an erratic sequence of drops angular across the panes of the window. The street was narrow, little more than a laneway, and one had to lean across, close to the glass, to see down into it. I looked out and down, hoping to catch a glimpse of Francis, all the time trying to absorb and assimilate the rich but fragmentary detail of our coming together.

'But what about me?' I said.

'It was only Francis, to begin with.' She paused. 'You see, Aunt Julie and *your* father...' The emphasis was exaggerated, yet seriously given; but then she stopped and looked sharply at me. 'He's *ours*, isn't he? Mine as well? It's so stupid.'

I ignored that. 'So it was Francis decided?'

'Yes.'

'And he included me?'

'Well, you're here, aren't you?' Again, the expression was assured, and the hint of a smile coupled with the questioning look in her eyes, reached across the table towards me as palpably as though she were reaching out her hands again to clasp mine. How difficult it is, in life, to define with honesty those details that matter most. Intent and eager though I had been, once the matter was raised by my brother, to be with him when we met Melanie, I must confess that there was an equal desire, ancient, instinctive, deriving from deep down inside myself, a desire about which I must admit neither pride nor shame, to be better than him in her eyes, to win, as it were, the essential, unending combat for affection. Other details fade away; that one prevails.

It also dictated another aspect of that part of our meeting:

57

that Father was hardly mentioned at all. I suspect that Melanie was motivated by a self-protecting instinct. I never asked her; and in a relatively short time events engulfed and obliterated any chance of disentangling such obscure issues. For my part, there was the self-asserting instinct, equally strong. Just as I had already made the best use I could of being ahead of Francis, purely, as I thought, because of circumstance, so in an unforced but probably instinctive way, I was cautious about drawing in, too early, references that might show an immediate concern about Father and any urgency in my design to bring us all together.

Do I portray myself as some kind of juggler of the emotions? Maybe it is only the truth, not just for the rather bizarre circumstances which surrounded Melanie, Francis, myself and him, but for all families, everywhere? Maybe that is the game we are engaged on, no matter how carefully enshrined it is in our culture, in our manners, in our conventions? I cannot tell. I certainly could not tell, then, as I came to terms with Melanie and with the very idea of suddenly having what I had not had before: a sister. Inexperienced as I generally was where girls were concerned, I was totally without knowledge as far as sisters went, and vaguely uneasy that Melanie behaved, and indeed seemed actually to be, older than me, a situation further emphasised by the fact that she was already out on her own while I was still a boarder at school. It added to my resentments about Coppinger; it endorsed the secretive, folded-in approach of the previous evening; it may also have provoked, subconsciously, my sister's next question.

'Tell me more,' she said, 'about your school. Aunt Julie says you were both there, and that it's special. I want to know what you do in English, what you like best. I was good at English. We had a terrific teacher. Of course, it was only a State school; not private, like yours. He was very good on modern poets, Eliot and MacNeice. Do you like them?'

I did not have time to answer. Francis came into the room

and crossed over towards us. He was with Albert, and talking to him, pulling off his gloves, finger by finger as he did so, his hat, streaked with rain, still on his head. I caught the phrase 'and I'll have it with soda, Albert,' and waited for him to greet us.

But it was the waiter who spoke first. 'So you're all together, now then, are you? Party's complete. Mr Francis and guests, eh?' I was puzzled by his familiarity. 'Different crowd from your usual, sir? Family?' He looked at us. 'If I may say so, sir, it must be. See the likeness. Know you all, now I see you together. With respect, sir.' He winked at me, smiled at Francis, but ignored, as far as I could see, Melanie.

Francis sat down beside her. The smile he gave us both was very restrained. 'I'm sorry I'm late.'

On a sudden impulse Melanie leaned across towards him. 'Give us a kiss, then. Brother!'

It took him by surprise. His eyes opened wide for a moment. He glanced at me. Then he kissed her on the cheek, and his face softened for a moment or two. I watched them as they exchanged greetings. The words were brief but affectionate. Then Francis said: 'Have you ordered? What's on the menu? Steak and kidney's good here.'

'We haven't had time to look at it. Too busy talking.' Melanie put out her hand and touched his arm.

'I'll have that if it's good.'

We ordered. Francis asked for a wine list. When Albert came with it he gave a little bow. 'We have it by the carafe,' he said. But Francis went through the wines, and Albert went away. He perused the list, that is the correct word for it, his lips pursed up, his brow wrinkled in a frown.

I said, meaning him to hear, 'Francis doesn't approve.'

'Of what?'

'Of Mr Eliot.'

She smiled in disbelief. Francis looked up, and with dreamlike convenience Albert was there again. He mentioned a number and handed back the wine list. Then he turned to us. 'And what is it of which Francis does not approve?'

'Do you not think T. S. Eliot is a great poet?' Melanie asked. She made the possibility of him not so thinking seem quite outrageous. Then she laughed and took his arm and leaned against him. 'You don't have to answer. It doesn't matter, anyway.' She looked from one of us to the other. 'You're quite alike. Am I like you? The waiter was a bit saucy, wasn't he? Talking like that about us. Mum—*my* Mum—would have had a fit. Sort of familiar, wasn't he?'

'Albert's an institution here.'

'How does he know you? That way, I mean.'

'It's a favourite place. A bit gloomy today. When it's nice the sun comes in on these tables.' He paused. 'I meet people here. It's convenient. Central. And private.' He said it with just the faintest hint of mystery, evoking for me the tone of the previous evening. I wanted to give Melanie some perception of this; but looking at her, sharply in profile as she stared at Francis, I realised that she was under the more direct spell of his authority as the eldest rather than of any mystery attaching to the wider aspects of his life.

'Who do you meet?' she asked. 'Girls?'

He laughed, a bit shyly, glancing at me, then looking sideways at her. 'All sorts of people,' he said.

'But girls as well?'

'Sometimes.'

'But not often?'

'You're very persistent.' He took a drink and looked round the room.

'But we've so much catching up to do.' She turned to me. 'It's true, isn't it?'

'We've all day.'

'That's true.'

Francis frowned. 'I haven't, I'm afraid.' He looked at Melanie first, then at me.

'But Francis! You said about keeping the whole day free. Didn't you?'

60

'I know. That was you. I hoped it would be the three of us. But something has come up.'

'Nicholas?' I asked.

He shook his head. 'Not exactly.'

I was going to press him, but the waiter arrived with lunch, and engaged us all, as he served it, in broken flights of conversation directed first at one, then another of us, and borne with patience rather than enthusiasm.

The gusty, showery rain, which had been beating against the windows, stopped and there were breaks in the cloud.

After we had settled to our lunch Melanie asked who Nicholas was, and Francis merely described him as a friend from Oxford. It released further questions which flew from her both with natural curiosity and with the apparent desire to see him talking and responding to her. She hardly had time to eat, wanting to concentrate almost more on the answers than on the questions.

I was astonished by her assurance. It was so much greater than my own. It was as if being adopted had taught her a whole range of convention, from which assurance derived, and that, now she had met us, she was throwing the convention over with a dedicated purpose related, if I could judge at all from the sparkling enthusiasm in her eyes and the animation of her features, entirely to the impact of her encounter with us. Certainly, Melanie more than came up to expectation; and, though I was more diffident about myself at that stage in the day, I could see that Francis and I, together, satisfied certain real expectations in her.

We were not altogether satisfactory. For one thing, there were girls. To be more precise, there were no girls. Neither Francis nor I could produce a convincing interest in, or evidence of, girlfriends, and to Melanie this was almost a source of astonishment. Francis pleaded work, as did I. And though I was able to mention the name of a girlfriend called Janet, and camouflage the fact of my interest in her being at that time very much a thing of the past, I was still able to present a picture of only very limited vigour under the

61

compelling curiosity she directed at these different facets of our behaviour. In her turn she confessed to boyfriends, but not to any serious involvements.

Her curiosity, like the hooves of stampeding cattle, thundered over almost everything. And yet, just as such beasts will respect impediments—the tree stump, the rock, the bluff in the ground—so she avoided for quite some time those questions which I had seen as inevitable, and yet which neither Francis nor I had discussed: his relationship with Father; mine; the possibility of hers.

Perhaps it was talking of girls that released her from some hidden restraint. After it, she finished off her lunch, or as much of it as she wanted. Then she said, turning sideways, 'Was it Aunt Julie persuaded you to leave him? Father, I mean?'

He glanced at me, then down at the table. He did not look at Melanie. Just shook his head, and then, almost to himself, said, 'No.'

The quietness made her hesitate, and she searched his face for a moment before saying, 'What, then?'

'We just didn't get on.'

In the light of other days it seems legitimate cause for teenage rebellion. Yet on that wet afternoon, in the close, smoky atmosphere of that restaurant room, and spoken by Francis with obvious hesitation, the superficial reason carried sombre weight. It was, of course, far from being the whole story. But there was no chance, then, that that would come out.

Melanie looked at me. 'And you're still with him?' It was a statement as well as a question.

'Not exactly.'

'What do you mean?'

'I still see him. I don't live with him any more.'

'Where do you live?'

I told her, answering her brief questions, explaining what I suppose is not so unusual, though limited experience made it seem so to me at that time. I think she was relieved at the way this slanted the conversation away from Father. She certainly followed carefully all that I told her about Mr Porphyry and school. Perhaps all she had sought was an initial reaction, from us both, by which she could gain a measure of Father's shadow, and come to terms with it.

Francis remained silent. He made no comment on Mr Porphyry. He seemed, in fact, to have withdrawn quite suddenly. And it was only when talk about Mr Porphyry led the conversation back to Coppinger, and to the questions of fact which inevitably arose, that he joined in again, and became quite animated, even to the point of imitating all over again, for Melanie's sake and to her evident enjoyment, the ancient ogres of childhood.

We sat on, drinking wine, then coffee. The restaurant, which had filled up after us, slowly emptied again, and there was left behind in the air a faint but not unattractive pall of smoke and warmth. And we talked on; our first compulsion being to straighten out and make common the uncertain ground which our coming together had raked up under our feet. It was soft and crumbly, and we needed to firm it down, flatten it out, rake it over, before there could be any seedtime or growth.

We worked prodigiously enough. Francis had the facts, I had the instincts, Melanie had the doubts, and we all furrowed away, imagining, I suppose, that we were recovering the past. I hardly noticed when Francis said, 'I think we should go.' And I looked blankly at him when he caught Albert's eye and made a scribbling gesture in the air.

Melanie said: 'I'd like to meet him.'

'Who?' I said, without thinking. 'Mr Porphyry?'

'No. Of course not. Father, silly.'

'Okay,' I said.

Francis said nothing, but looked at me.

I remembered Mr Porphyry's expression, as he stood and cautioned me, in the grey light of the flat that morning. And I felt something crumble within me. It was as if some aspect of integrity was falling down, as if some commitment was

63

being withdrawn; and the unspoken, secret failure of resolve, though perhaps it did not matter greatly, predominated in my mind. I actually felt it giving way, and it obscured another feeling, one of doubt at the way in which Melanie had said that she wanted to see him. There had been something not quite right about it, and that something, hanging in the air, then vanishing, was connected with the validity of her statement. It was as if she wanted to please me rather than herself. If was not that she wanted to see him. It was that she wanted to please me, please us, be part of us. And in her own uncertainty, which I did not recognise, she caught after this commitment as a way of underlining her own feelings. I might have seen this more clearly had it not been for the burden of Mr Porphyry's feelings about Melanie meeting my father. I might have acted differently. And the course of events, which I now see I plotted with such determination, would have been different.

There was no possibility of going into further detail, for Albert appeared, and Francis finished paying, and then, almost as if he wanted to block further conversation, he got up, and we left.

It seemed an ill-omen when he said he would have to leave us, there and then. I at least had hoped he would direct in some way our afternoon. But he was leaving that to us. It had stopped raining when we came out, and though the narrow side-turning off Monmouth Street was in shadow, there was watery sunlight on the buildings at the end, and shiny cars and buses, still wet from the rain, gleamed and glistened in the light. Francis took from his pocket a white envelope and gave it to me. 'Those are the Christopher Fry tickets. With my compliments.' He beamed at us both, and bowed to Melanie.

'But when will I see you again?' she asked.

'I'll be in touch,' he said.

'Oh, Francis!'

He gave her a hug, and kissed her on the cheek.

64

'I'll ring you tomorrow,' I said.

He nodded. Then he walked briskly away.

III

We took a bus to Westminster and walked along Millbank.
There were still the gusts of wind, blowing down river
towards us, and from time to time they blew cloud across the
sun so that the brilliance of its light in our faces was
intermittent. I showed her where the flat was, and told her
about Mr Porphyry; but she seemed only vaguely interested.

'Did you think about meeting me?' Melanie asked.

'Sometimes,' I said. 'If ever I mentioned it to Father it
would make him bad-tempered. He would be, well, kind of
morose.'

'Morose?' She spoke the word as though it belonged to
another language, handling it with curious respect.

'Yes. Moody. A certain look in his eye.'

'Why didn't he send you to Aunt Julie?'

'He hates her.'

'*Hates* her?'

'Yes.'

Neither of us spoke. I tried to reassure myself, by
remembered word or gesture, that I was right in what I said.
In my mind I could see him saying, on one occasion,
'Reproach me, the bitch! Reproach me!' And repeating it
endlessly during some agonised evening of recollection in
which he had been examining certain details out of his life.
But on the occasion he had been hopelessly drunk, and in
my heart I could not really accept that it amounted to hate.
Yet what other word could describe the tangle and confusion
of feelings which had so effectively blocked any action of
mine that might have brought about this meeting earlier? In
any case, Aunt Julie would have blocked it.

'Can you understand it? Hating people?' We had stopped
to look across the river, and Melanie was facing into the sun.

She had put on a headscarf, but it did not completely cover her light brown hair. The wind rippled the end of her scarf back behind her.

I shook my head, but not with any certainty. Turning over the idea of hatred, and relating it to the only world in which it could have application, that of Coppinger, I realised that it was real enough. 'There are boys at school,' I said. 'Not so much now. But when I was smaller. Bullying types. You could do nothing. You were just—' I clenched my fists as I had done on countless occasions when the frustration was too hard to bear, '—powerless.'

'What about Francis? Did he hate Father?'

'I don't know.'

'But to leave him—?'

'It was difficult for him, cutting off. But it wasn't really *leaving*. There was nowhere to walk out of, not permanent.'

'What do *you* feel about it?'

I did not answer straight away. I looked out over the brown waters of the river, whipped up by the gusts of wind. The tide was on the ebb, and a tug with barges was making slow progress upstream, nudging its way clear of Lambeth Bridge and into the glow of sunlight from among the clouds.

'I'm sorry, most of the time. Then, when I'm angry with Father, sometimes, I wish that I could do it. Just leave.'

'But you wouldn't?'

'No. Not that it's the same now.'

We walked on.

'Did Francis ever have doubts?' she asked. 'Did he ever think he'd made a mistake?'

'Never,' I said, without hesitation. 'He *never* has doubts.'

She laughed, and I turned and looked at her, smiling myself as I realised how emphatic I had been.

'And you? Do you have doubts?'

'Always,' I said.

'So do I.' She took my arm and cuddled against me, and we walked on, into the wind, and in step.

'Well, Brother,' she said, after a while, 'what does it feel like to have a sister again? You're one of two, remember? I'm unique.'

'It feels like magic. One day you don't exist. Just in memory. Then you're there. But all those years...' They piled up in front of me, in front of us both, like the buffeting of the wind. 'It seemed ridiculous, not knowing each other.'

'It *was* ridiculous.'

There was a lively enthusiasm in the way both of us set to and unravelled, all over again, with different episodes, in different contexts, the lost years. In a flood both of detail and of generalisation, the chronology of our separation was plotted in all its uncertainty and fragmentation. Some episodes were used to give a picture of the general pattern of life at a given time; others were glossed over. I came to some kind of understanding of my sister's adoption, partial, subjective, limited, a bit judgmental. In my eyes it had the unexceptional merit of regularity, security, comfort, care. If I could not detect in it more than that, the reason must have been the very subjective, if perhaps forgiveable as well, belief which we must have come to that afternoon, each in our own fashion: that all was ordinary that did not belong to the world we created around the extraordinary phenomenon of being brother and sister. We extended that, of course, to include Francis, since he was not only part of it already, but its chief engineer. And bit by bit the inescapability of Father manifested itself.

'When can I meet him?'

I hesitated. I was again impressed by the way she seemed to have taken hold. She governed what she was, what she did. 'I've only another fortnight. Then I have to go back. I was hoping we could meet. For a picnic. Go to Kew. If the weather was warm. What do you think?' I looked a bit nervously at her. Of course she could not know that a good part of my hesitation derived from Mr Porphyry, and the imponderable question of how I would explain to him, if I explained at all.

67

'It would be lovely,' she said. 'It would be the best kind of meeting. Shall I try and get free this Sunday?'

A brief shadow of desperation raced through my mind, then was overwhelmed by the warm and confident response I felt towards her. 'Yes,' I said. 'Yes, that's exactly what we'll do. I'll tell him. He's bound to be free. Francis will have to be. And we'll go.' I laughed, and raised my clenched fist in the air. It was as if shackles fell from my wrists. It had really been so easy.

Chapter Three

I

'I haven't found it easy to advise you,' Mr Porphyry said, 'and I've tried not to. I'm overjoyed that I've been able to provide a home for you during this particular holiday, and I genuinely mean it when I say you can always come. But you must realise she has had a very different upbringing.'

'I do realise it,' I said. 'But she was all right. It went very well.'

'I'm sure it did.'

I waited for him to go on, but instead he poured himself more coffee. He placed the cup and saucer directly in front of himself. Then, with his long, sensitive hands, he moved other things away with a finality that indicated his breakfast was over. He was clearing space absently, and deep in thought; the delicate movement of his fingers made me think of Mr Parker at the organ at school, preparing to play, his hands moving between the manuals, his eyes checking the stops, as he waited for the hiss of air that would tell him the bellows had been filled. And only then would he look up, and focus on the music, and the wavering hands would become certain and descend upon the keys.

'Don't you believe me?'

Mr Porphyry's eyes came up from the table and focussed on me. 'Of course I believe you. I do much more than that, I believe *in* you. But how can you be certain that she's all right?' More calmly he said: 'Tell me what you mean when you say it went very well.'

I looked directly back into his large, sad eyes. His tone was gentle. The soft, prodding, mildly interrogative mood in which he approached me was carefully adopted in order not to give offence or silence me from responding. Even so, I felt faintly crushed. 'I just *know*,' I said. 'From the feel of things.'

He nodded. Again he surveyed the table between us. It had a well-ordered appearance, even among the crumbs and eggshells of our meal, his housekeeper's hand serving as an extension of his own influence over me. 'Go on,' he said, looking up.

'She said it as well. It was as if we'd never been parted. She'd have known me just as I knew her. We like the same things. It was amazing! We'd read the same, thought the same, felt the same! It *did* go well.'

He smiled; it was a faint, mocking expression of his agreement. 'Don't you think,' he said, 'that's natural? Haven't you been taught much the same?'

'But it was much more than that,' I said. 'You must realise it was instantly different.' I clenched my fists and held them up in front of me, against my chest. I felt defiantly sure of myself, and anxious to convince him out of a mood of what I took to be merely wavering uncertainty. If I could only get the feelings across he would in due course accept my interpretation of Melanie's reactions.

But it was not to be so easy. 'It's what you want, isn't it?' he asked.

'Of course,' I said.

'And it's now that you want it because it's now it has come about.'

'You didn't want me to meet her, did you? You said it might be better—'

'No.' He laughed, and held up his hand. 'Wait a minute. I didn't interfere. Remember what I said. You don't know what effect it might have. These things cannot be predicted.'

'But it had a good effect. It did.'

70

'So far.'

'But it was the most important. It was the first meeting after twelve years.'

He smiled again, but this time with a look of resignation lifting his eyebrows. 'But years more may be involved.' He paused. Then more positively he said: 'It's lucky you got up early this morning. We wouldn't have had this chat. Perhaps you don't think it's lucky?'

'You didn't meet her,' I said. 'You didn't see how she was.'

'No. You're right. Tell me what you did with yourselves.'

While he drank his coffee I gave him an account of the day. He listened attentively, seeming to nod with approval at the easily evoked images of the two of us, walking in April sunshine, parading through the Tate, sitting together in the theatre.

'And what was your brother doing, that he couldn't be with you?'

'Well, he managed lunch. Then he had to go off.'

'And you say he really arranged it all?'

I nodded.

'Odd he should arrange the day and then go off.'

'Well, there's this problem,' I said. 'A friend of his at Oxford has got into some kind of difficulty, and Francis and Philpotts are trying to help him out.'

'Money?' he asked.

'I'm not really sure.'

'And was Philpotts with your brother yesterday?'

'They may have met in the afternoon.'

'I see.' He had finished, and, in the tidy, precise manner he had, he now pushed the cup in from the table's edge, wiped his lip with the large white napkin, returned it to the silver ring, and looked across the table at me.

'You don't think—,' he said, and paused. 'Francis wasn't avoiding spending the rest of the day with you both?'

I looked blankly at him, then shook my head in dismissal of the idea. 'Why would he do that?' I said.

71

'It's just a feeling I have. Arranging it all, like that.' He frowned, and shook his head. 'And then something coming up, more important. It doesn't altogether make sense.'

He got up. He was still holding the napkin. He put it down on the table, and it made a tiny noise in the stillness of the room. 'The main thing is,' he said, 'that she shouldn't meet your father. That *could* be distressing for her.' The weight of his experience, a life concerned with young lives, filled the room. I did not know quite how to react. Perhaps expecting agreement, perhaps, with that experience of his, sensing the guilt that had seized hold of me, he asked: 'Nothing *has* been arranged, has it?'

Truthfully, I was able to answer: 'No.' But I could not leave it at that. 'She *wants* to meet him,' I said.

He reacted sharply: 'She asked?'

'Yes,' I said. 'She told me she wanted to meet him.'

'And what did you say? I hope you put her off.'

My discomfort increased. 'Not exactly,' I said. 'How could I?'

'But these are quite different things!' He seemed really quite shocked. 'You and Francis and...and Melanie—,' he had to recall the name: 'You are all of an age, and, though I do have reservations, I can see there are arguments in favour of what has happened. But your father! I mean, with a young girl, a daughter he hasn't seen in years, it could have a disastrous effect.'

'What will I do?' I asked. I knew what I was going to do, and it was dishonest of me to raise the question.

'You must do your best to put it off.'

I did not answer; nor did I meet his eyes.

'You will, won't you?'

'I'll do my best,' I said.

'I'm glad,' he said. 'Relieved. I don't want you to feel I'm putting pressure on you. But I do think all this is very serious.' He looked at his watch. 'Goodness! Must get moving. Join me for Q.T.?'

I shook my head.

72

'You don't mind dealing with that client this morning. Up until lunchtime? You sure?'

'Quite sure,' I said.

'And what about this evening?'

I looked up at him from the table. 'I'm going with Francis to see him, tonight,' I said.

'Who?'

'My father.'

He stood still. His eyes, staring apparently in the region of my chest, had lost their focus and were turned inward upon the rising mists of doubt about my present course of action. He seemed about to speak. His long fingers tapped on the back of the chair. Then he faintly shrugged his shoulders and went out.

I heard him crossing the hall to his bedroom. Then the door closed. The sun flooded the room, yet I felt overcast by a faint shadow of doubt about my own enthusiasm for the course of action on which I was embarked. I also felt the burden of deceit. It was crabbed and complicated; there were ways round it; it was amenable to justifications of a sort; yet it was still deceit. All along, there had been no doubt in my mind that Mr Porphyry would not understand. I had forced him into that mould. In my eyes he had no experience, no terms of reference, to apply to the wild and fitful behaviour of our family. I was almost self-righteous in asking myself the question: how could I have expected him to understand? And yet his conscientious, thoughtful, unemphatic hesitations about the wisdom of it all acted now as a dampener upon the furnace of my conviction. He did know. He did have experience. He did have knowledge of such things. I could not harm my father. My brother was his own keeper. To him I had given the choice and he had taken it. But Melanie? What options had been hers? The blankness of refusal? Or the rich and varied complications, of Francis, of me; now, of Father.

She had been given no choice at all. Sitting there in the April sunlight, my eyes passing from object to object in the

73

brilliantly bathed dining room of the flat, I consciously suppressed what doubts I had. That which was happening was right. Nature, destiny, fate had so ordained. It was no more possible to keep us apart than it was to bring the stars together, changing, altering, the fixed associations which my father had proudly pointed out to me on crisp winter nights in childhood. Francis had acknowledged this in his agreement to meet me that evening and go and see him. Melanie had done the same in more or less accepting the plan for a weekend picnic, a picnic that was conveniently not yet confirmed. Yet the tide was set in its purpose, direction, timing. Only momentarily did I consider Mr Porphyry's caution, his measured, responsible doubt, the gentle Christianity that pushed him forward. I thought briefly of him, kneeling now no doubt in prayer, that 'Quiet Time' which on occasions in the past I had shared. In the sharp spring sunshine I bowed my head, closed my eyes, and whispered to myself, 'Pray God what I do, what *we* do, what is being done, the direction we are all taking, is right.' But the gesture was hollow. It was like Hamlet's uncle. I sought no guidance; only endorsement for my stubborn acts. My meditations were upon earthly passions, not on spiritual things; self-centred, they were brief and didactic. Doubt suppressed, I was ready to start the day.

II

The mood in which I had started the day was sustained and strengthened by the cool, fresh spring weather, the sun shining through intermittent cloud until, by late evening, when I made my way to Francis's flat, it was warm and still, almost summery.

He was working. I looked around for Philpotts, then asked where he was.

'He's gone back to Oxford for a day or two.'

'Wedmore?' I said, putting on an appropriate expression of concern.

He looked up at me rather sharply, and seemed to be adjusting to our previous meeting, reassembling the details of what he had told me. 'In part,' he said. 'Keeping an eye on things.' Then, more sombrely, 'But there's not much can be done.' He paused. 'He has work to do in the Bodleian. Facing exams, you know.'

I nodded. I got the impression that Wedmore's fate required no further examination, and that even Philpotts had been safely disposed of within the crumbling library walls where he was studying.

'How was the rest of your day?'

'It was wonderful,' I said. 'Isn't she terrific! We really did have a very good time.'

'What did you do after you left me?'

I gave him an account of the afternoon and evening we had spent together. His usually rather tense features, with their expression of command, a strict generalship over the emotions as well as over other people, softened as he listened to my recollections of what we had talked about, and what we had done.

'Do you think it is wrong?' I asked. 'Seeing her?'

'Wrong? What do you mean?'

I hesitated, not wishing to introduce a discordant note just at that time, when we were about to set out and see Father, but all the same seeing no alternative way of explaining what was, in effect, someone else's doubt rather than my own. 'Does it disturb things too much, to meet her, after all these years?'

'But she's a sister!'

'I know. But she belongs elsewhere. We have shifted things, not just for you and me, but for her.'

'What's made you say all this? Is it what you think?' He looked carefully at me, his interrogation now purposeful.

'It's not me, really,' I said. 'It's Mr Porphyry. I told him, of course. I thought his feelings would be like mine. I thought he'd say it's marvellous, to have a sister, just like that, out of the blue. But he didn't. He didn't seem to think it marvellous at all. He wondered if I should meet her, and what might happen, and where it would lead.' I stopped, looking at Francis, my own position more or less wide open for his inspection.

'We all make our own decisions. You wanted to meet her. She wanted to meet you. You are brother and sister.' He looked straight at me, his eyebrows raised, not in a spirit of inquiry, seeking from me some kind of response, but challenging my doubt; and, indirectly, or so it seemed, challenging the intrusion of this shadowy figure behind me whom Francis had never known at Coppinger, and had not so far met.

'You think Mr Porphyry's wrong?'

'I don't know how he could know enough to be right.'

It dismissed any argument. But it also had the effect of stopping our discussion for the moment on Melanie. And we stood face to face in the room, slightly awkwardly.

'Should we go?' I said. It was still early, if we took the Underground. 'We could walk.'

He looked at his watch, then round the room.

'Yes,' he said, 'we'll leave now. We can walk over Campden Hill. Chesterton country. When did you say we would be there?'

'Seven.'

'We've plenty of time.'

'He'll be frantic if we're not punctual.'

Francis laughed. 'He'll be frantic if we are.'

He looked a bit like a mountain climber as he stepped smartly along the upward slope of Holland Park Avenue, his walking stick swinging upward, the tip of it coming close to his shoulder. Instead of the broad-brimmed hat he had worn at our first encounter, on the station platform, he now had on a cloth cap, in tweed, not of a workman's cut but of a kind that might have fittingly graced the head of a racing gentleman or an officer in 'mufti'. I felt he was 'equipped' for the evening's encounter, and, from being the responsible catalyst, I was now relegated to a role that was really the equivalent of his 'squire'.

'Do you mind if we go this way?' I said when we got to Holland Walk.

'I don't like it as much. I prefer to go up by the tennis club.' He made to move on.

'I haven't walked this way for ages,' I said. 'I want to tell him.'

'All right. Why is it significant?'

I shrugged, then smiled at him. 'He once told me a story, long ago, when we were walking up here together. He told me a story which I've forgotten. He started it at the other end, and finished it just there.' I pointed to the wall. 'I don't remember the story, what happened or anything like that. I don't remember where we were coming, or going to. I don't remember where we lived at that time, or what job he was doing. There was something magical about the story itself, some mystery, about a child going through a gate in a wall, or a gap where the bricks had fallen, and finding a garden with other children, and playing with them. And either the child never comes out of the garden again, or he comes out and never finds his way back again. It doesn't much matter', I said, looking at Francis who was intent on my words. 'It's just that, if I want to remember those days, that time, all the feelings I had, then walking here does it.'

'All right.' He turned rather abruptly, and set off. He was giving in, something he never liked to do, and I felt at the time that this was all.

Hurrying after him I said, 'Do you think he told me the story because I never had any friends, alone on holiday with him, living in a bedsitter, sometimes working with him?'

Francis shrugged.

'Where were you then?'

He shrugged again. 'When was it?'

'That's it. I can't tell.'

He strode on, and casting a glance sideways at his face it seemed to be set in an expression that deliberately excluded

77

recollection. He was concentrating on walking, and on the way ahead. The evening sunshine was fitful enough until we came down into Kensington, and it caught on the sides of buildings to our left.

'We could slacken the pace a bit,' I said.

'Too fast?' Francis could always outwalk me.

'We've time.'

'But he'll be there anyway, won't he?'

'Yes.'

We walked on up Kensington High Street. It was a lovely evening, the sun now quite low behind us, the traffic intermittent and slack.

'Do you think he'll come on the picnic?'

'He will of course.'

'Are you looking forward to it?'

Francis laughed. It was a short, almost harsh sound, and it was accompanied by a brief glance in my direction. 'In as far as I look forward to anything other than in a mood of polite inquiry, curiosity, I look forward to a picnic with my family at Kew with something that could be described as pleasure. I just hope it doesn't rain.'

III

He told us to come in. I went first, turning with my back to the door as if ushering Francis in. I was proud and curious, both. I felt that I was the great reconciler. I was offering each to the other as a prize, a tribute to some great force of love that could solve the hurt of many years. I did not really understand, then, what lay between them. I am far from sure that I ever understood it. In later years, when Francis and I spent long evenings dissecting each other's feelings, attitudes, actions, lives even, it was one of the unexplored areas. It has always been under a curious unspoken interdict. I had enjoyed—if 'enjoyed' is the correct word—unbroken years in the precarious company of this man. Francis, by his own choice, had not. The time had passed, and the inescapable effects of this decision, like the motives which in the first instance had led to the decision, were fixed and irreversible. By coming to him Francis had not changed. By bringing about this reconciliation, as I saw it, nothing had been turned back. It was just that a phase was ended.

They stood and looked at each other. It can only have been for a moment or two, and yet it seemed that an absolute infinity of time and space was crammed within that shabby, ill-lit room. More, perhaps, than at any other time in my life I felt myself the spectator.

Father said: 'My son! Good of you to come and see your father.' There was a catch in his voice. He waited where he stood on the far side of the room, his great fist clenched and resting on the corner of a small table, his body bent over it, so still, so concentrated, I felt at any moment that the cheap, nondescript piece of furniture would collapse.

From his fixed expression, mainly of anticipation, I looked at Francis. He seemed also visibly conscious of the drama of the encounter, yet not overwhelmed by it.

'Hello, Father.' He did not move. Just stood there, on the other side of the room, in from the door, his hat and stick in his hand.

'It's very small. They want to get me out. It's the Coronation, you see. It would only be for the end of May, part of June. I'd come back then, you see. It's not that I have any trouble. Rent's always paid. Alice helps sometimes. He'll tell you how it is.' He gestured in an off-hand way towards me.

'He's probably told you already. Alice is very good. Sit down. You'll have to sit on the bed. It's not much, really. But now that I'm on my own it does me well enough. Keeps me shipshape, you see. Nothing superfluous.' He moved away from the table more or less to the middle of the room. I waited to see whether they would touch each other. I felt that, as with a man and woman drawn to each other by desire, who have never kissed, occupy, in those moments

79

before the first physical encounter, a special zone of air, thickened and intensified by feeling, that in the case of my father and brother, the same was true, and could, just then, have led to a gesture, an embrace, an unspoken statement, by hand or arm, of forgiveness, of reconcilement, of the ending of estrangement.

It did not. Close as we all were, in the confiines of his single room, there remained between us—though I felt I was entirely marginal—a detachment that was as powerful as the magnetism that had drawn us together in the first place.

'I thought we would go for a drink,' Francis said.

Father looked at him. 'Good idea! Let's get out in the spring air. Glass of beer for us all! Nothing wrong with it, in moderation.'

I came near to laughing. It struck me as strange that I had never suggested a drink, for a variety of reasons that embraced moral scruples and the recollection of past disasters; and yet here was Francis proposing that we should go drinking, and my father treating it as a healthy novelty.

'Pass me my cap,' he said. 'It's behind the door.' The order was peremptory. He looked briefly at me, and his eyes were stern, quite the opposite of the mannered indulgence with which he was treating Francis.

I did as he ordered.

He looked from one of us to the other, first Francis, then myself, then Francis again. 'Wallet, key, money, cigarettes, penknife, matches, handkerchief.' He touched lightly the pockets of jacket and trousers, and seemed satisfied that he was equipped for departure. 'Lead on.' He pointed me to the door. Francis followed, and we left the house.

It was natural that he should concentrate his interest upon the son he had not seen for years. That was the purpose behind my gentle persuasions, and I was pleased to go along with it, their silent companion, listening to the interrogation about Francis's studies, his travelling abroad, his interests, even his emotional life, though in this realm little progress was recorded. Yet, having more or less brought it about, I felt

80

vaguely jealous, and very much on the fringe of things. And this feeling was to be further emphasised.

We drank modestly enough; he had a pint to begin with, we had a glass of bitter each. And we sat outside the South Kensington pub to which he had led us, in the fading light of an evening just warm enough for *al fresco* conversation. For a period during which he had been drinking quite heavily, it was very restrained. Francis broached the idea of the picnic at Kew, and it was received with enthusiasm.

'You're too young to remember, but in the old days we used to go to Kew, didn't we, Francis?'

Francis nodded.

'It's a good time of course. The blossom will be out, the cherry blossom. Glades of it. Wonderful. What's that variety, now? It'll come to me.' He tapped with his fingers on the ridged skin of his brow, his eyes looking up at the evening sky. 'Not *tomentosa*. No. That's small and later. The Kilroys had that. But I didn't think it special. What I like best of all is the pendulous white. It's quite early. Japanese, of course. *Prunus serrulata* ... ' He had closed his eyes. With each of the two words his fingers had come quite sharply down on his skull, only to be raised again. And now they were poised while a look of intense agony crossed his features. '*Prunus serrulata* ... Oh, God, why can't I remember? I knew them all, these names!' His voice was anguished. But now it calmed, and he looked at us. 'I have walked underneath these glades of white in springtime, my sons, and it was a sort of heaven. A close panoply of soft white flowers filling the air with their scent. It is like a low ceiling. It changes the very texture of the air, the way the light falls on the ground. *Prunus serrulata* ... *sachalineusis*?' He paused, 'Sach—No. That's wrong. That's pink.' He looked at us both. 'That's in flower at this time.' He saw that we were waiting, indulgently patient, and the intense expression softened into a smile. 'I used to know them all. All! But it's gone. I don't need the information, see? And it fades. The mind can't keep these things.'

81

'Didn't you used to send us to read the names off the labels? And then you'd write them if you'd remembered wrong?' I spoke with a clear recollection of playing this game.

'That's right! I didn't think you'd have remembered. You remember, Francis, don't you?'

He nodded, and drank from his glass.

'Would you like another?' he asked.

'Indeed I would!'

'And you?' He turned to me.

'Yes, please.'

After he had gone into the pub, Father turned to me. 'So you do remember? You were very young. They were the days, my son, gone but not forgotten.'

'It's hard to remember, isn't it?' I said it tentatively, as an enticement.

'It comes back to me. Those days. I think you did the running and the shouting, you with Melanie trying to keep up and shrieking with excitement. Francis did the reading of the labels. Ah, well.' He looked out across the street.

'We had lunch with Melanie yesterday.' I said it as calmly as I could, but the bubbling sense of excitement swelled up inside as I watched his sad, reflective eyes suddenly light up with the quickening flash of excited inquiry.

'What!' he said. 'Melanie? My daughter, Melanie! Why didn't you tell me? Where did you meet? Who arranged it? Where is she?' He suddenly looked up and down the street, as though we had temporarily hidden her away in a parked car, or down a side street, in order to check first whether a face to face meeting would be possible. But then he looked back at me, and almost crossly said, 'Sonny Boy! Out with it, now! You must tell your father what's going on, and no mistake.'

'Oh Father!' I said, unable to suppress my own excitement. 'It happened completely out of the blue. It just—'

'But how did it happen? When? Who organised it?'

I laughed. 'I'm trying to tell you!'

'But I mean!' He spread out his hands. 'Your father must know! Everything!'

'I'll tell you everything,' I said.

But at that point Francis came back with the drinks, and was met with a rapid volley of the same questions.

'What's this about Melanie, son? What's this about meeting her? The two of you? I want to know everything! Everything!' His voice, aggressive, demanding, became quite high-pitched. It was almost angry.

Francis smiled at him. 'Yes. We had lunch yesterday. We rather enjoy—'

'I know that already! But how? Where did you find her? Why did it happen just now?'

'You'll have to listen,' I said, 'if you want the answer.'

Francis told him about Aunt Julie and fixing up the meeting. I let him describe Melanie, what she was doing, where she lived. I was glad to fall back on his much more precise outline. He, after all, was more in possession of the facts. But what I really valued was being able to see my father's face as he gradually absorbed details of Melanie's eruption into our lives. In a strange way the account subdued him. At the end there was even a pause, and he looked away.

'She wants to meet you.' I said. I spoke quietly. He was looking away from us both.

He was strangely hesitant. Turning back towards me he asked: 'Does she?'

I nodded.

'Will she come on Sunday?'

'I think so,' I said.

Francis said: 'She will of course.'

'Melanie!' he said. 'My little daughter, Melanie! So many years passed over me in vain.'

The urge to laugh, which I felt, was overwhelmed by sympathy for his own feelings, which were as intense as all his reactions. He seemed burdened by regret, if only momentarily, and it was as if to shake it off that he rubbed

83

his hands together and asked us what arrangement we had made.

'None, yet,' Francis said. 'But we'll organise it.'

'Have you time? What about your work?' He was filled with thoughtful concern.

'It's all right.' Francis smiled.

'How will it go? Will you get a good degree?'

'I haven't done enough for a first. I'll get a good second.'

'What do you mean? A good second? A son of mine, defeated before he starts?'

'It's not like that,' Francis said. 'I just haven't done the work. I did other things, theatre, politics. There's nothing can be done about it.'

'And you know, do you?'

'More or less,' he said.

We paused and sat there while he absorbed this information. A fattish man had come out on the steps of the pub and had glanced once or twice across at us. He was wearing a blue blazer. His shirt was open, but the space at his neck filled by a carefully arranged scarf, the paisley pattern predominantly yellow in colour.

'Shall we come and collect you on Sunday morning?' I said.

He looked sharply at me, then at Francis. 'No. We'll meet at Francis's flat. I'd like to see it. That okay?'

Francis nodded.

'Good. And what about Melanie? She wants to come?'

'Yes,' I said. He was looking closely at me, anxious to detect any nuance of doubt or indecision. 'You're sure?'

I nodded, and smiled at him. 'I'm sure.'

'We'd better pray for good weather.'

Francis turned to me. 'You'll do the praying, won't you?'

Father said, 'My God, it's old Chobber! Hello, Chobber! You back? Come and meet my sons!'

The fattish man moved over towards us. He was holding his drink, which appeared to be gin, and a half-smoked cigarette in one hand. The other, the fingers flat, was slipped down into his hip pocket, the thumb outside, pointing forward. He nodded. 'Hello, George! Came back last night. In time for Molly's party. Feel a bit wobbly still. Why weren't you at it?'

'You know I can't stand Molly.'

'I expect you wanted to get some serious drinking done. Shouldn't say it in front of your boys. What are their names?'

Father told him. 'He's at university. He's at school. Both doing well. Both'll make a success of things. Not like their father. He's a ne'er-do-well, isn't he, Chobber?'

'You can say that again, George.' Awkwardly he took a puff from his cigarette followed by a sip from his drink.

A rather tense look had come over Francis's face. The line of his jaw jutted forward, and with a slow and deliberate movement of his shoulder he reached forward, took up his glass and drank from it.

'Well, I'm for the tiddlypush,' Chobber said. 'This is my third for the road. Can't seem to get the old engines started tonight.' He drained the glass.

'Won't you stay and have another?' Father said.

Francis looked at him.

Chobber paused, glanced down into the empty glass, then across at us. His eyes met my brother's, and they stared for a moment at each other. 'Don't think I will, thanks, George. Might see you tomorrow.'

After he'd gone, Father laughed. 'He's all right, Chobber. Not a bad sort. Got a good job. Sells second-hand cars. You know, one of the good firms in Piccadilly. At least, he was there somewhere. May have moved to South Ken. What does it matter?' He suddenly laughed again at Francis. 'Saw 'im off, didn't you.'

Francis stared back at him. Then a thin, aloof smile flitted across his lips. 'And what was Chobber in the war?' he asked. 'He has the look of someone who was something in the war.'

This time the laughter seemed to be surrounded and

suffused by the smiling happiness of his whole face. He looked at me as well, and I felt drawn in by the tide of joy which momentarily was lifting us all.

'Oh, Francis! Oh my sons! You're so alike! You're different as well, I can see that. But...' I could see he was moved. An added layer of moisture, far too slight to be called a tear, had overlaid the surface of his eyes. And as the laughter dissolved and faded, the soft, indulgent look that was left turned equally between us. Almost to himself he said, 'I did try. If I could have the time over again...' He seemed then to shake himself. He pointed at me. 'Another drink?' Without repeating the question he pointed at Francis.

'No thanks,' I said.

Francis shook his head.

'Quite right! Moderation in all things. Learn from my mistakes, my sons!'

We walked back together. It was growing dark, and there was a chill in the air. I felt that we had gone perilously close to some kind of vague disaster. Walking away from the pub the two of them were ahead of me to begin with, and I looked carefully at Francis, swinging his stick, his shoulders back, and at the slow, easy, more relaxed movement of my father, keeping pace, swinging along, the slight dip of his left shoulder indicating, it seemed at the time, that all was right in his small world. And I briefly delayed catching up, pleased to see Francis pointing with his stick at something on a building, and making a comment to which Father responded with a quick and easy remark.

IV

I felt curiously inhibited, alone with Francis, afterwards. My natural inclination was to ask him what he felt after all these years and what his thoughts were. My own mind had been passively attentive: when I might have laughed at my father, or made some quick response to what he was saying, I had restrained myself instead, deferring to my brother, whose claims that night were paramount. But now the encounter was over I wanted a reaction that would tell me whether it had been worthwhile. I could not think of what to say. Indeed Francis was forbiddingly engrossed in thought, striding along up Gloucester Road in the direction of the Park, making it difficult for me to keep up with him.

'I say, Francis?'

'Yes?'

'Shouldn't I be getting a Gloucester Road tube?'

He thought for a moment. 'We can walk together as far as Kensington and you can get a Circle line there. Give us the chance to talk. Suit you?'

'Okay. But not so fast—'

We fell into step at a more moderate pace.

'Do you think Sunday'll be all right?' I said. 'With Melanie?'

'I don't see why not.'

There was another pause.

'Mr Porphyry doesn't think I should have seen her.'

'Oh. Why not?'

'Upsetting.'

'What does he know about it? What does he know about her?'

I felt the need for caution. 'Not much, really. It just came up, that I was meeting her.'

'Has he met Father?'

'No.'

'Doesn't want to?'

'It never came up. I mean, Father never suggested it, and…well, Mr Porphyry didn't, either. I mean, they wouldn't get on.'

'How do you know? Surely there's no telling. Look at that perfectly frightful man, just now. Chobber? Was that his name? Well, he seemed to get on.'

'Weren't they very alike?'

87

Francis shrugged his shoulders. 'Does he have many friends like that?'

I was puzzled by the question, realising how little I knew, apart from chance encounters earlier in my life waiting for him outside public houses, of that casual band of drinking companions, men and women, that he seemed able to assemble and dismiss again with such remarkable ease.

'I don't really know,' I said. 'There always seem to be friends. I think he finds it easy to get on with people.'

'There were always people like Chobber, in the old days. he used to bring them home. Mother couldn't stand them. Sometimes she would tell him what they were like. And he would look at her, like someone waking from a dream, and say she was absolutely right. And then he would be more against them than she was. And if they met they would have a row, and he would say terrible things. Complete dismissal.'

I looked at him, bemused by his recollection. 'I can't remember,' I said. 'I can't really remember her.'

But he ignored this. 'Oh, yes. Absolutely complete. And then, weeks afterwards, perhaps months, they'd meet, and he'd come home and mention the encounter, in an off-hand way. I knew from Mother's face, resigned, a bit sad, that it was starting.'

'I don't remember.'

'You were too young.'

We turned out of Princes Gate and headed down towards Kensington High Street. The traffic was light. It was chilly.

'He seems to think,' I said, 'that he'll have to move out. With the Coronation, I mean.'

'Yes,' Francis said. 'I'm worried about that.'

'Why are you worried?'

'Well, we're meeting on Sunday at the flat. It may give him ideas.'

'What? That he'd move in with you?'

'Not exactly. I won't be here then. But *he* will.'

I thought for a minute or two. 'Should we change things? Meet somewhere else?'

Francis shook his head. 'No. It'll be all right. I can control him.'

I laughed. 'No one's ever been able to do that!'

'We'll see.'

We reached the Underground station and paused there in the dusty, warm breeze coming out of the entrance.

'I'm going to walk,' he said. 'Over Campden Hill, this time. A faint smile was on his lips. 'No holes in the wall for me!' So you'll bring Melanie on Sunday? And we'll start at ten? Okay?'

I nodded. Faintly dissatisfied, I wanted to keep him there, ask him something, anything, to prolong the conversation. I did not know what it was I wanted, reassurance, encouragement, some indication that what I had done in bringing them together was right. But again I had the awkward feeling that I could not put into the right words whatever it was I sought from him, and that it would in fact be better to let the occasion pass without further exploration.

'Okay,' I said. 'We'll be there. See you on Sunday.'

Chapter Four

I

'Who is Philpotts?'

'He was at school with us. He's older than me. About the same age as Francis. They're at Oxford together.'

'Why did he go to Coppinger?'

It was, of course, the most obvious question of all. Boys went to Coppinger for a reason. And in most cases that reason would be as clear an indication as one could get of background; not exactly of class—it was too turbulent for that—but of 'kind', of social displacement; perhaps, most of all, of psychological attitude. Melanie was not delving consciously into that. But her question revealed her understanding of Coppinger's essential character, gleaned in part no doubt from Aunt Julie, in part from things I had told her. Yet I could not answer.

'I don't know,' I said. 'He lives with his mother.'

'And his father?'

I shook my head. 'I've never heard about him.'

'He wasn't your friend, then? Not specially? Or was he?'

'Oh, yes.' I looked at her. Apart from a slight touch of lipstick she wore no make-up. She had on a summer dress, and over her shoulders a blue cardigan. Her hair was held back from her face by a ribbon.

She frowned, waiting for me to go on.

'He doesn't ever talk about it,' I said.

'And his mother?'

'Nor that.'

She sat thinking about it. We were in a 52 bus, heading north-west from Pimlico, where I had collected her. It was dry and sunny; too early, that Sunday morning, for many people to be about.

'He won't be there today?' she asked.

'No. He's gone back to Oxford.'

It suddenly seemed surprisingly difficult to explain to her the different ways in which Philpotts was both Francis's friend and mine. I wanted to; no one had a greater right, just then, to know all that I could tell her about myself. And if this sounds as though I saw it as a duty or an obligation, it was supported by an almost passionate desire to draw her into the web of feeling and knowledge already occupied by Francis and Father, as well as myself. That the task should be approached by way of Philpotts was natural enough. He was close to both Francis and me. He did not belong to the past. I had already spoken to her of him, telling her about Wedmore, testing carefully with her what Francis had said about Eliot. Yet even so I felt a certain unsatisfactory compression of time within my mind: it was as if not only a large portion of the past had to be telescoped and summarised for her; but much worse, that there was no guarantee, for the future, that it would be lasting and relevant. Would she ever meet Philpotts? Under what compulsion would she and I, even, retain and pursue the meaning of our kindred blood? What was that meaning? Did it reside in a common response to poetry, in the recognition within each other's eyes and features, hands and gestures, of kinship, or simply in the knowledge that our blood was common? Much as all these things seemed true at that time, and combined together to convince me, more or less completely, that everything would be all right, I was nevertheless a little overwhelmed by the pace and intensity of it all. Our encounters were taking on a breathless quality. I felt momentarily that we were being carried, at too fast a speed, into a web that had

91

been spun by foolish spiders between two vehicles parked together only for a night.

'What do you normally do on a Sunday?' she asked.

'When I'm staying with Mr Porphyry?'

'Yes.'

'We go to church.'

'Always?'

'Yes.'

'And did he mind you going off?'

I laughed. 'Of course not.'

'Do you tell him all about us?'

'Mostly,' I said. Her question provoked in me a sudden feeling of guilt. I had told Mr Porphyry that I was meeting Francis and Melanie for the day. I had not mentioned my father. And of course he had not questioned it, not believing for a moment, I suppose, that I would go directly against his advice.

The feeling of guilt provoked me to ask Melanie: 'Are you looking forward to the day? Are you excited about meeting him?'

'I'm sure it will be all right,' she said.

'But not excited?'

She had been looking out of the window. Now she turned directly towards me, her face faintly troubled. 'I wish in a way it was just the three of us.'

With some hesitation I asked her, 'How can you say that?'

'I really don't know. I am excited and it is important. Of course it is. I have to meet him. What I said before, that I wanted to, it's true. I do want it. But, only...' here she faltered.

'It's too quick?' I said. 'Too soon?'

She shook her head. 'No. It's not that. It's not the time that matters.' She paused. Then she linked her arm into mine and smiled at me. 'It's nothing at all. I don't know what it is, but I'm sure we're going to have a wonderful day. Just look at the park!'

The bus was passing by Palace Gate, and the park, with

people walking, seemed bathed in gold. Calm day, clear blue sky, bright sunshine, and over the spring grass and in the trees there was to be seen the faintest evidence of a breeze. I was reassured into thinking nothing of Melanie's doubts. Father would put them right, anyway.

I did not ask her about her Sunday, and what she would normally be doing. I thought of it. But in doing so I revived a strange and irrational feeling of resentment against her adoptive parents. This same feeling, on the previous day, had prevented me asking questions about them. It had led me, at the same time, to concentrate on her school and her teachers. It rose in me again, and I was perplexed by it. I should have been grateful for their very existence. I should have been pleased if normal Sundays took her back to them. Real resentment should have been directed almost exclusively at my father, rather than at them. Yet he I wanted to protect from blame, while at the same time already seeing in them a callous meanness in not letting Melanie go to university, a meanness which I translated into prejudice against her blood and therefore against me. While Francis, educationally, was soaring upwards, with me in hot pursuit, Melanie had been curtailed in her aspirations and was already set on a course of limited reward. It was they who were to blame!

'Francis is worried,' I said. 'Father's got to move out for the summer. Something to do with the Coronation. He has this special arrangement about his room. When he heard about the flat, he told us. Now Francis thinks he'll want to move there.'

'And can he?'

'No. The flat belongs to a Miss Filgate. She'll be back in May.'

'She probably has it let for June, anyway. There'll be thousands of people here.'

'London'll be packed.'

'Will you come?'

'I don't know,' I said. 'I have my "A" levels. I may be sitting a scholarship. University.'

93

She looked at me, her eyes shining. 'Oh, you are lucky,' she said.

'I haven't got it yet.'

'You will. I know you will. And I envy you.'

II

Father took charge of the picnic from the very beginning. When we arrived at the flat he was already there, sitting in the middle of the room, repacking bags, the food, fruit and drink spread round him on the carpet. Already the full force of his mind had been applied to the task. I could see that straightaway. I saw also that he had brought with him a familiar hold-all of his own: small, and at one time smart and well made, with leather reinforcements and handles, it had been the object, over the years, of much domestic repair, with his needle and fishermen's twine, and it stood now in the middle of the array of things on the floor, more a monument to his determination, and his distrust of our capabilities in the practical business of carrying things, than of anything else.

The front door was open when we arrived, so that we walked in unannounced. Francis, who was standing back in amused contemplation of something he could not, and did not wish to, control, looked up at us, nodded, smiled, but said nothing.

Nor did Father speak. Not straight away. Reluctant, I suppose, to relinquish his position of power, if only over the modest array of things we were going to eat and drink, he nevertheless sat for a moment or two, making no other gesture than to raise his hands and spread them out in silent welcome. It was the regal greeting of an enthroned potentate, solemn, studied, and self-protective in the sense that I felt he did not quite know how to handle the encounter, and was not disposed to be hurried. He hardly looked at me at all, but fixed his eyes on her. Then, slowly, his

94

hands still spread out, there appeared on his lips a smile in which the suppressed excitement, the welcome, the pleasure, were all mingled with a profound sadness.

'Melanie!' he said.

She did not answer him straightaway, and he got to his feet, still looking at her, still surrounded, hemmed in even, by the paraphernalia on the floor.

'Melanie!' he said again. 'My daughter!' Then he moved out, with surprising agility, stepping over things, and engulfing her with a huge hug and kiss.

She responded, and kissed him back, though still not speaking; and then he held her at arm's length, looking into her eyes. 'You've returned to your father!' he said. 'You've returned! Come back!'

I had the urge to laugh, as a relief more than anything else. I felt foolish, just standing there. And I could see that Francis was almost gaping at the two of them.

Father looked sharply sideways, first at Francis, then at me. The expression on his face had become stern again, almost cross, but a certain thin layer of moisture in his eyes betrayed the turbulence of his heart.

'Who is she like?' he said. 'Which of you?' He looked back into her eyes.

'We're all alike,' she said.

He stared over her head at the window. 'Look at the sunshine. We must go!'

Suddenly, swiftly, he returned to his place, and began packing. It became obvious that he had already thought out where things were to go, and he packed them with precision. He had not gone far, however, when, glancing in my direction, he saw that I was still clutching a small carrier with food in it.

'What have you got there?' he said. He almost shouted it, his face angry, as if he needed to compensate for the earlier display of emotion.

'More,' I said, stepping forward and holding out the bag.

'We've a positive feast,' he said. 'Positive feast.'

95

Melanie had knelt down in front of him and she took my bag and unpacked it, handing the things to him, with little or no regard for his 'system'. She actually began to put things into his bag, and he stopped her, saying sharply, 'No! Just a minute.' She looked up at him, astonished, puzzled, two bananas in her hand. And they stared at each other. Then he smiled, and rested his elbows on the arms of the chair, and said, 'Go on, go on. What does it matter? We're on our way to Kew, my dears, we're on our way to Kew!'

After that, he let Melanie finish the packing of the picnic. Once or twice, watching her closely, he seemed on the point of interfering. But all he actually did, from a distance, was to make little, pointing gestures, and then to nod his approval. From Francis he demanded mustard, pickle, an extra sharp knife, a small towel.

'Must get it right,' he said, 'Eh?'

We had to agree.

Eventually, we were ready. 'My children!' he said, looking round at all three of us. 'My children!'

We departed. Between the four of us the load was light enough. But on the steps of the house, pausing in the April sunshine, Francis, about to close the door, looked at him and asked: 'Are you sure we have enough?'

Father frowned at him, then laughed. 'Feed an army, my son. But we could get lost out there.' He pointed downhill towards Shepherd's Bush. He saw himself, I feel sure, as leading an expeditionary force; and in a curious way I suppose he was, charting all four of us through territories of the heart and the emotions which were unfamiliar at the very least, and unknown in certain respects. Yes, we were on the scrubby fringes of a jungle only parts of which, that day, we would enter and map out.

Melanie took his arm. I walked with Francis.

'It's going to be all right,' I said.

'The day? Or him?'

'Both.'

III

We sat in sunlight and ate our picnic. There was far too much. We were close to the cherry trees, the deceptive cherry trees, which tell us that summer is come before it is true. The weather joined in the deception. Though there was a slight breeze the sun was warm and we sat on coats spread out on the cut grass.

'You've all grown up,' Father said. 'You've already made something of your lives, worked hard, done well.' He paused, the weight of his shoulders down on one elbow where he lay propped up to address us. With the other hand he prodded at the short grass. 'You're a credit to me. All of you. And you'll go on, and do better. Won't you, Melanie, my love?'

'I don't know if I'll do better,' she said. 'I don't know how.'

'Oh, you will, you will. We must all do better.'

'No,' said Francis. 'At what we are, we must be best.'

'That's the spirit! You know what you're going to do, you know what you're going to be, on and do it.' He looked up at me. 'And you?' There was an unexpected sharpness in his voice.

I was sitting cross-legged on my raincoat, my hands resting on my knees. I shrugged. 'I don't know. Get my exams. Get a scholarship if I can. I don't know after that.'

'Oh, you do! You do!' Melanie said. Her voice was urgent and her eyes shone. She was pressing on me responsibilities which I had no more than hinted at as a future possibility. I looked at her, in no sense checking the swift spontaneous flood of feeling which lay behind her words. I welcomed it rather as a demonstration of her faith in what I might become, and saw in her eyes a flicker of happiness at something between the two of us from which the others were excluded. Francis was impassive. But Father heard the exclusive, faint echo of a confidence.

97

'What's this?' he said. 'Something I've not been told about?' He looked sharply at Melanie, then at me. Neither of us spoke. 'I have to know. I have to know everything. Isn't that true, Francis? Do you know what Melanie's getting at?'

Francis did not exactly shake his head. He seemed unwilling to place himself on the same level of inquiry, and instead adopted an enigmatic expression which he turned towards us.

It seemed so slight a *contretemps*, swelled by Father into proportions which, if pursued, might embarrass me. In her wisdom Melanie sensed this. In mock solemn tones she began to recite:

' "What is the late November doing
With the disturbance of the spring…" '

She did not go on. I could have followed with further lines, but instead let them run unspoken through my mind. I do not think she meant the words in any cruel sense. I am not sure, even now, that they have that sense, though the passage is a compelling prelude to questions about the wisdom or folly of age. But Father took her up in good-humoured dismay.

'Steady on, now,' he said. 'I may be growing old, but I'm not yet in the November of my days. There are things still to be done. The capacity is there, the strength.' He looked down at the grass beside the coat on which he was half-lying. With his hand, the fingers spread out, he pressed down upon the soft green herbage. The indentation was slight. The gesture had a poignant quality.

'I didn't mean that,' Melanie said. 'It's just that there are things which are difficult to say.'

'You mean "the disturbance of the spring"?'

She nodded.

'It's a good line. Who is it?'

She told him.

Francis snorted.

Father looked at him. 'No good? Is that what you mean, Francis? Come on, now. Out with it. If he's no good, say it.'

98

'Francis doesn't think much of him,' I said. 'Melanie and I do.'

He sat up now, looking at all three of us in turn. 'This is serious,' he said. 'I'll have to look into this fellow.' He took out his spectacles and put them on. Then he produced a notebook and pencil. 'Have to get him out of the library. Read some more.' He stared at Melanie over the top of spectacle frames. 'One "l" or two?'

'One,' she said. 'And one "t" as well.'

'Dates?'

She was nonplussed.

'What are his dates? Period? Where does he come?'

She laughed. 'He's alive now.'

'Oh. My age?' He seemed a little put out at the uncertain prospect of a living writer. 'Is he in the September of his days, Melanie?'

'Oh, no,' she said. 'With him it's November.'

'He's an American,' I said.

The look he gave me was quite severe. He had moved his glasses down his nose, and he was able to stare from one of us to the other, holding us all in the pauses of his interrogation as though we were all accountable for aspects of the poet's life. 'American?' he said. It was treated as a significant clue and he added the word to the few brief notations he had made on the page of the notebook.

'It's not really fair to say he's American,' Melanie said.

'He should not be taken up lightly, though.'

'He should not be taken up at all,' Francis said, rather sourly.

'I shall judge that.'

I was impressed by his determination, a little bit moved by the notebook and pencil, and I watched with secret feelings of pleasure and involvement in his affairs as he produced his small and intensely sharp penknife and began, quite unnecessarily, to trim the point. It was an ordinary pencil, but with a metal guard for the point. What would he make of Mr Apollinax? I could not tell. He had two distinct

99

views of poetry. At one level it epitomised the effete world of art, quite the opposite of that world of action, sport, power, immediacy which he prized most highly. And yet, on the other hand, he found that poetry, the odd ragbag of fragments acquired along the way, memorised at school perhaps, and fairly rich in Shakespeare, seemed to echo deep within his nature mirror-image impressions of what his life was about. I had witnessed enough instances to be sure of both the force and the confusion. And though I could not tell what he would make of 'the disturbance of the spring' when he found it in its correct context, if he ever did, I knew even then that the words, perhaps because of being surrounded by the three of us, all in our different ways facing 'disturbance', had caught his imagination and had perhaps suggested a swift route back into all our lives.

'Will you read him, then?' Melanie asked.

'I'll get him out of the library. Read him up. We must go on learning, all the time.' He looked round at us all, sternly. 'If you have things to teach, I will learn.'

We were all silent in the face of his solemn invitation. For a moment I thought he would make demands, there and then, on our intellectual resources, making us offer up further names or ideas in this cerebral *déjeuner sur l'herbe*, where the selective nakedness was of mind or spirit or heart rather than flesh. Indeed, looking at Melanie and Francis I was surprised at the opaqueness of their expressions. Were their thoughts, like mine, folded in? And upon what scene, present or past, or even future, were their eyes fixed?

Almost to himself he repeated, 'Yes, my children, if you have things to teach, I will learn. Gladly. But time hurries on. I see the embers of my days. What do you think, Francis? Am I right?'

'About time? Or about learning?'

He laughed briefly. 'I know I'm right about time. I have only to look at you all to realise that. But to learn. At my age. To press on, and on. New people, new ideas.'

'You're right,' Francis said. His tone was not encouraging.

He did not seem to be enthusiastic about this learning process which might well involve him far beyond the limited commitment he had so far made by coming on the picnic.

Father's thoughts, however, were pursuing a line which did not necessarily require from any of us a direct undertaking on his behalf. He was more interested in a wider, looser examination of his theory. 'You are all in the midst of it,' he said. He swung his arm out in a gesture that seemed to invite a response from an audience far greater than the one he had, and his eyes and voice were fixed on a point some yards away where the bank of mown grass rose gently up towards a clump of shrubs.

'You must make a complete commitment,' he went on. 'Tooth and nail, utter dedication, to the limits of your endurance. I know. I have travelled the road before you.'

How did one ever reply to him? He sat there like Socrates divulging wisdom that could not be challenged and had got him nowhere. The slack hand, resting now on the grass, palm upwards, and empty from the previous gesture of dramatic invitation, invited our pity and love as so many words and gestures had done before. Only now, looking at him from the position I occupied opposite on the grass between Francis and Melanie, it was of them I was conscious, of their feelings, their response in the warm stillness of the April Sunday afternoon. I wanted them to speak, not me. I wanted Francis to speak for us, Melanie to coax him towards it. And I looked at her where she sat, her eyes turned down towards the grass in front of her; and I looked at Francis, who stared back at me. And I suppose I knew then, in my heart, deep down, that it was no good.

'The map,' Father said. 'Who has the map?'

'I do.' I handed it to him.

'We must go and find the azaleas.'

He did what once he had made us do. In distant childhood he had dispatched Francis this way and that to read names and check upon his knowledge and memory. And I had stumbled to keep up with my brother's headlong enthusiasm, his obedient involvement in what had really been a huge game. Now it was he who went from tree to tree, trudging across the grass to find and read out the metal labels, sometimes to make brief notes in his notebook. And we followed, the three of us, our path a less precise echo of the determined zigzag with which, for example, he seemed to devour individual glades given over to a single species, the maples, the walnuts, and of course the cherries, then coming into full flower. Moving among them there were moments when the mass of white blossom on a single tree seemed to create so great a halo of light that his severe and reddened features became radiant, his eyes glowing and sparkling at us.

'See the bark?' he said to me. 'See the lateral lines? That broken, flecking effect, a bit like a birch tree?'

'Yes,' I said, nodding, following the movement of his hand.

'Prunus,' he said. 'Not just cherries. Plums, peaches, apricots, almonds. Distinctive feature. Lovely bark.'

He looked round at us all for our approval.

'Funny,' I said, 'they're associated with pretty girls, aren't they?'

'What do you mean?' he said. He looked severely at me. Surrounded by so many of us he seemed ready to feel that he might be mocked. It gave to the glare in his eyes a hint of suspicion. Francis also looked at me, without expression. He was standing under a bough heavily laden with white blossom. In his case the close shadow of it fell across his face, darkening his features and giving them an added severity from which his unblinking eyes seemed to start out.

'Well,' I said, 'you'd say she's a peach, or lips like ripe cherries, or eyes like almonds. That kind of thing.'

Melanie, who was standing beside me, squeezed my arm and with a short, soft laugh said, 'You're right, of course. It's all to do with spring, and love, and the heart turning over.'

102

'And you, Melanie?' Father said, his voice still severe, but suddenly redirected in its intensity along a quite different route of inquiry. 'Are you in love? Do you have a man? Who is he? Tell me?'

'No,' she said. She shook her head, a faintly indulgent expression in her eyes. 'No. I have nothing like that to tell you. No excitement.'

'I have to know,' he said. 'I have to be told. Everything.' He pointed his finger suddenly at Francis. 'Girlfriend?' It was spoken with inquisitorial sharpness, as if he might catch Francis out, and get him to stumble forth an admission of emotional involvement. But Francis shook his head. He swung round on me. 'And you?' He had begun to make a game of it.

'Yes,' I said. 'Several. But I've had to call a truce until after my exams. What about you?'

'No,' he said. He drew the word out until it became a rattle in the back of his throat. Then he repeated it, this time until it became a chuckle. 'No! Women? That part of my life is over.'

'And Alice?' I said. 'What about Alice?'

He had put his hands into the sidepockets of his jacket, and had adopted an attitude, his shoulders hunched forward, his head stuck out, one knee slightly bent. Now he straightened and relaxed inside himself. Pausing, in thought, he moved his feet. He was looking at nothing in particular, and his expression was faintly bewildered. Momentarily, he looked weary, and older than his mid-fifties.

'Oh yes, Alice,' he said. 'She stands by me. She's a brick, ever faithful. But the rest?' He made a dismissive gesture with one hand. '*Finies. Toutes finies.*'

Later in the afternoon, standing with Francis under the dappled light of a walnut tree, and watching Father and Melanie some way off deciphering the name of a shrub with white flowers, I said I thought we had made him happy.

'No,' Francis said. 'You are wrong. We've made him sad. Not just sad. Unhappy.'

'Will he not think the day has been good for us all?'

'No. Good for you, me, Melanie perhaps. But for him it just invites regrets. He'll get drunk tonight. He'll be angry at what he calls the lost opportunities.'

'He's upset we're not spending the evening with him.'

'I can't,' Francis said. 'I must work.'

'And Melanie's on duty.'

'And you?'

'I said I'd meet Mr Porphyry. I could ring him. But it wouldn't be the same without you and Melanie.'

They were walking towards us, Melanie with her hand through his arm.

'We're all meeting on Wednesday, aren't we?'

'Yes.'

'And Melanie's free?'

'Yes.'

When he reached us he said, 'What are you two talking about?'

'Mainly about you,' Francis said.

'Talking about your father? 'hind his back? Can't have that!'

'We're always doing it.'

'Always? Talking about me?' The angry urgency of the questions, all rhetorical, barely concealed the absolute delight which flooded through him. He was hugely stimulated. It was so obvious. So wonderfully unsubtle. He glowed in the mixed fire of our affection. I admit, I see it through my own eyes only. I cannot speak for Francis, or for Melanie. I believed I perceived in their faces too, the sweet balm of affection pouring forth upon him. But it is quite possible that I was imposing an unsurprising benevolence, which anyone might feel in response to him, upon them, and seeing it as deeper levels of love simply because they were present in my own breast. That is the eternal possibility in defining and measuring love, and one always hesitates to check too nakedly the reality behind benevolence. His features softened. Still holding Melanie's hand, linked through his arm, he looked round at us all. 'You're wonderful children,' he said. 'Wonderful.'

We travelled back on the Underground, the remnants of our picnic in bags between us where we sat in double seats opposite each other. Melanie and I were face to face beside the window, where the evening sun, between houses and trees in those first few stretches from Kew, broken and flickering, glanced in.

Father seemed to feel his control over us slipping.

'Sorry we can't be together this evening,' he said. He looked round at each of us. There was reproach in his eyes. No one answered. 'We could have gone for a few drinks,' he said. 'Not a binge, you understand. Finished with all that. But a quiet evening together. A family evening.' The phrase pleased him, and he repeated it: 'A family evening.' To the word 'family' he gave an expressive note. There was a hint of unctuousness in the way he said it. He looked round for some response.

'I do have to be on duty. I'm sorry.'

I stared out of the window.

Francis said, 'I must work. I have so little time.'

Staring at Francis he seemed suddenly caught by another thought. 'Francis? This flat you're in? What's the position? What's the absolute basic position? You can be perfectly frank, you know.'

'I will be,' Francis said. 'The position is very simple. It's let for June and July. I think it may be let for May as well. That's it, absolutely basic.'

'And you'll be gone? Back to Oxford?'

He nodded. 'I go next week.'

Father paused. He was staring hard at Francis, his face a little pinched. Melanie and I were both looking at him, and though I felt he was conscious of this, he did not turn. 'And there's nothing you can do? No odd room there? Don't need much space, you know. Keeps everything shipshape, George does. You know your father.' He laughed shortly, but the sound ended abruptly, and he looked keenly into Francis's eyes, searching there for a hint of encouragement.

105

Almost imperceptibly Francis nodded, but the eyes were cold, and if anything they became colder. It was as if the father he knew did indeed keep things shipshape, but had other, grosser vices in his son's eyes which outweighed the meagre advantages of tidiness and the promised compression of himself into a little space. 'There's nothing I can do,' he said.

Father shrugged his shoulders. You don't mind my asking?'

'Of course not. Wish I could help.'

Francis got off the train at Hammersmith, saying that he had to go back through Shepherd's Bush. He did not explain why. He just said we would meet on Wednesday. 'We'll all come to you,' he said, shaking Father's hand. He had already told Melanie to come to his flat, and me to do the same.

Then Father left us at Gloucester Road. He waited on the platform for the train to go out. But it was not done for our sakes. Though his hand was raised in casual salute the expression in his eyes, the pensive, fixed lines in his face, reflected inward upon his secret, unsatisfied thoughts. And I imagined him still standing there, lost in contemplation of his inner soul, as the train carried Melanie and me further eastward, towards Sloane Square. We both got out there, and I walked with her intending to go on from the hostel by bus, but quite unsure about returning directly to Mr Porphyry.

'What did you think of the day, Melanie? Did you enjoy it?'

'He is a fine old chap,' she replied. 'He enjoyed it most of all.'

'And you?'

'It was a nice picnic. Kew's wonderful.' She looked back at me. I suppose my expectation showed too clearly in my eyes. 'I did enjoy it.'

'And we'll meet again on Wednesday? For the evening?'

She nodded. 'It'll be his evening.'

'It'll be ours. The four of us.'

'All right,' she said. 'The four of us.' Her eyes were acquiescent. Part of her seemed remote from me. There were faint forebodings in the air. Perhaps she sensed this. 'Will he read Eliot?'

'I'm sure he will,' I said. 'Out of curiosity.'

'It isn't enough. And it's too late.' Then she spoke again, slowly, consciously describing him:

' "His soul stretched tight across the skies

Impatient to assume the world." '

I was nonplussed by what I thought of as her wisdom, and dissuaded from agreement or comment. We travelled the rest of the way in silence. I saw her to the door of the hostel.

'We'll see you at the flat, then? I'll be with Francis. We'll go on to meet him afterwards.'

'All right,' she said. 'At seven, isn't it?'

'Goodnight.'

IV

I had half intended to go back to Mr Porphyry after leaving Melanie, but the closer it got the less attractive it became. The thought of supper in the flat, and answering his questions, put me off. I had no real intention of sustaining what had been a lie. It was too complicated. Much more important, of course, it was too good. The day had been a success. The encounter had worked. He had been wrong. Everything with Melanie had been all right. And by and by I would explain it to him. But to tumble in on top of his Sunday evening peace of mind seemed obviously mistaken. Luckily, it had been left fairly open, and I had no compunction about wandering off alone on that clear spring evening to think over, and settle into some kind of order, the experiences of the day.

One thing disturbed me: the recollected sternness in my father's eyes when they were turned upon me. I had made little of it during the day. The encounter with Melanie, the joking with Francis, the odd reconstruction, after so many years, of something that I saw as both good and essential, had to be achieved at some expense. Whether I thought about it in such terms, subconsciously I must have accepted that the price I paid was that of being forced into a minor role. After all, had I not been the self-elected engineer of reconciliation? And was this not, on the day itself, an exhausted function? No, I certainly did not think of it quite like that: yet through the day I had been content to see the main axis of feeling and conversation lying either between himself and Francis or between him and Melanie.

Now, detached from the living tide of affection, what I recalled was a strange look of hardness in his eyes when they were turned on me. It had been so, I recalled, on first walking in to Francis's flat that morning, clutching the picnic, ready to start. His greeting of Melanie had been effusive; all, and more than I could have desired. And the wave of feeling, then, had compensated for the cursory expression of notice in my direction.

Similarly, during the day, there had been other moments when a swift and sudden glance had revealed in his eyes a harshness of light, a glint of steel, that now, in recollection, worried me. Then, it had been absorbed in the general flood of conviction that everything was going well. He had, in my judgment, 'Come up to scratch'; completely. Francis and Melanie had been themselves. And the course of all of us was set fair for the next encounter. So why the stare? Why that strange, harsh glare in his eyes that I recalled so vividly as I walked up Buckingham Palace Road under the blue evening sky, the graceful trees and buildings bathed in the slanting golden rays of the April sun? He was not angry with me. He was not reproaching me. Everything I had done had given him pleasure, and he had responded to it with good sense, and with feeling, and this had been a relief. And yet, while I did not know what to expect from him in response to encounters which were extraordinary, I felt that something was wrong, and that it was contained in the brief and unspoken message of his eyes.

Perhaps it had not even been directed at me. For looking back, it seemed almost as if I had been a mirror. And if I had been able to say to him: 'Why do you look at me like that?' he would have shaken himself and said: 'Like what?' and then smiled, and the confrontation would have passed. In other words, he was looking for the reflection in my eyes of a reproach against himself that only he felt. And it was this that gave the grave, hard colouring to his gaze.

I tried to dismiss the thought. After all, the moments of catching his eyes in that way had only occurred infrequently during the course of the day, and had been completely overwhelmed each time by the full, swift passage of affection. But it still persisted. And in the end I found myself recalling also the warning Francis had given: 'He'll get drunk tonight.' For one brief moment I was tempted to go to him, to prevent so unfortunate an end to the day. But I did not. Instead, I walked on towards Piccadilly, intent on resolving in my mind questions which still remain, to this day, unresolved.

Was I callow? Mawkish? Struggling vainly towards maturity? Thinking that in some way it was easy? That an instant rearrangement of lives was possible? If so, then it kept me busy, that evening, preparing my mind with all its explanations for Mr Porphyry; and preparing, after that, for the next occasion when we would all meet, and it would be as good as that day had been.

In Piccadilly Circus the uneven conflict between the light of day and the glow of colour and movement from the neon signs and lamps was given an unreal quality by the residual purity of the evening sky. It was so clear, and it had been so warm and sweet-smelling a day that the rhythm and jerk of the mechanical evening of the city, coming to life, lacked its usual impact. Nevertheless, with a new and now diverted determination, I turned my attention to the brassy images of vicarious sensuality. Seeking an interregnum in noble self-examination, I turned, first up Shaftesbury Avenue, then off again and up into Soho, curious, guilty, filled with vague and not to be satisfied desires.

It was much later when I got back to the flat. In my frustration I had gone to a film, and it had replaced or suppressed for a time my faint nervousness about facing Mr Porphyry. When I eventually presented myself in front of him he was sitting in the drawing room, in an armchair, reading. A cup of half-drunk coffee stood at his elbow, and he was wearing gold-rimmed, half-moon spectacles. A record of the overture to Rossini's *The Thieving Magpie* was playing softly on the gramaphone. He looked up with one of his rare smiles. It was as if he were compensating for too many strictures on my behaviour.

'Did you have a good picnic?'

'It was wonderful,' I said. I stood in the centre of the room.

He took off the glasses and put them away. 'Francis and...and Melanie? Did they enjoy it?'

'Very much,' I said. 'It was such a lovely day. We used to go to Kew when we were children.' I paused. 'My father was with us as well.'

I expected some kind of exclamation, and certainly a hint of anger at my having gone in precisely the opposite direction from that which he had advised. Instead, he smiled slightly and said, 'I thought as much. You know best, then.'

I felt, smugly, that perhaps I did. But I replied, with more self-doubt than in fact I felt, 'I think it was all right. The day went very well. We're meeting again on Wednesday evening.'

'And what will you do?'

'I hope we'll go to a concert,' I lied. Having told him the main truth I felt justified in wrapping up our next encounter in more sober colouring than in fact it would have.

'And did you do that when you were a child?'

'With Francis, yes. Not with Melanie. It was after she was adopted.'

'The Albert Hall?'

'Yes.'

'What's on?'

'I have to check.'

The record came to an end. He put his books aside and got up to take it off. I watched him as he put it away, an almost laboured precision in his movements.

'You've only another week, haven't you?'

'Yes.'

'What about your work?'

'I...I haven't done enough.' I paused awkwardly. 'I'll do more now.'

He sat down again and reached for his book and the blue case in which he kept his glasses. The 'interview' was at an end. We were guardian and ward, but there had been a subtle change in the comfort I derived from this. I put on the face of respect, he that of concern; but we were going through correct procedures, and on this occasion the over-whelming shadow was the happy, carefree family love that had come to life that afternoon. Faced by such an unfair balance I could only tear myself away and return to my room where I looked in a kind of miserable desperation at unopened books and unused folders. Whether he felt the same sense of defeat or not, I cannot tell. How, in the privacy of his own mind, he measured the wisdom of what had happened, I cannot tell, either. But the encounter is still there in my own memory, an occasion on which, however fractionally, that process, by which independence is asserted, moved forward.

Chapter Five

I

Francis went on working. I sat in a chair and tried to read, but could not. I wanted to watch the way he worked. He had rearranged the room, moving the two tables together, and he had different piles of notes, clipped together and laid out in rows. There were neat piles of books as well, and from the pages of them there emerged pieces of coloured paper with words scrawled across them. It was as if the engine of his mind had been spread out in working parts around the room, cleaned, oiled, and ready to work. It was absurd of me to think of it in this way. His mind, of course, had been working all that day; these were the tools by which it was maintained, not the engine itself. Yet so opaque and silent, so impervious to the penetrations of another's eyes, so secret, that only by the tools did it seem possible to understand the machine. It would be a long time, many years, before I could apply judgment based on output. Others, of course—
—his teachers, examiners, assessors—were about to do this. But for me Francis was surrounded by a protoplasm of intelligence consisting of notes and essays, books and their annotations, whose vital properties were as near as I could get to an understanding of his mind, and therefore to an appreciation of the nature of work.

I looked at my watch. Melanie was already twenty minutes late, and we would now inevitably be late meeting with Father. I could already envisage the cross expression, the poised, suspended anger. But I was still disposed to make light of it, knowing that the three of us, each approaching it differently, would neutralise his impatience, and bring round his essentially forgiving nature.

Francis turned over another page of the papers piled immediately in front of him. Then, with a pencil, he made a heavy mark in the margin. He repeated it two or three times, laid the pencil down, and reached for a book which he opened at a marked passage. He read it with complete absorption, turning over to read a few lines at the top of the next page, and then closing it and returning it to the pile with its marker still in place.

I tried to read again in the book which I was holding, but the sense of the words eluded me. I wanted to be inside his mind, to see and understand the assembly of information from that still, pulsing point in his brain which captured and controlled the myriad elements of it which in their crude form only were contained in books and papers. He could teach me more than I knew. Francis could show me the way. He was so far ahead of me, his mind galloping towards an examination which made my own efforts seem, in anticipation, of little real importance.

In the hall outside the room the telephone rang. Francis went out to it immediately, but closing the door after him as if he knew it was for him. I crossed over to inspect more closely his work. There was a clipped precision about it all. A card in front of him was headed 'Trade—1300', and underneath a short list of words 'Wool, wax, leather, timber', then a line across the card, followed by 'Metals, mining'. At the bottom were the letters 'P.T.O.' But I did not. I moved away again, thinking how like Father he was. His notes were like the shopping lists which had governed much more than what my father bought, listing his movements and encounters in a way that equalised everything down to one common requirement—that the pursuit of everything should be 'methodical'; it had dictated my

113

movements as a child; the only difference being, in the notes before Francis, that nothing was scrawled out. But the same force was there, the same visible expression of determination. With Father, 'toothbrush', 'bread', 'library books', 'Ring Alice' had been, perhaps still were, the pegs of memory on which the unhappy, blank sheets of his day were hung.

He appeared in the door. 'Melanie can't come,' he said.

'What?' I stood up.

'She can't come. Extra duty.' He paused. 'At least, that's what she says.' He had the same expression on his face that the Wedmore tensions had provoked: a suppressed anger that gave a flinty edge to each word.

'But they can't do that to her! It was all arranged. Surely nurses' duty doesn't work like that?'

'I wouldn't have thought so.' He crossed over to his place and sat down again. He went through the motions of shifting another card, but I could see he was not concentrating.

'We'd better go.'

He did not get up immediately. He was still lost in thought.

'What is it you're thinking?' I said.

He looked across at me, his expression calm, his eyes level. 'She didn't want to come.'

'How do you know? She must have wanted it. After Sunday? Everything going so well?'

'We don't know how well it went. For her.' He now got up and crossed over to the bed where he had placed his coat and hat. Putting them on he turned back to me, his face grim and severe, the muscle in his jaw moving with the regular pulse of his frustration.

'What about this extra duty? Did she invent that?'

Francis shook his head. 'I would say she volunteered.'

'We'll be late,' I said.

'We're already late, *and* we don't have Melanie.'

It was suddenly as if we were little children again. We had gone off to play, and 'lost' Melanie. Now we had to return, and face awful retribution for not taking better care of her. I smiled at the thought of it.

'It isn't funny,' he said. 'I can see you're going to give me trouble.' He was trying to make a joke of it.

'I know,' I laughed. 'I am.'

'Tricky!' He paused, pulling a face. Then he relaxed.

'He'll be furious.' He said it with feeling. Then he smiled.

I laughed again. 'He'll blame us. He'll say it's our fault, her being on duty.'

'He'll certainly make us responsible for that. And being late as well. Perhaps we shouldn't go at all.'

'What'll he say?'

'He'll call us fiends. He'll shake with rage.'

A sudden wave of fear went through me. My careful plans were not quite working out. If Francis was right about Father's anger then perhaps he was right about Sunday as well, that he had been unhappy rather than happy, and that he had drowned his sorrows. So what did that threaten for the evening ahead of us?

'Francis?'

'Yes.'

'Why *are* we going?'

He crossed the room to the window, looking out on the wide avenue. He had on his hat, and had taken up his stick. 'It's because you want it,' he said, turning towards me.

'And he does,' I said.

Francis nodded.

'And you?'

He smiled. The look in his eyes was faintly cynical. 'I'm curious,' he said.

'And nothing more?'

'What more could there be?'

II

'What do you mean?' he said. 'Melanie not here? It was all arranged! It was quite clear! All of us agreed!'

His voice had taken on that tense, high-pitched tone that

115

struck within me a note of doom. It was like relentless, rapid *pizzicato*. Each of the short sentences ran together, like one word, rising to an exclamatory climax. Then he paused and glared angrily at both of us. We were in the bar of a pub. He had left a message, and we had found him there. When he spoke again his tone had softened, though it still contained reproach. 'I mean, Wendy came along to meet you.' He placed huge stress on the name, and spread out his arm towards the woman in question. She did not seem too enthusiastic. She sat on a chair in the uncrowded bar, her handbag on her knee. She must have been in her forties, softly attractive, her hair down to her shoulders, the brown tinged with grey, little make-up, and around her mouth there seemed to hover all the time an uncertain, nervous smile. It was as if she were still unfamiliar with this sharp, hectoring tone in my father's voice, and she was treating it with an indulgence which she had obviously been allowed to apply to other aspects of his behaviour. He was by no means finished. Having held out his hand towards Wendy, indicating her presence there, and emphasising her importance, he let it fall. But his angry eyes were still fixed on both of us where we stood before him in the lounge bar. 'It's a simple matter of organisation. When you say you'll do something, you do it. That right, Wendy?'

'I'm sure she had something which kept her, George.' Her voice was clear, the tone conciliatory.

'She had extra nursing duty,' Francis said. 'She just couldn't come.'

'Can't come to see her father. I mean, you make an arrangement, you just have to keep to it. And you two, you're late as well!'

'We were waiting for Melanie.'

He produced a ten-shilling note and handed it to Francis. 'You'd better get yourselves drinks. Wendy?' She shook her head. 'And a scotch for me. Double. No water.'

I hesitated, nodding at Francis when he suggested a beer, not knowing whether to go with him or stay.

116

Father resolved the difficulty. 'Well, get a chair. Sit down. Don't stand there like a fool. Go in beside Wendy there.'

I did as I was told. He continued to stare angrily at me.

I felt inclined to turn to her and say, so where did you come from? And the thought may have brought to my face the faint shadow of a smile.

'What's so funny?' he said. 'What are you laughing at?'

'I wasn't laughing.'

'Looks to me as if you've got a damn-fool grin on your face. You'll have to treat my sons like halfwits, Wendy. Be patient with them.'

'I'm sure you've very intelligent,' she said, turning to me. 'Are you doing exams?'

'This summer I do. And Francis is doing his finals at Oxford.

'And what will you do after yours?'

'Well, it's National Service or university. I don't know which yet.'

'Isn't that a difficult choice? I mean, how do you know?'

Initially grateful to her for diluting the truculence with which our encounter with him had begun, I now felt a faint hesitation, a reluctance to embark on the necessary explanations of things about which she seemed wholly ignorant, and was surely not greatly interested. 'It depends,' I said, 'on how I do. If it's good enough, the result, I'll go to university. If not, the army I suppose.'

'Son of mine! Not good enough! Piffle! This time next year and you'll have taken his place.' He gestured towards Francis where he approached carrying two glasses of beer and a whisky. 'He's the able one,' he added. He took his drink. Without waiting for us he drank from it. The neat liquor passed down his throat like water. 'He'll do well,' he said. With the hand that held the glass he indicated Francis. 'You'll do well, won't you?'

The smile on Francis's face was faintly supercilious. 'Yes, I'll do well,' he said.

117

'Confounded cheek! Saying you'll do well like that! How do you know?'

'Well, you asked me. And I will.'

Father's face became serious. 'Make sure you do, then. Put everything you've got into it. Everything.' Like a general with a group of staff officers before a crucial battle he looked sternly at Francis, then at me, then at Wendy. He would have included others in the bar, had they been near enough. But at that hour it was fairly deserted, just two women sitting up on stools, chatting, and an elderly man at the other end who seemed to be watching us while at the same time pretending indifference.

'Go hard. Play the game. Run the course. Don't panic. Isn't that the way, Wendy?'

She smiled at him. 'I'm sure you know,' she said. 'I was never any good at exams. I always did panic. Never did the right number of questions, either too few or too many. I was quite hopeless.' She shook her head in embarrassed recollection.

He suddenly held out his hand to her, a sharp imperative gesture between the two of them. 'Hold my hand, duckie.'

It would have been ridiculous, and I would have laughed, had there not been in his voice a current of need which charged the command with a certain flood of sweetness. It was in moments such as these, potentially absurd beyond the point of childishness, that a sudden stabbing comprehension of his charm as a man seized me. Good women give their lives away when appealed to in a manner such as he now displayed in that imperial gesture, in those spoilt words, in the look of soulful expectation which could not be denied.

With a faintly embarrassed laugh she placed her hand in his. Perhaps hers was the greater need. He clutched it, as if he might crush it, but then bent swiftly, briefly over it to kiss the willing flesh. Her eyes were fixed in fond amusement on him.

'Oh, George!' she said.

Francis and I were nonplussed. He looked at us both,

118

imperiousness of a different kind in his eyes. 'Have you nothing to say for yourselves? My sons! Silenced! You fail to bring Melanie! You come here for an evening out! You sit here drinking my drinks!'

'They've only just come, George,' Wendy said, disengaging her hand.

He responded to her attempts at conciliation, and seemed to calm down, asking us odd questions about what we had been doing. It was as if he were putting us on display for her benefit, a parade for our aspirations, but in almost brutal terms. I could see Francis drawing into himself. And yet, experienced as I thought myself to be in his ways and in his moods, I welcomed this development as an improvement on the hectoring manner that had preceded it. As we talked I cast occasional glances in his direction, noting a certain haggard look in his faintly bloodshot eyes. Unwillingly, I had to admit that Francis had been right: he had been drinking.

We had another round, too soon after the first, and I paid for it. The barman frowned, and I anticipated the indignity of him asking my age. But, glancing over at my father, he thought better of it.

Later, it was his turn, and he took it long before we were ready. Polishing off his own drink he got to his feet. He looked at Wendy's glass first, and nodded to himself in limited satisfaction that it, too, was almost empty. Whatever else were her limitations, she seemed well able to keep pace with him. He frowned at my glass, almost full, and Francis's, about half empty. He did not ask us, but crossed over to the bar. We sat still, listening as he ordered. 'And a scotch,' he concluded. 'Treble.'

I went over to the bar to help him carry back the drinks. They were not ready, and he was staring at the bottles lining the back of the bar. I stood beside him.

'Heigh-ho!' he said. It was an automatic phrase, its only merit that it indicated the temporary softening of his manner induced by what he had drunk so far. He seemed preoccupied. A brief, automatic smile crossed his features as he

119

turned to acknowledge my presence. It did not penetrate as far as his eyes, which seemed to draw their vision momentarily in from the contemplation of some far distant shore.

'How's Mr...' he had to pause and recollect the name. '...Mr Proffery? Can never remember his name.'

'Porphyry,' I said.

'Looking after you all right?'

I nodded.

'Better than your father, of course. *He's* a washout.' He looked at me directly now, a flash of anger in his eyes.

'I couldn't come to you,' I said. 'You didn't have room. You said so.'

'You could have called more often.'

I looked at him without answering.

The barman said how much the drinks were, and my father counted out silver from his hand. There was change to wait for. He looked again at me, his head held high, his eyes haughty and accusing.

'You're ashamed of your father.' It was a statement.

'I hope I never shall be,' I said.

He snorted. 'Getting above yourself. That's your trouble. Think you're too good for us. I suppose your Mr Prophet told you to see less of your father. Bad influence.'

'He never said that.' I looked at him. I felt crushed and hurt at the injustice of his attitude. But I did not trust myself to begin an explanation or a defence. 'Look, Father,' I said, 'I go back to Coppinger in a few days. I'm worried about—'

But he did not let me go on. 'Pick up those two,' he said, 'and follow me.' And carrying his own glass of whisky and Wendy's gin and tonic he set off back to the table.

III

'Sons o' mine!' he said. His voice had become rich and slurred. He and Wendy were on one side of the table, the wall behind them; Francis and I, beside each other, were opposite. The bar was fuller now, the lights on, the sky almost dark outside the window above his head, the atmosphere heavy with talk and smoke and laughter. It seemed that he liked the phrase, and he repeated it again. 'Sons o' mine! Sons o' mine!' To the last word he gave a throaty resonance, faintly off-key, so that one or two people who were standing round turned their curious eyes upon us. 'If I were damned of body and soul.' He looked from one of us to the other. 'Fine boys, aren't they, Wendy?'

'Shouldn't we go now, George?'

He had his hand on her thigh, a mark not of desire but of possession. And her own slimmer hand rested on top of his, and for a moment or two moved in an effort to reinforce her appeal.

'Of course we're not going,' he said. 'Don't be ridiculous!' He moved his hand from her leg and reached for his drink. He could have used the other, which was loosely at his side, a cigarette between the fingers, the smoke curling up to thicken the bleary atmosphere which surrounded us.

Francis said, 'I shall have to go soon.' I was debating whether I would add 'And me.' But I decided to let that be understood.

'Not yet,' he said. He seemed not quite sure of Francis. Had it been me alone I felt the order would have been more peremptory, a designation that I would go when he told me, and not before. 'We'll have just one more. Have you money?'

Francis nodded.

He drank from his glass. 'If I were damned of body and soul, I know whose prayers would make me whole.' He stared at both of us. Just at that moment no conceivable prayer could possibly serve for his wilful predicament. 'What I can't understand is why Melanie didn't come. What's she got against her father? You haven't met Melanie, Wendy. She's a nurse. Fine girl. Her father's daughter, of course.'

'What does that mean, George?'

121

'Oh, chip off the old block. Knows her mind. Probably why she's not here now. Go and ring her up. Here.' He plunged his hand deep into the pocket of his jacket, fumbling among coins, and then drawing forth a bunch of them from which he took twopence. 'Find out where she is, when she'll be back.'

I took the coins unwillingly. 'She's on duty,' I said. 'I don't think it'll be much use my—'

He flapped his hand, silencing me. 'Don't then. It doesn't matter. It was her decision. She made it, not to come. Good luck to her. God bless her.' His voice made one of its familiar but unpredictable swoops upward on the last sentence into a high register, and though it was said benignly, a modulated cry rather than a shriek, it attracted attention. Heads turned, words being uttered faltered. He was quite oblivious. He drank the rest of his whisky and put the glass down. He looked at Francis. 'What d'you think, son o' mine?'

That inward-turning smile that covered hidden meanings for what he might say crossed Francis's features. 'I'm sure she's on duty,' he said. 'These things happen.'

He did not answer. But he raised his hand, the one which rested for much of the time on Wendy's leg, and held it in the air, fixing on Francis at the same time a look of command and inquiry, both. His forehead was wrinkled, his eyebrows raised; and he made an oddly familiar gesture, one which, as a child, I had seen many times, though in precisely what context I could not remember: he turned down his hand, forefinger pointing, and following with his eyes, indicated the empty whisky glass.

Francis looked back, then across at Wendy, an expression of inquiry now in his face not unlike Father's. Wendy's glass was more than half-full, and she shook her head. He looked even more briefly at me, with too much on the table and too much already inside me. Then he reached for the empty glass and got up. The strange mime had worked without any words. But as he was turning from the table Father said,

'Treble. Son o' mine!' The command was sharp; the words which followed even more drawn out than before, and attracting, once again, the interest of other drinkers.

I felt returning, once again, the familiar miseries of childhood. Only now, the protective shields which he himself had erected in different forms and through different strange devices had been stripped away. It was as if my age now qualified me for a more naked, more direct assault. In addition, because of my supposed desertion of him, there was also within him a motivation to punish me. And Wendy, our initial audience, seemed not to be enough. He wanted the participation of others, and looked around now at the talking and laughing faces with an expression on his own of bemused appraisal.

It was only when I saw Father staring hard at the bar that I turned and glanced over. Francis was in conversation with Chobber, who had just arrived. It was hardly an animated exchange, although Chobber was puffing with the exertion, either of his walk from Gloucester Road, or of having to buy a drink on his own; on my brother's face was a look of polite curiosity, as if Chobber's words, even at that distance predictable enough in their general intent, were of certain if limited interest. But he pointed over to us and at one point indicated Chobber's glass as if offering another drink. They came together. A chair was found, with difficulty, and he sat down between Francis and myself.

He raised his glass. 'Hello, Wendy. How's the form? Keepin' 'im under control?'

She smiled at him but did not answer. And then, looking across at my father, Wendy's smile faded. His eyes had a flinty look to them. He was sitting bolt upright, his hands on his knees. He was looking at none of us, and the drink was on the table in front of him, untouched. If anything, the expression on his face was one of distaste. But it may just have been a passage of time during which he was simply removing himself from us all in his mind.

He refocussed on me. 'Where is your friend sending you next?'

'Mr Porphyry?'

'Nobody else sends you anywhere.'

'He doesn't exactly send me,' I said.

'Where are you going next?'

'Nowhere. Nothing's planned. I only have a few more days, then I go back.'

'No prayers?'

'No prayers.'

'Tub-thumping?'

I shook my head. Wendy looked puzzled, Chobber a bit uneasy. Francis was sitting in a bentwood chair with arms, his elbows resting on them, fingers intertwined in front of him. He looked down at his hands and flexed them, inspecting the nails.

'He's too good for his father these days. Moving in exalted circles. Prays for him. Doesn't come and see him. That right, son o' mine?' He had raised his eyebrows, and those deep, clear ridges across his forehead over which my small hands had traced out their infant wonderment and incredulity at the mahogany hardness of flesh, emphasised the cold light of disdain in his gaze. I did not answer. I felt uncomfortable; prickly with sweat, dizzy, and bloated from too much beer, though all I had drunk was a couple of pints.

'Yes,' he went on, the word curiously ugly, nasal and attenuated. 'Sons o' mine. But they don't stick by their father. Treat him as a curiosity. Probably laughing about him behind his back. Loyalty. Must have loyalty.'

'Easy does it, George. Fine pair o' lads. You should be proud of 'em. Growin' up well. That's my opinion.' Rather hurriedly, Chobber took a drink from his glass. The venturing of a contradictory view had taxed his courage.

'You think so, do you Chobber?' The stony eyes were turned away from me towards him, the words vaguely slurred. 'That's what you think, eh?'

'Well, I'm never one to get into family rows, George. You

124

know me. Keep my nose out of things, that's my motto. The odd drink. I never go overboard. It's never the whole hog with Chobber.' He laughed uneasily, and I saw him glancing at the glass of golden liquid which still stood on the table in front of my father.

'You'd be interested if you knew what these sons o' mine thought of you, Chobber.' He paused. He had made a gesture towards Francis with one hand. He now made it towards me with the other. My growing discomfort took a considerable leap forward. Chobber looked uneasily to either side of himself, as if the pair of us, young though we were, might seize him and add physical indignity to the reported but unspecified judgment.

Wendy put her hand out, resting the fingers lightly on his arm.

'Don't,' he said, his hand going up, finger pointing to the ceiling, not looking at her, the sound sharply imperative. And people turned to stare. 'Don't touch me.' His voice was almost squeaky. 'Yes,' he said. He looked at Chobber. 'They don't think much of you.'

I felt disgraced.

Chobber grunted. 'Can't have everythin',' he said. 'Can't win 'em all. Life has its ups and downs, George. You always say so yourself. Cheerio.' He raised his glass and drained it. He made as if to rise, and I felt a small measure of relief ameliorating my embarrassment.

'Now, hold on, Chobber. Don't be rushing off yet. I haven't finished.'

He sank again into his chair, staring down into the empty glass which he had in his hand.

Father reached forward and picked up his drink. He looked at it, an expression of positive loathing on his face. He drank about half of it, and I watched the careful, controlled movement of the muscles around his lips, and then in his throat and neck, as he swallowed. He put the glass down.

He looked at me. In spite of the fact that his increasingly

malevolent soliloquy seemed to have mesmerised us all, I had the strong desire to smile at him, even to laugh at the essentially miserable occasion. He seemed, inside his threats and the truly outrageous comments which had placed us all in invidious positions, to be flailing around in a hopeless fashion, looking for some route back to a normality that had not just deserted him that night, but had really been crumbling away for years, if, indeed, in the fullest sense it had ever been there at all. And unhappy as I felt, I was sorry for him.

The edge of my compassion, useless as a force but real enough nonetheless, lapped over Francis where he sat in frozen detachment contemplating I knew not what action. It spread no further than that. Chobber could look after himself; so, I supposed, could Wendy. If anything, they were guilty parties. Their very presence, swelling the audience around him, had acted as an inducement to be that much more demanding, aggressive, brutal. But Francis was there because of me, and I saw the small cycle of our encounters coming to an abrupt conclusion which mocked my youthful endeavour. Fearing that there was worse to come I wanted to leave then. But I could see no way of extricating him and myself, certainly not with me taking a lead. And looking briefly, almost surreptitiously across to where he sat I sensed that at least part of him was enjoying the awfulness of the occasion. There was a reward in it for him; he was proving himself right.

IV

'Sonny boy,' Father said. He had his right hand vaguely raised in the air beside his face. In a futile attempt to attract an attention he already commanded, even as bad performers in pantomime manage to exercise a hypnotic fascination, he was moving the middle two fingers up and down in a childish kind of wave. Creeping inebriation had flattened the tone in his voice, bringing the sounds back into his larynx,

126

filling them with a dull, viscous quality. He seemed to like the sound, and repeated the words: 'Sonny boy. In life the important thing is to get rid of it all. People. Possessions. Everything. Understan' me?'

I nodded.

'Just alone. Oneself. Running the whole show.' He put his hand on his head pressing the palm of it hard down on his skull. He closed his eyes, and the effort seemed enormous; in order to do it he had to open his mouth in an ugly grimace that had the look of a yawn, but none of the relaxation. For a moment he was like a hideous gargoyle. Then his eyes opened again, and were fixed on me.

Again I nodded, not knowing what to say.

Wendy, looking at Francis first, then at me, said: 'You haven't told me about the picnic. And Melanie.'

He lifted his hand, this time the forefinger pointing upwards, and looked sideways at her. His expression was cautionary rather than angry, but it had the desired effect: turning nervously in his direction she let fade from her face the look of inquiry. A number of people around us were unashamedly staring, their own conversations abandoned in favour of eavesdropping on us. They did so a bit surreptitiously. I assumed, as regulars, they had some knowledge or experience of my father's temper and did not wish to provoke it. Their interest exaggerated my feeling of humiliation, within which was now growing a bitterness against him.

Now he looked at Chobber. 'You see, Chobber, my old fruit, it's like this.' He waved his hand a couple of times, on this occasion a gesture indicating my brother. He seemed for a moment or two uncertain about his name; then it came to him: 'Francis, Francis here. Son o' mine. He has this flat, Chobber. Perfectly normal, satisfactory place. Absolutely ideal. He knows my difficulty. But will he do anything for his father? No! Blank fucking refusal. I mean, what are sons for? You'd think he'd do something, Chobber, no?'

Chobber said, 'Well I don't know the details, George.' He

127

looked across at Francis, who had put down his glass and was looking directly back at Father.

'Don't be so bloody feeble, Chobber. Can't you speak your mind? Ever? It's absolutely clear. Open and shut. Could help. Won't.'

Francis said to Wendy, 'You'll excuse me if I go now. It was pleasant meeting you.' He made as if to put his hand out, thought better of it, and turned to Chobber. 'Perhaps we'll meet again,' he said. Then he looked across at Father.

'You're not going? You stay there!' He pointed angrily, jabbing his finger in the air in the direction of Francis's chair.

'I explained about the flat. There was, there is, nothing I could do. You know that, you knew it.'

'Son o' mine! Speak to me like that!' He had clenched his fist, and was shouting, now sufficient even in the crowded bar to attract ever growing attention.

Francis got to his feet.

Wendy put her hand on his arm. 'Calm down, George.'

He shook it angrily away. 'Shut up, you stupid fart!'

'Hey, steady on!' Chobber said.

'I'll chin the bastard! I'll chin 'im.' Father attempted to rise, swaying sideways, and then plunging back again into his seat. He began the process again. His eyes were wide, and staring up at Francis in amazed disbelief. The flash of anger had faded, but he seemed determined on assault. His movements were childishly slow. Francis regarded the scene quite coolly. He looked down at me. 'Are you coming? Or staying?' he said.

I was as remote from him as everything else. It was entirely my decision. Dizzy, uncomfortable, nauseous, prickly with a sweaty foreboding, the bile of distaste, I suddenly felt a complete disgust with Father and all that he had done. With a suddenness that outstripped his ponderous efforts to rise I stood up and said, 'Coming, Francis.'

Once again he subsided in his chair, this time more slowly. He looked up at me, a puzzled, uncomprehending

128

frown on his face. It spread and altered into a range of reactions which, for all their slowness, were real enough. He opened his mouth to speak, then closed it again. From his face there seemed to drain away all the tension and hysteria that had been building there during the preceding period of time, and which he now seemed to be putting from him, though too late to change back our disposition, which now had about it an inevitable finality. Someone nearby laughed. It was a nervous ejaculation, no more. My father began to look, then thought better of it. He stared at Chobber, still seated between Francis and me where we both stood in front of our chairs. Then he stared at Wendy. She was still looking pained at his earlier brutality, but nevertheless responded with her eyes to his silent appeal for sympathy. It did not satisfy him, and he swung his gaze once more towards Francis, then finally back to me.

'Et tu?' he said.

There seemed to have come a sudden lurch forward in his drunkenness. He was slithering helplessly around in his own mind, trying to recapture control of something he had never controlled, the balance of heart and mind, his judgment.

I thought he would cry. There was this crumpled look of defeat on his face, and he had raised his hand to make a gesture only to forget what gesture it was he wanted to make, so that his futile fingers moved in the air for a moment or two without purpose; then his hand sank down to his knee again. He did not cry. No. He did something worse. Sitting there, weak, defeated, his jaw and hands slack and resigned, his eyes bloodshot, the haggard look of wounded pride, wounded dignity upon him, he smiled up at me, a sad smile of capitulation and farewell. It was gentle and sweet; full of love and kindness and affection. But brief: just an interruption, quite unplanned, with no devious intent, a mute appeal, one day, to forgive him. Then it faded.

His voice unnaturally deep and theatrical, he said: 'Then die, Caesar!' He sat there, as though waiting for a burst of applause. But it did not come. And the expression, which

129

suggested he was feeling inwardly quite pleased with himself, faded as rapidly as had the smile. And when he looked up again he was held once more in the slack web of resignation.

I suppose he was signing off. I suppose he was accepting the accomplishment of fate. In his heart always stoical, he saw the precipice on which I stood, knew the decision was mine not his, knew that it was a critical moment for me rather than for him, seemed indeed to read correctly through his inebriation the essentials, and waited patiently for me to confirm them. Wendy and Chobber were the audience for this strange wrenching, and in deference to a moment that would hold its place in eternity were both silent and still.

Francis, for all his own silence, was a more critical figure than he could possibly have known. If the ill-defined, vague, loose, infuriating concept of 'family', which he was to come to value increasingly with the passage of the years meant—means—anything at all, then it wrapped round and enclosed that strange moment in the noisy atmosphere of the bar, with him standing and waiting for me to make a decision I had already made, and for Father to accept a decision that he had already absorbed deep into his wounded heart. Francis, standing aloof, mattered; the absent Melanie, too hurt long before perhaps, too troubled now to be there, mattered; and this bemused and puzzled man, through the clouded vision of his heart and the steadily darkening forest of his mind, did perhaps perceive that what was happening, in its curious and painful way, was right.

He was still not quite willing to let things go. I cannot understand why we waited. But we did. And perhaps part of it was the distortion of time itself, where moments are strung out by the tension of feeling. He said it again: 'Et tu?' There was a faintly proud wobble to his head as he spoke. It was almost as if he was coming to enjoy the phrase. Far from it having the tragic, Shakespearian connotation, with its fatal corollary of death, the words took on a debonair,

130

insouciant colouring, as though life, his life, could now go on again, but liberated still further by my departure.

It was this which made it easier for me to leave. Together, we walked out. And the last image, fixed within my eyeball and my brain, was of that faint, self-contained wobble of his drunk head as he directed, towards me specifically, the undeserved rhetoric of betrayal.

Later, fitting the pieces together in an attempt to measure out what it all meant, I imagined him saying under his breath, 'Then live, George!' And this imagined optimism, this threadbare defiance, gave to the faint shake in his head, to the look of surprised recovery in his eyes, to the decision in his heart that though we mattered to him he did not need us in order to press on with his life, gave to all these things the magic of survival.

It was an ending of kinds. He was to live on for more than twenty years. We were to see each other, and go on seeing each other, our paths crossing in love and companionship right to the end, with many further 'adventures', 'encounters', 'events', call them what you will, to exercise mind and heart, and in the passage of time to bring a certain peaceful harmony to his last years. But the necessary freedom started then in that most unpromising atmosphere of betrayal and disgust. If I ever understood Samson's riddle about strength and sweetness, then it was in absorbing the atmosphere at that strange parting.

It took time to get quite away. In an alleyway not far from the pub I was vehemently sick, with Francis looking on. Then he took me back to his flat and made tea. I was filled with lassitude and a certain self-pity. I felt I had messed things up, for him most of all, and I said as much. It had all been a failure, I said, a mistake. One could not organise life in that way.

'No,' he said, and there was brotherly kindness in his voice. 'It was right, what you did. I shall go and see him again. Next time I'm down from Oxford, later in the summer.'

131

'You will?'

'Yes. Why not? It was quite amusing. He does pick up some awful types, doesn't he?'

I thought of Melanie, and her judgment of him: 'He's a fine old chap.' I was surprised, and rather pleased at the rational and balanced way in which Francis had re-absorbed Father after so many years. Perhaps I had not been entirely wrong. But my pleasure in this was marred by resentment towards Melanie. She had slipped away. I was convinced there was a purposeful evasion in her 'duty', and I was hurt by it. Relieved as well, I must admit; the evening, with Melanie, might easily have been even worse. But setting this aside I felt betrayed by her. It was grossly unjust of me. I, who had known him all those years, and was simply imposing him, a virtual stranger, on others, was expecting a great deal more than was fair. And I did come to realise that later. But not then. In my mind, then, I felt dismissive. I saw as unfair her pulling back. Years and years had conditioned me to give to my father, always, the benefit of the doubt if blame was in the air. And after that evening it certainly was.

In my mind I turned towards Francis: I would emulate his example, where work was concerned. I would leave aside everything else and cram into the next few days the holiday work which had been hanging over me. In my heart I warmed to my brother, felt gratitude for his reaction, the calmness of his approach. I felt I could confide more in him, tell him in greater detail my fears about the approaching term at Coppinger, outline once again the prospects and dangers, the shadow of Bennett and Mrs Patterson, the dreary threat of my housemaster's limited responses, the looming challenge of work. But I was so tired. The tea settled my queasiness but failed to revive me. I wanted to sleep. He had arranged two armchairs for me, the second bed having been moved elsewhere in the house on Miss Filgate's instructions, and had even telephoned Mr Porphyry to say I would be staying the night. And I had let all this happen looking forward to the prospect of further discussion the next day, discussion which in the event did not take place.

'Will he be all right with Wendy?' I asked, stretching out in my makeshift bed.

'No.'

'Will he be all right at all?'

'No.'

'Does it matter?'

'Not really.'

Francis, by being right, was teaching me to believe him. At first unwilling, I now took a curious, relaxed pleasure in considering as correct a view that in other circumstances might have seemed outrageous. But as I drifted towards sleep there came to me again the tug of pity which had held me in those last moments before leaving the pub. And once again I reconstructed him in my imagination, hand raised beside his face, eyes accepting the inevitable, yet still expressing puzzled surprise, and his voice, clumsy and thick, dismissing my dismissal: 'Et tu? Then live, George!'

Chapter Six

I

'I told him to move, sir. It's entirely on my responsibility.' I looked calmly back at Patterson where he stood beside his desk, pulling on his tattered gown.

'But why didn't you consult with me?'

'I did, sir. Last term.'

'Last term? I don't remember that.'

'I told you Bellamy would be gone, and asked if it would be all right to move up Wickham.'

He looked searchingly at me across the room. It was large and untidy, a big roll-top desk at one end, and a table, both covered with books; and at the other a sofa and fireplace, lamps and a radiogram, and two or three chairs. All along one wall was a window looking out on to shrubs, and it was the indirect sunlight on these that illuminated in uncertain light our faces as we looked at each other. His was more in shadow. He ran his big hands over his sparse hair, smoothing it down. There was a vague look of annoyance in his eyes. 'And I said yes? To that?'

I remembered vividly the cold and hurried encounter, the faint smell of whisky on his breath, the other, end-of-term decisions he was obliged to make and would not make. 'I think you agreed, sir.' I could not avoid the slight hesitation. He had not agreed. He had said nothing, putting it off, and I had hoped, during the holiday, that my suggestion would have stuck in his mind so that coming back I would just have found Wickham's name there on the dormitory list, in with the seniors. But it had not been there. Nothing had been done at all. No new boys, at that mid-point in the school year, had forced forward any action, and none had been taken. In the light of that I had told Wickham to move up.

'I don't think I agreed,' he said. His voice was flat, but determined enough. 'No. I didn't agree. Wickham's too young, anyway.'

'But he's Lower Fifth, sir.'

'That may be. He's able. But he's young for the form; you must see that.' He pulled into place the padded and pleated shoulders of his gown. They were the only part of it which held firmly together, and even there the black material had turned a faint and dusty green colour, a mixture of age and incipient disintegration. The rest fell away in tatters.

I stood and waited for him to go on. There were other things we had to discuss, but I was in no mood for them. The issue of Wickham was all important. I knew I was wrong. I shouldn't have moved him without consulting my housemaster. And, looking at him across his study, I knew, deeper down, that he would not have countenanced the change. 'I felt you'd leave it to me. When you hadn't put any names—'

'You should have asked.'

'Last term, sir. I came to you last—'

'I didn't agree.' He shook his head slowly from side to side. It was not a certain recollection. But it had already been enough to provoke from me an answer which told him he was right. 'You'd best move him back.' He did not look at me. He had half turned towards the crowded roll-top desk, and was pulling from it some papers. Several books slid to the floor. He looked at them but made no effort to pick them up.

I felt intensely annoyed. 'I would rather you left him now, sir. Now that I've moved him.' I could not keep out of my voice the despising tone. He should have been more decisive

135

at the end of the previous term. He should have answered. He should have corrected the lists. There was so much he should have done and should be doing.

He looked up at me. 'I'm not prepared to do that.'

We stared at each other. I wished I had never come to his house. I thought: you need me, and you undermine me. And it was true. In his eyes I could see both distrust and uncertainty, and I remembered the curious experience, many months before, of being told that I was to move from Forrest's to Patterson's house. The occasion, even then, had been surrounded by vague disquiet, that strange shiver across the face, in the eyes, of deceit. Had it been Forrest, wanting to move me, for the sake of his daughter, Janet? Had it been Patterson, genuinely looking for a boy to replace Franklin? Or had it been Merchant, manipulating them and myself, with altogether a larger design in mind? I was never quite sure of any of them, and suspected Forrest most of all because he was right. But at that moment I wanted to be back where I had been. I wanted to be there in place of Danby, once again near Janet, with her willing, earthy affection, her ready smile, her open arms. I had let it all pass without due consideration. Perhaps there was nothing I could have done. But it was gone completely now.

'It will make me look a bit stupid, sir.'

'I don't think so. Say it was a mistake. Say it was my instruction.'

He had once been handsome, once had the visage of a hero: long jaw, broad forehead, the penetrating eye of courage. But it had crumpled a bit. The black spread of his moustache, turning grey, no longer quite concealed the weakness of his mouth; and his eyes, bloodshot and tired, hinted at anticipated defeats.

Even so, I suppose I was foolish to press what I thought was a just claim. 'May I ask you what the reason is?'

'Oh, don't be so stubborn. He's too young for the seniors. Can't you see that? Just take your orders. Arrange it as I say.' There was a flash of anger in his eyes. He only glanced

136

at me, looking again at the papers in his hand. 'We have several other—'

'Who shall I put up in Wickham's place?'

He paused and pulled out the list of house names. Then he looked down at them, placing the sheet of paper on top of the other things he held in his hand. 'Bell?' he suggested. Once again he seemed uncertain.

'He's already up,' I said, trying to keep from my voice the pitying tone. It was typical, I told myself, that Patterson should not have known this. What else did he not know about his own house? He went right through the lists this time, and then he looked up at me, an expression of almost smug certainty in his eyes.

'Move Skinner up,' he said.

'Skinner?' I said. 'He's only Fourth Form.'

'I know. But he's older than Wickham.'

'He's a lout,' I said. 'He causes trouble wherever he is.'

'We all have our crosses to bear,' Patterson said.

I thought, viciously, that he was one of mine, persistently burdensome, impossible to set down. Being head of his house was tiresome and difficult, without being rewarding. Deep down, I had not really become part of it at all. I was an exile among Patterson's boys, a mercenary, his adjutant for a brief enough period, now mercifully coming to a close.

'What about the other moves?' I asked.

'What do you mean?'

'Well, with Skinner gone, who'll go into his place?'

He looked a bit slyly back at me. 'Did you do nothing about that?'

I shook my head.

'I'll deal with that at assembly.'

'There are some other points you've to deal with, sir.' I waited, watching him stare around at the general untidiness which he made no move to clear up. Then he looked up at me.

'Oh, yes?' he said. 'And what are they?'

'Well, the cricket boots. There's no place for the cricket

boots. In the bootroom. You said you'd arrange for the extra shelves.'

'So I did. Meant to do that. Carpenter's shop very busy during the holidays. Couldn't seem to fit it in.'

He looked at me, a bit bleakly. I raised other points with him. I tried to feel concern about cricket boots and shower fittings. But they were incidental. Administration, which I supposed was an end in itself to him, was a means whereby I could assert and then exercise power, and at that time power seemed interesting. It disturbed me, the way he blocked my initiatives, and I expect I let it show.

'Will there be anything else, sir, before house assembly?'

He shook his head, but not with absolute certainty. 'Something else about Wickham...' he frowned. 'Oh, yes. His pills. He's back?'

'I saw him earlier,' I said, 'to tell him to move up.'

Patterson went off down the long, low room towards the fireplace at the other end. 'They're here somewhere.' He looked along the mantelpiece, and then reached for a package.

'Is he still on those same pills?' I asked. 'He seems to have been on them since I came to the house.' I had never questioned this before, but my growing concern for Wickham made me puzzle over his health.

Patterson looked at me a bit oddly. 'It's better he keeps on them,' he said, 'for the time being.'

'What's the problem, sir?'

'He gets dizzy spells. Nothing serious. Bit of a fuss, really. But doctor's orders.'

I took the package. 'I'll call assembly for nine, then, will I, sir?'

He nodded. 'I want to get off on the right foot,' he said. 'And I want us to keep in step, you and I. Understand?'

'Yes, sir.'

'Can't have the captains and the generals at odds, can we? Can't run an army and win battles, when everyone's at sixes and sevens?' The flash of stern order and military discipline appeared momentarily in his eyes.

I shook my head, but said nothing. For the sake of our working together perhaps I should have spoken. But nothing came to mind. All I could think of were his stories of Spain; all I could wonder was whether, distant in space and time as it had all become, it was also distant in reality.

He tried once more to stir me. 'Important term, this one. We've got to win back the cup.'

'Yes, sir.'

But the light of battle, as he would have described it himself, had somehow faded back into an uncertainty that reflected the real nature of all war. We were etched against the pale bright sunlight on the garden foliage through the window that ran down the side of his study. We were like two champions of two quite different causes, and it was almost with a note of appeal in his voice that he said to me across the shadowy space between us, 'Winning's what it's all about, isn't it, eh? Good tactics, good strategy, all working together, the details right, the support right? That's it, eh? We can't be at odds, can we?'

'No, sir,' I said. But I didn't mean it.

II

'Wickham?'

He turned in the window of the Common Room and looked at me. He was with two others of his own age, Baron and Cooper. I stood by the door.

He showed no inclination to come over, so I beckoned him. There were others in the room, waiting, talking, testing the newness of their return to the ancient, ineradicable smell of countless generations of boys.

'Yes?' He had sauntered across the room and stood in front of me, a slight smile on his parted lips, his brown eyes sparkling in his somewhat dark complexion. The texture of his skin seemed to have been dusted already by the heat of the early summer sun; he seemed possessed of an inner warmth.

'You're as untidy as ever, Wickham. It's phenomenal.'

He laughed at me. 'You're not so smart yourself.' For one who was still the leading treble in the school choir, though he must at this stage have been well over fourteen years old, his speaking voice was surprisingly deep and resonant.

He was untidy. Most of the knot of his tie, which was large and loosely done, had slipped up under the rather grubby points of his shirt collar. This was crumpled by the lapel of his jacket, and the top button was undone. His grey suit was creased from the day's travelling. His black shoes were filthy. Yet in a curious way the laughter in his eyes, the expressive features, the apparent absorption of summer into his skin, made quite unimportant and incidental a general appearance which, with a different kind of boy, would have seemed raw, clumsy, uncouth. Wickham carried it off. I felt he knew it, too. He had style.

'Well, what is it you want?' he said. 'Can't keep my friends waiting. We're having a discussion.'

'Are you indeed!' My own attempt to simulate polite surprise and counter the faint thread of impertinence in his voice concealed a feeling of constriction, even embarrassment. There were quite a few boys in the Common Room, standing in groups. It would soon be time for assembly. The long room, with its several windows, was filled with the evening sun. I felt suddenly serious, and angry with Patterson. 'I've made a mistake,' I said. 'You're not to move up. You're to stay where you were last term. Mr Patterson wants Skinner in the senior dormitory. I'm sorry.'

He laughed at my look of concern, and pushed his hands deep into his trouser pockets, making his general appearance, if that were possible, even more untidy. 'It doesn't matter,' he said. 'I'll be with them.' He nodded over his shoulder towards Baron and Cooper. 'It's all right.'

I felt suddenly foolish at my unnecessary concern on his behalf. The concern was entirely on my own. 'That's okay then,' I said. 'Is Skinner back?'

He shrugged. 'I don't know.'

'You'd better move your things. If you see him, tell him. He should be back by now. He's to go up.'

Wickham looked up at me. His generally mobile and expressive features were still, the look in his eyes serious. 'It's your last term, isn't it?'

'Yes.'

'You working for this scholarship?

'I will be.'

'I hope you get it.' He turned to go. I had in my hand the packet of pills.

'Oh, Wickham, Mr Patterson gave me these for you.' I handed them across.

The laughter in his eyes died a little. 'Oh, those.' He took them.

'Don't you like taking them?'

'Not much.'

'But you have to?'

'Yes.' He spoke quietly, turning away and tucking the package into the hip pocket of his grey jacket, where it bulged out.

I wanted to ask him why, keep him talking; but he seemed disinclined. I watched him go back to his friends and speak briefly with them, earning from both a smiling response that indicated to me that my own dismay at Patterson's reversal of my orders was not shared by them. Then Wickham went out.

I wondered later why Patterson had bothered to give me Wickham's pills when, in the general flurry of term's beginning, he could so easily have sent some other messenger or brought them himself to house assembly. And I think that the act of so wondering was itself an indicator of the restless, swirling, spiralling shape of my thoughts from the very beginning of that term. I had to ask myself about

141

everything. I had to question whether, after the reprimand, Patterson was offering some kind of antidote, feeble, marginal, but faintly ameliorative. It made me conscious of being watched. And it heightened my own predisposition also to watch. For there was doubt between us, and uncertainty, and from these derive cancerous growths which multiply.

To say at this stage that it was an interference with my work would be an exaggeration; yet it did foreshadow difficulties. One is wrestling, during the closing stages of school, to come to terms with living as well as with learning. And at Coppinger most boys had odd enough foundations for the intellectual and emotional structures which were slowly going up.

I watched Wickham go back to his friends. The constriction within, the strange tumble of anticipatory feelings, eased. So, too, did my annoyance with Patterson. I even considered the possibility that he was right. I looked round the room, taking in groups here and there, confident of my position, contemplating with equanimity the shift that faced me into order, routine, authority; at the same time aware that everything I did would be just faintly overshadowed by the fact that it was being done for the last time.

I crossed the room to give orders to a group of juniors, then moved down to the end where three older boys, not house monitors but in the senior dormitory, were sitting in the deep recess of a window. They looked up at me as I approached, pausing in their conversation.

One of them, Cartwright, said: 'Wickham's moved up to our dorm, then?'

'No,' I said, standing in front of them.

'He told us he had. He moved his things in, didn't he?'

A heavily-built boy called Blake nodded, and the third, Atwood, said 'It's true. He said he was told to move up. By you.'

'It was a mistake. Skinner's moving up, not Wickham.'

'Skinner!' They seemed appalled at the thought.

142

'He'll turn the dorm into a bear garden.'

'Does he wash?'

'What about his toenails?'

'Uncouth fellow.'

'He has claws, not nails.'

'He can be managed,' I said. 'A little diplomacy, my friends.' I looked at them, but they did not seem greatly encouraged by my words. 'Have any of you seen him? Skinner?'

They shook their heads.

'I'd better go and find him.'

I was almost at the door when Skinner came in. To say that he 'came in' is, as with everything else connected with him, an understatement. He tumbled through the door, looking backwards over his shoulder and shouting something to a group of boys in the hallway outside the room. I had to put up my hand to stop him banging into me, and, through the material of his jacket, I felt the muscles in his over-developed shoulder. He stopped and turned, with mock surprise, hauling himself backwards like an animal character out of a film cartoon, the words being delivered over his shoulder coming to an abrupt halt.

'Cor!' he said. 'You!' His blue eyes were open wide, his big freckled face shone with sweat, and he automatically put up his hand to smooth down his long, untidy mass of fair hair. 'Nearly knocked you down, didn't I? I'm sorry?' He turned the apology into a question. He said it rather hopelessly, as though aware that it was a familiar leit-motif, heralding the augmentation of his careering progress for the term, through which he would undoubtedly bang his noisy way.

'It's all right, Skinner. We were beginning to miss you.'

'Yeah?' There was an expression of surprised inquiry on his face as he looked round at a room which had received with some interest his arrival. Then a broad smile spread across his face, and he raised his fist and gently punched me in the chest. 'You're 'avin' me on, aint you?'

143

My own smile was guarded. 'Not at all, Skinner. You would be greatly missed.' I inspected his growing bulk. He seemed, in the brief month of that Easter holiday, to have expanded disproportionately. As untidy as Wickham in his dress, he was infinitely more of a mess to look at, large, clumsy, gangling and awkward. His pale skin, his freckles, his great blank eyes, his untidy fair hair always badly cut and stark-looking, and the sense one had of his limbs almost audibly creaking with further growth, all contributed to a larger than life impact on the house. It seemed inconceivable that he was only a month or two older than Wickham. Standing there in front of me, almost my own height and certainly destined in time to be taller and much stronger, he was a young giant, contained and finally disciplined more by his own good nature than any other force.

'It is with mixed feelings, Skinner, that I have to tell you of your elevation in seniority. You are—'

'I am now in the senior dorm!' He nodded as I spoke, grinning broadly, taking the words out of my mouth. 'Wickham told me! Said 'e was greatly relieved to be able to announce the fact. I clipped 'is ear, for cheek. 'E was too quick, though. Eyes like an 'awk.'

'You'd better move in, then.'

He drew himself up in height, pulled in his chin with a frown, and gave an exaggerated, American-style salute, his hand jerking down in front of my nose. 'Aye, aye Cap'n!' Then, swinging a canvas bag which he had been holding, he left the room, laughing to himself.

III

Patterson wore the trappings of responsibility with a certain grimness that first evening; and yet he seemed to have gathered himself together by the time he came to house assembly into giving an account of himself which, if not

144

compelling, was, in the light of the way he had seemed to me earlier, convincing enough.

Though I saw, behind the conventionally handsome physique, a certain crumpling away, as though deep down inside the man a will to triumph had died away, I was constantly surprised at the manner in which he succeeded in reconstituting himself when he needed to do so. He had not gone to seed in the conventional sense. He was still physically spare, and his movements were determined. But he gave the impression that he was pushing himself on. Now in his late fifties he was coming to terms unwillingly with age, with stiffness, with grey, thinning hair which he wore cut short, with the need to wear glasses, his black-rimmed pair being an instrument which he handled with clumsy ostentation.

Conscientious in small things, he kept a tight control over the use of electricity. I always thought him curiously circumspect about it. He had been at Coppinger before it came of course, in the days of gaslight. But it was more than that; an attitude of mind, a mannerism. So it was, that although the sun had set, he came into assembly in that curious end-of-daylight stillness, that interval before the turning on of lights, when the glow of evening, of what had been a faultless sun-filled day in early May was fading imperceptibly into dusk.

One side of the long room was lined with lockers, the door in the middle. Made in beech, their light, golden colouring was marred by the wear and tear of many generations of schoolboys. Some failed to close, others were stained, blemished in different ways, even broken. Collectively they had as much character as shelves of books. Certainly they gave to the room, which otherwise was sparsely furnished, a feeling not just of being lived in, but of being filled with the essence of boys' possessions, past, present and to come. Three windows, each deeply recessed, broke up the wall opposite, and faced out over falling ground towards the south-west. At one end there was a

145

fourth window; at the other a fireplace and above it a large steel engraving, in a maple frame, of a Victorian cricket match. Patterson was fond of the engraving. He used to make jokes about it, criticising the stance and dress, but claiming that the enthusiasm was right. And he used to try and avoid standing directly in front of it, as though allowing its attractions to help us in our general attention to what he was saying.

From a position in front of this it was normal, on the first day of term, in the early evening, for him, together with Bennett and the house prefects, to give out the term's announcements, their weighty nature projecting forward for us all to a similar gathering with which the term would end. Rarely, if ever, did the house tutor attend with Patterson other than at the beginning and end of term. For the rest, it was either him or the housemaster; and on occasion myself rather than either of them. The prayers we said were perfunctory, a fact that in itself emphasised the ritualism.

'Well, Skinner, you made it back here for another term?'

'Yes, sir.'

'You were nearly in time, I hear.'

He grinned, his freckles suffused with a pinkish glow of pleasure. He pushed his hand up through his hair, making it a good deal more untidy.

'The reason I've moved you up to the senior dormitory is not so that you make life more difficult for everyone there, causing trouble and strife, but that you should become more adult and responsible in your behaviour. Is that possible?' For a moment he looked grimly at the ungainly giant who stood out above the other boys in the centre of the room. Then a slight smile traced its way across his features, and Skinner responded with a broad grin and a nod of the head.

'Yes, sir!' he exclaimed.

Patterson looked round the room. 'And I want that spirit from the rest of you. We've fine opportunities this term. We must make the most of them. All of us.' He paused, looking at a list in his hand. 'Page? You're to move up,' he said.

146

'And Uttley. And we've a spare place left in the junior dormitory.' He looked sideways at me for corroboration; possibly for something more, to see that I had accepted his disposition of the order of things. I nodded only, looking at him for a brief moment and then staring out over the heads of the boys at the window at the end of the room. I only half-listened as he talked over details of administration. He was announcing nothing that was new. He issued the familiar rallying cry about house cricket, followed it with the equally statutory injunction about work and the examinations which would come, in one form or another, at the end of term. He seemed, then, to gather his thoughts for a moment, debating upon some further issue which might or might not be raised. We waited, conscious of the deliberations. One or two boys fidgeted. There was a tension in the air. Then, gripping the tattered borders of his gown and lifting them in front of his chest where they would have created an impressive dark shroud if there had been any material, but where they resulted instead in a curtain of faded, uneven, ragged ribbons falling in front and around his tweed jacket and corduroy trousers, he eyed the boys in front of him for a moment in troubled silence.

'Let's put last term and its troubles behind us, once and for all. It's over, it's past, let's forget it. We must work together this term as a unit, disciplined, determined. Above all, loyal. Your loyalty to the house is paramount.' I think he would have liked to leave on that note, but he looked sideways at Bennett and rather grudgingly asked him if he had anything to add.

Bennett said he wanted to talk with a group of boys, about athletics, and he read out their names, so that assembly began to break up without any flamboyant departure, and in fact with Patterson himself surrounded by other boys who had queries for him.

There were none for me. I was relieved of the focus of any attention, curiously suspended in an isolation that was made more potent by the crowded, noisy room. I watched both men, thinking them imperfect. It is odd how, in later life, we look with equanimity upon those things which, in youth, provoke moral, social, human outrage. I felt it then. If I were to seek within myself for an understanding of puritanism, I would endeavour to reconstruct my mind's attitude towards Bennett, toward Patterson and his wife, an attitude of mind reinforced by strong feeling. I disapproved; and it was moral. If the judgments had been human they would have been directed against myself. And so odd is the structure of any school, made even odder by the circumstances surrounding Coppinger, that no easy social view was possible.

In later life, a man might entertain his mistress, his wife's current lover, other women with whom he has had affairs, other men who have had affairs with his wife, or just desire her, and reconcile within himself all objection. But in youth, how differently we see it all! How we burn with indignation!

I felt it specially because of Bennett's formal involvement in the affairs of Patterson's house by being house tutor. It was the regularity of his being there, the calm acceptance by each man of the need to work together, that seemed to me so much of an assault upon what was right and honest. And I cannot believe, in spite of everything, that living it all over again would make it any different. It was a travesty of example and behaviour, even if I was the only boy to perceive it; and I was not. Yet ritual, convention, 'form', clouded it over, so that watching the two of them, each surrounded, listening and answering, I simply felt a slow, inescapable amazement.

Over the heads of the boys around him Bennett suddenly said to me: 'I'd like a word with you later.'

I nodded. How fine he looked, I thought, his expression lively, vital, his answers sure and precise. And yet studying the two men, at the end of the room, as I moved away with no particular task facing me, down towards the window, I could not quell or neutralise the essential outrage I felt at the duplicity manifest in one, if not both of them: with Bennett it was a robbery, a rape, with deception, a sustained dissimulation; with Patterson it could have been ignorance still, but I doubted that. He was living out a husk-like travesty, or so I judged it at that time.

Circumstance had isolated me, also. The move to Patterson's house, more than a year before, had given me greater responsibility but less contact with contemporaries whose attitudes I valued. The result of this had been beneficial for my work. Perhaps a trifle loftily, I had emphasised the burden of study and used it as a final refuge from the demands of my housemaster. And the principal compensation had been Bennett. His evenings on duty in the house, the occasions he seized for other visits, the times when, quite conscious of the vague irregularity, he would arrive out of the blue with an essay to talk over with me, were the highspots in my learning, so that even now I can trace back certain perceptions to odd and often intense conversations which would spring up between us.

I was his best excuse for visiting the house as often as he did, and though he clearly seized on the opportunity more frequently than he would otherwise have done, and this may have been noticed, he did always fulfil the unspoken obligations towards myself implicit in his visits. I was the only Upper Sixth pupil going for a scholarship, and no matter what other emotions drove him, he gave to me what I believe was the best he could in teaching.

Nevertheless, there existed between us, always, an unexpressed tension deriving from instinctive reservations on both sides. I could never fully adjust to the knowledge I had about his most inner feelings: not instinctive, but factual knowledge. And this, in turn, must have relayed something back to him, creating an impediment. Never spoken, never alluded to in the slightest way, it was contained, like a faintly moving fragment of dust catching a reflection in the light of a sunbeam, in that short space between our eyes. Looking directly at each other, intent upon the intractable issue of Hamlet's mother or uncle or father, there existed always between us an additional human shadow.

He found me later that evening in the prefects' study, a small, rather stuffy but comfortable room which I shared with the three house monitors and in which I had a desk of my own where I was able to work. Even this was a concession specially made by Patterson, and I derived benefit from it more because the others were not intent on work or solitude or the peace it offered, and generally left the room to me.

'Did you get much done, in the holidays?' Bennett asked.

'I read.'

'Any essays?'

'Two.'

He raised his eyebrows. I gave him details. They had been done, as had much of the reading, in those last few days following the episode in the pub. Chastened, shamed and following Francis's example where work was concerned; unable to bring myself to seek out Melanie, I had suddenly engulfed myself in all the neglected work planned for the Easter holiday.

'And that's all?'

I nodded, a bit put out at his severity. 'I did as much as I could.'

'I hope you realise what you're up against.' He was frowning at me. 'It's not just passing. It's competitive. They're greedy for the best, not just the good. You do want to go, don't you?'

I nodded again.

'You must be ruthless. Not with others. With yourself.' He paused, staring at me. He was tall and spare, athletic in his build, and he looked down at me slightly, his frown intensifying the penetrating directness of his brown eyes. 'You won't be taking on anything this term, will you?'

'What do you mean, sir?'

'You're not in the cricket?'

'No.'

'Swimming? Athletics?'

'I have to run for the house.'

He nodded, almost absently. It was his own responsibility, and yet he seemed prepared to excuse me from any involvement beyond the bare essentials.

'Nothing else?'

'I suppose music,' I said. 'We gave the madrigal concert last summer. Parker's doing it again.'

'That's all right, I suppose.' His expression was preoccupied. 'We'll get down to detail tomorrow.'

IV

I saw Patterson last thing before going to bed. His wife was with him, in the study, reading on the sofa. Bennett had left.

He was at his desk. Turning, he said: 'Skinner's moving up? How has it gone?'

I said, with a shrug, not meaning it to be disrespectful, 'Well, he's moved. And we all know about it, sir.'

'Noisily?'

'Skinner'll be a handful wherever he is,' I said.

'No one would dispute that.'

'I think he's improved,' Mrs Patterson said. She had laid aside the paper, her dark eyes fixed on her husband.

'Has he been polite to you?'

She laughed. 'Well, not actively rude. We mustn't expect too much.'

Patterson looked rather sternly at me. 'He'll need watching, you know. He's a source of trouble. You must see him that way.'

Imitating one of my father's favourite phrases, which he employed in order to give a quite opposite meaning, I said, with a faint smile, 'He's all right. Skinner's all right, sir. I can manage him.'

Patterson did not respond to my confidence about Skinner, and I think I saw why. And what I saw encouraged my sense of impending gloom. His assumption seemed to be

151

that boys are conditioned to misbehave. And I accepted it as a normal one among schoolmasters. But I wondered: with adults, did he feel the same? And if so, did the feeling extend as far (or, more properly, as near) as his wife? Or did that other schoolmasterly conviction, just as strong, that the world divides into 'them', the boys, and 'us', which was everyone else, exonerate her from blame or suspicion? For it had seemed, up to that time, that what we, his pupils, had witnessed, and increasingly believed was the situation, had failed to create in him any serious reaction or antagonism. Whereas, in contrast, the slightest whiff of suspicion about any individual boy's behaviour, or more particularly that of a small group of boys, set him off in hot pursuit of the imagined fault. It was not that we thought it unfair, even; it was just that we considered it a bit foolish.

As if reading my thoughts, Patterson said to me: 'There's something in the school called the "Confrérie"?' He spoke the word awkwardly, lending equal emphasis to each syllable. 'Means brotherhood, I think. Know about it?'

'I've heard the name,' I said.

'Anything more?'

I shook my head.

'I suppose it's a schoolboy thing. Headmaster was asking. Seems he's curious. Any of our boys involved?'

'I don't think so,' I said. 'But I don't know.'

For a moment or two he looked at me. 'Well, if you find out anything, let me know.'

I did not reply to that. I could not see myself volunteering such information. I would judge for myself, if he asked again later in the term, what I might say.

Mrs Patterson had been watching us, her intense, level gaze first on him, then on me. 'I suppose your father's coming into his own?' she said.

I was completely bewildered by the question, and must have shown it.

'Gardening. It's the busiest season. We talked about it when he was last here.'

'Oh, er, yes. Yes, he is busy.' I felt only embarrassment; not just at lying to her, for there had been no real evidence of my father having many 'clients' as he liked to call them, the last and disastrous occasion we had met; but at the sour recollections I had of that time, which removed far from me any concern I might have felt for him and his love of the soil.

'I wish he were here. I need help. I don't know what to do with the rose trellis on the back wall.'

'I'm sure he'd help if he was here.'

'Will he be down?'

'He may come for Prize Day,' I said. I felt certain he would not.

'It'll need attention before that.'

'I'm sorry.'

'So am I. Your father always makes his presence felt. He gave me useful advice about lilies, I remember.'

'If I could help?' I said.

'I might hold you to that,' she said.

I paused, looking at her. 'He's not been well lately.' I don't know what made me say it. Some wish to draw sympathy from her, perhaps; to build a little structure upon the feelings she had for him.

'Nothing serious, I hope.' It was said coolly. She was not curious to know the nature of his trouble, and I felt sudden relief at not having to explain the vague, bronchial disorders which were beginning to form an ominous adjunct to any bout of drinking which became heavy or prolonged.

I wanted to respond more warmly to her. Quite apart from any feelings I might have had deriving from knowledge or speculation about her and Bennett, she was an attractive woman, admired to the point of desire by many boys, perhaps conscious of it; certainly able to turn it to advantage in the general run of house encounters.

Patterson, who had moved away, now got up from his desk and came back towards me. 'We've a chance of the cricket this year. Hope you'll be playing.'

153

I paused, looking down at the floor between us, at the worn texture of the patterned carpet. 'No, sir,' I said. 'I've too much work. I'm not doing cricket.'

'Oh.'

'I'll do athletics. Later in the term. But my scholarship comes up in July. I don't have time.'

Mrs Patterson was looking at us.

'I see,' he said. 'I hope you get it. It won't be easy.'

'Thank you, sir.'

'That's all you'll be doing, then? Athletics?'

'Yes, sir. More or less.'

'More or less?'

'Well, there's the music, sir. We have the madrigals. With Par— with Mr Parker.'

'You've time for that?' The tone was faintly sarcastic.

'I wanted to do it, sir. Yes.'

'I see.' He paused. 'Wickham's also a singer, isn't he? Leading treble in the choir, or something?'

I nodded.

'It's better he stays down.' He looked at me for a moment. His expression was cold to the point of being angry. 'He's young, you know. Has a long way to go. Got his own friends. Better that way.'

I made no response. I looked briefly at Mrs Patterson, then back at her husband. The truculence which I seemed to have provoked hovered around him. 'You know, when the headmaster suggested you to help me out in the house I thought the commitment would be better. I really did. I really did.'

The repetition perhaps guarded him from upbraiding me any further; and I was grateful in a way, since I would have defended myself against the implications of not pulling my weight. But something in what he said tugged more deeply at my mind and made me pass over the minor irritation my less than total involvement in the life of the house represented to my hard-pressed housemaster. 'I didn't think it was Mr Merchant's suggestion,' I said.

154

'What are you talking about?'

'What you just said, sir.'

'What did I just say?'

'That Mr Merchant suggested me to move to your house.'

'Well, that's right, isn't it?' He frowned.

'I think it was Mr Forrest.'

'Mr Forrest?'

'Yes.'

'Well, we all agreed. I know that. I always thought it was the Headmaster picked on you. Does it matter? What's important is that you give of your best.'

I could think of nothing to say to that. I had been reminded of a certain inescapable vulnerability in my predicament, common to all boys at school, compounded in my own case, and possibly in the case of Coppinger boys generally, by a certain imposed gratitude for our presence there at all. And it made me vaguely, perhaps subconsciously, vindictive in my final reaction.

After a pause I said, 'I've told Mr Bennett.'

'Told him what?'

'About doing athletics.'

'I see,' he said.

'Will that be all, sir?'

He nodded.

Chapter Seven

I

I held the bell upside down by its clapper so that it should make no sound. I stood in the open doorway of Main Hall staring down its length towards the figures at the piano, and I listened again as Danby played over the short passage in the music he was practising with Parker. Parker said something and then played a few notes on the piano. Danby repeated the phrase. Then Parker. Then Danby again.

I looked at my watch. It was getting late. Outside, there were shouts floating up from the sports fields below Main School, multiplying, coming closer. I had left the other prefects in the study talking, and had come out on my own to find Danby and bring him in for a brief meeting before assembly. 'Finding Danby' was a euphemism, much of the time, for listening and then tracking down the mellow mournful notes he produced. On this occasion he was close enough, but as usual had lost all sense of time, and looked at me almost blankly as I came slowly down the length of Main Hall and approached him where he stood beside the piano, playing, to Parker's accompaniment, a melody for which he needed only occasional reference to the music in front of him.

I raised the bell, and my eyebrows at the same time, but he went on playing to the end of the passage. Parker looked sideways at me once or twice, as he ran through the last bars; then, when it was finished, turned on the piano stool and smiled up at me. 'You've come to claim your leader, then.'

'I suppose you could say that, sir.'

'Have you any wish to be claimed, Brian?'

Danby shook his head. He looked across at me. He was pulling the mouthpiece away. Without interest, he said: 'You could do it all yourself. You'd prefer to, anyway.'

'I think you ought to come. The first day.'

'I suppose you're right.'

I stood and waited, the bell in my hand. Sunlight flooded across from one side of the hall to the other, but from windows high up. Where we stood was more shadowy. Parker was pulling over the black piano a fitted baize cover. He did it carefully, reluctantly. 'You should practise the new piece,' he said to Danby. Then, to me, he went on: 'And we must get practices going again. Before the weekend, if possible.'

We had left too little time to arrange prefects' duties before assembly. When we got into the study, and when everyone was quiet, Danby searched through his pockets and eventually found a crumpled piece of paper. He read over some duties, then he said, 'And Merchant wants us all at three o'clock. The usual set of instructions for the term.' He looked round. 'Anything else?'

There was a pause. His dreamy eyes surveyed the other prefects. With the exception of myself they were all younger, this being in most cases their first year of what is best described as ultimate responsibility and power for boys at Coppinger. His eyes came to rest on me. I said nothing, but nodded towards the handbell which now stood on the table round which we were sitting.

'Oh, yes,' Danby said. 'You take duty prefect for the rest of this week. That all right?'

I said it was.

'Alphabetical after that?'

I took up the bell again, this time by the handle, and stood up. The clapper brushed the side and sent forth a faint note. By carrying it carefully, but hanging free, a tentative resonance of sound could be coaxed forth as one made tracks towards whatever point was chosen to announce change of class or the gathering together of the school. I said generally to the room: 'We're a bit late. Let's move. Get them in.' And I paused to check on the response. Even Danby got up to follow.

Boisterously, the school assembled. There was that collective freedom from guilt, the willing turning over of a new leaf, that would soon disintegrate into the unevenness of an erring flock, the chiding of which would be Merchant's ever weightier task. Streaming in from the playing fields below to the summons of the bell swinging in my own hand, they came to the narrow pass of the main entrance to the school and scrambled on into Main Hall.

It was an assembly with staff, and the flurry of gowns and the sheer numbers added to the sense of occasion, the ritual catalogue of injunctions designed to carry us through, and falling from Merchant's lips with a relish and precision which once had been ominous, and now seemed to me admirably precise and commanding. I had grown to admire his authority, to see in all he did a sense of purpose and direction which was framed in large-scale ambitions for the school to which we were all commanded to contribute. It was a different perspective on him that I now had. I stood beside, rather than against, and I was disposed to believe that he was the constant, I the variable, not admitting that there could be change in him also.

He led us through a catalogue of minor matters. Then he paused. Looking round for a moment or two he seemed to be debating whether to end there, or go on. Then he said: 'I will deal very severely with any repetition of last term's trouble. That is all.'

On Patterson's face there was a pinched and hooded look. He stared straight ahead of him in the brief silence that followed, and just for a moment or two the serried row of boys on a lower level, looking up, and the double line of gowned staff on the platform, faced each other in the silent, hostile challenge which was derived from Merchant's brief warning. Then he left the stage, and was followed by the others, the swirl of movement watched closely by us all.

Naughton said to me: 'What was all that about?' He was a prefect, one who enjoyed authority. He was good at work, too, and ambitious.

'The boys he beat for drinking.'

'But why did he mention it? The fuss last term was kept fairly quiet, wasn't it? Not many would know what he meant.' He was genuinely bewildered.

I saw in it an oblique reference to Patterson, as though Merchant wished to introduce a faint but persistent tension not otherwise called for by the clean slate of term's beginning. But I saw no point in discussing so obscure an aspect with Naughton just then, though of all the boys closest to me at the top of the school, he was the most obvious for that kind of debate. 'It's Merchant's way of doing things,' I said. 'Keeps everyone on their toes.'

'A bit sinister?'

'Effective.'

II

Later that first day we had a prefects' meeting. Like assembly the occasion was part of the ritual by which the machinery of the corporate life of the school was set in motion once again. No longer indifferent to such processes, of which I had once moved through Coppinger in blissful ignorance, I noted with care the precision with which Merchant handled detail and set in motion certain tests and checks by which our performances as adjutants to his larger design were monitored and measured. He allocated responsibilities, he made demands on our allegiance, he endeavoured to define and absorb our loyalty.

He told Danby at the end that he wanted to see him later, after he had prepared certain lists, and he then asked me to remain behind. When the others had left, and the door was closed, he said to me: 'Have things gone well so far with Mr Patterson?' I had expected some quite different inquiry,

159

about my work, or examinations, and was puzzled by this repeat of a query that belonged to an earlier and more tentative period, closer to the time I had been moved to Patterson's house. It seemed a bit out of place now.

'Yes, sir,' I said.

He looked at me with an expression of inquiry, inviting some elaboration. 'There have been no difficulties?' he said eventually.

'No, sir.'

'And you get on?'

I nodded.

'You're very non-committal.'

'Sir?' I filled my voice and my face with simulated evidence of my bewilderment.

'You seem to have become rather closed in on yourself of late. As if the burden of the house, together with your school duties, was bearing down too heavily. It made me wonder if there was something on your mind. It reminded me that we haven't had a proper talk for a long time.'

I thought of the times when these words, or a similar formulation, would have set off presentiments of doom. Even now there were faint vibrations of uncertainty. I looked at him and considered as swiftly as I could, and with a rational objectivity that had to range across several possibilities, the likely intention of his mind.

'I think at this stage in the term, sir, everything's all right.'

He took what I had meant as a witticism rather coldly.

'I'm glad to hear that. Pull over a chair.'

I was a reluctant recipient of this friendliness. I looked for a moment at him, where he sat behind his large desk, the mullioned windows behind him placing his face in slight shadow. From the semi-circle of chairs on which the prefects had sat I selected one and drew it closer to the desk. Then I sat down.

'You've been a credit to Mr Patterson since you moved over.'

'Thank you, sir.'

160

'It must have been difficult at times?'

'It's a good house.'

'But Mr Patterson is not the same kind of housemaster as your old one, Mr Forrest.'

I didn't know whether to shake or nod my head. 'They're alike in some ways, sir. Different in others.'

'But you rub along?' He was leaning forward. He had raised his pale expressive hands into a fragile, cathedral-like structure of stiff fingers and knuckles, the pointed forefingers making an inverted vee which, after he had asked the question, he pressed against his pursed lips.

'It's the boys that matter,' I said. 'In the house I mean.'

He nodded slowly, absently, his lips still against the tops of his forefingers. 'Of course,' he said. 'It's the boys. And they're a good bunch. None involved in last term's troubles?'

'Not that we know of,' I said, and smiled. It was a trifle sycophantic, the attitude of mind into which his question had manoeuvred me, and I determined on asserting my independence from such base collusion.

'Skinner a handful?'

I shook my head. 'Skinner's all right,' I said. It was an automatic defence of myself rather than of Skinner, who was increasingly a handful, and, to have come to the specific notice of Merchant, could not have been otherwise. Looking at him I could see the doubt in his eyes.

'And there's no one else making life difficult?'

There flashed through my mind the idea that I should offer up some name or other from those within the house as a form of sacrifice to Merchant, so that he should not feel that I was blocking too completely his obvious attempts to be helpfully involved on my behalf. And the mad thought suggested itself that I should name Wickham, not as a perversely cruel form of betrayal—since it would immediately bring upon Wickham unwanted and undeserved attention—but simply in order to confuse the trail of Merchant's persistent curiosity, which had me sitting there in front of him still not clear as to why we were going through this tedious catechism. And the thought of this bizarre line of action made me smile inwardly. Fortunately, no vestige of my odd line of thought appeared on my face, and my eyes, fixed steadfastly on him, had learnt in the long years of our association sufficient of his skill to be emotionally just as opaque. Only with the eventual realisation that he was expecting an answer did I shake my head.

'Good,' he said. He repeated it: 'Good. I'm glad.' He moved his hand down from his face, adjusting the papers and books on his uncharacteristically crowded desk. 'You, of all boys this term, need a clear run at your work above everything else. You can't cut off completely your responsibilities as head of your house and the second senior prefect. But you don't want any special difficulties, do you?'

'No, sir.'

He looked sideways across the room at a portrait in oils. It was one of the Llewelyns, a woman of stern appearance, painted in the 1860s, dressed in a house bonnet of a puritan cut.

'And how does Patterson cope with it all?' It was said as an afterthought. Or so it seemed.

'I think he finds it hard going at times.' I said it almost unthinkingly. I was puzzled, even as the words came out, that Merchant had not called him 'Mr Patterson'.

Merchant had fixed on me a baleful, unwinking stare. 'Hard going?' he said.

'Well...' I stumbled, trying to think ahead.

'Yes?' Lynx-like, his eyes were fixed. He seemed ready to spring.

'He... Mr Patterson seems tired at times. I'm sure it's nothing, sir, just his age.'

'Hard going? Tired? Do you know how old your housemaster is?'

Hopeless about age as we are at that time in our lives, I was further confused by the intensity of Merchant's interest. 'I... I suppose he's in his fifties... don't really know.'

'And surely he gets help from Mr Bennett, doesn't he?'

162

'Yes, sir. He does.'

He seemed not to hear me. 'I mean, he's your house tutor, isn't he? He visits. He's often there, isn't he? In the house?'

I couldn't understand why he was repeating the questions. 'Well,' I said, 'it's his duty. He comes—'

Again he swept aside my reply. 'He likes coming, surely. He likes being in the house. It's not just duty.'

I shook my head.

'And when he comes, does he spend time with you? Working?'

'A bit, sir. Yes.'

'Not a lot? You're his star pupil. That's what he tells me.' The smile was fleeting and wintry, incidental to the main drive of his thought.

'Well, there are other things.'

'You mean house duties, of course.'

I nodded.

'And do they get on together?'

I looked blankly at him. Surely he wasn't asking me about Mrs Patterson and Bennett?

'I said, 'Who, sir?'

'Why, Bennett and Patterson, of course. Who did you think I meant?'

I shook my head but did not answer.

He paused, and seemed to be regrouping his thoughts. He was staring hard at me, and his look made me answer the question: 'Yes, sir. They get on very well.'

'I'm glad to hear that.' His voice relaxed again; became almost silken in its texture. 'It's important for a house that the tutor should feel completely at home in it. We could always do with more staff. We're not a rich school. It's important that everything goes smoothly, that everyone plays his full part. I think you realise that, don't you?'

I nodded.

Merchant said to me: 'You had to be on your own. You realise that, don't you? We were not sending in a rescue party. Just one boy, who had to be capable of taking over.'

163

I nodded my assent.

He seemed not to be aware of me, although his eyes were fixed on mine. 'We needed someone strong enough,' he said, and paused. And I thought he would look down, or away, and relieve me of the chilly expectation that hovered in his eyes. But he did not. 'And loyal,' he said, the tone in his voice sepulchral. 'We knew we could trust you.'

No man I had known in my life up to that point spoke with less legitimacy of any collective expectation than Merchant, whose autocratic hand was governed by an egotism that brooked little interference from anyone. And to talk of 'We' merely underlined this fact. There *was* no 'we'; it was he alone who had dictated all the action, who had plucked me from Forrest's house, handed me over to Patterson, and persuaded me that the course of responsibility would give added purpose, direction and accomplishment to my days at Coppinger. And I had believed him. How could I have done otherwise? Even though conscious, at the time, of a certain deception in the air, and accepting, it now seemed wrongly, that the motivation had been Patterson's when a willing part had also been played by Forrest, I had seized on the recognition of my talent at face value, and had become a willing vehicle of Merchant's design.

He spoke now without feeling, his tone mechanical and passionless: 'Your loyalty must be unstinting, unqualified. Loyalty to the school matters greatly. You realise that, don't you?'

Again I nodded. The flashes of tension in the air were fading. But I was still nervous of some further, hidden question he was holding in readiness for the moment of relaxation which he seemed now to be consciously encouraging.

'You'll come to me,' he said, 'if there's anything? Any trouble in the house? Any difficulty?'

'I don't expect there will be, sir.'

'I want to know.'

'Yes, sir,' I said.

164

'Everything. You understand? Your duty is to the school. First and foremost, that's it.'

Again I nodded. Then I said, 'I do have to concentrate on work, sir. There's the scholarship, and—'

'Yes, of course, of course.' The tone softened again. 'Your work comes first. Your results must bring credit to Coppinger. We shall all be watching you in that regard.' It was a perfunctory gesture towards possible academic achievement, something which was out of the ordinary to him as to everyone else. Having said it, and paused long enough to give indeed the kind of expectant stare which seemed to him appropriate, he went on: 'But if you do run into difficulties, no matter what, boys in your house, in the school, problems with staff, anything, you'll come and see me. Is that clear?'

'Yes, sir.' I was unnerved by his choice of phrase, the order clarified by the question.

'That'll be all,' he said.

I got up and went to the door.

'Oh,' he said, and I turned. 'Don't mention this to any other boy. This chat of ours. It's strictly between us. And nothing of it to Mr Patterson.'

III

One adjusted quickly enough to the beginning of each term, the flurry of activity sweeping boys and staff forward together in a multitude of different directions which nevertheless had a common purpose and a common goal. But no time of year had quite the impact at Coppinger as those first days back at the end of April or in early May. In the month of absence Nature did more then than was possible in either of the other two holiday breaks which so firmly severed our school and home lives. And we came back to a prodigious lushness and growth which seemed everywhere to echo the strange mixture of diversity and common purpose in the pursuits and ambitions of the

165

school's inmates. We left, as often as not, in a late winter atmosphere of cold and blustery winds coming in at us from the east, from the flatness of Northamptonshire; we returned to the soft uncertainty of prevailing winds which blew up the Severn Estuary and came on across the whole of Gloucestershire, taking their tentative and benevolent character from the succession of wolds broken up by warm and comfortable valleys. And even in the uncertainty of that particular year, which was to become worse rather than better, a wash-out of a summer in fact, those early days in May, the grass thick and fresh and intensely green, the leaves on the trees waxy and lemony with growth and moisture, intensified for me the sense of climax and fulfilment.

On the night of the practice I walked up from the house towards Main School with Wickham. We were the only two boys in Patterson's house who took part in Parker's madrigal group, a more select choice of ten from the choir, and I felt a perversity in keeping on with this one diversion when I had dropped virtually every other activity in the interest of work. Patterson, who frowned on it in my case, was prepared to tolerate it in Wickham's because the younger boy was developing into a capable bowler and a reasonably sound batsman, and was clearly seen by our housemaster as a serious and potentially vital element in winning the house cricket. This redeemed his pursuit of music, more or less. Even so, in seeking permission after prep to leave the house for the hour or more during which Parker would want us, he managed to indicate a vague disfavour towards both of us, and our stubborn determination to go and chant English madrigals.

'Is it that he doesn't like Parker?' Wickham said.

'He has nothing against Parker.'

'Us?' He looked sideways at me as we walked.

'What would he have against us?'

'Well, he moved me back down again after you moved me up.'

'That was nothing,' I said. I paused to pull a piece of grass from the bank beside the road. In order to stop him walking on I asked: 'Did you mind?'

He shrugged. 'Not much. I'll move up next term.'

'I minded,' I said.

He looked at me. 'Why?'

'Just did.'

'Him not backing you up? After you'd done it?'

'If you like, Master Wickham. If you like.' It was said with a hint of sarcasm, a protective folding over of a device, 'Master', that distanced him from me at a point that touched me more closely than I wanted to admit, and for reasons some of which worried me.

'David?' he said. The questioning note in his voice was accompanied by a raising of the eyebrows. We had been over this territory before; it concerned recognition.

'I'm sorry.'

'You don't have to be.'

'David.'

'That's better.' Then he laughed. 'Did you want to say something?'

'I did. Yes.'

'Well, go on then.'

'I wanted to ask you which you thought was best, of the madrigals.' This was not what I wanted to ask him, and I regretted the gauche flatness of the question immediately.

He just shrugged his shoulders.

'David?' Real names are real. It was as though we could not see each other: I was calling out in a darkened room, testing the air, measuring the resonance, setting up a tension between us. 'I wish I could write like some of these people.'

'What people?' he said.

'Campion, Dowland, you know.'

'Oh, those!'

'Don't you think what they do is good?'

'I don't really think about what they write. I just sing it.'

167

'Don't you like English?'

'It's okay.'

I felt I had crossed a patch of emotional gravel, trying not to crunch the small pieces against one another, thereby drawing attention to myself, but knowing also, wilfully knowing, that it was impossible.

'The thing is, you're serious about it. So is Mr Bennett. It's easy to see that. With us it's all clause analysis, parsing.' He said it disdainfully. I could not share in the dismissal. It all seemed worthwhile to me.

'Does our housemaster teach you?'

'Yes.'

'What's he like?'

'Don't you have him?'

'No. Haven't for two years.'

'He's tricky, isn't he? He doesn't like teaching.'

Wickham turned his face towards me as he walked, kicking occasionally at the grass verge. The phrase was one at that time which was in vogue, giving added and eccentric meaning to an epithet which otherwise might have seemed quite puzzling. For Patterson was straightforward in most things to the point of simplicity.

'He thinks you're too young. For the senior dorm.'

'And am I?'

I smiled at him. 'Yes.'

'But you wanted me to move up?'

'Yes.'

I confess there was a restrained fervour in my response, and we were silent for a while. We had come out from the group of houses, which were relatively close, and interspersed with trees and vegetation, to the more open space of playing fields and mown grass which surrounded Main School. Ahead of us were other boys of the small group then assembling, and Parker's battered Morris Ten already stood on the gravel.

'Do you get on with Archer?' Wickham said.

'Why do you ask?'

168

'He's the best of the prefects in the house. I just wondered.'

'He's all right,' I said. 'He's good. He's reliable.'

'Not that!' Wickham said. 'I meant just as a friend. Someone to talk to.'

'I don't talk to him that much. Keeps himself to himself.'

'You do the same.'

I shrugged. At eighteen it is possible to be uncertain in a way that does not trouble us at an earlier stage in our growing up. Drawing near to the school building as we then were, and to other singers bent on the same purpose as ourselves, I was silenced by impending restraints, and thought to myself that if we were alone for longer, some endless walk along summer laneways, I might be able to explain and soften for Wickham the image he had of my keeping self to self. That I had this wish to explain must itself, now, explain things which then I could not frame into words. I put my hand on his shoulder but he shrugged it away, and we entered the school building in silence.

IV

'It must be perfect,' Parker said. He touched, just once, the chord of four notes. He was standing, his foot pushed awkwardly under the piano to press down the soft pedal. He was making it difficult for us, and his face as he looked across seemed to be agonising over the efforts we were making to pick out our own notes. Then he raised his hands, and, holding them close together, brought us in, the miniature scale on which he conducted transferring into ourselves the burden of perfection he had placed upon us. We were not perfect, of course. But Parker had brought us already to a measure of perfection, and led us through the range of music so far learnt for the recital without any major difficulty. What he led us into, unashamedly, was a small and enchanted world of springtime and tears, of streams and

169

fountains, of love and rejection. Was it any less real, because
it isolated and then intensified extremes of feeling? Was it
precious, or true? ('Touch not, proud hands, lest you her
anger move'). It was so intense a world; as well as being
enchanted, one of apophthegm and epigram, it suited the
vague and uncertain pressures, multiple and at times
forbidding, which seemed, in that summer, to weigh down
upon me. One wanted them to weigh down. One sought, and
did not find, the circumstance for weeping. ('Alas, these your
springtides, methinks, increase not.')

For Parker, of course, it was the music. Casually, at times
a trifle embarrassed, he would refer to some phrase, and tell
us to think of the words, not knowing, I suppose, what
mixed responses he could engender in our minds. But within
the ritual of the harmonies he was safe.

Perhaps I wrong him. He was, to us, an ageing bachelor;
and I had grown familiar with his idiosyncracies, singing for
him as treble, alto, and now bass. It may not have been
embarrassment, solely the restraints which experience had
taught him were wise. He said: 'I have something new for
you.' He turned to a pile of music which he had on the
piano, and began searching through. We relaxed. We were a
group of fourteen or fifteen. Jennings, beside me, was the
other bass. A year younger, he was now a house prefect with
the Gaffer, in my old house. We had nothing to say to each
other. Instead, I watched Wickham where he leaned over to
make some joke with another treble.

'This is for five voices,' Parker said. 'We need to split the
altos.' He gave the music to one of the trebles and divided
the altos. It was towards the end of the practice, and, much
as we enjoyed it, a certain fatigue had descended on us all. I
read through the words of 'The Silver Swan' not really
comprehending their meaning; and I listened to the music as
Parker played it through, two or three times, commenting on
and repeating certain dissonances, without really absorbing
the essence of it.

'We shall end with this,' he said. He was playing as he

170

spoke. I sensed in his voice a special feeling for the music which made me look more closely at it. But I had yet to find the key to it, and the measured, sombre rhythm seemed curiously ordinary, the poignancy of death elusive, the meanings obscure.

He started the trebles on their part, and they seemed to come to it easily enough. He sang himself the bass line, and that brought some of us in. But he was really just launching the music among us, and there was no endeavour to pick out the intermediate parts. What was curious to me was the almost casual certainty with which the trebles, Wickham particularly, descended on their line of music, absorbing straightaway the essentials: melody, phrasing, the poignant arching of sound conveyed in the four notes which accompany 'Farewell all joys.'

Afterwards, walking back, I said to Wickham. 'You're silent. You're like the swan. What do *you* think? I tell you my thoughts. You're good enough to listen. I'm really grateful for that. But you don't express an opinion. Yourself, I mean.'

I felt that I was floundering towards a confessional status that I would not have admitted to anyone else. Not Philpotts, not Mr Porphyry, not my brother, not Melanie—why then towards him? The truth is, I could not have helped myself. There was within me an urge to turn his heart towards me, make him react, force him to swerve in the determined trajectory of his own actions, and in order to achieve this I had to lay before him evidence of my concern, my willingness to open the secrets of my heart to him.

I waited to learn the secrets of his.

'I dunno,' he said. 'I don't attach much importance to it.' He laughed. It was a lilting, silvery sound. Then he looked at me. 'You take it all too seriously.'

171

Chapter Eight

I

Bennett sculpted the air in front of him with his hands. They were powerful and expressive, and he used them as a visible cradle for his thoughts. Hunched forward, his hands held up, the fingers spread, he was filled with a vitality, a passion, which gave life to everything on which his mind touched. Even now, as we sat, the two of us either side of him, Danby and myself, in a moment of silence as Bennett paused and searched for the words that would express the abbreviated content of the particular moment of revision through which we were moving, his two hands, supported on his elbows, clawlike and vital in appearance, held us in tense anticipation of wisdom.

'You will soon look for universal things,' he said. 'You must understand it like that. This whole passage in the poem is another echo of the wonder he felt when he saw that huge peak, black and huge, bearing down on him. But he's not responding to the experience: he's responding to himself having the experience.' He looked at Danby, then at me. His face was expressive of concern, doubt, tension, inquiry. Had we understood? Did we grasp the grandeur of this mind whose growth was our study? He put his hands flat down on the library table, either side of the open book from which he had been reading. He looked down at them, as though inspecting them for blemishes. They were broad, almost coarse, the hair, black on them, giving a certain ominous rude appearance to their palpable strength. Then he looked up at us again, his face relaxing from the intensity of what he had said and thought.

I asked him: What are the "universal things"?'

'The nature of life. The redemptive urge in the human spirit. Changing men's hearts.' He said these things almost dismissively. It was not that he did not understand them. It was just that they were not for him.

Danby said: 'Is this where the idea of pantheism comes from?'

Bennett looked at him, his eyebrows raised into a frown, his eyes themselves inviting him to go on.

'Well, everything matters, doesn't it? I mean, nothing really big happens to him. It's not like Byron or Shelley. It's not like Coleridge. It's so ordinary. It could be us. We could do any of those things. But Wordsworth makes it sound spiritual.'

'It is spiritual,' I said.

Bennett looked at me. 'Why?'

'Well, it's happening to his spirit. It's not the events that matter. It's not just thinking about them, either. It's if he can take your breath away.'

'And can he? Does he?' He stared at me this time, the hand nearest to me raised in the air again, the fingers spread, the thumb and the first two more open than the others, ready to pull from my brain the idea that was growing there, an uncertain grasp of passion.

I gasped with nervous amusement. 'Well, yes, he does.' I paused. He stared at me, waiting. 'That bit you just read. I mean, it's religious, isn't it? He's waiting for some call, some sign. He's like Saul.'

Bennett looked at me. A faint smile appeared on his face. He turned to Danby. 'Do you agree?'

'Not exactly. He is waiting. But it's not for any sign. It's just for everything to make sense.'

'Perpetual logic?'

173

'Yes.'

'But it's more than that,' I said. 'He has to do something with it when he understands it, when it makes sense.'

'I suggest you read it over in that light,' Bennett said. 'You've already absorbed the experiences. They strike one first, are most memorable.' He was hunched forward over his book, his elbows on the table, his fists clenched close to his chin. 'But what you must look for—' he paused, and gradually opened his hands. The fingers were held stiff and straight and all together, at right angles to his palms, so that the two hands, touching together, made a box-shaped cradle in front of his face into which he stared, as though wishing to deposit there the collective substance of his teaching. 'What you must look for is the commentary he gives of his own mind's reaction to that perpetual logic. He wants to tell us how it happened, how he became a poet.' He folded the fingers down. Then he looked at his watch. 'We've three minutes. Very quickly, I think for next time we must get to grips with the twentieth-century poets. We've been ages on Wordsworth. Didn't we start with him? After your "O" levels? I suggest you each deal with a different aspect of Eliot. Here are three questions. It will be an interesting exercise in discipline to see which you leave out, which you do. But you mustn't do the same.'

'Will it do in note form?'

He nodded. 'At this stage, yes. But be sure and go on with the other work. You've little time. You've got to bring everything forward.' He gave us, separately, two sheets with notes and questions.

I said to him: 'Will you excuse me? I have to do duty?'

I left the library to ring the bell. Danby began to pack up his books. They did not speak. Danby was always the same. When the lesson ended, he stopped; it was mechanical, like an engine. I thought at times it annoyed Bennett, yet in his turn he had, as a teacher, a certain detachment, a neutrality; he only forced the pace in response to demand. By that late stage, of course, we were familiar with the pattern of his

174

teaching, familiar with each other as well. Yet I could still wonder at the diversity with which he wrenched at Wordsworth, to whom we had gone back in our revision: soul, mind, record of experience.

When I returned to the library Danby had gone, but Bennett's books were still on the table. He was in front of one of the windows looking out over the green fields.

I sat down again in my place and read over the notes he had given us. Danby had gone to a class in science, which I did not take. I had a free class and intended staying on in the library, a room in which, increasingly, I chose to work. I had not realised that Bennett also was free. He came over to the table. 'You've private study, have you?'

I nodded.

'You'll have to work extremely hard for the college entrance you're taking, not to mention the scholarship. You realise that, don't you?'

I nodded again.

'You'd best let house affairs take their own course. Leave things to Archer. The same goes for the school.'

'But I can't really do that, Mr Bennett.'

'They don't compare in importance, you know.'

'But I'm head of the house. I have a duty to Mr Patterson.' I looked directly at him as I spoke, expecting some kind of reaction to the name, anticipating that he might flinch or in some other way betray a detail of the emotion the name should conjure up. He must have known that I was not unaware of the general trend of his feelings, though he could not possibly have known the extent of my knowledge.

'What exactly do you owe him? He'll muddle through whatever happens. But you won't have this chance again.' He was leaning on the table now, looking down at me. 'You should cut out all but the bare essentials, and concentrate on work. How long have you?'

'Seven weeks.'

'And you want it, don't you? Oxford?'

'Yes.'

'You're doing these madrigals? With Parker?'

I nodded.

'Does it take up much time?'

'Not much. It's just singing. I have to have some time off!'

He laughed. 'I know. Madrigals. I couldn't sing a note.'

I frowned. 'There's one madrigal we're singing, by Orlando Gibbons. We've practised it two or three times, and it's very good. It's about a swan, singing in the hour of its death. Is that an Elizabethan idea?'

He laughed. 'More like Hollywood. Swan Song. Bette Davis. Jean Harlow. The great comeback.'

'But seriously?'

'No, it goes back. I don't know how far. Probably to Homer. Most good things do. He was known as the Swan of Meander.'

'Meander?'

'A river.'

'I never knew!'

He stood up straight, raising his hands from the table and clenching his fists in front of his body. 'Is there anything else on your mind?'

'There's just that,' I said, 'getting my exams. Getting in.'

He looked, rather than spoke, his question. The quizzical uncertainty of his eyes made him distant from me, so that I hesitated in the wish I had to confide further in him. I wanted so to confide, and there was in Bennett, in part of his makeup as I understood it, a hard, granite-like sense of purpose untrammelled by conventional restraint. He would probably give good counsel. Unfortunately, there was the blurring of this by his too-close involvement in precisely that area that troubled me. If I was troubled by Patterson, and the faint feelings of distrust between us, I could reasonably assume that, for very different reasons, Bennett was also, and to raise questions with him about how I felt might all too easily be misconstrued.

The same expectation of misunderstanding stopped me

176

from mentioning love and affection, even in abstract or poetic or philosophic terms, though there burned within me a curiosity about my own feelings for Wickham which the unconventional nature of Bennett's emotional life encouraged me to think would make him sympathetic. Yet he could take, in the wrong way entirely, any mention of feelings where the details were imprecise. And how could I possibly be precise?

I knew how I felt, but could not measure the legitimacy of that feeling. Nor could I easily talk about it. Perhaps never talk about it at all. Did Bennett read my thoughts? He said: 'You've had some trouble over Wickham, haven't you? About his seniority in the house? Whether he should move up?'

'It's nothing really,' I said. 'I made a mistake. Did Pat—. Did Mr Patterson tell you?'

He paused. His expression was thoughtful. 'It's not unreasonable that I should know the day to day goings on in the house.' He paused again. 'As your house tutor.' He added it as an afterthought.

'Yes,' I said. 'But it wasn't exactly goings on.' I smiled ruefully at him, and wondered whether he could possibly have more to say on the subject. I sensed within myself the vague and imprecise resentment against Mr Patterson, who I thought to be a man of limited sensitivity, spilling over to affect my feelings for Bennett, whose sensitivities, in a variety of directions, emotional and intellectual, I knew to be worthy of respect. Yet even this did not prevent me from beginning the process of erecting safeguards against any further intrusion by him into the way I felt and the things I did. That he so intended became apparent when, turning away, he asked me: 'You're fond of Wickham, aren't you?'

'Yes.' I said it more sharply than I intended. There was nothing to add.

He waited for me to say more.

School had settled down again; there was an infinite stillness, spread out, through the windows, and across the sunlit fields. In the untroubled air of the library, scented by many books, I felt at ease with Bennett, curious at his question. Yet at the same time coolly distant from him.

His next comment was a stepping back. 'He's able,' Bennett said. 'Constable's his form master and says he'll get into university. Did you know that?'

'No,' I said. It annoyed me more that I was not better informed on so crucial an issue as Wickham's intellectual potential. If I was fond of him I should have known this about him. 'He has to take some kind of medicine,' I said. 'All the time. Pills. He doesn't like it. Do you know what's wrong with him, sir?' I spoke with slow deliberation, and watched Bennett where he stood, half turned away from me, staring down the length of the library.

Without turning he just said 'Yes. I do know. He suffers from epilepsy. I probably shouldn't tell you. It may well be he doesn't know himself. So you keep it to yourself. Understand?' He stopped. He was frowning.

I nodded. The word itself meant little to me, but the possibility of it being something I shouldn't know, and perhaps something which Wickham didn't know about himself either, made me more curious. Involuntarily, I turned towards the row of broadbacked volumes of the Encyclopaedia Britannica which lined a shelf nearby.

Bennett turned back towards me, slowly, reflectively. He was holding the fingers of one hand in the other, and gently rubbing with the palm of one hand across the extended joints of the other. He was looking down at the finger nails and the flat, familiar terrain of vital, expressive flesh. Then he glanced at me. 'You will give everything to your work, won't you? Everything. You don't have room for mistakes. You don't have time to spare. Not really for anything.'

II

I sat on in the library after he had left, and in my mind I

attempted to reconstruct what had happened between us. It was not difficult. Predominant before me was his physical image; like a ghost it filled the room, so that wherever in my mind's eye I looked, I saw him standing, solid, alert, aggressive, his face with a questioning expression on it, his hands held as they had been during his interrogation. I was transfixed by his vitality. He was so sure. He knew about himself. He knew what he wanted. He wanted Mrs Patterson. The presence of Mr Patterson in the world did not deflect him.

The environment, surely one of the most difficult within which to pursue a love affair, did not deflect him either. And all of this was encompassed by his work. He taught with the same sureness. There was a fixed velocity which contained no sentiment, no real revelation of self, and no preference, either where subject was concerned, or pupil. He was as self-contained as a meteor, responsive only to some natural law, like gravity, which energised him and gave him his remarkable compulsion.

That he should have departed from it, or reapplied it in so uncharacteristically personal a way as he had done with me, raising but not resolving the 'question' of Wickham, and the diversifying of my energy and resources, seemed both strange and natural. It was strange because so personal; but natural because his concern could be narrowed down to one issue only, my work. The simplicity of his approach absolved him from any charge of intrusiveness, and left intact my admiration for him. At the same time it left me even more puzzled and bewildered. I could not easily see how to achieve the simple objective he had given me. I recognised that it was right. At the same time I felt overwhelmed by duty, affection, commitment, the rich stream of events.

I think that I did not, at that time, quite put into thoughts and words any conscious rejection of the blinding singleness of purpose implied in what he had said. Yet by my actions, then and there, subconsciously I was taking another path. In

179

the quietude of the middle of that period, with silent learning going on all round me, with Danby in another room somewhere absorbing equations or quantities, with classes filled with people hurrying on towards tests and challenges of one sort or another, in all of which singleness of purpose was an overriding condition, I spent the rest of that class endeavouring to finish the writing of a sonnet which might express for me the feelings I had about Wickham, a sonnet for which I had already assembled various portions and ideas, rhymes and phrases.

I can pretend that he was incidental to those first inner strivings of the soul towards an understanding of itself, and that it was the exercise in self-knowledge that mattered. Not so. My uncertain thoughts, weighing Bennett's words against my unco-ordinated feelings, centred upon Wickham; and further words and phrases came into my head at his remembered smile, turn of phrase, recollected laughter in sunlight. I saw, no, heard him singing. Perhaps saw and heard myself. And from the experience, so secret, so essential to that last soft fragrant Maytime at Coppinger, I assembled finally the stilted words and artificial phrases of what in retrospect must seem like some kind of memorial, perhaps just to a state of mind.

For truth's sake, and mindful of their youthful imperfections, I give them here, not from some kind of inverted vanity, but because they are part of my story. Indeed, they might even be said to have acted as the pivot upon which all the events from this point onward swung in that dizzying trajectory which brought to an end my last term at the school. I did not, for one moment, at least consciously, intend Wickham to have the poem. Not at that stage. And there were many drafts. But, as I wrote it then, I now present it:

> O, little swan, whose voice so resolute
> Determines now the purpose of my day,
> Kindles its start, awakes the morning flute,

Has certainty, as has the sun's first ray;
Respond, with mercy to my honest doubt,
My sense of moving blindfold through the dawn,
My solitary wanderings about,
My lonely questioning each naked morn.
I seek the simple purpose you possess,
Youth's certitude, its dreams, its urgency;
While I find work and words a wilderness,
A barricade against my potency;
So help me, little swan, and do your part;
Respond, reply, and so release my heart.

Poets struggle after subject matter. At times they wrestle with themes as a sailor might endeavour to gain control of a billowing sail in a storm in order to reef it, and then turn it to his purposes. But mostly the spirit is becalmed, and the mind's sail flaps in an uncertain breeze, waiting for inspiration. For me, then, this was not the case. My inadequacies were technical ones, or those of experience and depth of understanding. What was real was the gust of feeling, curving me into the wind, carrying me forward. I can even remember the sheet of blue, deckle-edged paper on which I so carefully wrote out the fair copy, and then folded it, putting it into a matching envelope, and tucking it inside a leather writing case which I carried around with my books.

As I have said, I had no clear idea of giving it to Wickham, or even of showing it to him. But in that curious way words have, the verbal commitment of intense thought to intense, if at times awkward, form, conditioned my reflexes, and began to shape the next and fateful cycle of my acts.

III

'Do you ever see that scholarship bloke? Porphyry?' Archer said. He was sitting on the radiator in front of the window of the small room which served us as a prefects' study.

'Why do you ask?'

'Just wondered.'

'I do a bit. Off and on.'

'Do you have to do anything? Or is it just you see him, like, because you want to?'

'He takes an interest. He writes to me occasionally. He's all right. He's really nice.' I felt within me faint surgings of guilt. I should have written; there were unanswered letters, a stony residue of indifference.

'You'd wonder, really,' Archer went on, 'at the growing numbers. Each year, and another one added. It must be like being a godfather, adding on new recruits and not forgetting the old ones like you.'

It seemed an odd but appropriate likeness, and I stared at Archer, questioning his curiosity with my eyes.

'Were you ever in for it?' I asked.

'Not that I've heard,' he said. 'What about this year? Have *you* heard? Does Mr Porphyry mention it to you?'

I shook my head. 'There'll be somebody chosen'.

'Who do you think?'

'Why?'

'I'd never get it, would I? Wouldn't mind, though. You had a good time, didn't you?'

'It was all right.' The memory was faintly disjointed, and not altogether unclouded.

'When does Merchant tell people who are in for it?'

'Around now.'

'I'll tell you something,' Archer said, and he waited, looking up at me across the room from where he sat.

And I said, 'Yes?'

'I'll never forget the day you got the scholarship.'

'Oh?' I said.

'Yes.'

We stared at each other. His eyes were shining with an inner excitement. I could not remember anything about the occasion or how Archer came into it at all.

'I don't remember—' I began.

'I've never told anyone,' he said. 'I had to see Merchant. Straight after you. *You* came and told me he wanted me. I was frightened. Didn't know what it was. And he was all friendly, the way he makes you uncertain, expecting the worst. And the first thing he told me was what he'd just told you, that you were the new Porphyry scholar. That's how I remember.'

He stopped again and seemed to be thinking to himself.

'So why do you remember?' I said.

He looked strangely embarrassed. Then he said: 'Because Merchant told me that day that my mother had married again.'

'*Merchant* told you?' I said. 'Why didn't your mother?'

'She just didn't.'

'But *Merchant*?' Not even old Patterson?'

He shook his head. 'I've never told anyone. Never.'

'Did your mother write to you?'

He shook his head again. 'Nope.'

'Not even later?'

He looked up at me and gave a slight shrug of the shoulders, smiling almost apologetically on her behalf. 'Couldn't bring herself to, I suppose.'

'And what happened after?'

He frowned. 'After?'

'Well, do you see her?'

He shook his head. 'It was all right. It worked out, really.'

'Worked out?' I said it gently. My curiosity was contained by feelings of sensitivity over so extraordinary an event as the casual loss of a mother.

'Well, my father. I go to him now. It's better.'

'And he's all right?'

'Oh, yes. He's okay. We get on, him and me.'

I had still not fathomed Archer's position; but I could not think of further questions. 'I hope you get it. It is worth having.'

'I hope so, too.'

For a moment I was silent. The thought of Archer's life

183

being founded on an insecurity not dissimilar from my own had not occurred to me before. The unique nature of my own experience was watered down by this new piece of knowledge. At the same time, sustaining the analogy, the watering gave life to new seed: I felt a surge of compassion for him. We were alike. But then, were we not all alike? And if Archer, then others as well?

I was staring down at my fingers. Without looking up, I said: 'What's the position now?'

'What do you mean?'

'I'm only asking because you mention it.'

'I know that. I don't mind you knowing. But I don't understand what you mean.'

'Well, if you want the scholarship there has to be a reason. You know, you have to deser—' I stopped short and looked up at him.

'You mean I have to be good? Or things at home have to be bad?'

I laughed then. 'I wasn't very good. And things weren't very bad for me. Not that I remember. I mean, my father had married again. And it didn't last. There was all that.' I think at that time I did not allow myself to remember very much. And probably I was selective as well.

'My old man's okay. He won't marry again. I get on all right with him.'

'And your mother?'

'I don't see 'er no more.' He smiled at me. Then he corrected himself, and in stilted, sombre words he almost intoned at me: 'I do not see my mother any more.'

'What was Merchant like when he told you? Was he all right?' I could not visualise the exchange. Yet at the same time, given the possible choice facing Archer, I could see that Merchant's sympathies might be preferable to hearing the news from Patterson.

'Yea. He was. It's just that he said about you getting the scholarship, and that I had become a possible future candidate, that's why I remember.'

184

Looking at him I felt the urge to trade further confidence for his confidence. Yet the real cloud overhanging me at that time concerned Wickham, and my feelings for him, and there was no way in which I could speak about that. I stood silently in front of him, watching our conversation trickle away one-sidedly.

On a sudden inspiration I said: 'I met my sister last holidays. It was the first time in twelve years. She was adopted.'

'I never knew you had a sister.'

'It never came up.'

'How old is she?'

'Seventeen.'

'Have you a photo?'

I frowned, and shook my head.

'What's her name?'

'Melanie.'

'Melanie.' He repeated it.

On the slender basis of name, age, relationship, he was asserting, in his mind, an interest. It made me feel ashamed. Her sudden arrival, and equally sudden withdrawal from the events at the end of the Easter holiday had left an unsatisfactory longing in the air.

'I must write and ask her for a photo,' I said.

'Would she come up? Prize Day? Old Boys' Day?'

'Hardly appropriate.'

'Didn't you have a brother here?'

I looked at my watch. 'It's time for assembly,' I said. 'Bennett's here tonight. He's taking prayers. We'd better go.'

When the house was assembled I left Archer in charge and crossed the hallway to the Pattersons' living room. Through the heavy, panelled pitch-pine door I could hear the ripple of her laughter, and hesitated for a moment with my knuckles raised, longing within myself to know what had provoked her pleasure. Then I knocked.

'Come in!' she called.

I had learnt, by then, to step fully into the room rather than peering round the door, and I did so now, looking across at her in the window of the large and comfortable room. Her slim form was silhouetted against the pale green light which the evening sun shed upon the shrubs outside the window. She was half-sitting, half-leaning on the large and clumsy radiator, her arms straight down at her side, the heels of her hands close to her thighs. The pose deprived the front of her body of any shapeliness, the faintly crumpled folds of her summer frock falling in awkward, irregular confusion. And the light behind her concealed from me the expression in her eyes. I was conscious of a certain tension in the air. The laughter had stopped as soon as I had knocked, and now she waited, and watched me, as if it was to her that I wished to address myself.

I thought she would speak, if only to say hello, or to inquire, rhetorically, if I was looking for Bennett. And I waited in the doorway, imagining, in my expectation, a greater expenditure of time than in reality was taking place. Always, with her and with him together, there was this false atmosphere surrounding us, distorting time's flow, creating anticipations which were never realised. There was nothing between us to justify it. Yet my conviction that they were lovers, my knowledge about the actual declaration of love between them, overheard long before, had stimulated attitudes which in turn had created unnatural tension. I cannot know what they felt or said to each other. I believe, in the light of experience, that they would have detected in my youthful attitudes the suspicions which in later life I would have better concealed, and because of this would have acted a trifle strangely. They seemed then, as on previous occasions, vaguely to resent the way I stood, spoke, looked. Yet at that stage in the term I still retained an openness towards them and towards the relationship which I was convinced existed between them.

It was unquestionably that of lovers. I could see it in their eyes, their gestures, the occasionally overheard word. Across

186

the width of a cricket pitch the turn of her head, the raising of just one of his expressive hands, were noisy declarations of passion to me. And so obsessed was I becoming, not just with their relationship, but with the fact that I could discuss it with no one else, that I felt I was being drawn into it. I was part of their love, a spectre, an unwelcome participant, a solemn judge whose suspended deliberations were frozen in the air above their heads. Even as I stood there I felt, through my own eyes, that I was betraying the knowledge I had. I could not keep it from them. It was there. It was true. And it was a judgment. The thought flashed through my mind that perhaps they were both just a little frightened, and that this was in part contributing to the tension.

Bennett said: 'All ready?'

'Yes, sir.'

'I'll come, then.'

He did not move. I waited. They looked at each other, and I stared, first at her, then at him. The shrug he gave was very slight, the movement of his eyebrows no more than a faint flicker. But I noticed, and still stood without moving, waiting for him to get up and come. It was the way things were done. It was expected that I, as head boy in the house, would accompany him back in for prayers. And I was not disposed to let slip away a ritual that time had honoured. But as he got to his feet, and came across the room towards me, I felt the vague resentment deepen between us.

That it could exist side by side with his encouragement for my work and the forthcoming examinations was no real surprise to me; for there was in him a directness, an objectivity, quite at odds with the guarded, rounded 'performance' of other members of the staff who had been at Coppinger for longer, and had developed—as an actor might develop a particular part in a drama—a more self-conscious and circumspect representation of themselves. Bennett was not like that. And as he passed me in the doorway he gave me a direct, cool stare which seemed to be saying a number of things, most notably that he and I were close through the

meeting of our minds, over poetry, over exam tactics, over a
dreamed of university future: but that there it ended, and
should I seek to drive forward into other aspects of his life,
should I intrude into the affair of the heart about which I
ostensibly knew nothing, then beware.

'Are there notices?' he asked, over his shoulder, as we
crossed the hall.

'Just one, Mr Bennett.' I held a slip of paper in my hand.
'The head, Mr Merchant, wants to see three boys at eleven
tomorrow.'

'Oh. Who?'

I handed him the list. He stopped and looked down at the
three names. One of them was Skinner's. His features
softened, and his brow slightly perplexed he looked up at
me. 'Skinner? Again? What is it this time?'

I shook my head. 'I don't know.'

'Why do I have to announce it now? You haven't told
them?'

'Mr Merchant particularly said to get the names read out
at evening assembly.'

A slight curl of scorn was on his lips. For a moment he
said nothing. Then, more to himself than to me, he
murmured:

> 'There came a Tyrant, and with holy glee
> Thou fought'st against him.'

He looked into my eyes. Then he folded over the paper
and gave it back to me. 'You tell them at breakfast
tomorrow. And not before. Understand?'

'Sir?' My doubtful expression, my unwillingness to com-
ply, must have shown in my face.

'Think of them,' he said. 'Think of the other side.'

'I'll do what you say, Mr Bennett.' I put the slip of paper
into my top pocket. I felt a sudden stab of regard for him.
From beyond the open door there came the shuffle and
murmur of the attendant house.

188

IV

House assembly was at about nine each evening. Prayers
were followed by talk, games, relaxation. Bennett usually
stayed for an hour or so, on the evenings on which he was on
duty, and was popular, the object of query and argument.
Then, dormitory by dormitory, boys went off to bed.

There was ritual in everything. A pre-ordained pattern of
events governed nights and days. A change in the pattern,
however slight, either swiftly became part of the pattern or
was challenged and dropped. But there was no serious gap in
the grid of obligations through which we all made our way,
day after day, week after week. Vacancy of expectation, that
most odious burden of later life, was never part of those
days.

Bennett came to the house on Friday evenings when the
Pattersons went out. Once every month Patterson went on
his own somewhere. Unlike his predecessor, Bennett had
come on those evenings, and, as with everything else, had
established yet another aspect of the pattern to which we
were all ready to adhere. Natural at first, it was only later
that it seemed to have been constructed to facilitate his love
for Patterson's wife. I say 'seemed'. Speculative rumour in a
house full of boys is quickly generated. I saw it and heard it
from the unique position of certainty. Biding my time,
keeping my counsel, I was yet in possession of incontrovert-
ible fact. I had *heard*. I *knew*.

I see now that the conclusions which all too rapidly I
drew from that summer afternoon when Lytton and Pritchett and I had crouched in what seemed like a dugout,
listening to the sounds of the warfare of love from immediately above our heads, may have been precipitate. The speed
with which youth draws conclusions is not necessarily the
speed at which people live out their lives. Nevertheless,
what I knew was guessed or supposed by others.

189

Skinner said to me that evening, 'Mrs P.'s 'appy tonight.' He laughed into my face. We were in the washroom. His big, open, freckled face was splashed with water which he was about to dry off.

'Oh?' I said. 'Have you seen her this evening?'

His eyes went blank, the smile fading. 'Naw,' he said, and plunged his face into the towel, rubbing it vigorously. Emerging again, he added: 'But we know, don't we? Wiv Bennett 'ere it stands to reason, don't it?'

'Does it, Skinner? What stands to reason?'

He was threateningly close to me, big, clumsy, loose-limbed. And he was staring, open-mouthed, wanting me to endorse his speculation. Responsive to his good nature I could not maintain the sternness which I felt appropriate to the occasion. A brief smile flickered over my face.

'You're smilin',' he said. 'Look, 'e's smilin', everyone! 'E knows what I mean. 'Ere, Wickham. You fink the same, don't you? You're friends, ain't you? See? 'E knows exactly what I'm talking about.'

Wickham was on his way out of the washroom. Stripped to the waist, his shirt over his arm, he stopped beside Skinner and looked at me.

'Of course you know,' he said. When I did not respond he said 'Come on!' And he smiled, challenging me to admit what I had already said to him.

'They're good friends,' I said.

'Good friends! Blimey!'

'Now then, Skinner.'

Others in the room, briefly attentive in response to Skinner's appeal, had now resumed their ablutions and conversations about other things, so that the three of us stood more or less alone.

Skinner became confidential. 'But truthfully, you must admit, they do see each other quite a lot, don't they?'

'I can't deny that,' I said.

'And what does 'e think about it?

'Who?'

'The old man?'

'Mr Patterson?'

'Who else? Cor, you're really making me work, ain't you?'

'Have you cleaned your teeth?' I said.

Wickham, who had been watching us both, laughed and repeated my question: 'Have you cleaned your teeth, Skinner? Let's have a look at them. Open!' He peered up into Skinner's face.

'What would you feel, Skinner, about Mrs Patterson, if you were Bennett?'

'I don't need to be Bennett. I feel it anyway.' His throaty laugh was subdued and suggestive.

'You've vulgar,' I said. 'How can I have a conversation with you? It's impossible.' I looked at Skinner's big, raw features, his inquiring eyes puzzled by my unwillingness to endorse in words what I admitted by my prevarication. I was glad that he did not know what awaited him the next day, and was myself puzzled at what it could be, but could see no way of finding out without revealing that he was wanted by Merchant. 'Do you like Bennett?' I asked.

''E makes you work. But 'e's very fair. Yeah, I like 'im.'

'And you?' I looked at Wickham. Then, suddenly, it did not matter what Wickham thought of Bennett. I was overwhelmed by what I felt for him, a deep flood of affection, concern, relief that his name had not been on the list, frustration that I could not give any clear expression to my feeling. O, little swan, I thought, as I watched him begin to answer me, and all I wanted was to give him the poem. Let him judge the words. Let him read what I felt. Could I just give it?

Bennett himself came in. 'Bit slow getting to bed tonight aren't we?' His arrival induced a quietness, and he went on to me: 'There's a racket somewhere upstairs. You'd better go up.'

'I will, sir. Come on, Wickham. Up you go. No more idling around down here.'

'I'm not idling.'

191

'Bed anyway.'

There was a movement towards the door. I followed in its wake, leaving Bennett in charge.

On my way up, stopping in the prefects' room, I found and took out the blue envelope, and read over again the words I had written. I did not then feel about them any of the critical restraint or emotional self-doubt which now afflicts me. They glowed on the page, redolent with innocent commitment and, I suppose I must confess it, desire. Not of the flesh; at least, not oppressively so, but of the essence of my being. I wanted Wickham to be an audience to my endeavour, a commiserator in my all too possible failure. Of all the people by whom I was then surrounded he was the one to whom I wished most of all to turn. Ill-defined as my needs were, I felt that they could be satisfied by him. I would go even further, and suggest that perhaps I was not above manufacturing some self-doubt or threat or intellectual danger in order to be able to turn to him.

Stuffing the envelope into my pocket I went upstairs to quell the modest and good-tempered riot which, in Mr Patterson's absence, had gained in momentum and noise beyond what was normal or acceptable. Gradually, the sounds of going to bed abated. First the junior dormitory was silenced for the night, then the next, then the one in which Wickham slept was brought to a measure of control; finally, there was my own.

I said goodnight to Mr Bennett, and watched him as he crossed the hall. The light from above, fading now into dusk, fell on his figure. There was vitality in his movement; seen from behind, his broad shoulders, and his arms out at his side, swinging slightly, the hands open and alive with expectation made him seem fine and heroic.

At the door into the Pattersons' living room, in shadow from the balcony above, which ran round and overlooked the centre well of the hall, he turned and said 'Is everybody upstairs now?' He glanced towards the corridor which led to wash-rooms and bootrooms, the back end of the large old house.

'Oh, no, sir. Archer's having a bath.'

'Will he be long?'

The question lacked logic. I shrugged. 'I don't know, sir.'

'Very well. Anyone else?'

'The other house prefects are up, sir.'

'Good.' He hesitated, and glanced again at the darkened corridor. 'Just Archer, you say?'

'Yes.'

'Well, you go on. You'll be up early, working?'

'I will.'

'Goodnight then.' It was said as a form of dismissal, without expectation of further reply. I waited without moving as he turned and opened the door. A warm glow from the lamplight silhouetted his frame for a moment, and at the same time there flowed from inside the room the soft sounds of music from a gramophone. At that moment, for some incalculable reason, he seemed suddenly less heroic, a man magnetised by his own nature.

I passed on up the stairs, and turned my head, as I did now by habit, to look upon the sleeping or waking form of Wickham, where he lay in the dormitory bed visible through the door, and through the bars of the balustrade surrounding the landing. In the fading light I could not see whether he was awake or asleep, but he hissed at me, and I rounded the stairs and went across to the door.

'He's gone in, has he?' Wickham's attempt at a whisper was noisy enough for everyone to hear it.

'You're as bad as Skinner,' I said. I walked down through the dormitory to the other end and stood looking out.

'We was talkin' about cricket when you came in. We've won two matches. There's a good chance of winning the ovver two, ain't there?'

'I suppose so. Yes.'

'Why don't you play?'

'I'm not very good.'

'You can bowl. I've seen you.'

'You've got Wickham.'

193

'It could make the difference.'

'I have too much work to do. I shall be away in any case on the day of the final match. Scholarship.'

'It's all Mr Patterson cares about.'

''E doesn't care much about Mrs Patter—'

'That's enough of that,' I said.

Baron said: 'Is it true? All that stuff about Spain?'

'You mean him being there? That's true. Yes.'

'And her? She come from there?'

'As far as I know.'

'He'd tell you, would he?'

I thought of the exchange between us, and laughed inwardly. Patterson had never once touched upon his early, heroic life with me, and I did not expect it. Our encounters were at best neutral, more often baleful. 'It's not the kind of thing we talk about. But surely, some of you...?' I left the question in the air. There was a pause.

'Skinner said last term, when they came back from Caulfield's, Patterson had a few drinks and they were in with him. He told them of fighting in the north, and about this village where they shot a landowner and his wife and family. Skinner said he went all funny.'

'How do you mean? Funny?'

'Well, sort of regretful. I dunno. You'll have to ask Skinner. He said Patterson'd drunk quite a lot.'

'Does 'e drink much?'

'Lots.'

They went on talking, and I listened. I was only vaguely curious about their views, which were perceptive but free of judgment. Patterson was their housemaster, comprehensively so, as he would never be mine, and there was an indulgence towards his weakness for the bottle that was quite appealing. I realised, from what they said to each other, how large he loomed in their minds, and the thought tempered and qualified, more perhaps than it should have done, my own view of his importance.

A boy called Spenlow said: 'Did you hear the Council

194

of the Confrérie met? The word is out: there are vacan—'

Somebody interrupted him with a 'Shush—'

Spenlow said, 'What's up? What are you ...' And then he stopped.

There was an awkward pause.

'It's all right,' I said. 'You can go on. I know about the Council.'

Someone called Kidd said, 'That's more than we do.'

There was another pause.

'How many vacancies, Spinny?'

'Two. That's what I heard.'

'Are you a member?'

'No.'

'Is anyone?'

There was silence.

'Well, at least you obey the rules, whoever you are.'

There was faint laughter from the darkness. I waited, hoping that some new conversational departure would start us in another direction, but none came. I could tell, from the faint sounds of movement and breathing, that the dormitory was settling down. Though Archer had a great liking for soaking himself endlessly in his bath I knew he would be up soon enough. Almost, I wished him present, that he might pre-empt my intention. I felt I was stepping forward, gingerly, upon a surface that was less dependable than my habitually secure ground. I felt the envelope in my pocket and took it out. In the late twilight the settled breathing of sleep was beginning to take over, the indistinct features of the room and figures in the beds to merge together into a curiously vivid aspect of Coppinger, an etched outline for so many remembered episodes. Different dormitories would become one dormitory in my mind, different houses one house; boys would merge, fade, be forgotten, be recreated; but the basic structure was the same.

'Goodnight, then,' I said. And was answered by some of them only. 'Did you clean those shoes, Cooper?'

Cooper said he did.

'Did you finish that work?' I had paused briefly at the end of a bed occupied by a boy called South. He said he had.

I turned by Wickham's bed towards the door. 'Have you taken your pills?' My voice was low, so that only he could hear.

'I have,' he said.

'Good.' I felt a constriction in my throat. I leaned forward and put the envelope beside his pillow. 'Read that some time.' I went out, not looking back.

From my own dormitory I could hear the sound of voices, among them, most noisy of all, Skinner's. Archer was coming up the stairs, a towel round his shoulders.

'It's not mine you should be visiting,' Archer said. 'It's your own.'

'I know. There are times I can't face them.'

'Is it Skinner?'

'Not really.' I paused. 'By the way, he's in some sort of trouble. Merchant wants to see him.'

'When?'

'Tomorrow. At eleven.'

'Anyone else?'

'Why do you ask?'

'Curious, I suppose.'

When I looked at him, he looked away.

'Two others,' I said. 'Carter and Smith.'

'Have you told them?'

'Not yet.'

'Isn't it usually announced?'

'Bennett said to tell them in the morning. So that's what I'm going to do.'

'You won't forget?'

'Would you?'

'Poor buggers.' He laughed.

'Could it be anything to do with this Confrérie nonsense? Skinner in that? Or the other two? Merchant's hot on it these days.'

'I dunno.' He looked doubtful.

'Could be he's found out something. Ever since they decorated the tree in front of the school at Christmas he's been stalking them.'

'I don't think Skinner's in it. Or Carter. I don't know about Smith.'

'Who do you think's at the centre of it? Packer?'

'Maybe.'

'How does it work? Some kind of "dare", isn't it? We used to have something like it, Lytton, Pritchett, myself...' I left the vague implication in the air of others, but Archer seemed preoccupied.

'It is some kind of task. There's a council. The Council of the Confrérie. Decides. Sends a plenipotentiary. It's quite elaborate.'

'I suppose Merchant'll stop it.'

'That's not what he's on to now. If he knew something for certain they'd know he knew. It's much more likely it's their work. He's going to stimulate their minds.'

'Goes about it from an odd angle.'

Archer laughed. 'Works, doesn't it?'

'Goodnight then.'

He went in past Wickham. In my own dormitory I sat for a time on the window sill, contemplating, with faintly indulgent recollections, the mystique surrounding the 'Confrérie'. I had to admit that Packer, if it was him, had style. Dormitory conversation went on around me, but I was not drawn into it, nor did I attempt to bring it to an end. Gradually it died down, and I sat on listening to the faint wind in the trees, the distant sounds of the night.

I wondered, had I done a foolish thing? What could Wickham possibly make of my words? Down which particular avenue of disaster had I embarked?

Up the hill there toiled the small car run by Patterson at the time, a Ford Popular, black, very plain. Its lights and engine were a major disturbance. I thought of Bennett and Mrs Patterson in the room below, hearing from the large window the same approach. I realised how late it was, and that I should be in bed asleep if I was to wake early enough to work before breakfast. Yet I could not bring myself to move, and listened as the car stopped, doors opened, closed, opened and closed again. There were voices, and then silence. And then there was the crunch of Bennett's feet on the gravel of the roadway as he set off back to the staff house. I expected some comment on the sequence of sounds, but none came. The room was filled with heavy breathing, and I was alone on the broad window sill, my legs drawn up under my chin, the sweet scent of the night air blowing in.

Words were echoing in my mind about something being prefigured in the stars, and I could not remember where I had read or heard them. It must be Bennett, I thought; something he has said to me. And suppose it should come up in the exam? Did I really know *anything*? Did I know anything at all?

A board creaked on the landing. I turned my head towards the open dormitory door. I could see nothing.

Then a voice said 'Who's in the window?' It was Patterson. His tone was frail, high-pitched, uncertain.

I swung my legs down and walked quietly, swiftly towards him. 'It's me, sir. I was just about to go to bed.'

Indistinctly, I could see him as I came to the door. He was leaning against it.

'You're very late,' he said. An exaggerated sense of outrage seemed to pervade his words. 'Very late. Won't get the work done, you know. Anything happen tonight? Everything shipshape? House and boys in order?'

I could smell the drink on him, the familiar, mixed and oily scent of alcohol and sweat and tobacco. It induced no feelings, neither pity nor revulsion.

'No, sir. Nothing,' I said. 'Everything's in order.'

'I've been drinking a bit, you know. The old trouble's at me.' He put his hand on his hip and groaned quietly. 'Burgos.'

I stood in front of him, unable to see, in the dusk, the

198

expression in his eyes, but imagining them bloodshot. I could hear his breathing.

'You know, the trouble with you is you're not fully part of the house. Not fully. No. I've no complaint. Tell you that straight. But it's a question of your involvement. It's a question of being part of us.' He stared hard at me, his head forward. He was uncomfortably close.

'I was just going to bed, sir.'

'It's the house spirit,' he said. 'You see, the cricket. You're not involved.'

I half-turned towards my bed, and pulled out the pyjamas from under my pillow. 'I do my best.'

'Other things. It's all a question of being part of the team. Team spirit. In my youth, had it. In Spain. Wonderful. But now?'

'There are boys have to see the head tomorrow,' I said. 'A messsage came from Mr Merchant.' I was seeking to deflect him back to present reality.

'Who?' he said. 'Who are they?'

I gave him the names.

'Have you told them? Carter? What's he been up to?'

'I'm telling them in the morning.'

'Mm. Don't like it. Can't argue about it now.'

I could see the outline of his figure against the light from the door. He seemed undecided whether to go or stay. Then he moved away. It was almost a shuffle.

'Goodnight, sir,' I said.

'Yes,' he said. 'But I don't like it.'

199

Chapter Nine

I

It was the afternoon before Old Boys' Day. I had come away from cricket practice, back to the house, and was working in the small study. It was a minor breach of the rules, but I had, by then, obtained tacit support for this, in the interest of my rapidly approaching examinations. Emulating Francis, I was working away with precise notes on small strips of paper, the administration of it becoming more attractive than the work itself.

I heard someone in the hallway outside, and stopped to listen. I thought, apart from myself, that there was no one in the house. But the quick step approached, and I recognised it as Mrs Patterson's. She came to the door, knocked, and opened it. And I turned. Then I got to my feet. 'I was just working, Mrs Patterson. Revision.' I made a sweeping gesture at the table filled with books. It was untidy. I felt untidy myself, my thoughts not collected, and wondering why she was there.

She looked directly into my eyes. 'I need some help. Can you spare me ten minutes?' She was wearing a cream-coloured skirt and pink blouse. The sandals on her feet were elegant, with heels, though not too high. She wore no stockings, and no make-up.

'Of course, Mrs Patterson. What do you want me to do?'

'It's the trellis,' she said. 'It's still not done. I thought you, of all the boys, would understand it.'

'I'll try,' I said. I put the cap on my pen and left it on the table.

'You don't mind, do you?' It was said almost automatically. There was a faintly haughty expression in her eyes which made me wonder what she thought of us all.

I followed her through to her part of the house. In their kitchen she pointed at a toolbox. 'You will need that,' she said, and passed on.

I took it up. There was a hammer and nails; secateurs; other implements. Again I followed her through into the garden, and to where a wooden rose trellis had come away from the wall and was learning out at a perilous angle, pushed and weighed down by the branches of a rose.

'What is it?' I said.

'What?'

'The rose.'

'I think it's Albertine.'

I cast my far from professional eye over the trellis, and tried to think what my father would do. I moved along, looking for hooks or nails in the wall, or for wood pegs that could have nails hammered into them. I could hear my father's voice saying, keep calm, think it out. And I took my time assessing the problem, conscious of Mrs Patterson standing behind me.

It did not seem too difficult. 'I think I can manage it,' I said. 'We'll need to prop it back up again, while I work. And I need a ladder.'

'There are poles by the gate,' she said. 'And the ladder's in the garage.'

She came with me as I collected the things I needed. She pointed at the ladder, indicated various lengths of wood, and followed me back with them. But she did not offer to help.

It was a simple matter, really. I set to work, much as I had done with my father on similar jobs in gardens in London, and because I knew what I was doing I did not mind Mrs Patterson standing behind me. In fact, it emboldened me, in

201

a strange way, to question her as she might easily have questioned me.

'Do you remember much about Spain, Mrs Patterson?' I had paused in front of her, the hammer in my hand.

'I was only a child,' she said.

I could not ask her what aged child. I said: 'But you remember the language. You remember the people, don't you?'

'I suppose I do.' She seemed at first unwilling to talk. I went back to the trellis and hammered in another nail.

'Albertine. It's a nice name.'

'It's a beautiful rose.'

I fetched more nails. Coming back past her, quite close, I thought how remote she was, from us all. For all I knew, she despised us. I went back to where I was working and looked over my shoulder. 'What was it like?' I asked. 'Spain; then?'

She shuddered. 'It was terrible. I—the fighting was terrible.' Her dark eyes were fixed on mine, and I stood foolishly waiting, with the hammer up in the air. She said: 'I remember when they came to the village.'

When she didn't go on I asked: 'Who came?'

'The nationalists.' She said it in a tired, resigned voice. Then she bent down and picked up the secateurs which were in the tool basket. She began to trim back the straggling growth from an escallonia. I turned back to the trellis and put in another nail. Over my shoulder I asked her: 'Was it Mr Patterson, who came to the village?' I waited, but there was no answer. I finished putting the nail in.

'Not with the nationalists,' she said, shaking her head. 'He came before. He came first. Two of his men were wounded. My father was leader of the village community.'

I turned. 'Did you own much land?'

She smiled. 'No. A little land.'

'What happened to the two men?'

'My father took them in. He supported the Republicans.'

I was vaguely puzzled about which side was which. I tested one end of the trellis. It was firm. I moved along, not

202

looking at her. Bits and pieces of what I was hearing had come from Mr Patterson at different times. But to my knowledge no one had talked with her about Spain, although she was telling me without any apparent reserve. But I felt the need to be cautious and relaxed. I propped up another piece of wood. 'It's going to be all right,' I said.

'That's good.'

'What happened then?' I asked. 'What did Mr Patterson do?'

'He had to go on. He was fighting for Belarmino Tomas. It was the time of General Davila's advance. He thought it would be all right, leaving the men.' She stopped.

I began hitting in the nail, and the noise against the wall was hard and sharp. I propped up the ladder to do a nail higher up. Before climbing I looked over my shoulder. 'And was it? All right to leave the men, I mean?' I waited, looking at her.

She shook her head. 'No. They came. At dawn. They shot the men. They shot my parents. They would probably have shot me.'

I stared at her in the sunlight. From a long way away there came the faint shouts of boys. I felt the weight of the hammer in one hand, and with the other I squeezed hard on the two or three nails I was holding, willing her with all my heart to go on. 'And what happened?' I said.

She laughed briefly. 'I don't know why I'm telling you this. I never talk about it. Ben— Mr Patterson— talks about it. He loves Spain, you see. And I don't. I think it is a terrible country.'

'And did he come back?'

'He came back.'

'And took you away?'

'You ask too many questions.' She turned and walked along the pathway, looking at plants, occasionally bending to push a branch in, or pull out a weed. Her movements were graceful and relaxed. Her thick, dark hair fell forward when she did things, concealing her finely shaped cheeks, the dark

203

complexion of the skin. I put in two more nails, and once again moved the ladder.

'Have you much more to do?' she said.

'Nearly finished, Mrs Patterson.'

'Anyone you know coming tomorrow?'

'My brother. And Philpotts. They're coming.'

'Really? I've not met your brother. And I hardly know Philpotts. Wasn't he head of Mr Forrest's house?'

I nodded. 'That's it, now.' I put my hand out, and pulled at the trellis to show her how firm it was. Then I took the ladder and laid it down on the path. I did the same with the pieces of wood. Standing in front of her, I said: 'What saved you from being shot?'

She frowned. 'I may tell you another day. Not today. Put the things away, then you may go. And thank you for your help.' She turned and walked from me down the path, and I watched her easy step on the gravel. Through the pink texture of her blouse I could see the point where her brassiere was fastened, and on her shoulders the faint indentation of the shoulderstraps pressing into the soft flesh. I felt the stirrings of desire. She was, what? Ten years older than me? Twelve? I thought: with all that Patterson had done for her, how could she betray him with Bennett? But the answer was there, directly before my eyes. It lay in her vitality, her assurance, where she turned at the end of the path, and went into the house, not looking back. Patterson was too old for her. Patterson was too tired.

II

'You say everyone's talking about it?' Philpotts looked at me quite sternly, as if suddenly aware that what we were discussing related to real lives.

'Yes, more or less,' I said. 'I mean, juniors in the house talk about it as if commenting on cricket.'

He laughed abruptly. 'It will come to a head soon, then.'

'I'm surprised it hasn't already.' It was Francis who spoke, to Philpotts more than to me. 'I'd have thought Merchant would have moved faster on it.'

'What could he do? It's a slippery business.'

'What's odd about it,' Francis said, 'is I don't remember you telling us.'

'But I told you everything,' I said. 'Before Easter. I told you about Bennett and her. And about him. And Merchant. Everything.'

'Funny, isn't it? I just don't remember.'

Philpotts looked at my brother, then at me. 'I do,' he said. 'We just didn't believe you.'

'Do you now?'

He nodded. 'Yes.'

We were standing in the late May sunshine, on the close-cut grass in front of the school buildings. We had already done one circuit of the cricket pitch, and looked now at distant groups of old boys, some of them with boys still at school, moving or standing, acclimatising to the shock of recovering time.

They had come down from London in a coach which was now parked in the shadow of three huge elm trees, and had reported that no one else of their generation was included in the London contingent. Nevertheless, they both occasionally looked round in the vague expectation of seeing some other familiar face that might recall further dwindling memories. Philpotts was on the lookout for the Gaffer. Both of them had expectations of an encounter at some stage with Merchant, and had already indicated a certain relish at the prospect.

'Why have you changed? Your minds, I mean.'

They looked oddly at each other. Then Francis said, 'It must be coming back to the old school. Reversing into unreality, you might say. It breathes of complicities and plotting. Looked at from London, and it isn't credible. But down here it is.'

My brother stared round him at houses, trees, the general

blanket of green everywhere, all of it, every detail, so familiar to each of us. And I looked at his face and eyes, inscrutable, expressionless, dear to me in an ancient, exact, inescapable way, and recognised how important it had always been to me to please him, to gain his admiration; and yet how hard to do so. I could not fathom what his feelings were. I wanted to, every one of them. I wanted to know, not what he thought about Coppinger, but what he felt: how had his time been, compared with my own? I suppose, in a vaguer way, I had the same instinctive curiosity about Philpotts. But with Philpotts there was a light-heartedness in the way he would edge back from self-revelation, shrugging off the demands made by my occasional stabs of importunate curiosity. Francis was more barren in his reactions, a hungry look coming into his eyes as he recalled, perhaps, those lost or frustrated opportunities of his childhood and youth in that place.

I felt that I perceived this now, in the strangely frozen regard with which he scanned around him. And it halted in me any wish to upbraid him for not believing me before.

'And how will it end?' I asked, deferring now to their wisdom, having supplied them with what knowledge I could.

'That's an interesting question,' Philpotts said. 'Francis? What do you think?'

'Well, what are the possibilities?' My brother raised his left hand in the air with all the fingers spread out. 'They are quite limited. Firstly, from Merchant's point of view: he can sack Patterson, she goes with him, and he's left with Bennett.' As he spoke he seized hold of the little finger of his left hand with the fist of his right.

'Bennett would leave and follow, wouldn't he?' I said.

'Why would he leave?'

'Doesn't he want Mrs Patterson?'

'We'll come to that, now,' Francis said, and opened his right hand to take hold of the second finger as well: 'Secondly, alternatively, Merchant sacks Bennett. Bennett goes. Key question: does Mrs Patterson follow?' He raised his eyebrows and looked from one of us to the other. Philpotts shrugged, and looked at me to answer.

I thought of her dark eyes, looking into mine with their haughty splendour, their Spanish fire; I saw the swing of her pleated skirt, the firm, braced step of her sandalled foot on the gravel. 'I think she would go,' I said.

'It's a big step,' Philpotts said. 'What would happen to Patterson?'

'He'd crack up. Drink,' I said. I was enjoying the detective fiction level of our conversation; motive and action, or at least potential action, were in a frozen conflict which, though it did not quite obsess us, provided a stimulating subject for our heartless speculation.

'I thought he'd done that already,' Francis said.

'Well,' I answered, 'it could be covered over.'

'It doesn't bear thinking about,' Philpotts said. He put an exaggerated note of tragedy into his voice.

Francis had dropped his hands to his side again.

'Is that all?' I said.

'Of course not,' Philpotts said. 'The third possibility is that Merchant does nothing.'

'Not a possibility,' Francis said. 'It's clear he has some action in mind.'

'Fourthly, then, look at it from Bennett's point of view. Does he stop? Resign? Leave?'

We shook our heads.

It was Philpotts now who held the whole of his left hand inside his right. 'Fifthly, Mr Patterson. What does he do?' He looked from one of us to the other.

'He's trapped,' Francis said.

'Cherchez la femme!' Philpotts said, and he spread his arms out and looked up into the sky. 'She is at the heart of it all.'

'And she's the one person Merchant can't sack,' Francis said.

'We shall tour the estate now,' Philpotts said. 'Are you free?'

'More or less,' I said. 'There's just the game, starting at eleven. We don't have to watch. We've plenty of time. Lunch is at quarter to one.'

'How is Merchant reacting to all this?' Francis asked. 'What's he actually doing?'

'There's no decision,' I said. 'Not that I know of. Merchant doesn't really *know*. He asks me about Patterson, about Bennett, about the house. But I don't really tell him. What can I tell? And why should I?'

'Don't. Say nothing. Get on with your work. That's what matters.' Philpotts had stopped and half-turned towards me. 'How is it, anyway? You look as though you're overdoing it. How much longer do you have?' He looked at me with an expression of penetration and concern, as if suddenly he wanted to know everything, to take charge, to help. We were grouped on a roadway leading down into the valley. On one side was a hedgerow; on the other a field of young, green wheat. It was quiet, but for the singing of birds. There were larks in the sky above us.

The responses to my difficulties, such as they were, and for which I had sought in vain, at Easter, seemed about to manifest themselves now in a more perceptive understanding of what I faced. Perhaps too much perception. However, it was too late. The day was wrong, the time was wrong; I could not labour to reconstruct those different stresses, side by side, which had weighed upon me through the intense encounters the previous holiday. If Philpotts had been alone, it might have been possible. But with Francis there as well, the questions had to be dealt with in a straightforward, even a dismissive way. I did not know what he was recalling in his mind, what feelings were going through him. Nor did I know what I felt. I was just conscious that he had at last grasped within himself a sense of my turmoil and was responding to the need I had unsuccessfully given expression to when I had been with them both at Easter.

Instinctively I looked across at Francis where he stood on the other side of the road. He was staring at me, and obviously had been watching us both. From his mouth there dangled a piece of grass, the full green seedhead weighing it down at the end. He munched on it, slowly. There was no perceptible wish in his eyes to speak. If anything, there was the pinched look of being excluded, of resenting some level of friendship between Philpotts and myself obviously different from anything that existed between them.

'I get up early,' I said. 'About six. I work for an hour, at least.'

'Do you still have cold baths? Everyone?'

'Yes.'

'I never could come to terms with that. Makes me shiver still.'

'I used to have mine when I got up,' I said. 'But Patterson didn't like that. I needed to set an example, he told me, having it with the others.'

'And the work itself? Going all right?'

I nodded. 'I love it. I lose myself. It's the best time of the day.'

'And Bennett? He's good?'

'The best, Phillers. Really the best.'

'Pity he can't behave himself,' Francis said. 'Seems to me he lacks self-control.' He paused. 'Will we meet him?' It was said as an afterthought. With it he seemed to be generating a new diversion which made me faintly nervous.

'You can if you want to.'

'It might be instructive if we did.'

We moved on down the hill. I asked them about Wedmore. Francis gave a clipped evasive answer. We moved slowly along in the warm sunlight. There were patches of black tar showing through the yellowy, beige gravel that had been used to surface the road. Remembering hotter days I tried one or two of them with my foot, to see if they had softened. But they did not respond. The air around us was still. Only birdsong, and the occasional cry of cattle, disturbed our thoughts.

Was there a certain restraint between them? I felt only the

209

possibility of it, and of it extending over me. On the surface I felt free in their company, and more relaxed than I had been so far throughout the term. But if I had been able to predict securely their arrival, I would have had an expectation which was not being fulfilled. I was free to talk of things at Coppinger which otherwise demanded circumspection, yet I did not feel the same impulse to do so; I was free to reveal to them secrets or confidences which I could trust to no one else, yet there again I held back; and in that most general of all impulses—the seventeen-year-old's desire to be expansive and perhaps confessional in the company of young men of twenty-two or twenty-three upon whose indulgence he can depend—I felt beneath the surface the faint thud of obstruction. I could not talk with Francis about whether or not he had seen Father, because I did not wish that subject to come up with Philpotts. I felt hesitant about talking to Philpotts about his work for fear it would exclude Francis. And I could talk to neither about Wickham. I chose the easy course.

'Where will you be in the summer, Phillers?'

'The V and A.'

'Working?'

'Looking.'

'What at?'

'Miniatures.'

'All the summer?'

'I'll be in the Courtauld as well.'

'What's that?'

'It's a bit of London University. For the study of art. A library. A collection. Very important.'

'But will you work all the time?'

He smiled. 'Not quite,' he said. 'There are other things to do, people to see.'

'Your mother?'

'Yes. How do you remember? The old lady and I will go to Brighton once or twice. But I don't move her around too much.'

210

He seemed, with his words, to close her off, as he had always done before, into a privacy that I had never begun to penetrate. For a brief moment I had a vision of her in a wheelchair, being trundled along the seafront at Brighton. And I wanted to laugh. Philpotts's mother was an unimaginable person. Since I had first known him she had been part of his character; put another way, he had, in the strangely unbalanced world of Coppinger, represented for me that which I could not possibly understand: a boy who had grown to manhood under the sole influence of a woman, and one whom none of us had ever met. He had once told me that his earliest instruction to his mother, when he came to school, had been never to visit him at Coppinger. And she had obeyed. Through a talented youth of conventional achievement, never once had his mother emerged to give that linkage in understanding between Philpotts growing up and the family background which I would have seized on to strengthen friendship. It was entirely characteristic of him; it fitted in with gesture, word, the tenor of advice. It did not always impose predictable responses. But it did seem to justify most of what he said or did. It was always possible to say of Philpotts, yes, he *would* say that; or, how typical. Yet it was not so. In his discretion, in his cool judgments, in his patience, in the care with which he made comments upon events, really in his whole behaviour, totally different though it was from my own, I was detecting the moulding of a pattern in life derived largely from this unknown woman.

We came down to the valley floor where the road ran along beside the river meadows. The sunshine warmed us; the air was scented with hawthorn; and across the flat fields the willows and poplars, silver and lemony greens in the golden sunlight, defined the ancient winding course of the familiar stream.

'The pool still there?' Francis asked.

I looked at him. Then at Philpotts. Momentarily I was perplexed. 'Yes,' I said, 'why would it not be?'

'They think up reasons for changing the course of rivers.

You probably don't remember, but when you were first here, when you were very small, we used to come here.'

'That was when Father came to see us.'

Francis nodded.

I looked at Philpotts who was leaning on the gate, staring out across the field. Then I turned back to Francis. 'Have you seen him?'

He nodded. 'He's giving trouble.'

I laughed. 'What's he doing?'

'He rang Miss Filgate. Went direct to the top, you might say. I was quite annoyed, but what can you do? She was cool about it all.' He paused. 'You see, I haven't been much to London.'

'So you've not seen Melanie?'

He shook his head. 'Just once. Briefly.' He looked away, towards the trees that lined the stream. I was relieved. His reply was a simple absolution: from jealousy. Too busy, too disappointed; whatever the reason, both of us had turned temporarily away from a reconciliation which at the time had seemed momentous. And if I was puzzled at Francis's reasons, I was more relieved on my own account, and felt less guilty.

'We used to come here, Phillers, didn't we? Do you want to go over?'

We all now leaned on the gate. The meadow was tall with grass ready for hay. The distant edge was bounded with the thick undergrowth covering the bank of the stream where it wound its way towards the pool, more distantly outlined by tall trees.

Philpotts shook his head. 'It is enough to see, at a distance,' he said. 'It does come back to you, though, doesn't it?'

'The past, you mean?'

'Scruffy times, they were. Must shake them off.' He laughed to himself. Then he pushed himself up from his leaning position on the gate and, turning away, walked on. I followed, and then, after a brief pause, heard Francis

coming after me. After that we were together again, and
walking back.

III

The expectation of what they might do, coming down to the
school for Old Boys' Day in what I imagined must still have
been much the same mood about Coppinger that I remembered having left them in at Easter, had evaporated. And
instead of being disappointed, I was relieved.

It was not that the mood had changed. They felt much the
same. Their curiosities were the same. So were their
judgments. It was just that they were not going to disrupt or
challenge anything. Across water already rippled by the
breeze of events their presence sent only a brief, additional
cross-hatching of tiny waves, which were visible as a sudden
gust of wind can make itself felt to the eyes, but which had
no further impact, disturbing neither hair nor cheek, since
stronger currents intervened. It was instinct that told me
this, a sense of scale that measured them, and I suppose
myself, against the great curved back of the hillside down
which we had walked into the valley, and decided that the
force was not there to shift and alter events. In that first
glorious hour of May sunshine it came to me that we were
not just puny, but isolated as well: Philpotts and Francis,
Francis and myself, myself and Philpotts, the three of us
leaning on the gate, the two of them arguing over the merits
of Merchant or the appropriateness of the Gaffer retiring,
crowned with the full harvest of his integrity as a teacher
and a man. I am filled with a sense of remembered despair at
how remotely we were able to grasp upon the action around
us. I exonerate them entirely. What had they to do with the
real events? How could I ever fully tell them? Could I
explain Patterson? Could I encompass Bennett's passion?
Could I confess how I felt about Wickham? Could I
translate for them the sense of doom, ominous, inescapable,

which I felt at the silken persistence of Merchant looking for detailed expression of my loyalty to Coppinger? No, none of this could be more than just hinted at, superficially absorbed, used to provoke vague words, laughter even, and then consigned to some secondary memory cell in their brain. They were not living it. It was as artificial and as constructed as the fate of Wedmore was to me.

Into this overall sense of scale, and with an even sharper disappointment, I fitted a reduced Philpotts. The giant of my early youth, who had loomed over sad and eventful days, was smaller now, and though I think he was as assured as one would expect of a young graduate preparing to make his mark in post-graduate research at Oxford and London, it had distanced him from me and from the concentrated, enclosed passions of Coppinger.

Francis, too, was reduced by his more pronounced remoteness. What was it that had brought him down? Curiosity? Concern? Affection? Love? He set *my* dilemma within *his* Coppinger, and it did not add up. Philpotts, possibly with greater understanding since he had left later than my brother, did the same. And by the time we came back from our walk, any nervousness I might have felt about them intruding had gone.

This was emphasised in the brief encounter that took place with the Gaffer before lunch. Mr Forrest, to give him his proper name, had been my housemaster for much of my time at Coppinger, and had then offered me, like some reasonably capable commander in the field, to Patterson to take over his house. That was in the past, and the severance had been swallowed up in time, so that I looked on Forrest now from a distance, the former familiarity with his more intimate character replaced by an equal, if less affectionate set of feelings about Patterson. But Philpotts had not only been with Forrest throughout his time at school; he had also been one of his more successful pupils, and he bathed a bit in the reflection of this.

His delight at seeing Philpotts was genuine. 'We thought

you'd got above us, you know. All this Oxford thing. And now post-graduate work. We thought you'd forgotten your old school.'

'Difficult to do that, sir.'

'How many years is it?'

'Three, isn't it? I won't embark properly on post-graduate work until the autumn. And it does rather depend on my finals.'

'Do you have to get a First?'

'Something like that.'

'And will you?'

'Probably.'

'There've been some changes here. But overall it's much as before. My daughter's gone away. Danby's head of the house. School as well, as a matter of fact. You remember him? And *he's* head of Patterson's.' He pointed a hand at me. It was a brief recognition. 'Doing a good job, by all account. And this is your brother? Francis, isn't it? Yes, I remember. You left before the houses were changed, didn't you? Days of gaslight, and all that? You must find it very different.'

Francis was almost shy in his facial response to Forrest's surprising recollection of his name. He did not speak, merely nodded and shook hands.

He turned back to Philpotts. 'We don't have many for university. He's going,' he said, nodding at me. 'And Danby. That's all. But there are one or two promising younger ones. And we have to find places. It's a question of putting Coppinger on the academic map.'

'Surely there are no problems about that?'

Forrest paused and looked at him. He sucked ruminatively on his teeth. 'There are always problems,' he said. 'Mm, always.'

I turned away beside Francis, and we paced off from them across the grass. It was an uncertain, tentative move, a deferential recognition of their former respect for each other, broken, resumed, and now the source of a warmth in Forrest's manner which, considering the time when I had

215

known him better, was a relatively rare departure from his essentially pessimistic nature.

I said to Francis: 'Tell me about Father. Ringing Miss Filgate? What happened? Did you go and see him?' It was the first opportunity properly to broach family matters. And, apart from the brief exchange in the valley, I had been waiting for this opportunity.

He smiled, now, then laughed. 'Yes,' he said, 'but I don't know where it will end. He's an impossible man.'

The warm feeling I had that they were at least seeing each other was faintly tinged by jealousy, and the opposed instincts see-sawed in my mind. 'What kind of trouble is he in?'

'He can't find a place to live. He's been thrown out of that room. He's now in an old and beaten-up hotel in Gloucester Road.'

'Did he come to you when he left the room?' I had visions of his figure, wild with anxiety, on the steps of the house where Francis lived and where we had gathered at Easter.

'No. What happened was this.' He had turned towards me, an expression of excitement in his eyes as he recalled the events. 'A phone call came while I was out, and a message was left. Something like "Come at seven. Serious crisis. Father." So I went.'

'And I suppose he was in a frightful rage, pacing about, cursing people?'

Francis put his hand up to stop me, not impatient, smiling even at the interruption. 'No. Wait a minute. I knew imediately what it was. The only crisis he could ring me about was a lodging crisis. It couldn't be money. He knows I don't have enough to be any help. It couldn't be women. And if it had been health or the police the message would have been different.'

'So what did you do?'

'Well, I was rather clever. I went to Gloucester Road, found this hotel, booked him a room, promised to pay in advance and then went round to him.'

216

'And that's what it was?'

He laughed. 'Yes. I was right of course. He'd been thrown out. You only need to get drunk once in some of these places. And that's what had happened.'

'But it will happen again.' I felt a baleful sense of doom about the future.

'Probably.'

'Did he want to come to you?'

'Of course.'

'And you couldn't have him?'

'I thought I handled it rather well.'

I felt enormous admiration for his instinct. I could see myself floundering in similar circumstances, or simply running away. I would have identified too closely with my father's self-pity, brought him back under the pressure of his appeal, and then become hopelessly enmeshed in a situation that Francis had quite cleverly pre-judged and avoided.

'And how is he?'

'He's surviving.'

'Isn't it better than that?'

'Not really.'

I visualised his 'surviving': the tidy table with the spring-clip of his daily intentions, sternly noted down, with no discrimination between them on grounds of importance; 'Cheese', 'Rent', 'Alice', 'Library books', 'P.52', 'Mend Shirt Collar', 'Blue Thread', 'M and B', 'Ephedrine'. And as sternly struck through when accomplished. For in his life even 'Alice' was from time to time 'accomplished'; she was contacted when needed, an appeal made, telephoned, met, relieved of money, told a little of what was going on, embroiled for a time in the agony, and then discarded.

Pausing in those moments of sad resignation which his all too familiar report inspired, I considered the gap between us, and realised that he could never catch up, never acquire what I had. We must have looked a glum enough pair of young men, as we ambled across the close-cut grass, alone among many other groups of boys and visitors, close to the flow of the day's encounters, and yet lost in a reverie that had little to do with Coppinger. But perhaps I am wrong. Perhaps it had everything to do with that place. My being there, Francis having been there, the special bonds of affection and dependence which rooted us there, all related back to the turbulence with which my father had disturbed and undermined our world. Did my brother feel as I did? I doubt that. The sources of his pity were different. He never witnessed, as I did, the futile 'accomplishments'; at least, not in so sustained and so agonising a way. He had turned his back on them, much as one might turn away from a strongly patterned wallpaper, one of an inspired quality, where the subtlety and richness of imagination was sufficient to sustain interest, but where the strength of the repetition, the predictability of every precise detail, eventually drove one to seek something else, wallpaper being, in the end, only wallpaper. So Francis had changed the background of his life while I had kept what I had, the sharpened pencil in the half-pint milk bottle, the oiled secateurs close to his idle hand, the framed photograph of one of us on his table, the rest of himself packed in a battered suitcase on top of the wardrobe in the innumerable bed-sitting rooms in which we had lived together, or folded away in the green morocco wallet in which the few painful secrets of his existence were kept under the imagined security of his tidiness and the way I feared or respected it.

It conditioned for me a single source of feeling, a spring of clear water whose endless resources went back as far as I could remember. It had never been broken. That it had not been the same for Francis was no source of regret for him. As, in time, he was to tell me, the reasons were deep and still in a sense compelling. But the divergence in our ways lay between us.

It was emphasised by the fact that he was telling me how things were, filially speaking, a rare reversal of our situation.

'And Melanie?' I asked.

'Vanished,' he replied. 'Into thin air. She changed her

218

nurses' lodging, and they were unco-operative about telling me where she had gone. I left messages. But she did not reply. Her time as a student nurse is almost over. She could well move out of London.'

He spoke with authority and finality. We had stopped under the shadow of a small group of silver birches, and had half turned ready to go back towards Philpotts who was still talking with the Gaffer. The light dappled shade fell across him, and I looked carefully at his face to be sure of the expression in his eyes. Did they contain mockery? There was reason for it. Had I not set in motion a series of encounters which had more or less come to nothing? Yet Francis was too philosophical to mock. He might become angry in time, but the time for that was not yet.

'And you only saw Melanie once?'

'Yes. Shortly after you came back here. A fortnight or so.'

'And did she say anything about me?'

'Only that you had not written to her. You said you would write. She was most emphatic. Something about T. S. Eliot, or literature. I don't remember what.'

'It's true. But, Francis, I've been so busy. I've had so much work to get through.' I wanted him to see my point of view. He would understand the work. He had also been through it. But all he did was shrug his shoulders and turn back the way we had come.

Philpotts had left the Gaffer and was coming across the grass towards us. I was relieved. I felt ashamed at the way in which my own efforts in the spring had come to nothing: Father a burden, Melanie having made some kind of emotional departure from us, and Francis, at his most inscrutable, the bearer of tidings which faintly reproved me.

The bell had begin to ring for lunch. From the main school buildings a stream of younger boys, less interested in the previous generations, was moving down through the May sunshine for the midday meal. Philpotts stood in front of us, looking thoughtful. 'One cannot entirely dismiss the Gaffer,' he said. 'He has certain qualities.'

219

'Oh?' There were times when Francis could put on an expression of polite surprise which undermined one's assertions. 'What are these qualities?'

'They are not exceptional. He has a certain stern perception of the character of others, impregnable to sentiment, patient, resigned, at heart good.'

'You think so?' The inflexions in Francis's voice, which hardly made it a question at all, put the onus on Philpotts, underlined that it was his judgment of the Gaffer.

To me, such talk was refreshingly adult. My own judgments, much less concerned with character, were subjective. And at that stage in my time at Coppinger, having moved from the Gaffer's house several terms earlier, I viewed him from a distance and not altogether with benevolence. I realised the wisdom of what had come about. It would have been unfair for Danby and myself, at the head of the school, to be also in the same house. Nevertheless, I looked back with regret from the present to the past: uncertainty seemed to surround me now, whereas then there was trust, and the warm, encircling comfort of Janet's arms. I was thinking of this, and regretting that she had gone away from Coppinger, when Philpotts spoke. 'He seems to think you might make some mistake or other.'

I looked blankly at him. 'What did he say?'

'He said he hoped you wouldn't make any mistakes.'

'Did he explain?'

'No. He said it in that way he has, turning aside, going on to something else, you know, the way he always used to tell us important things. That's why I mention it.'

They were both looking at me, and I thought to myself, tell them everything, tell them all that is going on, ask their advice, involve them, they are on your side. But instead, I said: 'I don't know what he can mean. It must be to do with my work. We'd better join the others for lunch. We go in this way.'

IV

We met with Merchant late in the afternoon. It seemed to me he did not want the encounter at all, but ran into us in circumstances which made it unavoidable. We had been wandering together through the school buildings, Philpotts and Francis looking at old photographs, while I listened and absorbed. And it was coming out into the sunshine, and rounding a blind corner, that we came face to face with the Headmaster.

He said to me, 'Is everything set for tonight?'

'As far as I know it is. Yes, sir.'

'Good. I trust it will go well. Wickham the soloist?'

'We're singing madrigals, sir.'

'No solos?'

'No, sir.'

'But he's the leading treble?'

'Yes, sir.'

'Good?' It seemed an absurd question.

I said: 'I think so.' I was puzzled. I felt a slight flush of embarrassment, and concentrated myself so as not to let it show. And all the time Merchant watched me, ignoring the others.

Then he turned to them. 'And how do you find everything?' He had, of course, met them briefly at lunch with the other Old Boys, leaving him now with less to say. Even so, I was surprised at the question.

Philpotts said: 'I think you're doing a good job, Headmaster. A few of the photographs are crooked. But everything else seems in order.' He smiled blandly at Merchant, then indicated me. 'He's having to work rather hard in Patterson's house. I hope it won't prejudice his chances of a place at Oxford?'

'That's up to him,' Merchant said. 'You two did it. He will as well.'

'The school does have to play its part, though.'

'I think you can leave all that safely in my hands.'

'I do hope so,' Philpotts said. 'Being head of a house can present problems, strains and stresses, you know.'

Merchant's eyes narrowed, and he looked towards me. Then he said: 'He does very well.'

'It's his work that matters.'

Merchant stared back at Philpotts, then glanced at Francis. 'And what are you both going to do when you come down?'

Francis said: 'I haven't made up my mind yet.'

'I suppose it will depend on the degrees you get.'

'Not really. I shall get a good degree. It just depends on me making up my mind.'

I was faintly distressed at the frostiness of the encounter. It was studied insolence, of a kind that would have been swiftly reproved, had they still been at Coppinger. I looked at Philpotts with an expression of vague appeal in my eyes. Philpotts winked.

Merchant said, turning to him: 'And you?'

'Well, I shan't be coming down. I'm going to stay up and do some post-graduate work, Headmaster. A doctorate. Working in London, of course. But still at Oxford.'

'And National Service?'

'It seems they're prepared to wait for my contribution to the defence of the realm for a further couple of years. Some sort of exemption. That is already agreed.'

Merchant nodded. 'And what will your subject be?'

With a cool glint in his eyes Philpotts said: 'Hilliard. Nicholas Hilliard. You know his work, of course?'

Merchant looked back at him, then glanced at Francis and at me. He seemed to be debating how to answer. 'Of course,' he said. 'Excellent subject. I suppose not a great deal of work has been done on him?'

'Oh, yes. A great deal.'

He looked at his watch. 'Well, you know, time is short, and the demands upon me are heavy. You'll excuse me if I

222

leave you without going into Hillier's career.' He eyed us all, in a general way, with distaste. In the act of turning away, however, he voiced a further question: 'What aspect will you be covering?'

'His links with European colleagues. You know the most important of these, don't you?'

'Yes, but you will be dealing with others, surely?'

'Yes. That's what I'll be doing. Dealing with others. But nothing is very certain.'

'I shall see you before you go. At the concert.'

'At the concert, then,' Philpotts said. 'And remember the photographs.'

He left us, heading on into the school buildings.

Philpotts frowned at me. 'Well, you can't have crooked photographs in a school, can you?'

'He always was a failed perfectionist,' Francis said. He spoke moodily, as though he felt far distant from Merchant, and sought to be even further away.

'The question is this,' Philpotts said, and he began to move away from where we were standing. 'What does he think Hilliard did? He called him Hillier, didn't he. Ignorance. What we must work out is a question to ask him later, so phrased that he will not be able to cover himself.'

'Is that fair?' I said. I was less concerned with fairness than I was with avoiding an encounter that might be unpleasant, and lead, in some vague way, to subsequent retribution against me.

'No. It's not.'

'Then—'

'How fair has he ever been? Why should we not treat with him as he is?'

I did not answer the question. 'I've to leave you now,' I said. 'I've house duty. I'll see you after the concert.' I walked away from them realising that there would be time only for a hasty farewell. I was put out by the encounter with Merchant. It introduced an element of uncertain threat which overshadowed me on my way back to the house.

223

Later, leaving the house again after tea, and in advance of the other boys, since Parker wanted the singers ready early, I had the chance to talk with Wickham. It was the first time that day.

'What's the matter?' he asked. 'You look really fed up. Has something happened?'

'Hello, little Swan. I was—'

'Don't call me that.' He interrupted me, his voice sharp and penetrating.

'Why not?'

'Just.'

'Okay. What will I call you? Wickham?'

'That's all right. Names don't matter. David. If you like.'

'Will it be all right, the concert, this evening? Are you nervous?'

He laughed. 'No. It'll be fine, but you don't seem very happy about it.'

I shrugged. 'It's nothing. Nothing to do with that. When are we to be there?'

'Half-past. That's when Parker wants us.'

'We're in good time.'

Wickham said: 'Can I ask you something?'

I felt a constriction, anticipating something about the poem. 'Of course,' I said.

'You know the talk there was, in the dormitory that night?'

I was disappointed. 'You mean about Patterson and Spain.'

'Well, no. About the Confrérie."

'Oh, that.'

'Well—' He looked down, and moved his head from side to side. Then he swung his arm in an eloquent arc over his head, as though delivering a ball down some imaginary wicket. 'Well, what do you think?'

I laughed. 'The less I think about the Confrérie and its Council, the better. I know nothing, anyway.'

'You're kidding! You must know.'

I shook my head. 'You're obviously interested. Be careful.'

'What do you mean?'

'I don't know, really. Just be careful.'

'You're not against it?'

'How could I be?' I looked down at him for a moment, then I said: 'I've never told anyone this, but once—' I stopped.

'Go on,' he said. 'What happened once?'

'Nothing.'

'Go on. You can tell me.' His treble voice was soft, unusually deep and mellow, matching the dark and dusky colour of his skin, the tumble of black hair.

I had never spoken of Pritchett, Lytton and myself, and the things we had done, to anyone. It was not the secrecy that mattered. It was that it belonged in the past, and had not really amounted to very much anyway, so that I was restrained by a diffidence over the impact on Wickham of midnight walks and tunnel exploration. Yet I had to tell him.

'Do you remember Pritchett?'

'Yes.'

'And Lytton?'

'Not really. He wasn't here at the same time.'

'He was. Well, nearly.'

'What did you do?'

I looked at him, shrugging my shoulders as if emptying from me the recollections of our tiny enterprises. 'We went out at night, climbing through windows when we could have used doors. Or could we? I can't remember. Perhaps they were locked with a key in the Gaffer's house. We explored under the floor of the school. That's all changed now. We did other things.' I tailed off, rather lamely.

'Wasn't it fun?' He seemed a bit put out by my dismissive approach.

'Yours is better,' I said. 'It's competitive. This setting of tasks. It's a kind of dare. I like it.'

225

'I'll tell you how it goes.'

'No,' I said. 'Don't tell me anything. Don't involve me. I haven't heard, and don't want to.' I paused, staring at him. 'And that...other stuff.' I hesitated. 'What I did, what I gave you. Forget it. Okay?'

'You mean...the poem?'

'Yes,' I said, firmly.

He pulled a face. 'Okay,' he said.

I meant the opposite, of course. So often we do. I had unburdened myself of feelings, he had adsorbed them, and pressing him for reaction would achieve nothing. My self-consciousness had taken a new direction, a more stimulating form. Fourteen lines of indifferent verse had altered the texture of the air between and around the two of us. And instead of embarrassment, which to some extent I feel now, the overriding feelings were confidence, even pride. I walked beside him, fiercely aware of myself and of my own set of determinations, instincts, targets. Seeing my brother and Philpotts with Merchant had sharpened the edge of something within me analogous to courage but somehow deeper and more lasting. And now, Wickham's appearance in front of me, his questions, the look of trust and affection in his eyes, had strengthened the earlier conviction.

Looking back, it all seems so trivial. Time has made even those events of slight importance to me now. Once I felt like that, I can now say; once I did those things. And at the time I believed myself to be right. Others judged me then. Others will judge me now. But what is done is there, and if there are moments when we decide, turn, take a new direction, and by it alter the course of lives, our own and those of others, then I did so that evening in the odd measure of inner self-assertion, as well as in the curiously irresponsible answers I gave to Wickham's quite innocent questions.

For myself, I can see now that this instinct, deeper than courage, is that hardening-off within oneself which defines character, and derives often enough from reading within others points of limitation which vaunt and expand self-

226

confidence in oneself. If Merchant did not know who Nicholas Hilliard was, and yet could not bring himself to admit the fact, that initiated in my mind a new perception, not just about Merchant, but more importantly about myself. If Philpotts, wishing to tease Merchant, wishing to engage in a very mild form of vengeance for past aggressions, was determined to pursue the odd engagement over his chosen subject for post-graduate work, then once again there was the double perception: brief, straightforward, easily absorbed, where Philpotts was concerned; but much slower within myself, as I laboriously judged of its effectiveness, and came eventually to the conclusion that I would not do the same thing in similar circumstances. Likewise with Francis. He had handled Father in a way that I could not have done. I felt admiration. Even envy. But I also felt, deep down within myself, a hesitation at the clipped, pre-emptive sharpness of their acts. And I wondered myself into a state of gradually growing confidence about what I was doing and what I had done, on that afternoon, walking to the concert, as the sun slowly settled in a clear sky, spreading out across the soft green grass our youthful shadows.

Chapter Ten

I

I stood for a long time on the pavement on the other side of the road, watching the doorway to the building, and trying to make up my mind whether to cross over and go in, or simply to turn and walk away. I had time. I was free in that faintly irresponsible way, where no arrangements had been made, no commitments given. I could depart, and he would not be any the wiser. Yet some compulsion, hovering between love and pity, had brought me there, and deep within myself the decision had already been made. I had not told Francis, and rather suspected he was not in London at all, but at Oxford, working.

Philpotts was, but the arrangement I had made with him was for the day after the Coronation. We were down in London for three days. With all the work, it was still not an occasion to be missed. With some excuse, not too well received by the master in charge, I had managed to break away from the others, Wickham among them, and come on this reconciliatory mission. In spite of my hesitation, standing on the edge of the pavement, on that damp afternoon the day before the crowning of Queen Elizabeth, I knew I had intended all along the recovery, more on my terms than on his, of the uneasy equilibrium that had been lost in the spring.

The building had a seedy look about it, made worse in the

dull greyness of the afternoon. The stucco was peeling off, or had flaked away altogether, leaving ugly, leprous scars in the blue painted plaster surface. And from the word 'Court' above the heavy, pillared porch the letter O had fallen or been torn away. Since it was called, oddly, The Court Mantle Hotel, the accident was a rectification of sorts; but it left an ugly gap in the lettering, and added to the unkempt appearance.

This was what Francis had chosen for him, and it fitted his sad, frustrated hunt for an elegance which his behaviour in the end always pushed further away. It was different in kind from what had gone before, in the days that preceded Laurie and in those that came after. It was more pretentious, of course, and nastier. It lacked the anonymous security of the ordinary private houses in which, since as far back as I could remember, he had rented for himself and for me reasonably satisfactory, even respectable bed-sitting rooms. They had always been precisely described and priced, answering the ringed and pencilled advertisements in the local *Advertiser* for Kensington with an accuracy that he had come to rely on. This was different. All I could think of, as I crossed the street, was that he had moved onward and away, slipping from me, downward.

I only half expected him to be there at all. But he was, and the first sound I heard from his door, as I raised my hand to knock, was a violent fit of coughing. Perhaps I should not have knocked until it was over; but I did, with an instinctive relief that he was there, coupled with nervousness, and he shouted out, hoarsely, in the middle of a sustained run of chesty explosions, 'Come in! Come in!'

He was sitting on an upright chair beside a table, stripped to the waist, his braces hanging down over his hips, his shoe laces undone, his shoes lacking their normal high polish. In one hand he held a towel; though full size, its crushed and crumpled appearance, and the way in which his fingers curled around it, made it seem quite insufficient for whatever purpose he contemplated. In the other hand, even

229

more crushed, was one of his large spotted handkerchiefs. On the table stood a half-bottle of whisky. It had not yet been opened.

He stared at me, unsmiling, as I peered round the door. The force of his coughing made his eyes bulge and his cheeks blow out. And after the second bout he went on with small, wheezy expressions of a continuing irritation in his throat. With a finality of gesture which did not match this grumbling reminder that all was not quite right within his barrel-shaped chest, he wiped his mouth with the handkerchief, his whole face and torso with the towel, and motioned me to sit on the edge of the bed. With time to look at him a little I was disturbed to see how thin his chest in reality was. The great trunk-like shape was still there; but the substance was meagre, and his ribs showed.

'You!' he said. 'What are you doing here? You haven't run away, have you?'

I shook my head, trying to laugh at him, with him. 'We're down for the Coronation. Quite a few of us.'

'And you've come to see your father, eh?'

'Well, I was passing.'

'Passing, were you? Where were you passing to?'

'Well, I wasn't exactly passing.'

'But a passing visit, eh? A passing visit to George?'

'I couldn't find the hotel name in the book. I got the spelling wrong.'

'So you came on the off chance?' He was tense. Unsmiling. Unfriendly, even.

'You don't seem well.'

'I'm not dead yet.'

'Going to the Coronation?' I thought the question might make him smile.

'Don't be a blithering idiot. Can't you see I'm sick?'

'Have you seen a doctor?'

'No. They know nothing. Useless bloody fools. Only ever had one good doctor, and that was a woman. Dead now. Cancer. Couldn't do much about that, could she?'

'Are you taking anything for the cough?'

He pointed to the whisky, staring hard at me, then swung his finger towards a brown bottle further back on the table. 'Mixed together,' he said. 'You've got to bring it up—' The words seemed to inspire action deep down inside his lungs, and he erupted into another bout of chesty coughs which turned his browny-red face purple and made his bloodshot eyes bulge again. As the bout went on he pointed urgently at the whisky, then at a glass which stood near the bottle, indicating to me what I had already begun to do. When he could manage it he took a small gulp of the spirit. It eased his distress.

'Shouldn't you put a shirt on?' I asked.

'I suppose so. I was trying to rest.' The antagonism had faded from his voice.

I picked up the shirt and stood up close to him, holding it. I could smell the good, clean smell of his clothes, which he always washed himself, nightly. I looked at the pale colour of his skin. It must have been many months since he had last worked out in the sun, and its whiteness emphasised the unhealthy, sick appearance of the figure sitting beside me.

'Leave it,' he said, quietly, waving his hand toward the bed.

'You should put something on your—'

'Leave it!' His eyes suddenly flashed with anger.

I sat down again on the edge of the bed and looked at him, not knowing what to say.

'You come here, fussing over me like a woman!' He glared at me.

'I'm not fussing,' I said. 'I just came to see you.'

'Why don't you write to your father? Haven't heard a word, not a word. Don't know what's going on, what you're doing. You could be dead!'

'I've been working very hard.'

'Well, it wouldn't take long. Just a few lines. I'm alone here, you know. Day after day, nothing. A day's work here

231

and there, but they drive you all the time. Never satisfied. I can't take it much longer.'

'Alice?' I said. 'Have you seen Alice?'

He shook his head. 'I can't cope with Alice.'

'And Melanie?' I said. I knew what the answer would be.

He looked up, one eyebrow raised. 'Didn't see her again. She didn't come back to her father.' He paused, staring at me. 'Have *you* seen her?' He was ready to accuse us of joint conspiracy.

But I shook my head. 'No. I've seen nothing of Melanie. Nor Francis.'

After a bit he said: 'It's better to be free. It's better when I'm on my own.'

I looked at him and then round at the dreary walls of the room, the thin counterpane on the bed, the sparse furnishings. I could have argued on the merits of freedom, but decided that it was better to keep quiet.

We sat in silence for a while. But mentioning Alice had triggered off another thought in his mind. Looking up at me he said: 'I'll put that shirt on, old son. Hand it to me.'

He put the handkerchief into his pocket, and draped the towel across his knee. I passed him the shirt without getting up and he began to put it on. 'Good of you to come,' he said. 'I shouldn't have shouted. I know you're working hard.' He began to do up the buttons. 'By the way,' he said. He paused, turning up the collar and looking round for his tie. 'Do you have any money?'

'I have a bit,' I said. 'Do you want some?'

'Come in handy. If you had a pound. I could get another half-bottle. It'd tide me over. Medicine, that's all it is. I'm off it otherwise.'

I wanted to laugh. I had to choke back the urge to do so, and look away.

'I can give you two pounds, Father. That'll leave me enough.'

He looked sharply at me. It seemed he was debating within himself whether this example of independent

232

thought, coupled with a precise decision as to how much I might give him of the money I had brought with me, was a form of insult, and should provoke anger. But he thought better of it, and nodded his head. 'Good,' he said.

I was glad that he said no more. I would have been shocked, pushed perhaps to the brink of tears, if he had expressed gratitude. The haughty look in his eyes, the clear fact that he could not bring himself to soften any further his own reaction to the successful appeal for money, was, in my eyes, right. It was a slight added portion to the bewildering confusion of debts and duties we owed to each other.

I took from a leather wallet given me by Alice the two notes, and handed them over.

He took them, and crumpled them quickly into the palm of his hand, stuffing his hand into his trouser pocket to deposit them deep down in its safety. And he looked away as he did it, for all the world as though it had been a surreptitious act that might breed bad feeling between us. Then, his eyes back on me, the briefest of glances cast at the wallet still in my hand, he said: 'You've enough? You sure?'

I wanted to smile at him some kind of reassurance, but held back from doing so for fear it would come out as a patronising expression. And so, solemnly, I nodded and said, 'Yes, Father.'

Another brief glance swept down towards my hands, and I anticipated him asking me how much I had left. In fact, two pounds still remained in the wallet, which I now put away in my pocket, and I hoped it would be enough, though I was by no means sure.

He looked sternly at me. 'You all right for money, these days?'

'Yes,' I said.

'Get it from Mr Porphyry, do you?'

'Yes.'

'Regular allowance?'

'Yes. Sort of.'

'It's better, old son.' A sad look came into his eyes, and he

233

stood up and turned away. He crossed the room to a cupboard and took out a jacket. When he had put it on he turned down the white collar of his shirt over it. 'Shall we go and have a cup of tea somewhere?'

I looked at my watch. 'Okay,' I said. 'But I have to be back. We're staying in Barnet, at a school, and we've to start at three tomorrow morning.'

On the way out, he stopped at a door marked 'Inquiries'. For a moment or two he leaned against its frame, his eyes turned down towards the floor some five yards or so in front of him, but not focussing at all, so that quite openly I could stare at him, assess him, without any response. Still with the fixed expression, his lips slightly pursed, almost in disdain, he ran his powerful hand flat across his hair once, then again, then a third time. He seemed to have recovered morsels of dignity and self-respect. Focussing his eyes on me he knocked on the door, and when a voice inside answered he looked in and asked if the *Daily Telegraph* was free. It was handed to him.

'I try to keep up with things,' he said. 'Read the papers. They're good about lending it. They're not bad sorts, you know. They have a certain tolerance.' He was squinting down at the front page, but he folded it and tucked it under his arm as we went down the steps of the house. He looked at me, and a faint, uncertain smile played briefly on his lips. 'One day I'll read about you in it, your successes.' He shook his head gently from side to side, as if in contemplation of what seemed far off, if not wholly impossible. 'But I'm afraid it's not for me. I won't get there. Not now. Won't make the grade. My day's over.'

As we went down the steps together he began crooning to himself:

> 'When there are grey skies,
> I don't mind the grey skies,
> I'll follow you, sonny boy.'

234

I thought then that he must surely die. I thought it without sadness, without regret. It was an unexceptional occurrence, made inescapable by his behaviour, by the batterings he gave himself. The thought was qualified by the recollection of the other occasions when I had felt the same; but it was not banished by the fact that he had not died before. Rather, it was reinforced: it was as if this was really the time towards which the other remembered occasions pointed the finger. And what strange occasions they had been, waking alone, at dawn, to see his sprawled and senseless frame close by me in some vaguely remembered bed-sitting room of my childhood, half-clothed, dishevelled, wheezing or snoring or groaning in his sleep, for all the world, to my eyes, as if he were on the pitch of death itself. It was on such occasions, in the half light, in the queer unreality of dawn, that I used to make those same intrusive speculations, tinged with a hardness of heart that belongs to childhood's unbalanced judgments about what is possible, what is likely, what is dreamed, what actually happens. Easily, dispassionately, with a hint of melodrama pervading my imagination, I would consign him to his coffin, then his grave, and picture myself beside it, orphaned finally, and alone. It was different now; colder, with less melodrama, fed perhaps by the partial wisdom of literature, I regarded the crumbling edifice of the Court Mantle Hotel as an appropriately faded and battered mausoleum for his last rites, and quietly, in my mind, I consigned him to it, that wet afternoon, as we made our way down to the Lyons at Gloucester Road Station, for cups of dark brown tea.

In fact, he seemed a bit better. There was still the coughing, bouts of it interrupting our conversation. But he did ask me about my work, about Oxford, about what would happen in the autumn. I told him about Mrs Patterson, and mending the trellis. He took a keen interest in that. I told him about her and Bennett, and he listened carefully. 'Well, good luck to them, that's all I say,' was his only comment.

He was reluctant to tell me about himself. None of the

235

familiar names meant much to him at all. He had already dismissed Alice; and in turn he denied contact with the others; Ursula, Madge, Laurie. He had already registered his bitterness over Melanie. And Francis, having found the hotel for him, also had moved on. I began to want to stay with him, but he became anxious about me getting back in time, though in fact I had invented the six o'clock curfew. I stretched out the minutes, assuring him that it would be all right. But once the demon of departure had seized on him there was nothing that could be done.

On the pavement we parted. There was powerful pity in my heart for him then. He said little, raised his hand in a small economical wave; smiled with equal restraint; and then paused: for when I reached the corner and looked back he was still standing in the same position. Just as I passed out of sight I saw that he had begun to cough again, the coloured handkerchief fluttering up to his face. And there have been few occasions in my life since then when I have looked upon a man and been more sure that he stood alone in the world.

II

The image stayed with me that evening, of his humped figure on the edge of the pavement, coughing into the blue and red handkerchief. From dawn the next day I had the vague expectation of him joining us at some point, a wild imprisoned look in his eye, his lean face and spare physique turning this way and that in the crowds along Piccadilly, trying to spot us, his handkerchief again held up to his face, partly to stem the choking coughs, partly as a banner that I might recognise.

He did not come. I was relieved. As on previous occasions my knowledge of the city gave me an advantage, even over the staff who were with us, and I did not want it to be submerged in a problem as complex as handling my father could easily become. But the expectation overshadowed my enjoyment so that in a sense, in my mind and heart, I was handling the problem anyway.

This showed. To Wickham at least it became apparent that there was something on my mind. And I felt a curiously intense response to him when eventually he asked me what was wrong. It did not happen for some time. It must have been one of the longest mornings any of us had experienced. We got up at three when there were only traces of light in the sky, and we were in position by four, somewhere along Piccadilly on the corner of Arlington Street, with our backs to the solid but hardly very protective walls of the Ritz Hotel.

It rained. People laughed and sang. We drank lukewarm coffee, ate sandwiches, and were gradually caught up in the excitement of the throng. I tried at first to be restrained. It was an attitude forced on me by my sense of expectation about him rather than the Queen of England. But slowly it evaporated. Looking up at the windows with their crowded faces it seemed better to be there on the street, even with the rain streaming down upon us.

But I write of what is known, the innocent laughter and excitement which pageantry inspires. What of the shadows which were crossing my heart, slowly fading, being replaced by patriotic thoughts? What of the muffled echo in my memory of his bronchial coughing, accusing me of neglect?

'Where did you go yesterday?' Wickham said. 'You just disappeared.'

I was leaning against the grey granite wall, preserving part of our space for when the parade should pass by. And I looked down at his open, inquiring expression, unloaded, I felt, of feeling for me other than curiosity and friendship; certainly free of the sense of need that made serious and no doubt a little portentous the replies which generally I have to his queries.

'I went to see my father.'

'How did you find him?'

237

I took his question up wrongly. 'It wasn't difficult,' I said.

'No. How was he?'

I laughed. I think at that stage I had gone past any contrivances by which I might conceal my father's derelict health and the basic cause; at least, from Wickham I had. But I was not prepared for his concern. It gave me momentary pleasure. 'He's all right,' I said, euphemistically.

'What did you mean? About it not being difficult?'

I hesitated. 'Well, I did have to find him. He'd moved.'

Wickham nodded, but did not speak.

'He's actually not all that well,' I said. 'Something wrong with his chest.'

I was relieved when Wickham changed the subject. 'What do we do after the procession?' He asked. 'Do we have to go back?'

'Only for tea. We come out again tonight.'

'But do we have to stick together?'

'No. How could we? We'd get separated anyway. You can stay with me if you like.'

Thinking about it and frowning to himself Wickham nodded. 'Yes,' he said. 'I'll do that. You know London, don't you?'

'We'd find our way. We'd be all right.'

'Who else?'

I shook my head. 'Just us two.' I felt curiously excited at the simple prospect of going about in London with him.

'But what do we do?'

'We'll go down the Mall, to the Palace. There'll be millions of people. Then through the Park to Westminster Abbey. We'd better see it.'

He seemed uncertain at the prospect of so much walking. He turned away. I was anxious as to whether he would come with me, or drift away with the others.

Danby had been sitting on the edge of a low parapet, reading. I envied him his composure. It seemed that what he was inspecting were notes. I wondered if he would do better than me.

I said to him: 'It's filling up. We'd better make sure of our places.'

He looked up, a blank expression in his eyes. 'Does it matter?'

'We want to see, don't we?'

'We'll see all right.'

'But what about the smaller ones?'

'Do you mean Wickham?' He went back to his reading.

We saw all right. After the many hours of standing and sitting the steady rattle of horses' hooves and carriage wheels was like music ringing through our numbed and fatigued heads. Then it was over, and we were streaming away from that place, caught in the throng of people; and all I could think was that he would not find me now.

And Wickham stayed with me. But so did Archer and the others, so that the pleasure of guiding them back was diffused. And when Philpotts rang that evening, as he had promised, it was with a sense of relief that I arranged to meet him the next morning.

The night revels were better. For a while it stopped raining. Packed among the crowds in the dusk we moved down towards the Palace once again. I kept close to Wickham; but he kept close to the others, and in the end we gathered together near the Victoria Memorial without having lost anyone, not even Danby.

It was then that he came up to me. 'Let's shog off somewhere,' he said. 'I'm bored.'

My eyes must have visibly brightened. 'Okay. We want to head back, then up Marlborough Road, if it's open. Or by Carlton Terrace. There are steps there.'

We stood together a short way from the others. I noticed Danby looking, and beyond him Merchant talking with three boys, and pointing up at the Palace balcony. He drew their attention. Even Danby turned away.

I touched Wickham's shoulder and walked off into the crowd. He followed, and it closed behind us, an anonymous, seething, impregnable throng that soon filled the space

239

between us and them like a forest.

'Have you any money?'

'I've got a bit. Have you?'

'I've two quid,' I said. 'It's enough.'

'I've two pounds twelve and three. I didn't spend anything yet. Some of the others bought flags. Daft.'

'Where do you want to go?'

'It doesn't matter. Could we go to Piccadilly? Is it safe?'

I laughed. 'On a night like this? Of course it is.'

'And other nights?'

'I never worry. What's there to worry about?'

'Nothing, really. It's just what you hear.'

'Would you like to live in London?'

'Yes. My place's a dump.'

'What? Hurstmonceaux?'

'Yeah. A real dump.'

'It sounds interesting. By the way,' I said, 'have you heard from the Confrérie?'

He looked up at me, quickly. 'Do you think I'd tell you if I had?'

'I don't know,' I said. 'How can I tell?'

'Well, you said knowing would make things difficult for you.'

I nodded. 'I suppose so. You make me curious.'

III

The attendant laid down the tray and went away to a far corner of the room where he sat at a high desk. There was nobody else there. He was quite impassive. I wondered if he had watched the Coronation, but could not imagine it. The previous day's excitement seemed very far away.

Philpotts picked up from the tray a small oval portrait and held it in his hand, more for me to see than himself. 'The first Elizabeth,' he said.

'Crumbs,' I said. 'Look at the jewels!'

240

'No,' he said. 'Look at the face. Look at the eyes.'

I stared and stared. 'They're not attractive,' I said. 'She's not very pretty.'

'But they're real.' He held it close to his own face and then produced a small glass and began to study it. 'She's not pretty at all. And she's not even old. But she knew a thing or two about ruling England. And the artist knew that she knew a thing or two. Look how slight his brushstrokes are! I wonder how he did it.'

I looked at him. 'Don't you know?' I asked. 'Don't *they* know?' I spoke quietly, but indicated in a general way with my hand the structure of the museum around us.

Philpotts smiled, more to himself than at my question. He handed me the glass and the portrait. 'Look at the curls on her cheek and temple. Look at the straight bit of hair, and the shadow in her ear. It is all so delicate.'

I peered closely at the glowing surface of pale flesh, magnified in the glass. Then I just looked at the miniature itself. 'It's beautiful without making her beautiful. I wonder what she thought.'

'There is somebody here who's good. I've written to him, but I haven't met him yet.' He was answering my earlier question. 'Not a great deal is known. But we do know quite a bit about what she thought. A bright lady, you could say. And she liked him. He was her favourite limner.'

'Her favourite what?'

'Limner. Painter. Another word. Portrait painter really. We don't use it any more, but she did. And so did he. They talked about it together.' He put back the small oval into the tray, and took up another. He went over several of them, pointing out different features, emphasising the economy, the coolness, the objectivity, the concentration in the eyes.

'Did he do many?'

'There would be thirty or so recorded works. Not much for a life. There are more on public display. We'll see them on our way out.'

'Don't you want to do some work?' I did not know quite

241

what I meant by 'work'. I was curious about it. The idea of Philpotts studying Hilliard had not really progressed much beyond him staring at the individual miniatures with the aid of his glass, and noting different points of excellence in the technique. I half expected him to produce a notebook and write something into it, but he did not.

He looked at me. 'You said you wanted to know what I was doing. This is it. This is what I shall be working on.'

'Do you want to meet this man here? The one who knows about it? I don't mind waiting.'

He laughed. He got up from his chair and crossed over to the high desk to say something to the man. Then he came back. 'We'll look at the other ones on our way out. It won't be as good as seeing them like this, but we're lucky there aren't more on display.'

I stood up and watched as the attendant checked the cards in his hand against the miniatures in the tray. Someone else came into the room and sat down at a box of drawings or manuscripts, I could not see which.

The attendant said 'Thank you, sir,' and handed back the cards. When he had gone away again, this time with the tray, we turned towards the door.

'I'm not ready to see anyone yet,' Philpotts said. 'I have to prepare myself. I need to know what I'm talking about. We all need to know that first. You need to know it right now, with your exams coming up. I hope you do.'

I didn't answer. His words had suddenly brought home to me how close it all was, how little I knew. Why, I did not even know what a limner was!

'Are you still looking after Wedmore?' I asked. 'Is he still a problem?'

He looked at me, one eyebrow raised. 'We lost Wedmore. To the others.'

'*Lost* him?'

Philpotts nodded. 'Your brother still thinks he can be redeemed.'

'And do you?'

242

'I'm not sure. I expect he'll have another crisis before the end of the summer.'

I followed Philpotts through part of the museum, and we came to a room in which there were flat display cases filled with miniatures. I wanted to linger over them, absorbing everything. But he was impatient to deal only with the one thing.

'We concentrate on the matter in hand,' he said watching me as I identified another portrait of Queen Elizabeth, this time by Isaac Oliver. 'He was good,' he said, pointing at the work in front of me, 'but this is great,' and he shifted his hand across the glass to another work, this time the face of a young man with dark hair, and wearing an earring.

'He's wearing an earring,' I said.

'And a jewelled ring on his finger. And a brooch on a golden chain around his neck.'

'Why the flames?'

'They are the flames of passion.'

Later, sitting at a table drinking coffee, I said to him, 'You know, I never knew what it was like for you, doing exams, when you used to talk to me. I didn't know what you were going through.'

'And you do now?'

'I do, in a way.'

'And is there anyone you...talk to?' His hesitation was momentary.

'Well, there's a boy called Wickham.'

'And do you think he understands?'

'I don't know if he understands. It doesn't seem to matter. He listens. He asks me how I'm getting on.'

'Same house?'

'Yes.'

'Does it help?'

I nodded.

'Good. That's what you want.'

I had thought of all sorts of things I wanted to ask. But I realised they were pointless and impossible. If I had been to

243

Philpotts what Wickham ⟨   ⟩ me, then so be it. It was sufficient. And it had passed on into the morning's encounter and the rich inspection of the limner's art. It was a new dimension replacing the old, and it was more powerful, more impressive, than what might have been with other friends, notably Lytton and Pritchett, with whom I could not easily see myself renewing any acquaintance. And the realisation of that was enough.

Looking across the cheap surface of the table in the tearoom at his calm, reserved expression; thinking of the premeditations he applied to his work; and remembering how like this he had been at Coppinger, I was reassured in my own feelings about Wickham. We had returned to the place where we were staying, tired, but by no means late, the previous evening, and I had left him and the others the next morning to come and meet Philpotts knowing that I had to be back in time to leave at lunch for the coach journey back to Coppinger. The imprecise curiosity which had brought me to this encounter, a curiosity about his work and feelings which shadowed an equal curiosity about my own future and about how I felt, had not lost its imprecision. Instead, it had been overwhelmed by a deeper and more fundamental conviction of rightness. To be loved, to love, in the senses in which instinct made me understand the words, even if I could not bring myself to form them into such explicit terms, was an acceptable course along which to allow my own heart to seek its fulfilment. That is how I felt. I looked at Philpotts and wondered if he knew what was in my mind. I decided that he didn't, and that even my own perceptions were muddled and terribly unsure, wavering on the brink of shame or embarrassment only to be pulled back by the rocky outcrop of love.

'Do you know Wyatt's poem "They flee from me…."?' I asked.

'Are you thinking of the Flames of Passion?'

I nodded. 'It's a marvellous portrait.'

'One day,' Philpotts said, 'if I'm lucky, and work hard on

244

it for about twenty years, I might find out who he is, and why Hilliard painted him in that strange way.'

IV

We drove out of London through districts I had always regarded, more or less, as 'home'; from the Bayswater Road up near Lancaster Gate to the bottom of the long incline down past Holland Park, I could point to left or right and say, 'There is "home"!' 'And there!' 'And there!' I did not do so, of course. The most I permitted myself was to indicate to Wickham, who sat beside me in the coach, the house where Francis had a room, and to tell him that which was not entirely true, though might in certain circumstances become so, that I also might have a base there. As for the rest, it was over. My father had moved away. He no longer made provision for me, and the need for it no longer arose. Combinations of circumstance, notably Mr Porphyry, had rescued me from dependence on him, and with the change there had drifted away also the strange and hungry urge to claim territory that had, on past occasions, made me proud to regard this part of London as 'home'. When I had done so the claim had been very inexact, deriving from innumerable shifts here and there, often accompanied by painful memories. But that did not matter. What I could say was that here I lived and grew up and experienced what I suppose were as much 'adventures' as anyone has in life. And passing through in the coach as it moved quite swiftly westwards, far too swiftly to allow for even the most rapid mental documentation of where and when, I had a clear sense of something being over, past, finished. I did not know what it was, but it seemed to be contained in the recollected events of those two days in London, events which had almost nothing to do with the historic occasion which had brought us all to the city. Somehow, seeing Father, meeting Philpotts, being with Wickham, had created within me an

245

expectation of alternatives which freed me from the curious geographical anchorages of Clanricarde Gardens, Campden Hill, Ossington Street.

My last sight of him, as he stood on the edge of the pavement, looking sideways at me, coughing into his large coloured handkerchief, made me think of him as small and, in a new and different way altogether, vulnerable. That view was to be rectified in no uncertain terms; he was to come roaring back, quite literally, and in most unfavourable circumstances. But just then he took on a reduced stature. There was compensation for this in the secure feelings I had about both Philpotts and Wickham. And I suppose it was this that liberated me from place and latched my dependence on to people.

Comfort in the present, a certain confidence within myself, diluted the normal feelings of regret with which, on past occasions, departure from London was suffused. Now, I felt relief. On that afternoon journey, through rain and, for June, a cold wind, the return to Coppinger—the last I would make as a schoolboy from London—was surrounded by the comfort and confidence of carrying within myself certainty about all the ingredients of my future happiness. Friendship, affection, love, work, goals towards which to direct my energies, they all whirled around in my mind, and I was invincible. Or so I thought.

But I had not reckoned with the savage, unheeding hand of fate which can set in motion with such terrible and dismissive disregard for a lifetime's preparation a small but fatal sequence of events. When Wickham came to me shortly after we got back I could see straight away that something was wrong, but could not accept it as serious.

'What is it?' I said. I was in the prefects' study with Archer. We had been looking at the photographs in the newspapers to see if our part of the route had been taken. Wickham was standing in the doorway. He was rather pale under his dark complexion, and it made him look ill.

246

'Can I see you?' He nodded his head sideways to indicate that he wanted me to go out to him.

'Of course.' I got up and went out.

'There's been a locker search,' he said.

'Yes?'

'The Old Man found your poem.'

'What, Patterson?'

'Yes. He took it. He just sent for me. Asked me about it. Did you write it. Did you give it to me. He wanted to know what was behind it.'

'There's nothing behind it. The man's mad. It's just what it is.'

'He wants to see you. He told me to send you.'

I shrugged my shoulders. 'I'll go and see him then. Are you all right? Are you upset?'

'Why's he making so much fuss?'

'He's probably been drinking. Don't worry, little—' I stopped myself from completing what would have been, in the circumstances, an inappropriate expression of my concern. But I reached out my hand to give his shoulder a squeeze.

He stepped back, still staring at me. It was as if he had bitten me.

'Where is he?'

'In his study.'

I went directly to the door and knocked. I felt frightened on Wickham's behalf, angry on my own. I prepared nothing in my mind, for there was nothing to prepare. All was there, on the sheet of paper. I could not pretend there was a word I did not mean. I meant it all.

'Come in.'

'You wanted me?' I did not call him sir. If he noticed he chose not to make an issue of it. I recognised immediately the sheet of blue paper in his hand. I closed the door behind me and walked into the centre of the room.

'What's the meaning of this?' He raised the bit of paper so that I could see the envelope behind it.

247

'Have you read it?'

'Of course I've read it.'

'Well then, you must know the meaning.'

'But did you give it to Wickham?'

'Yes.'

'Yes, sir!'

I did not answer. I waited for him to repeat the injunction. I had the awful feeling that I was precipitating a crisis that could, possibly, have been avoided.

He went on: 'Is Wickham the "little swan"? Are these lines addressed to him?'

I looked at him in the comparative gloom of the room. From the corner of my eye I could see the yellowy light of the sun, after the day's heavy rain, falling on the bank of green shrubbery outside the window. It had a threatening appearance.

'Yes, sir. They are,' I said.

'But this is a love poem!' He uttered the word love as if it referred to some quite loathsome act, and that writing about it was a desecration of human life and behaviour.

'If you think so, sir.'

'What do *you* think? You must know! I mean—' His voice angry, his eyes glaring, he looked from me at the paper. 'What's this here about "the morning flute"? What do you mean by "each naked morn"? And "potency"? And "release my heart"?' He stared hard at me, expecting answers.

I was trembling. There was a crumbling feeling inside me; it was in my stomach and in my head. But I was determined not to let it show. I was determined not to give way.

'It means what it says, sir. What *I* think is in the poem. I meant it.'

'I hope you didn't.'

I looked at him for a moment or two, slowly realising that he did not have anything more to say. Then I stepped forward towards him. 'May I have it back now, sir?'

'Have it back?'

'Yes.'

'What do you mean? Of course you can't have it back. This is a very serious matter.' He folded the letter in two, as it had been, and replaced it in the envelope. 'I've been watching you and Wickham. And I don't like what I see. I shall take this matter further. You can go now.'

I left without a word. If I had behaved coolly with Patterson it was because I despised him. But after I had left the room I found myself shaking with the shock of the encounter and with own pent-up coldness towards my housemaster. I half expected to find Wickham nearby, but mercifully no one was in sight, and I was able to slip out of the house, and walk away.

I could not understand why Patterson had raised the matter at all. But I now felt a hollow, sick dismay. My sense of confident anticipation about the Oxford examinations, if not about everything else, had evaporated.

Chapter Eleven

I

The building was a huge rectangle. At each end was a lift. On each floor corridors ran round the outside. Unbroken they ran, both ends, both sides, except where they came to where the lifts were.

On each floor there was one room. The same in size, it was also the same in appearance. It resembled the great hall at school. It was not quite the same. Instead of having double doors at one end and a dais, or stage, at the other, it had double doors at both ends leading out to the lifts, so that looking into the large room on each floor, no matter from which end, was like looking towards the back of the school hall.

The corridors which ran round the outside were unnecessarily broad. They seemed immensely long, but light, as if the outer wall were either made of glass or even open to the weather.

The lifts were like cages. Not only did they have metal grille doors, which clanked over on wheels, leaving one able to see through them; but they seemed open in every other way, so that even the floor gave a feeling of insecurity, though it was apparently solid. The mechanism for raising or lowering was entirely visible: one could look upward into the great open shaft, and see people standing, waiting, staring through the grilles...

And there were many people...

They moved along the corridors in an unending flow. They were busy, preoccupied, silent. It was as if they were doing a regulated circuit of a sportsfield; certainly, that was the size of it. But they came to a stop at the lifts. In some curious way the lifts clanked up and down in the middle of the corridor, their grilles opening on three sides. This meant that only when the lift was on a particular floor could people move freely round, continuing the unending circuit. Otherwise, they were checked and controlled, at each end, by the lift-shafts. And to get into the room on each floor one had to wait for the lift, enter it, and then leave it through the grille and then through the double doors. Yet no one did so. The rooms remained empty. Sometimes, the double doors were open, so that it was possible to see row upon row of empty chairs, and to know that no one was in them. But usually the doors were shut, and people hurried by.

Sometimes the lift doors opened in sequence. Sometimes they opened altogether. It was all very difficult. Whenever one came to the lift at either end a small group was there, gradually growing, waiting to see what its chances would be. That was what the expressions on their faces meant. Expectant, solemn faces upon bodies poised to move forward again, they seemed acutely aware of having been brought involuntarily together.

But then I realised that the expression, a bit guilty, a bit self-conscious, a bit the look of someone who does not want to be noticed, was on everyone's face, not just when waiting for the lift, but moving along the corridors, turning at the corners avoiding each other. Trying to be indifferent, they nonetheless could not avoid the guilty glance of non-recognition that strokes one over with a brief, incurious inspection.

I knew none of them. I only knew that among that huge and anonymous crowd of people, floor upon floor of them, floors that I could not number, was Wickham, and I had to find him, and give him the bottle of pills I clutched in my hand, and discover why he had not let me offer him some comfort.

At each corner of each floor in this prison through which I hurried in various stages of panic, fury and despair, stood some member of the Coppinger staff. They were on small wooden platforms so that they could see clearly the passing people and inspect their faces. They, also, were searching. But for what? I did not know. They were ominous, like guards in a concentration camp, and the threat was emphasised by the downward-turned gaze of everyone who moved there, backward and forward, and from floor to floor. It was emphasised in the opaque reactions of the universal, grey anonymity of all the people, blocking the penetration of the inspecting eyes.

At first I thought they would stop me, and perhaps subject me to some form of punishment. Then I thought it was Wickham for whom they were searching through the crowd. But it seemed to be neither. They never shifted from their positions. They were always there, always staring.

The search was fruitless and exhausting. From time to time, finding myself in different places, I would see Wickham, and cry out to him, my voice mute or so faint as to make no impression among the shuffle of silent people. I would race after him, dodging through the indifferent throng. But every time I came close, and reached out to touch him on the shoulder, he would move back and away, slipping from me into the crowd, or dodging beyond the grille of the lift to be carried up or down to another floor. Then I would lose track of myself even, and find that I was suddenly in a different part, on another floor, and I would have to start all over again. My eyes were wet with tears of frustration and fatigue. The stern and bulky women attendants in the lifts would stare at me in a hostile way, just as they might have done in a London store years before, reproving me for playing with a machine designed for serious workers of the world. They did not stop me, but their hostility pervaded my aching sense of loss.

I would ask at the corners of the building on each floor, looking up at Merchant or Parker or the Gaffer, whoever had control of that section. But they did not answer me. They looked reprovingly down and shook their heads. They did so, sadly, mockingly, as if they could not tell me what was wrong.

And then I would set off again, and Wickham would be there, and I would plead with him to stop. I would hold up the bottle. But always he just slipped away from me, shaking his head, his eyes also filled with sadness and a faint aspect of mockery.

I seemed to spend all of that short summer night in that strange building of my imagining, hunting through its corridors and among its grey inhabitants for someone I had found, and lost, and would never hold again. At dawn I got up and went to the window of the room I had been given. It looked out, not on the quadrangle of that particular Oxford college, but on a narrow street along which, on the other side, ran a high wall. I could see over it into another college garden where a huge weeping ash trailed its deep green leaves on the clipped lawn. In the greyness I took in the detail of what I saw without any pleasure or comfort. I felt exhausted by my night's search. It had been neither a dream nor a nightmare. It had been both, and something more beside, since each time I awoke and lay in the narrow bed trying to purge my mind of the wasteful exercise upon which it had embarked, nothing happened; and when I slept again it served only to send me back into the same prison to embark yet again on the same futile quest.

For a time it was better just to sit in the window, feeling the cool morning air blowing in upon me. I did not want to go back yet again to the prison. But the long hours stretched ahead of me. I kept saying to myself, 'Oh, little swan, Oh little swan!' And beating with my fist on the painted wood, chipped and discoloured, of the window frame. I could not bring myself to complete the poem. I could not remember it.

Wickham's was the only copy. And now it lay on Patterson's desk or was tucked inside his wallet.

The morning air was refreshing. My eyes were heavy and I felt my head nodding forward. I did not know how I would be able to cope with the papers that day, but it no longer seemed to matter. I was resigned to thinking, even then, that I would not come here anyway. It was just too difficult.

I went back to bed. On rare occasions, sometimes years apart, I have revisited, in later life, that particular prison; and I have spent time traversing its corridors. Sometimes the outer walls have not existed, so that people cringe away from the nightmarish fall over the precipice. Sometimes they have led straight out into open countryside. Sometimes the lift has been simply a platform, so that the people using it have crushed into the centre to avoid that same fall which shadows so many of our dreams. I have sought other loved ones in the maze of humanity. And alongside my fear of returning, there has grown up, not quite an affection, but at least a recognition of visited territory of the mind's own creation, so that even Wickham himself can be restored, on occasions, as he flees from me. But it is a sour restoration, redeemed only by the fact that it is better than what was yet to come.

II

I returned to Coppinger from Oxford by train. It was a Saturday. I had been told before leaving that they could not offer me a place at the college. I felt nothing. There was nothing I could say to myself. I still had my main examinations ahead of me. I would do better with them. Time was on my side. I thought about Wickham, and felt a great emptiness inside me. I did not know how to make it right. Then I thought about Patterson, and felt angry and cold and full of a bewildered determination to act.

It was the day of the cricket match between Patterson's

house and the Gaffer's. It was the final, and everyone would be there. It was early afternoon, and as I walked up towards the house I decided simply to find and take back the poem which Patterson had held in his hand that night, and which had blighted, it seemed to me, the innocent love I felt for Wickham, blighting also my frail chances of admission to an Oxford college. No one would be about. The match was as sacred as Memorial Day. And if it was there at all I would find it, and then I would destroy it.

I felt disembodied. I had not reported back. There was no one to report to, not even a junior boy, whose acknowledge-ment of my presence would make it real and could be used in evidence. Until I found someone, anyone, I was not really there, so completely empty was the place. Acres of sweet, familiar countryside that I had known so well, and for so many years, spread around me where I walked as though the whole school had been spirited away, as in a fairy story, and would be deposited back perhaps, but in a different era, so that younger colleagues, departed old boys, different staff, all part of the vanished cast, would be able to play tricks on my memory, or on my imagination. I thought to myself that I could commit some dramatic crime, some act that would be memorable, and then walk away and arrive all over again, as from a later train, with a cast-iron alibi. Yet all I wanted to do was retrieve my poem.

Instilled with this intent, girded by a Raffles-like sense of justice, I moved silently through the hallway of the house until I came to Patterson's study. I paused briefly, then opened the door, quite silently, and went in. I could not understand why the curtains were half-drawn, but did not care much, thinking that the room had not been used in the excited anticipation of the day's match. I was halfway across the end of the room where the door was, heading towards the large roll-top desk, with its untidy debris among which I felt I would find the blue envelope, when I heard a sound from the other end of the room, and turned to see the grappling figures of a man and woman, he with his buttocks

255

crudely lodged between her thighs, the motion as he drove himself into her seeming to me pitifully inadequate. I could see her face, indistinctly in the gloom, turning from side to side, her mouth groaning and gasping, her eyes opening upon me with a shriek that froze me completely in the act of turning and hurrying out.

Bennett looked as well, and his expression, less abandoned than hers, was angry, flushed, startled, as indeed it well might have been, given the unfortunate circumstances.

'Get out of here!' he shouted. 'Get out!'

Mrs Patterson was saying 'Oh my God! Oh my God!' and pushing him away, and dragging at her skirt to bring it down over her thighs, and trying to sit up, and pushing her hand up through her dishevelled hair, all at the same time, in a frenzy of action. Most of all I was struck by the untidiness of everything. Bennett's crumpled trousers, and the difficulty he had pulling them up quickly; her awkwardness, and the curious position in which his violent assault on her body had placed her, half on and half off the sofa; their dishevelled hair; their flushed faces.

Appalled though I was by what I had intruded upon, I yet had time to think to myself, so this is what it is all about: not the sweet and gentle folding of arms and pressing of flesh, the hand on a young girl's breast, the touch, the kiss, the endless cycle of embraces; no, not that, but this urgent, flushed, uncontrollable, and hungry pumping of the buttocks in a chaos of crumpled and discarded clothing, with limbs spread-eagled over sofa and floor, the whole world a disregarded chrysalis for each individual act of copulation.

I stood outside the door, suddenly and totally appalled by what had happened. It would be years before I would apprehend the enormous delight of such risks, and look back upon my intrusion with a compassionate understanding of the reality behind our perception then of what Bennett and Mrs Patterson meant to each other. But in the shock of what had occurred all I could think of were the towering difficulties of absorbing and living with what I had seen.

Where could I turn? What could I do? How could I possibly expunge my previously unnoticed arrival and go back and start again, walking past the house and on to the cricket match, as I would surely have done were it not for the poem?

With all the amazing speed of which the mind is capable, I went over the whole cycle of their love: how its chronology had been monitored by our youthful vigilance, yet never properly understood; how its impact on Patterson had worn him down, making him tired and suspicious; how Bennett had really been admired, Mrs Patterson desired, her husband pitied.

Thinking these things I moved slowly, step by silent step, across the hallway heading towards the door of the small prefects' study. I felt, foolishly it must be admitted, that I should have told Bennett about Oxford. And I wondered if he had had similar thoughts. And just for a moment the absurdity made me laugh to myself before the awfulness descended again.

Suddenly the study door opened behind me and Bennett called out. He stood in the doorway as I crossed the hall towards him, and I hesitated, not knowing how angry he was, and what he might do. But he stood back and said, in an almost gentle voice, 'Come in. Don't worry. I want to talk to you.'

I went in. I stood where I had stood before. Mrs Patterson was sitting on the sofa, smoking a cigarette. She had smoothed her dark hair. She looked tense and withdrawn, staring straight in front of her. Having closed the door, Bennett moved down the room to the far end, turning in front of the fireplace, and picking up from the table there the packet of cigarettes and box of matches. He looked at me as he took one out and lit it, and I watched in a kind of envy as he drew deeply on it and then blew out the smoke staring directly at me.

'How did it go?' he said.

I looked from him to her, faintly astonished at the

257

question. She looked up at me, an expression of curiosity about my career on her face for the very first time. Never before had I had any sense of being a person to her. Now my fate seemed to matter. She also drew on her cigarette, and then looked at Bennett. Perhaps she was wondering what should happen next, and why I did not give an answer to his question. Boys, as far as she knew, answered when their masters asked them things: that was the impression she gave.

'I didn't get a place.'

'They told you?'

I nodded.

'Bad luck. What went wrong?'

I shook my head. 'I don't know. I seemed to fluff all the papers. The viva was hopeless.'

'Were you worried by anything?'

I looked at him and frowned. 'What do you mean, sir?'

He also paused, looking down at his cigarette. Then he drew on it, inhaling deeply once again before blowing out the pale cloud of smoke. 'I mean Wickham,' he said. 'What did Mr Patterson say to you about Wickham?'

Mrs Patterson was sitting forward on the edge of the sofa looking down at her cigarette, perfectly still. Her dark hair fell across her face, masking the expression, so that I did not know quite how to go on.

'Did he tell you about the poem?' I asked.

'Yes.'

'Did he show it to you?'

'You came in here to take it back, didn't you?'

'It's ours, Wickham's and mine. It's not his.' I felt a tide of distress flowing through me. I did not really want to talk about it to Bennett. There was no one to whom I could turn any more. It was over. Finished. The words did not matter. They and the feeling behind them had been sullied by Patterson, and I was only waiting for Bennett to add to the damage done.

He took from the pocket of his jacket the blue envelope. It was beginning to look a bit crumpled. He walked towards me. There was a table with books on it between us, and he leaned over it, holding it out. I took it. His face was quite serious, and I thought to myself it would make it all right if he said something about it, about the poem, that it was beautiful, perhaps; that it was well written. Even if it were not true it would still be all right.

But he did not do that. Perhaps because of the passions that lay behind the quite extraordinary encounter we were all having, he felt constrained to lighten the occasion. He said: 'Don't worry about it. We all have these feelings at school. It does happen. Nothing to be ashamed of.'

I was suddenly and intensely angry at his patronage, angry in the immediate and ill-controlled, throbbing way that can seize upon us at seventeen or eighteen, and is never quite the same later. 'I'm not ashamed,' I said. 'I'm proud. And *it* didn't just happen.' I put my hand over my mouth, which was quivering, and turned towards the door. I walked over to it, and had my hand on the handle when he told me to wait. I did so, without turning round.

'I want to ask you a favour,' he said.

I waited, not answering, still not turning.

'I've been in London for two days. I'm not due back until late tonight. I don't want you to say anything about my being here.'

There was a long pause. Eventually I turned and looked at him.

Beyond his shoulder Mrs Patterson was standing up, looking at me as well. I took my hand away from my mouth which must have looked both ugly and pitiful; certainly that was how it felt. I could not trust myself to speak. All I could do was to nod at Bennett, my eyes filling with tears. Then I went out.

III

It was grey territory now. Years before, at Coppinger, there

259

had been games of Cornish football played, large numbers participating in a wild and ragged rout, across pitches, round houses, through spinneys, down laneways. And it has often seemed to me since those days that there is in the game's exclusion of most rules and inclusion of anyone determined or strong enough to take part an analogy with life's endeavour as the novelist attempts to encompass it: the ball is the story; not the people. Kicked and carried along, first by one group, then another, provoking conflict, leaving characters behind, bringing on new figures, in the end it is always one's final concentration on the ball that concludes the story.

Bewildered, now, at what was happening, and stumbling out into the grey territory of my own dismay at having lost between myself and Bennett one of the final threads of reliance which I believed I required, I was plunged once more into events which seemed to have taken hold of me by the scruff of the neck. Like a ragged schoolboy I ran headlong down the hill because that was the way everyone else was going. I was no longer doing what I chose. I was now to be plucked, shaken, thrown about, by a fate which I had only ever really believed affected my father, and people like him.

Blundering from the house into the sunshine once again I tried to tell myself that I should never have gone in there. But it did not work. Somewhere within the churning recesses of my mind I was pleased to know and have confirmed all the innuendoes which had derived from a collective sequence of evidence that went back to an earlier experience a long time before. But such a confirmation!

I did not believe it possible, yet had to believe it. In my imagination I had constructed passionate embraces between them, but in the summer fields or autumn bracken, under gorse, or under the stars, on beds of pine needles or dead leaves, and never with quite that precision that envisaged his broad buttocks shaking and jerking between her hungry thighs. In one flashing, terrible moment all the evidence and suspicion had been overtaken, and lay now in useless, chaotic profusion around me. So, Mr Bennett, what I felt was 'nothing to be ashamed of'? What strange world did we inhabit?

From the match ahead of me, over the brow of a steep bank of grass, I could hear shouts and clapping and then quiet again and the crack of a cricket ball being struck. I was in time. But after the stroke there was a roar of approval, and as I topped the edge of the pitch I realised that my arrival had coincided with the end of the game.

It had become traditional to draw the stumps with the winning stroke, and not to play things out to a quieter end, and in the confusion of seeing this it took me a moment or two to realise that we had won, and that Patterson's slow tread as he walked out to meet the last two players, with Archer and others beside him, was the step of a happy man.

It had been Wickham, in fact, who had struck the last ball, and he now walked off rather jauntily, with his bat over his shoulder. There was no need for me to hurry. Being there was at least a gesture of having tried to get back in time, and little that I could say would measure up to the collective pleasure that was already apparent in what I was watching. I felt doubly excluded, by both tardiness and guilt. And saying well done to Wickham earned the small glance and nod which it deserved.

It was the same with Patterson. He acknowledged my return, but did not ask me how I had done. I think he did not realise, just then, where I had come from, nor that I might know the outcome of my attempt to get into Oxford. Why, in any case, should it matter to him?

'This merits a celebration,' he said to me later, as the excitement began to die down.

'It does indeed, sir. It's very good.'

I felt I was forcing out an enthusiasm which was not really there, and I wondered if he sensed this. 'When did the house last win?'

'We won it four years ago.' He looked at me, and I realised I should have said 'we' instead of 'the house.'

'Well, it's very good to have the cup back again.'

He just looked at me. 'I'll tell you the arrangements later. We'll get the team together for a bit of a party, and a few of the seniors. Mr Bennett as well. I'll ask the Head if he'll drop in.'

'Shall I arrange anything?' I asked.

From somewhere within his mind he seemed to recollect other issues that lay between us, sources of animosity and doubt. And I saw in his eyes what I can only describe as a remote fumbling for balance, a sudden grasping for an equilibrium that was absent. 'I want to see you, anyway,' he said. He looked at his watch. 'Come in to me at six. I'll be back by then.' Then he turned away towards the crowd now milling around the pavilion steps.

It was at this point that I saw Bennett. He came from the administration buildings, the opposite direction to the house, and he walked briskly yet easily, with a swing to his step, along the pavilion path towards us. He was slowed up by the boys, but made his way through them, heading towards Patterson. I think he had noticed that I was there, though it would not have mattered either way. And strange feelings ran through me as I saw some boy exchange a word with him, no doubt telling him the result, and the smile on his face, full of genuine pleasure and congratulation, as he went up to Patterson and spoke to him.

So, I thought, that is how it is done. How strange! Like Judas kissing Christ, we lay waste around us all trust, all faith, all certainty.

And Patterson replied. And his weak and craggy features smiled and melted with a pleasure that was unalloyed.

The cup each year was presented there, at the end of the match, and carried off in triumph by the winning house. It was an undisciplined occasion, and Merchant made it brief and fairly clipped. He was not greatly interested in cricket; and the additional friction between himself and Patterson, which had manifested itself sufficiently in my experience to mean that it was more widely known, cast a certain coldness over the presentation. But Archer, who took the cup, was loudly applauded, and I watched with pleasure the light of excitement in Wickham's face as he stood close beside his captain immediately afterwards. I saw Patterson speaking with Merchant, and Merchant nodding.

Wickham came up to me then. 'How did you get on?'

I smiled a bit bleakly. 'I didn't get a place,' I said.

'Bad luck. What happens next?'

'I try again, I suppose. See how the other exams go. I hear you won for us?'

'I got a good score.'

'I was late getting back. Just in time for the last ball.'

'It was a good one. I hit a four.'

'I know. Well done.' I smiled at him, but he turned away. And then he moved off with others of his friends, drifting now with the dispersing spectators towards houses and teas, roll calls and diversions.

I watched him still for a moment or two, and was vaguely troubled to see Spenlow and Kidd approaching the group he was with, and all of them moving away to stop and talk. What was it that Archer had said about them? Were they the Emissaries of the Council of the Confrérie? Was that it? Briefly, I recollected what I had been told; but then the recollection was engulfed by greater worries, and I hurried on back to the house in the glowing mellow light of late afternoon.

IV

It was curious how substantial the distancing was between myself and everyone else as a result of my having missed the match. The tide of excitement did not carry me along at all. I could evince some pleasure at victory, but that was the extent of it, and I knew nothing more that could furnish out

263

any exchange about the day's events. It was probably a good thing. My own somewhat damaged feelings were over-looked. No one, apart from Wickham, asked me how I had done at Oxford; and as for myself, my own disappointment had already been swallowed up by the encounter with Bennett and Mrs Patterson.

I felt calm about it, detached. I was not yet awakened, not yet aware of the disgust I also felt, deep down, about what had happened. It was building up within me. Quite unfairly the close connection in time between the cold voice of the assistant master of the Oxford College telling me I had no place, and the quite collected way in which Bennett had returned to me the poem wove together the two events, so that I felt the same cold hardness about both. And all the time my mind kept bringing up before me the untidy, frantic scramblings of the two of them, half on the sofa, half on the floor, caution forsaken for passion's sake. If only I had commanded greater wisdom then. But I did not. I stalked in cold fury, allowing my resentment at Bennett's patronage over the poem and over Wickham to distort and poison my judgment of his own love for Mrs Patterson.

At six I went into the study. Patterson was on his own. He was standing, just as Bennett had stood, at the end of the room.

He was relaxed, and looked so pleased with himself. 'Ah,' he said. 'Yes.' Then he stopped and frowned. 'We'll have a small celebration. In the senior common room. I'll go down for beer and cider. You'll arrange it.'

I stood looking at him, waiting.

He stared out of the window, then down at the sofa. I noticed how tidy it was now, the cushions plumped up, the rug in front of it straightened. 'I've decided to give you back the poem. I...I shouldn't have made such a fuss. I'm...' I thought he was going to say 'sorry', but the phrase petered out. I think if he had been able to give it to me then, it would have been all right. But I am by no means sure. He chose, however, after a fumbling, uncertain pause, to go on;

264

and the words were foolish words. I wanted to stop him; but the only way I could was by telling him I already had the poem, and I could not bring myself to do that.

He said 'You must be more careful, you know. I'm sure there's nothing underhand going on between you and Wickham. But you have to think about your position, what the others will think. You know, we've had trouble in the house before. There was Franklin. Had to be expelled. You remember Franklin?'

'Franklin's why I'm in your house, sir. It was because of his expulsion that I was moved here by Mr Merchant.' I spoke very quietly.

He paused just for a moment, but not looking at me, not aware of the slightly frosty edge of disdain in my voice. I did not want him to be aware, and had spoken quietly in order not to convey to him my inner sense of dismay. But there was rising within me a sick feeling that he should even mention Franklin.

'Yes,' he said. 'Remember what happened to him. I mean, you've got to be careful. Responsible.'

I suppose I should just have dismissed him as ridiculous; a man fumbling for answers to paradoxes which were outside his range of experience. But I was too angry, too filled with disgust.

'Do you mean,' I said, 'that I might get myself expelled? For the poem?'

'Of course not. Look. Let's forget the whole thing. Only you and I know about it. Just the two of us. Let's keep it at that—'

'And Wickham, sir.'

'Well, yes. Of course. Wickham. But he's not likely to betray any—'

'And Mrs Patterson, sir.'

'Well, she's my wife...'

'And Bennett, sir.'

'Bennett?'

'He gave it back to me, sir. This afternoon.'

265

'Gave it—? But Bennett was in London this afternoon! He only got back at the end of the cricket match. You were there.' He walked across to the desk, suddenly certain in his movements, and looked down at the papers and books. Then he turned his head towards me, frowning. 'Did you come in and take it?'

'No, sir. I came in here on my way up from the station. Mr Bennett was here, with Mrs Patterson.'

The frown became a puzzled look, and he turned slowly, leaning back against the desk. 'But my wife was out this afternoon. Shopping.'

I did not answer. I felt the constraining embrace of something larger than my own predicament. Looking down the room in the slanting light of the evening I could not imagine at all clearly what I had seen there only an hour or so before. I wondered, had it happened at all? But I could not go back now. 'You told Mr Bennett about the poem, sir. And he gave it back to me. He told me to be more careful. He told me it was nothing to be ashamed of. Will I arrange the party, then? Will I get things ready? We'll need glasses, won't we, sir? And plates?'

He paused, just standing there, not knowing what to do.

He looked crumpled and defeated. He waved his hand and nodded. 'Do it,' he said. 'Yes, do it. Get things organised. You know how. I'll be along at nine. They did well, the team. It was a good effort. I'm proud of them. We're all proud of them, aren't we?'

I went to the door. When I looked back at him he was fumbling with a bottle wrapped in brown paper. He must have bought it for the evening's celebration. I supposed it to be whisky. But I did not wait to see.

V

'It was Wickham did it,' Skinner said. 'Bloody marvellous innings, weren't it, Wick?'

'Just marvellous'll do, Skinner,' I said.

'I'm sorry. But it was better than marvellous.'

The two of them were sitting side by side among the others, and Skinner had draped his long, ape-like arm around Wickham's shoulder, so that his red and freckled hand fell round the younger boy's neck. Dressed still in their cricket clothes, and flushed now with the excitement of recollection as they had once been flushed with the effort of winning, they seemed to belong to a different, more remote tribe.

'Did you hit any fours, Skinner?' I asked.

'Yeah. Two. I got fourteen runs altogether.'

'His first four was terrific. Straight down the pitch.'

'Can we start another bottle?' Archer said.

He looked across at me and I nodded. It was about half-past nine. The sun had only just gone down beyond the fold of hills seen distantly through the window, and the sky was gloriously suffused with reds and mauves and faint tinges of green.

'He said he'd be in at nine. He won't be long.'

'Surprisin' 'e ain't 'ere now. 'E's usually 'fore time when we're celebratin'. Remember the Christmas party?'

'Yeah! We won't never forget that!'

The laughter ran round the room, good-natured, indulgent.

'What I say is it doesn't matter, him drinking an' all. He's a good sort!' Skinner had stood up and turned, with his back to the door. 'What I think is this, a vote of thanks is in order. Here's to Mr Patterson. He may take one over the eight, but he's a good sort.'

He raised his glass. Only the indifferent quality of the response he got told him that Patterson had appeared in the doorway behind him, and was standing in bemused uncertainty at the qualified praise he had heard.

Skinner turned and looked at him, his eyes wide open. Then he laughed, a great bold guffaw. 'I didn't see you, sir. Come to join us, 'ave you?'

Patterson stared at him, and I realised that his face was not quite right. The eyes, half-closed, were not responding; the left hand remained against the post of the door, supporting him.

Then his lips began to move, and after a time words came. 'You're good sorts yourselves. All of you. Grand fellows. Grand. I'm really very proud of you tonight. Yes. Proud. There are times one has to win. It's like a war, you see. I fought in one war. In Spain. Of course we didn't win. Not the war, anyway. But after a time it all becomes so confused that winning and losing are battles that take place inside you.' He attempted to demonstrate what he meant by placing his left hand across his chest. It was only when he then fell sideways against the door that I noticed he was clutching a fairly empty whisky bottle and a glass in his other hand.

Nobody spoke or moved. I could not tell what effect this strange spectacle was having on the others. All their eyes were on him, and from the expressions on their faces I vaguely assumed a lack of familiarity with the phenomenon to which they were witnesses. Into the bargain, they did not have the knowledge that I had, and to which I now saw myself as a central pivot. Under other circumstances I would have acted then, and done more or less the same as I had done at the Christmas party, persuading my house-master that for him at least the evening was over. But I felt differently now. I was curious and at the same time detached. I was conscious of Archer looking at me, and frowning, and asking with his eyes what should be done. But I made no response, not even the shrug of uncertainty that might have held him in check.

Patterson now stood in the doorway, unsupported, swaying slightly. 'In the end,' he said, and paused, looking round. He had said the last word with a special emphasis, surrounding it with an aura of distaste. And now he repeated the phrase, twice more with modifications. 'In the end. At the absolute end of everything, it all happens in here.' And

268

he thumped on his own chest with his fist, in which he enclosed quite easily the whisky glass. A few tiny drops flew out of it. The gesture, his physical assault on the centre of things, seemed to affect his balance, and he took first one step backwards, and then two forward into the room, coming to a stop quite close to Skinner. He looked at him as though for the first time. 'You're all right, Skinner. You're all right. You'll do, you know. You'll make out. You see, Skinner, you're a good sort.' The mental agonising of working out how good or bad people were showed in Patterson's face to a degree that reminded me strongly of my father. Some instinct told me what was coming, but I was powerless to act. 'Others,' he said, and the word stopped him for a moment, as though it was hurting him to get it out. 'Others are not so good, Skinner. There are others you just have to watch. It's like active service. It's like war. Eyes alert. All the time.'

Had he been sober the movement then would have been brief and covert. It would have been no less noticeable, but perhaps open to varied interpretation. As it was his blurred vision fumbled around among us until it settled on me. Then it seemed as if he had to focus, and I felt some of the boys as well were now turning to look at me. 'Others,' he said, and paused, and shook his head from side to side. The impulse, whatever it was for, to deride perhaps, to upbraid me for what I had done, which seemed of no great significance, now faded, and he looked down.

Whatever spell his physical and emotional state had exercised over us now vanished. It was Archer who stepped forward and said to him: 'Don't you think you should go back, sir? Sit in the study for a bit?'

Patterson looked at him. 'Do you think so, Archer?' It was a question of genuine curiosity.

There was muffled laughter.

'I do, sir.' Archer said.

With that infuriating slowness of reaction which it is fatal to hurry, Patterson looked round to find another answer, and his eyes came to rest on Skinner.

'Well, Skinner, what do you think? Do you agree?'

'Oh, yes, sir. I agree wiv Archer. I'll come wiv you, if you like.'

I wanted to laugh. I was so impressed. There was something so admirably relaxed about Skinner's big, muscular frame as he stood close in front of Patterson.

'That's a very good idea, Skinner. We'll go along now. It's getting dark, isn't it? Did I come late? It was a very good match. Very good. I'm proud of you all. Very proud.' He turned to the door, Skinner at his elbow, not exactly touching his arm, but giving what might be described as moral support. 'And Wickham was good,' he said, more to himself. 'And Archer was good, and so was Parkin. It was a very good catch he made. Where's Parkin?' He stopped, and wanted to turn, but doing so brought him face to face with Skinner once again, and seeming to recognise him all over again, he changed the direction of his mind: 'And you were good, Clarke. Yes. Everyone. Everyone.' Again he paused. I suddenly realised, from my own experiences, many of them, at different times and in different places, that Archer and Skinner had made a mistake. In closing in too much upon him, one on either side, they had stirred some ancient, half-forgotten resentment about compulsion. And with it, Patterson turned once more. 'Hold on a moment. Where's Parkin? Parkin?'

He was faced back into the room, staring among the faces. Somewhere through the house I heard a door slam, and voices. It was muffled, far off, and yet it registered in some of the boys' faces in that pause in which our housemaster searched for Parkin.

He stepped forward rather nervously. He was a quite small boy who had played exceptionally well. 'Here I am, sir. Parkin.' Mentioning his own name, as a reminder so it seemed, provoked more laughter. But it seemed that the pace of the alcohol through Patterson's system was accelerating, and that he had passed beyond any subtlety in recognising the humour of what was happening.

Almost ominously he stared at Parkin, trying to adjust to his presence, trying to remember what his achievement had been, and then praise him. But the effort was too much. Some secret spring in his mind clicked, and across his face there seemed to be drawn a blind which rendered his responses quite blank and neutral. 'Very good, Parkin. Very good. Very good. Very good.' The third time he said it, it sounded as though he were testing the words for their fitness, for as he said them he stared ahead at the evening light to be seen through the window.

Might it, even then, have been all right? I think probably not. I could hear voices again. We all could. And, whether Patterson did also, or not, he turned more swiftly than he should have done, calling out as he did so, 'Archer! Skinner!' And then he slipped, on spilt beer, and went down. It was sharp and sudden: on his bottom, his legs straight out. There was laughter. There were gasps of astonishment. And then Merchant was standing in the doorway, Bennett behind him, and he was saying, over his shoulder, 'From the noise it must be in—' He saw Patterson and stopped. His expression froze instantly, and then seemed to go hard, so that his eyes, flickering from face to face, then back and down towards Patterson's ludicrously inelegant position on the floor, were the only mobile elements in his features. Patterson looked at him, and then seemed to shrivel a little at the intractable hardness in Merchant's gaze.

Patterson looked round at the floor. 'Who spilt that beer?' he said. The note of command hid the slurring tone which had developed in his exchanges with Parkin, Archer, Skinner. He pointed down at the smeared puddle of liquid, part of it under his trouser leg. He still held in his hand the whisky glass; the bottle had rolled away, but was still all too visible beside a table leg. He looked up at Merchant. His face, never of a particularly healthy colour, had taken on a more pallid shade. 'Somebody spilt some beer, Headmaster. Some careless boy. Too much excitement. Slipped in it.' He drew up the knee of one leg, and turned sideways, reaching

271

across to give himself the necessary leverage to get up. He puffed first with the effort, and then found that he could not manage on his own. He looked away from Merchant, searching in the faces of the boys, now all staring either at him or at the headmaster. 'Archer?' Patterson said, looking for him. 'Skinner?' He seemed not to be able to focus on either. He put the hand still holding the glass on his raised knee and stared at it for a moment; then he looked up at Merchant. 'Mild celebration, old man. Winning the cup. You've just dropped in to join us, I suppose. Bennett here, too. Very welcome.' Then his face, looking into the inscrutable hardness, seemed to crumple. When he spoke again the tone was anguished. 'I need a hand, you boys. Can't you see?' He held out his arms. Archer and Skinner stepped forward. They paused, even as they were reaching down to help their housemaster, and glanced briefly back at Merchant. But he gestured at them with his two hands to heave Patterson to his feet, which they did.

Once again, Archer and Skinner stood on either side of their housemaster, their attitudes now protective rather than restrictive. I admired the calmness in their faces. I wanted nothing to do with him or with the episode. I felt no involvement, no concern. I felt disgust.

Merchant turned to Bennett. 'Get these boys to bed, house tutor. The celebrations are over.' Then he turned back towards Patterson. 'Do you need these two boys? Archer and Skinner? Or can they go? I'd like a word with you.'

Patterson shrugged. 'Off you go, houshe. You've done ver' well. Ver' ver' well.' He raised both his hands, dismissing them both. 'Come along, then, Headmaster.' He stepped forward towards Merchant who stood back and to one side. When Patterson was level he stopped and said, 'I'll lead on, eh?' And he walked unsteadily through the door, his arms swinging, too much, I thought, as if they had suddenly become engines of balance and of locomotion.

Merchant looked once round the room. For the first time he saw me, and he stared for just a moment or two longer than at anyone else, his eyes hooded, and narrowing very slightly. Then, almost imperceptibly, he nodded his head twice and went out.

There was no reluctance about going after that. The rude shock of the encounter took the heart out of celebration and put it into speculation, which was whispered in washroom, lavatory and dormitory. Bennett suppressed or moderated it where he could, but the tide of gossip flowed on during the half hour or so in which the senior boys settled down.

I was too closely a part of the real events to join in. Cold as I felt, and filled with a sense of disgust at drunkenness unmitigated by affection, as it would have been in the case of my father, I saw all too clearly that I had played a positive part in bringing Patterson to what I perceived as his dismal apotheosis. For that is what began for him that night. Ill-disposed to join in any speculation, equally ill-disposed to encounter Bennett, who I felt might have some suspicions as to why Patterson had drunk the whisky, and with no special duties to perform, I cleared back to the staff pantry the bottles and glasses, wiped up the beer, opened wide the windows of the room which by force of habit, and the intensity of my own work I had made my own, and sat down with the door firmly shut. I had not been part of the triumph. I would not now be part of any dismay or defeat or recrimination. I did wish, in those moments sitting there, that Wickham might come to the door, and that I might just talk with him, tell him— But what?

There descended upon me the renewed urge to work. If I worked I would be carried away. I could lose myself, forget. A few brief weeks remained to me, and here, now, the events of the day had rescued me. They had turned all my energies in on myself. Almost nothing outside of me mattered. Involvement had been stripped away; commitment sacrificed. I had no more duty towards Patterson; none to Merchant; nothing to Mr Bennett. The web, the net, the paving stones of what they were to each other, meshed, knotted, interlocked, had released me or expelled me into a

273

void of my own. And if I had been weak I would, just then, have suffered the isolation, seeing it as a form of hell, a damnation for treachery that was not treachery: for being the flux, the catalyst, that instrument of change which is itself not changed. But I was strong. And I felt it, sitting there, a wave of energy passing through me, the pricklings of determination, to renew the attack, to make good the recent failure, to build up towards a new peak that I would easily conquer.

I pulled books out from where they had been packed onto shelves or inside cupboards. I opened up files and turned over the pages of essays with Bennett's tidy, precise comments in the margins where he had detected and approved the nascent physiognomy of my mind. The sense of that approval made me grit my teeth: it was judicious, impersonal, objective, real. It could not be taken away. It had a life of its own, on the page, just as the work which was now coming to its final fruition had a life of its own, in my mind. I felt that this was the real climax of the day: not the encounters nor the confrontations; not the passion nor the despair; not the wonder I had witnessed, nor the triumph, nor the dismay: just this inner recognition that engulfed me and brought me to life.

Once, Archer appeared in the doorway, and began to tell me that the boys were in bed, and that Bennett had left, and that Merchant had left, though later still. And I listened, but could think of nothing to say. I was incurious. And seeing that I was engrossed among books, and in no mood to talk, he mumbled some vague encouragement, asked did I never let up, and went off again.

I measured out the days and hours left to me and tried to fit into them the many tasks, the reading, the revising, the final preparation that had to be faced. Could I rise before six? Would that help? What would lock up for certain a good result now, at this late hour? Mounting the stairs I was surprised to hear a faint clearing of the throat behind me. It came from the doorway of Wickham's dormitory. In the faint passage light that shone from further up, towards the next door, I could see he was lying on his side staring out at me, one hand hanging down across him towards the floor.

He raised it and beckoned me in.

I stood at the doorway looking down at him. 'Why are you still awake?'

He made a shrugging gesture, but it was vague, as though the question did not matter at all.

'Is anyone else awake?' I looked into the dark depths of the dormitory from which the gentle breathing of its youthful inmates came, soft evidence of collective insensibility.

'No.'

'Are you sure?'

Again the slight, dismissive shrugging gesture. Then he pointed to the foot of his bed. 'Sit down,' he said.

I did so.

'What was wrong? This evening? Why was he drunk? He was, wasn't he?'

It was my turn to nod. But I did not answer his other questions.

'But there was something else as well. He's never been like that. Never. I expected him to be all relaxed, and tell us about Spain. But he didn't, did he?'

'Did he give you your pills?'

'No. He didn't have them.'

'You mean he was too drunk?'

'No. He'd forgotten. It doesn't matter. It'll be all right.'

I frowned. 'When did they run out?'

'Ages ago. Two weeks. It doesn't matter. I've been okay. I haven't felt dizzy. Honest. Nothing.'

'But he should have got them.'

'Have you had a row with him?'

I shook my head. 'Why do you ask?'

'Just the way you looked. When you stared at him. It was as if he didn't matter any more.'

'Oh, I—David,' I said, 'you're too clever for your own safety.'

275

'But something must have been said. When you got the poem back.'

With that painful mixture of simulated idleness and indifference which marks great desire, I took his hand. There was a refreshing warmth in his response to my touch. 'It's all too complicated to tell you,' I said. 'Bennett gave me back the poem, not Patterson. He was nice about it. But it means they talked about us. Then I just told Patterson I had it back. I think he's ashamed of all the fuss. But I don't know.'

'You'll be a poet,' Wickham said. He gently withdrew his hand from mine.

I laughed. 'No, I won't. I'll be a schoolmaster. That's how it'll work out.'

'But you'll write more?'

'I don't know,' I said. 'I just don't know.' And then, fishing, I suppose, for some further compliment or encouragement; prolonging, for moments more, the settled sweetness of the occasion; and feeling the curious moving intimacy of the night around, I asked him: 'Should I?'

And with his unusually deep treble voice, and with a certitude that moved me, he said 'Oh, yes. You must go on. You must.'

I sat for a moment or two longer, then I got up. 'Good night,' I said. 'I have to be up early. Time's running out.'

He did not answer. He just raised his hand from the bedclothes and winked. He did it so well I wanted to laugh. But I just turned away. I felt strengthened to the point of invincibility. The dawn already seemed to beckon. The books laid out on the table below were all within my compass. I would turn the next day to my advantage.

Chapter Twelve

I

I knew that something was terribly wrong. It was a quarter to six, and I had got up to work. It was already light, the sun glinting through the trees, and it emphasised the stillness in the house to hear the full rich song of the birds. Yet it had nothing to do with that. It was in the stillness that I sensed it. Going down the stairs in my stockinged feet a small change in the pattern of my habitual experience checked, and finally stopped me. I stood there, puzzled, my hand on the rail. Then I realised what it was. I had not seen Wickham's face through the bannisters as I passed down on my way to the study.

I retraced my steps. He was there, but his bedclothes were over his head. The prickle of unease increased. He never slept like that. I went back up and crossed to his bed. A fairly shapeless bundle of clothes lay down the centre of it. I pulled them back. There was nothing to indicate where he was. I looked round the dormitory. All the other beds were normal, with clearly defined bodies in them. I pulled back the pillow. Nothing. Then the sheet. Under it, with his watch and a pen and a small knife, lay a crumpled envelope. I could not understand how it could help, but I turned it over and unfolded it.

There was no stamp. In flowery, boyish script across it there was written: 'Confidential and for your attention only. To Cadet Apprentice Wickham.'

I knew it to be his task from the Council of the Confrérie. I opened it, quickly now, and read the message. 'In the waters of the pool lie three marked stones. They must be brought to the Council tomorrow for your admission.' On a second sheet of paper there was a map showing the pool. In it was marked a cross, and paces along the side and one end were indicated, giving a more or less precise indication.

I dropped it. Terror seized me. I went down the stairs three at a time. The back door was locked, as well as bolted, but I found in the bootroom the narrow window from which Wickham must have gone out. It was latched open. I pushed my way through, and then I was running across the dew-laden grass. Great fear had already taken my breath from me, but I pounded through the sunlight and birdsong with huge, frantic strides, my arms pumping away at my sides to get me to the swimming pool.

It came into view, and its surface was smooth and unbroken. I felt a great flood of relief. Then I felt foolish. Then bewildered. Where could he be? I stumbled to the edge, almost falling in. Then I saw him.

Not much of his body was above the waterline. There was the little cushion of his sunburnt shoulders, just breaking the surface, and the black smudge of his hair. One of his hands was stretched out, the fingers extended, as though reaching for the handrail which ran round the pool.

I plunged in, threshing my way through the shallow water, terrible floods of feeling crushing themselves behind my dry, panic-stricken eyes. Pushing the water with my hands, taking huge but ineffectually slow strides, I came to where he was, and reached out, towards him. He moved easily to my touch. Then I heaved him up on to the edge and turned him over.

The eyes were wide open, but the warm liquid brown iris and the black pupil were whitish now, and opaque: terrible to behold. Between his parted lips I could see that his tongue, bluish-purple in colour, was deeply wounded by his teeth where they seemed to have bitten hard on one side.

278

I vomited into the pool, holding on to the handrail. I began to shiver uncontrollably, and tried to wipe my mouth. But my hand was shaking too much. Water was splashed on my glasses and I saw that water had got into my watch, a small puddle of it moving under the surface of the glass. It had stopped at five to six.

I could not look at him again. I got out of the pool and ran to the nearest house, sluggish and wet in my clothes now, but once again pounding through the dew, this time hopelessly enmeshed in feelings of terror, and trying to gather my breath to shout. It was my old house, Forrest's. I rang the doorbell and beat on it with my fists until a window opened above me, and the familiar face appeared there, solid and reliable.

'It's Wickham!' I shouted. 'It's Wickham! He's drowned!'

Forrest came down. He did not say anything. He was half dressed. He set off immediately at a loping run with me beside him. He must have said something to his wife because I heard a door slam behind me and then a window opening, and a voice calling something. But he did not stop.

When we got to the pool I hesitated, letting him go forward toward the little crumpled form on the grass at the water's edge. Tears were in my eyes, but would not flow. I felt numb, but not with cold. I knew, of course, he was dead, and nothing could be done. The Gaffer knelt down, turned him over, and began straightaway to press on his back, counting to himself. From where I stood the first pressure sent forth from his mouth a gout of water, and I turned away, gripping my fists and not knowing what to do next.

Not long after that the Gaffer came up behind me and took my arm. He led me away from the edge of the water. 'I'm afraid it's no use,' he said.

Brokenly I told him what I knew. It seemed so futile, and the Council of the Confrérie such a pitiful engine in the tragedy.

Then others arrived, Parker, Mrs Forrest, Merchant, and after them Patterson. He looked old and ill. Someone had

279

thrown a coat over the body, and standing all wet with Forrest I saw Patterson set off across the grass towards us, only to be stopped by Merchant, who came instead.

'I think, Forrest, you'd better get him to your house. He's done in. He could do with a hot bath. Patterson's in a hopeless st—' He stopped himself without finishing and hurried back.

Mrs Forrest had brought up their old Riley, and they put me into it. Then they drove away. I did not remember much after that except sitting, first in a blanket, then in borrowed clothes, and listening to Forrest as he said to his wife, perhaps not thinking of me at all, 'There'll have to be an inquest. This'll be bad for Patterson, and that's the truth of it.' And he sucked on his teeth and gently shook his head from side to side.

II

The police officer was a uniformed man, a sergeant. He was so like one's expectation of the solid reliable figure that brought to a safe conclusion at that time the innumerable well-made comedies and melodramas pouring forth from the British film industry. It was enough to make me want to laugh.

'I come from these parts,' he said, his voice a soft, country burr. "I knows it all very well. I were born over th'other side o' Gloucestershire, but my father came 'ere to take over the station at Biddington when I was just so 'igh, an' I grew up in sight o' this place.' He had put his hand out to measure how small he had been at the time, and in my bewildered state I fixed my eyes on this imaginary nipper who had grown to be such a large and phlegmatic individual. 'Weren't a school then. Probably you know. It were quite different then. There've been big changes. But then you're aware of all that. I'm told you didn't come 'ere yesterday, nor the day before that neither.' He paused, his head vaguely, questioningly, turned.

I realised he wanted me to answer. 'I've been here ten years.'

I must have said it very bleakly, because he laughed. 'Well I don't 'spect it were all that like a prison, eh?'

I smiled back at him and shook my head. 'No.'

Then he said: 'I suppose we'd best do a stroke o' work.' He suddenly looked businesslike. 'I want you to tell me just what happened.'

'Will I begin with this morning?'

He frowned, and I thought he would ask questions leading me back to an earlier point of departure, but all he did say was, 'Why not?'

And so I told him. I was surprised at how long it took. Surprised, too, at some of the questions he asked. I had to spell 'Confrérie' for him twice, and while I was all for hurrying on, he wanted to know who its members were.

'And did you know he was an epileptic?'

'Yes, sir, I did.'

'And did the others?'

'You mean the boys, in the house?'

He nodded.

I shook my head. 'No. No one knew in the house. No one in the school, not the boys, anyway.'

'Are you sure?'

'Yes.'

He seemed puzzled at how emphatic I was being. 'How is it you're so sure?'

'I just knew about him. I just found out. I was curious about the pills he had to take.'

'Yes,' he said. 'The pills.' But he did not ask me about them. Instead, he said about the body in the water, where it was, the position, face down, legs trailing on the bottom. And I tried to tell him about my struggle lifting it out of the water. But I could not go on, remembering the soft and sodden weight of it in my arms, drooping, pinched head with its matted black hair. And all he said, speaking gruffly, was, 'We know all about that. You can forget that.'

But I could not. And the memory fed my unhappiness and resentment. I was puzzled he had not asked about the pills. What I thought important he glossed over.

It may seem strange, but I went back to my books in the library. To say that I worked is to encapsulate in the word a fitful and uneven pursuit of knowledge, punctuated by repeatedly going over the events of the day. But that is what I did. I was surprised, late in the afternoon, to see the police car still sitting outside the main school block. I could not imagine what had kept them so long. If anything, my own testimony had been devoid of those things that might have inspired detailed cross-examination. Yet in spite of this it seemed to me that something had precipitated a process, one of law, which was far more substantial than I could have anticipated.

It was not the time taken in the inquiry. Nor was it anything said afterwards. If it could be pinned down at all, it was quite the reverse: a pervasive silence in which the issue of Wickham's death and the statement which I had made and which the police sergeant had laboriously written down in his notebook were studiously ignored. I was the object of certain penetrating stares; I was the recipient of the careful, almost too-polite treatment of Merchant, of Forrest, of Bennett, and of Patterson most of all.

They no longer behaved like schoolmasters. Instead of summoning me, as he would have done, sending some hapless emissary simply for the sake of form, Merchant came to the library, after tea, when the police had gone, and I was collecting my books to bring them back to my house, and he stood by the table, clearly uncertain what he should say.

'They've gone, sir, haven't they? The police?'

'Yes. They've gone.' He paused, staring down at the table. 'I'm sorry this has happened. He was a close friend of yours, wasn't he?'

I nodded, not able to speak.

'They asked a lot of questions, I suppose?'

Again I nodded.

He drummed on the end of the table with his fingers, but slowly the tips of them all together, and coming down on the oak surface with little measured thuds. 'They asked about his illness?'

I stared at the pale gold patterning of the medullary rays in the wood. Then I looked up at him. For what seemed quite a long time we just stared at each other. But I did not answer. Then he said, 'Well, of course all you must do is tell the truth. That's what we've taught you here.'

He went out after that.

No one else spoke as directly as he had done about the events of that day, or about what had gone before. And in its own way it was even more curious than Merchant having exhorted me to tell the truth. It was odd, being in the house with Patterson, aware of his grey and harassed expression, and yet having no exchange at all about Wickham's death. And it was the same with Bennett.

I had not mentioned to the police officer the poem. And so one whole thread was missing from the texture, depriving it, except in the case of the three of us, and Mrs Patterson as well, of its full pattern. But no allusions were made to that. In fact, nothing at all was said.

Archer came to me the next morning to show me the *Daily Telegraph*. A tiny, two-line paragraph reported the incident. It simply said: 'A coroner's inquest has been ordered into the death of a boy of fourteen, David Wickham, whose body was found in the swimming pool at Coppinger School, Biddington in Oxfordshire yesterday morning. The inquest will take place later.' I was faintly disappointed that my own name did not appear.

When the time came the inquest was held in the school library. It began in the afternoon. It was expected to last a couple of hours at most.

The Coroner was a woman. I was surprised at how relaxed she was about it all; surprised, too, that we all assembled together in that long, comfortable, familiar room in which I had spent so many of my happiest hours at Coppinger. There must have been more than thirty people in the room, including a small group of outsiders who had nothing to do with the investigation. There were also two journalists at a separate table, one of them an elderly man in rimless glasses from the *Oxford Mail*, familiar from prize-givings, when he came down to report the sayings of the generals and admirals who addressed us. There were seven in the jury, only one of whom I knew, the local post-mistress, and she smiled across at me where I sat in the front row of chairs with Mr Forrest, and Mr Patterson beyond him. I nodded back at her, and I watched her face as the court was called to order, the jury sworn in; and then all of us were told that which we knew already, that we were gathered to ascertain who had died, where, when and how. I felt very remote. It was with relief that I heard my own name called and stepped forward.

I was directed to a chair facing the jury, and sat down in it, feeling uncomfortably stiff and tense. I undid the button on my grey jacket and smoothed down the blue house tie I was wearing. A prefects' tie would have been better, I thought, and then thought to myself, it does not matter.

She asked me if I had made a statement, and she pointed to the police sergeant. I said yes, and watched as she moved the papers in front of her, looking down at the typed sheet.

I said to her: 'What do I call you, please?'

And she answered, 'My name is Uttley. You can call me Miss Uttley. That would be best.'

And so I repeated to her, 'Yes, Miss Uttley.'

'Well, if you don't mind,' she said, 'I'm going to ask you to tell me in your own words again what happened. Take your time. Just do it your own way.' She waited, a look of polite inquiry on her otherwise inexpressive face.

I was surprised how easy it was, once I got started. I became quite pleased with myself, the way I was telling the story. And then I was suddenly ashamed, and remembered the feelings within me as I struggled to lift the small, sodden body out of the water.

'You've said in your statement you knew that your young friend was an epileptic. Did you know what this meant?'

'I knew he had dizzy spells. Sometimes he fainted.'

'And nothing more serious than that?'

'I knew what could happen.'

'You mean, worse than just dizzy spells?'

'Yes.'

I paused in the warm stillness of the afternoon and looked at the jury. I was vaguely aware of a faint rustle of movement down the room, where the others were sitting, but I did not turn towards them. I looked back at the Coroner who had glanced down at her papers. I thought to myself: She doesn't expect me to say any more. And yet I have more things to tell her.

'You see, Miss Uttley,' I said, and she looked up at me. 'You see, he had these pills.' I paused. 'Only he'd run out. He didn't like taking them. He thought they spoilt his bowling.' I paused. 'He used to say to me—'

'Just a moment,' she said. 'Let me stop you there.'

I stopped, and looked down at my hands. The noise in the room had increased. In front of me, by glancing upward, I could see that some of the jury were staring at the Coroner. I felt within me conflicting currents of emotion; a tide of longing and regret pulled one way, a tide of bitterness pulled the other. Nothing, in all the grey world, could bring him back, not anything I could say or do. Yet if there was an instinctive urge towards discretion of some kind, towards restraint, towards a glossing over, there was a still stronger tide flowing in favour of telling all.

'You say he took pills? And had run out?'

'Yes,' I said, nodding at her. 'I used to ask him, had he taken them. I used to worry, 'cause he didn't want to. I thought something might happen.'

'What did you think might happen?'

'I thought a fit, or something.'

285

'How did you know about epilepsy?'

'I read about it in the Encyclopaedia.'

'Did your young friend know about it?'

'I don't think so. I never asked him. He never liked to talk about it. I just used to say to him he'd get a dizzy spell if he didn't take his pills.'

The Coroner made a note on a sheet of paper on the table in front of her. She paused, still looking down. Then she looked directly at me. 'And you say he ran out of pills?'

'Yes, Miss Uttley.'

'He told you?'

'Yes.'

'Did you do anything?'

'I went to our housemaster to ask him to get more.'

'And what happened?'

I paused. 'Nothing,' I said.

'You mean—?'

I looked down.

'How many ti—' She stopped and raised her hand in the air, a frown on her face, her mouth frozen open for a moment or two. Then she said: 'No. Don't answer that. Just sit where you are for a moment and keep quiet. You've done very well.' She smiled at me, but I could not smile back. I did not know where to look. I felt the eyes of the jury on me.

The Coroner leaned across towards her officer and spoke to him. She seemed to be asking a question. He then beckoned the police sergeant who had questioned us, and they conferred for a moment or two. Then she looked up at the main group of people facing her in the library: 'Which of you is Mr Patterson?'

Patterson got to his feet, and for the first time I looked at him. His face looked grey and old, the mouth troubled and weak. I felt within me the vigour of my distaste. 'That's me,' he said.

'I think,' she said, speaking slowly, 'all things considered, that it would be better if you were represented legally. Do you have a solicitor?'

286

Patterson looked back at her, frowning: 'I do. Yes.'

'Could he be here tomorrow morning? Eleven o'clock?'

'I'm sure he could. He's local. Should I find out?'

'I'm going to adjourn this inquest until eleven o'clock tomorrow. Perhaps you would telephone your solicitor and tell my officer immediately, in case we need a longer adjournment. Please understand that I am taking a formal precaution only. That will be all.' Turning to me she said, 'And you, young man, will present yourself again in the morning. Don't think that this delay is anything unusual, or that you have said anything wrong.'

She had meant the words to reassure me; but they did not. It was clear from the stern, flinty expressions on the faces of the jurors, that it was unusual, and that I, as the only witness so far called, was entirely responsible. But I did not need their reaction to tell me what I had done. It was already clear within me, just as the words themselves had been deliberate, just as I intended, at that moment, to pursue the next day, that very course of objective truth which we are exhorted to pursue with the public voice of morality, even if the private whisper in one's ear advises restraint, discretion, mercy. That was the construction my mind put upon the circumstances in which the inquest broke up. There were hesitations as well. I did feel strangely alone. The physical isolation of actually having no one, no one at all to whom I could turn and talk in the confusion of the room emptying itself of people, was almost the equivalent of a series of blows. And, briefly, I even thought of retiring into one of the bays of books to escape into the pages of literature or history in default of some person to whom I might turn. And then, suddenly appearing beside me, there was this small woman, dressed in a blue summer skirt and flower-patterned blouse, a broad-brimmed hat on her head. And looking down at her hand on my arm, and into her sad eyes, I recognised Wickham's mother. An exchange of words at some school event or other was all the knowledge we had of each other, and yet, at that moment, she seemed very close and very necessary to me.

I looked down into her face. 'Are you alone?' I said.

She nodded.

I knew she was a widow, but thought that some friend might have come with her. 'I didn't know you would be here.'

'Oh, yes,' she said. 'I had to come.'

'I've caused a delay.'

'I know. I was interested in what you said, very interested. I shouldn't ask, of course, but what did happen about the pills? How many times did you ask Mr Patterson? Do tell me. I want to know.' Her eyes looked directly into mine, level and unblinking. Amid all the movement and noise the silence between the two of us was pronounced.

I wanted time to think about her question. I did not want to name, there and then, a given number of requests made to Mr Patterson. I was confused and a little frightened; I did not know what to think or what to say. It was enough to have to face the continued giving of evidence the next morning, without going over it in advance with Wickham's mother. In addition, there was a curious feeling of remoteness towards her. After the initial response, of closeness and need, I had detached myself once again. Her relationship to Wickham, which should have sustained feelings of sympathy, now did the reverse: she was suspect in the questions she was asking. I still might have answered them, but fortunately Merchant came across the room and joined us.

'I'm sorry I didn't see you before now, Mrs Wickham. I knew you would be here, of course.'

'I arrived late,' she said. 'I did not expect an adjournment.'

'None of us did.' Merchant looked at me. 'You can go along now,' he said. 'I'll look after Wick—, Mrs Wickham.'

I left them without saying anything. I felt a curious numbness in my head. I was glad of the excuse not to speak any further with her or with the headmaster. I wanted to be outside, in the damp wind of that miserable July day. Closed in, all around me, were the principal protagonists of my

288

years at Coppinger, and I needed to escape and think over again this present course of action.

When I came out in front of the school buildings, Forrest and Patterson were standing together in one place. Bennett was there with Parker, and there was a junior master called Lock. Several of the wives were also talking together, and one or two members of the administrative staff. Patterson looked across at me and our eyes met. To say that I stared back is not entirely true, but it was, in that trite phrase, a level gaze that I turned on him, and when he glanced away again I felt a certain strong disgust. He was to blame. He deserved to be punished. And I did not care.

Hate is a strange emotion. Like love, one sometimes has to tell oneself that it is there. Our animal instincts carry us forward; it is the intellect that arrests the forward motion in order to inject feeling, and time is perpetually modifying and watering down our passions. We could not survive them else. And now, years afterwards, it is hard if not impossible to recapture at all just how strongly I felt about that weak, sad man, whose suspicions had been an insult, whose negligence I believed had deprived me of something I loved, and whose fate at that time had fallen into my youthful hands.

If the inquest did not exactly promise to have Patterson brought forth from it, bound, to the gallows, it certainly foreshadowed an outcome almost as final, as far as his career was concerned. At least, that was how I viewed it. And I did so, from behind the protective armour of self-righteousness. It did not feel so good at the time. It was the first occasion I had experienced of that kind. I suppose it was a taste of power. Certainly it was a new dimension, one that in time would become both familiar and even enjoyable. But just then, to the freedom I felt, there was attached a loneliness, an isolation, which was almost breathtaking.

III

I thought something would happen. I anticipated some revelation; intervention, divine or human, had been made necessary by the turn of events. Yet the short summer night passed away, with no change in whatever resolution it was that held me fixed upon a course that seemed to have frozen away from me all contact and communication. Perhaps not quite all. There was Skinner, for one. And there was Archer.

Skinner had spoken to me about Wickham's death at the time. He had been most upset. He came to me on the morning the inquest was to resume and asked why it was going on a second day.

'Haven't you heard?' I asked. I imagined that no one was in doubt about that.

'I don't fink nobody knows,' he said.

I looked quite steadily at him. 'Our housemaster had to get a solicitor. The Coroner told him he needed to be legally represented.'

He stared back at me, not fully comprehending. I was disinclined to explain further.

'Will they take it out on 'im?'

'I've no idea.'

'I was real sorry; about old Wickie. Real sorry. An' you findin' 'im, an' all.'

'I know.' I nodded. 'You said.'

Emotion troubled a face that was generally bland and cheerful. It had caused him to revert to a looseness of expression, a more pronounced dropping of aitches and word-endings than was normal.

'I mean,' Skinner said, ' 'e were special to you, wern' 'e?'

'Thanks,' I said. 'You were fond of him yourself.'

'Yer!' His face flared up with life and energy, as though the act of remembering Wickham and his affection had brought him to life again. But the light quickly faded.

290

'Yer,' he repeated, more quietly. 'But that were different.'

'I don't know,' I said.

He frowned. 'But ol' Pa'erson! Wouldn't be fair, would it? 'im to get the chop?'

'I think it may already be too late to avoid that,' I said.

'You mean Merchant? Comin' 'ere?'

'Maybe.'

Skinner went off then to get ready for morning school. I was free until eleven. With a relentlessness that was justified by circumstance house activities continued their normal course. A short while before it was necessary for him to leave, Archer came in to the small room in which I had spent so much time working that year. I was not working then, but for want of something better to do I had opened a book, and it now lay in front of me on the desk.

He stood beside me. 'Getting some work done?'

I had the grace to laugh. 'Can't seem to make any sense of it.'

'Anything I can do?'

I shook my head.

'If I could help in any way...'

I looked up into his troubled eyes. 'Thanks a lot. But there's nothing.'

He looked down at his feet. His hands were in his pockets. 'You once said to me, it's always bad to get your name in the papers. Remember?'

I nodded.

'Yours is in. Bit in the *Telegraph*. Bit like that.' He held up his hand to indicate with his fingers a three-inch story.

'They've come? The papers?'

'Baron showed me. Do you want to see?'

I shook my head. 'Not really,' I said. 'I'll look at it later.'

Archer said, 'I'll have to go now. I'll be late. There's nothing you want?'

Again I shook my head. 'Thanks anyway,' I said.

After he had gone I tried to work, but could not. Then I wandered into the commonroom, found the paper, and read over the brief account low down on an early, inside page. It must have been the adjournment which had caught the attention of the news editor. I did not at the time, realise it was unusual.

We assembled, as ordered, at eleven. The Coroner knew Mr Patterson's solicitor, and the two of them were talking together before her officer called the room to order.

I sat in the front row of seats, facing the table at which she sat, and expecting to be called first. But instead she turned to the jury. 'I am sorry this has involved more of your time than was anticipated. It is a precaution only. I don't want you to attach too much importance to it. Now,' she said, turning towards where I sat, 'will you come back and sit up here?' Her voice was kindly, gentle, unstrained, as though we were all resuming a chat about an event that was unimportant and far off in time.

I felt to myself, yes, I will do it to oblige her since she is being so pleasant about everything, and I got up and crossed the short space of floor to the witness's seat for all the world as though we were rehearsing a school play and I was going through the necessary motions under the direction of someone who knew a great deal more about the ultimate design of things than I did. I was merely playing a part. And those strange yet familiar constrictions that had descended on me before singing a solo, the dryness of the mouth, the heart pumping, the curious conviction that the body does not belong to that tiny nugget of intellect which drives it forward to act, descended now again in the expectant stillness of the school library.

The feeling was probably illusory, but I seemed to be doing everything very slowly. I sat down opposite the jury, and looked at the six faces which were now opposite, for one of them had been excused the previous afternoon. Then I looked at the Coroner. Like a well-trained performer I refrained from surveying the audience, and waited for the conductor to set things in motion.

She did not smile. 'You were telling us about your young

friend's health,' she said. 'You knew he was not well?'

I nodded.

'You knew he was an epileptic?'

'Yes,' I said.

'Did you have any idea that he was in any kind of danger from the illness?'

'Do you mean having fits, getting dizzy?'

She paused, made a note, then looked up at me. 'That sort of thing. Yes.'

'Well, I knew he had to have these pills. I read about it. I knew it could be bad. I didn't know about him. I just knew he had to take the pills.'

'When he had them?'

'Yes,' I said.

'But he ran out of them?'

'Yes.'

'And where did they come from?'

'Well, they came from the San—the Sanatorium.'

'But who was responsible?.

'Our housemaster. Mr Patterson.' I half anticipated that Patterson's solicitor would get to his feet and say something like 'Objection!' But there was just another of the little pauses that preceded her questions.

'It was you went to Mr Patterson? To tell him, I mean, that Wickham's pills had run out?'

'Well, Wickham told him, first. But he didn't make a thing about it. You see, there was the cricket. He was playing for the house. Bowling.'

'He thought the pills affected him. Didn't you tell us that?'

I nodded.

'And did they?'

'I didn't know. I didn't think so. But I knew he had to have them.'

'And so you went to Mr Patterson?'

'Yes.'

'How many times?'

293

I stared back at her. 'I don't remember.'

She frowned. 'You must try to remember,' she said.

There came back to me the smell of drink on his breath in the half-light of dusk at the dormitory door. I imagined, rather than saw, in memory's eye, the slack jaw, the bloodshot stare, the haggard look of wounded pride and wounded dignity. The crooked line of stepping stones led backward across dark waters to that distant occasion when, in my secret hideout, I had overheard Bennett declaring his love for Patterson's wife. And I should have felt compassion. But I did not. All I felt was a hard need for judgment. Not remembering condemned him more. I gathered inside myself all my resolve. I felt again as a singer does, though now it was a different moment, a different surge of purpose stirring within me: having traversed certain difficult passages I was approaching that climax when there descends a sense of glory, a flood of accomplishment; malevolent glory, to my shame, and the accomplishment of spite. The room was very still.

'You must try to remember,' she repeated.

In the muggy heat of that July morning the windows had been opened, and the rain pattered relentlessly down on the green shrubs outside. The sound of it seemed to grow. I was not prevaricating. I felt an icy determination. Through my mind there flooded certain images, of Bennett and Mrs Patterson sprawled across the sofa, of the whisky bottle in Patterson's hand, of Bennett holding out to me the poem, of Wickham stepping away from me, putting his hand up, saying no; last and worst of all, of the lips drawn back from the teeth, the tongue protruding, the matted hair, the glazed, dead, unseeing eyes.

Then, suddenly, at the other end of the room the door opened. It did so noisily, with none of the deference that had attended the arrival of people before and during the early part of the resumed hearing. The door itself was concealed in one of the bays between bookcases, so that notice was taken of the sound of the door, then of voices, then of it being slammed shut.

Though up to then I had studiously avoided looking in that direction, keeping my attention fixed on Miss Uttley and the jury, I turned now to find heads and faces turned also towards the commotion. Voices were raised, and then, like an arrow to my heart, I recognised my father's. It was pitched high with indignation; and he said 'Leave me!' just once, the sound almost a scream.

It made me shiver, and I thrust my knuckle between my teeth. In all the world I would have known the heartrending indignity with which he seemed to cloak his most passionate acts. And with a frozen incapacity I waited for him to lurch into view, carrying with him his untidy bundle of anguish, concern, compassion, love. And this he did. He appeared round the corner of the bookcase, unsteady and dishevelled, spilling out of his wet raincoat and leaving it in the hands of the policeman who was trying to restrain him. Quickly free, he staggered on down towards where I sat, his hair ruffled, his clothing in disarray, his drunkenness barely contained within the agony of his hopeless caring. All the way down the room he spoke: 'Oh, no! Oh, no!' he said. 'Don't try and stop me!' He looked defiantly over his shoulder. But there was no risk of anyone stopping him. The policeman was following, but as yet seemed not to be contemplating any precipitate arrest.

The range of my father's voice occupied an enormous span. After the first phrases, which were delivered in an agonised falsetto, though with nasal undertones, it sank to a deeper, angrier disdain: 'Don't be so futile!' he ordered, and then savagely repeated the word, spitting it out: 'Futile!' He looked round him, even peering into an empty bay of books.

He had seen me from the other end of the room. But now he stopped for a moment, and a note of sepulchral unction crept into his words. 'My son!' he said. He raised one hand, a bit unsteadily. 'My son is there! Let me through!' He looked briefly over his shoulder, but no attempt was being made to apprehend him, and there was nothing to prevent him moving on. 'What are they doing to you?' He shuffled forward. 'What are they doing? What has happened?'

He had reached the space in front of the table at which Miss Uttley sat. He came to an abrupt stop, and swayed where he stood. 'I was told nothing! Nothing!' Again, the tone of his voice had risen to an absurd level, so that the last word came out as a suppressed and horrifying scream, mainly directed, or so it seemed to me, as I sat frozen before him, at some body of malevolent goblins terrorising his soul.

He looked quite formidable. His arrival had eclipsed the tension which had undoubtedly been gathering towards a climax before his interruption. There pulsed from him in waves the energy of his passion, and everyone waited, as though to see what he would do. The policeman, who had followed him down the room, trailing the wet raincoat along the floor, stood a yard or so from him, staring first at his shoulder then at the Coroner. And once again, for a few brief moments, there was silence and the distinct, relentless sound of pattering rain came in through the open windows.

He had stopped abruptly, and in doing so had thrown out his arms, with his fists clenched, in a dramatic, challenging gesture. Christlike, he seemed to be offering himself for sacrifice. And foolishly, frozen by shame, embarrassment, helpless anger, I just sat and stared at him, like everybody else. Though it can only have been for a moment or two, it did seem like an eternity; it was long enough for all the transgressions, with which by humiliating himself he had humiliated me, to be gathered into this moment and into this dishevelled, bizarre figure standing before us. His collar had come undone, his suit was crumpled, a corner of his shirt-tail had come out of his trousers and from his jacket pocket there stuck out a folded newspaper: the physical giant he had always been to me shrank before my eyes and I saw him, not just vulnerable, but meagre as well.

The policeman took a step forward, so that he came within range of the clenched fists, and looked for guidance at the Coroner. I looked as well. She had raised her hand, restraining further action, and now she spoke, quite softly: 'Are you this boy's father?' she asked.

Slowly, like an eagle folding its wings, his hands came to his side. The glare in his eyes faded, and that flash of intimidation softened over with a flood of what must have been so many different feelings. He did not answer her directly. Instead, and it seemed with agonising slowness, he turned his eyes fully upon me, half raised his open hands in a gesture of appeal, and said 'My son! My son!' He swayed slightly. I thought I heard a snigger of laughter from somewhere in the room. The Coroner seemed content to take his words as an answer, and waited patiently while we stared at each other.

I was not conscious of feeling anything. I just wanted him not to be there. And I felt a certain hopelessness in the defiance of his presence. It was so palpably central that I could not envisage any way out. Again, from the seats down the room which were by no means filled, there came a sudden rapidly suppressed whisper of laughter. He drew himself up and slowly turned to survey them. If there had been appeal in his eyes when he looked at me, it gave way now to authority, as though he were searching for evidence that would condemn them all for conspiring to keep him from a drama which in his eyes had engulfed me. I was all that mattered, and he seemed determined to pursue the lofty purpose of his misdirected assistance. With uncertain hand he fumbled in his hip pocket for the folded newspaper, and producing it he waved it in the air above his head. 'I read about it in the paper! That's the first I knew of it. Quite by chance. An accident! A discovery! My son, finding the drowned body of his friend. And nobody tells me! Nobody!'

He looked down the room, flourishing the copy of the *Daily Telegraph* above his head. Then he turned towards the Coroner, and gave her a stern, even malevolent stare, including her now in the conspiracy. Then he swung his gaze back to me. He sensed, I suppose, that the patience of the court was running out, and that he had little time left.

297

A look of sudden, frantic appeal came into his eyes: 'Why?' he said. 'Oh, sonny boy, tell me why? Am I no use at all?'

The Coroner called him by name, gently, twice. And he looked at her, turning slowly from me. And there were tears in his eyes.

I did not know what to do, or what to say. And I felt ashamed. I hated myself for not having brought him there. And I was suddenly conscious of the awful emptiness he must have felt, reading, in that brief newspaper paragraph which I had seen earlier that morning, evidence of the gulf between us. I, too, wanted to cry; but I could not, because I felt so ashamed of him.

Suddenly, his voice completely sober, standing in front of her, vaguely to attention, he said: 'What would you like me to do? I should not have come, breaking in. I'm sure he's all right.' He glanced over. 'Aren't you, old son? You don't need your father any more. He's just an embarrassment to you.' He again turned towards her. He now looked all crumpled and old. He stood almost as if *he* were on trial, as if waiting to be sentenced, at the end of the table.

She said: 'I think it would be better if you left. Your son is in safe hands. He is a model witness, and you should be very proud of him. He has helped us all greatly. But I think it might be upsetting if you stayed.' She looked beyond him to the policeman, and nodded.

Turning to go, he looked at me, and from the depths of his tear-filled eyes I could see a yearning expression coupled with a kind of folding-in, a conclusion, of love and regret, both, a visual apology for what he had done and what he was, a farewell, a blessing, an appeal for my compassion, a plea for my forgiveness.

Then he went. I watched him stride down the room, taking back the old raincoat and putting it on, glaring from side to side, his step far from steady, his knee giving slightly more on the left side than on the right, until, at the corner, by the last bay of books, he turned and disappeared from my sight.

I still sat where I was. I had not moved throughout the whole interruption. The Coroner said something to an official, who went out. Then she looked up at me. She smiled. 'Would you like to go with your father? You could come back in later. We can deal with other evidence.'

I shook my head. 'I would like to go on,' I said.

There were some gasps from behind me, and whispering.

'Are you sure?' she asked.

I nodded.

'You remember what I was asking? About Mr Patterson? How many times?'

Again I nodded.

'Well?'

'I think it was just twice,' I said. 'I mentioned it the first time, but he was busy. The second time was the night before the accident.'

'Was there any reason for thinking that they could have been got earlier? That they could have made a difference?'

'It would have been up to Wickham to take them, wouldn't it?'

'Nothing else that Mr Patterson could have done? Or anyone else?'

'Nothing that I know of,' I said. 'He just forgot. That's all.'

'Did he—?' She stopped herself, and looked down, making a note on the paper in front of her. Then she looked up. Her face seemed clearer. 'You're quite sure? There's nothing else you want to tell us?'

I shook my head.

'You may step down then. If you hurry you'll see your father. But I may need to call you again, so please stay nearby. You've done very well.'

IV

I did not see him. Whatever force it was that had brought

him tumbling once again into my life, however briefly, had already carried him away again, careering impetuously into the whirlpool of his own vexed passions, his own so readily recognised shame. And I was both hurt and pleased. He had come because he recognised, however dimly, however wrongly, a need ancient as time itself that floated there, amorphous, detached, between us. He had gone with equal precipitancy because, just as clearly, he had seen the need dissolve.

How much of this I recognised then I cannot tell. Perhaps it has taken all the years since to come to an understanding of the unfruitful seeds of glory that died within his breast years earlier still than the time of which I write. And this time was just part of the process, an uncompleted stage in my own growing up. I felt hurt, side by side with being pleased; but the bruising was uppermost: how could he have so shamed me?

Of course he did not shame me. In her wisdom the Coroner had recognised this, and perhaps had detected as well that by lurching by accident right into the middle of a crucial exchange, my poor blundering father had salvaged another and not dissimilar bird of passage from ignominy. Even I cannot tell this. I cannot tell what it was that stopped me in mid-sentence and ruled for me that I should carry no further my hate for the man on whom I laid blame for Wickham's death. But in part it was the spectacle of my own father's mute cry to me to love him, to forgive him, and only then to forget him. All three injunctions, of course, impossible to order. The words I have written, the words I have yet to write, bear testimony to that. But I hope they also bear testimony to something else: that slow process by which we acquire wisdom and judgment and compassion to compensate for the power and strength and determination which it is also part of life's aim to seek out.

Epilogue

Wickham's death was by misadventure. Patterson resigned that summer, and left at the end of term. Bennett left, also. To him, some time afterwards, went Mrs Patterson. And after that, his heart broken, or his health, or both, Patterson died, walking into the river Severn at dawn, on an early October day. I always wondered, since I regarded him as a cowardly man at heart, where he found the courage; and I presumed it came from that time in his youth, when he fought in Spain, when he first found the happiness of that young and beautiful girl who became his wife. Merchant maintained a flinty demeanour throughout the rest of that term, and no doubt long afterwards as well. Certainly, he remained for several years after my departure, improving and moulding the texture of Coppinger to his own pattern. Good or bad, it was inescapably his.

And myself? Well I have told all that really mattered, all the important events of that time. Everything else that happened will seem trivial. I worked intensely hard. I heard nothing from my father. Then I took the various examinations. In spite of everything, I passed. I had left Coppinger by the time I got the results. And they were good enough for a place at university. And that was where, in due course, I went.

But that was not the end of the 'story'. In reality it was the beginning; slowly, uncertainly, it was there and afterwards that the 'events' of that spring and summer, together with earlier and later encounters and tribulations, began to be folded and woven into a pattern. At first it did not work; it was tried again. Then, gradually, some sense and order emerged, pointing me in a certain direction. Are stories ever complete? I think not. They leave, palpitating in the atmosphere which they create, expectations which can never fully be satisfied. And this is right. The prefiguration of life is like the tracing of words in water, or the writing of messages in sand. The intensity, the feeling, may be there; but what is left is always imperfect.

Towards the end of that summer term, my last at Coppinger, I had a brief and hurried note from Francis. He and Philpotts were off on some mysterious mission, to Finland. Wedmore had gone there, to a conference, and had disappeared. They were off to find him. Francis wrote saying that I could use his bed-sitting room in London if I wanted it that summer until he came back. It suited me much better than going back to Mr Porphyry, who now had a new scholar on his hands, though not Archer. Francis sent me the key. At the end of his letter he said he had been round once or twice to the Gloucester Road hotel, but without luck.

On an impulse, I wrote there, telling my father I would be in London. But the letter came back with 'Gone Away' scrawled across it.

That was the last week of the term. On the morning of the last day I went to see Patterson to say goodbye. He was sorting through the papers on his desk. Whatever strain there had been between us, whatever differences, were buried now; so, too, though temporarily as it transpired, was the misery which in due course would drive him into the river.

'Well, you look transformed,' he said. 'I hope you are.' I smiled a bit sheepishly. I was wearing a spotted bow tie for the first time, and carrying in my hand a green pork-pie hat which I had recently acquired and had been secretly trying out during those later days. 'I thought it was the right style for university,' I said.

'It's deeper than that,' he said.

'I suppose so.'

'What'll you do in the meantime?'

I shrugged. 'Go to London for a bit, sir. I don't know what after that.'

'Well, I go to a well-earned rest, as you know. It's a relief.'

I could see quite clearly from his face that it was no such thing. He was packing up his life, no less. I suddenly felt a great surge of feeling for him; perhaps it was no more than pity, but even so I wanted to mark the occasion, which even without his death would probably have been the last meeting between us. It may even have been that the sudden feeling for him prompted what I then said.

'I have to go and find my father,' I said. 'He's disappeared.'

Patterson stopped the vague and uncertain moving around of papers, and looked up at me. 'Oh?' he said. 'Disappeared?'

'Well, the letter I wrote came back. It was marked "Gone Away". He usually tells me some address.'

'How will you find him?'

'There are people,' I said. 'Friends. Those he depends on. I'll trace him somehow.'

He looked at me, a slow, sad smile on his face. 'It was strange, your father coming, that day. The day of the inquest. I think he did me a good turn. Did he?'

I nodded.

'Thought so.' He moved down from his desk to the other end of the room. On his way he picked up from a table a pile of documents. He turned and looked back at me. We had the whole length of the room between us. 'I have the reports to write,' he said. 'It's for the last time.' He looked down at them, and began turning them over at the top, to see the names. He read some of them out, but more to himself.

303

'Archer…Atwood….Blake'….Cartwright…' He rifled through more. 'Parkin…Skinner…Tate…' His head came up and he looked at me, his mouth open. The room was filled with his sadness, the yearning regret with which he seemed to be saying goodbye to them all. Meeting my eyes seemed to penetrate his thoughts. 'So you're going to find your father, eh? I can think of worse things to do.'

'I…I did just come in to say goodbye, sir.'

'Yes. Of course.' He dropped the reports back where he had found them, and came down the room towards me. 'We're birds of a feather, I suppose,' he said, 'your father and me. Birds of a feather. Rough diamonds. Casualties. He's worth finding. Good luck.'

He put out his hand, and I shook it. We were friends, I suppose, for the first time. I said to him, 'Thank you, sir.' And I suppose I was thanking him for a host of different benefits. But most of all it was for the brief and fleeting tribute to the wild and passionate man whose whereabouts I was setting out to track down. I thought, then, it would be easy. I thought that, through Alice, through Laurie, through Ursula, somehow it would turn out all right, and we would soon be together again. Little did I know, then, how long it would be before the quest was over. Perhaps, still, it is not.